Praise for Novels by . . .

COURTNEY WALSH

Just Let Go

"A charming story about discovering joy amidst life's disappointments, *Just Let Go* is a delightful treat for Courtney Walsh's growing audience."

RACHEL HAUCK, *NEW YORK TIMES* BESTSELLING AUTHOR

"*Just Let Go* matches a winsome heroine with an unlikely hero in a romantic tale where opposites attract and we learn that sometimes there's much more beneath the surface than first appears. This is a page-turning, charming story about learning when to love and when to let go."

DENISE HUNTER, BESTSELLING AUTHOR OF *HONEYSUCKLE DREAMS*

"Just the kind of story I love! Small town, hunky skier, a woman with a dream, and love that triumphs through hardship. A sweet story of reconciliation and romance by a talented writer."

SUSAN MAY WARREN, *USA TODAY* BESTSELLING AUTHOR

"Walsh crafts engaging, believable characters who resist falling in love with one another because relationships aren't easy . . . especially when we struggle to accept our own brokenness."

BETH K. VOGT, CHRISTY AND CAROL AWARD–WINNING AUTHOR

For my sister, Carrie Erikson, who has taught me so much not only about letting go, but about moving on.

"I discovered Courtney Walsh's novels a few years ago and quickly added her to my must-buy-immediately list. Her stories have never failed to delight me, with characters who become friends and charming settings that beckon as if you've lived there all your life. You won't want to miss *Paper Hearts*!"

DEBORAH RANEY, AUTHOR OF THE CHICORY INN NOVELS SERIES

"Delightfully romantic with a lovable cast of quirky characters, *Paper Hearts* will have readers smiling from ear to ear! Courtney Walsh has penned a winner!"

KATIE GANSHERT, AWARD-WINNING AUTHOR OF *A BROKEN KIND OF BEAUTIFUL*

"*Paper Hearts* is as much a treat as the delicious coffee the heroine serves in her bookshop. . . . Like the matchmakers that surrounded the couple in the novel, I couldn't help cheering them on. A poignant, wry, sweet, and utterly charming read."

BECKY WADE, AUTHOR OF *MEANT TO BE MINE*

A Sweethaven Summer

"Walsh's touching debut will have readers longing for a visit to the idyllic vista of Sweethaven. . . . The touch of mystery, significant friendships, and a charming setting create a real treasure."

ROMANTIC TIMES

"Walsh has created a charming, inviting, homesick-inducing world with Sweethaven. I want to hug the ladies featured in the book and learn from them. . . . To fellow readers, this is a series you don't want to miss."

NOVELCROSSING.COM

Change of Heart

"Walsh has penned another endearing novel set in Loves Park, Colo. The emotions are occasionally raw but always truly real."
ROMANTIC TIMES

"*Change of Heart* is a beautifully written, enlightening, and tragic story. . . . This novel is a must-read for lovers of contemporary romance."
RADIANT LIT

Paper Hearts

"Walsh pens a quaint, small-town love story . . . [with] enough plot twists to make this enjoyable to the end."
PUBLISHERS WEEKLY

"Be prepared to be swept away by this delightful romance about healing the heart, forgiveness, [and] following your dreams . . ."
FRESH FICTION

"Walsh writes a small-town setting, a sweet, slow-building romance between two likable characters and a host of eclectic secondary characters."
ROMANTIC TIMES

"Well written and charming."
NOVEL REVIEWS

"A masterful word painting, *A Sweethaven Summer* is a story of loss, regret, forgiveness, and restoration. Novel Rocket and I give it our highest recommendation. It's a five-star must-read."
ANE MULLIGAN, PRESIDENT, NOVEL ROCKET

"This book captivated me from the first paragraphs. Bittersweet memories, long-kept secrets, the timeless friendships of women—and a touch of sweet romance. Beautifully written and peopled with characters who became my friends, this debut novel is one for my keeper shelf—and, I hope, the first of many to come from Courtney Walsh's pen."
DEBORAH RANEY, AUTHOR OF THE CHICORY INN NOVELS SERIES

"*A Sweethaven Summer* is a sweet debut, filled with characters whose hopes, dreams, and regrets are relevant and relatable. A great book club read!"
SUSAN MEISSNER, AUTHOR OF *A FALL OF MARIGOLDS*

"*A Sweethaven Summer* is a stunning debut. . . . With a voice that sparkles, Courtney Walsh captured my heart in this tender story of forgiveness and new beginnings. It's certainly a great beginning for this talented author."
CARLA STEWART, AUTHOR OF *THE HATMAKER'S HEART*

"Courtney Walsh weaves a captivating tale that taps into the universal desire for belonging and happiness. This delightful debut has a bit of mystery, a bit of romance, a beautiful setting, and an intriguing cast of characters."
MEGAN DIMARIA, AUTHOR OF *SEARCHING FOR SPICE*

"*A Sweethaven Summer* shines with moments of hope and tenderness. With interesting characters, a delightful setting, and a compelling plot, this is one of those stories that stays with you."
TINA ANN FORKNER, AUTHOR OF *RUBY AMONG US*

A Sweethaven Homecoming

"Courtney Walsh puts the sweet in Sweethaven. If you're looking for an uplifting, hope-filled story filled with characters you'll feel like you know, *A Sweethaven Homecoming* has it!"
MARYBETH WHALEN, AUTHOR OF *THE BRIDGE TENDER*

"*A Sweethaven Homecoming* is a triumph! With the foundations of family, love, and faith, The Circle grows through heartbreak, loss, and betrayal and emerges renewed in their love for one another and, most of all, their love of themselves."
SUSAN OPEL, CREATIVE EDITOR, *PAPER CRAFTS* MAGAZINE

A Sweethaven Christmas

"Readers will smell the pine of Christmas trees and the aromas of holiday food and will hold close the friendships they develop with the characters."
ROMANTIC TIMES

"Walsh's compelling writing style creates unforgettable characters readers come to know and love, while her story lines contend with issues common to us all. . . . Even though the ending is emotional (keep [a] box of Kleenex handy), it's a story of hope, goodwill, and good friends that is perfect for the Christmas season."
EXAMINER.COM

JUST LET GO

ALSO BY COURTNEY WALSH

Just Let Go

a novel

COURTNEY WALSH

Tyndale House Publishers, Inc.
Carol Stream, Illinois

Visit Tyndale online at www.tyndale.com.

Visit Courtney Walsh's website at www.courtneywalshwrites.com.

TYNDALE and Tyndale's quill logo are registered trademarks of Tyndale House Publishers, Inc.

Just Let Go

Designed by Libby Dykstra

Edited by Danika King

Published in association with the literary agency of Natasha Kern Literary Agency, Inc., P.O. Box 1069, White Salmon, WA 98672.

Just Let Go is a work of fiction. Where real people, events, establishments, organizations, or locales appear, they are used fictitiously. All other elements of the novel are drawn from the author's imagination.

For information about special discounts for bulk purchases, please contact Tyndale House Publishers at csresponse@tyndale.com, or call 1-800-323-9400.

Library of Congress Cataloging-in-Publication Data
Names: Walsh, Courtney, date- author.
Title: Just let go / Courtney Walsh.
Description: Carol Stream, Illinois : Tyndale House Publishers, Inc., [2018]
Identifiers: LCCN 2017055452 | ISBN 9781496421524 (sc)
Subjects: | GSAFD: Christian fiction. | Love stories.
Classification: LCC PS3623.A4455 J86 2018 | DDC 813/.6--dc23 LC record available at https://lccn.loc.gov/2017055452

Printed in the United States of America

24	23	22	21	20	19	18
7	6	5	4	3	2	1

CHAPTER

1

HE SHOULDN'T BE HERE.

A diner in some little tourist town in Michigan was no place for Grady Benson, but here he was. From the second he walked in the door, it was clear he'd made a mistake. Eyes found and followed him all the way to this table, conspicuously located at the center of the space.

A girl with glasses and wild, curly hair rushed over and set a glass of water in front of him.

If he had to guess, he'd say tourist season was over and this place was filled with locals. He didn't even catch the name of the diner when he walked in, but when Wild Hair handed him the menu, he read *Hazel's Kitchen: Harbor Pointe, Michigan* on the cover and figured that's where he was.

Where he definitely should not be.

So much for staying under the radar.

"Did you see the sign on your way in? It had all the specials written on it." Wild Hair wore a nametag that read *Betsy*. Now that

1

he looked at her, she was cute, in a small-town, innocent sort of way. Not like the girls he was used to dating. They were anything but innocent.

"I didn't." He opened the menu and kept his head down, but the whispers started despite his best efforts to disappear. Apparently Harbor Pointe had noticed him.

"Can I just get a cheeseburger with everything, fries, and a chocolate milk shake?"

Betsy's eyes went wide. "Are you sure that's a good idea?"

He glanced up at her, and she quickly swiped the menu out of his hand.

"I'm sorry. I shouldn't have said that."

"What do you think I should eat?" he asked.

She looked away, visibly ruffled. "Grilled chicken with a big plate of roasted vegetables and a glass of water?" There was a question in her voice.

He pretended to think it over for a few seconds but shook his head. "I'll stick with the cheeseburger."

She scribbled something on her notepad, then scurried away like a mouse. Grady sat for a few long minutes, feeling too big for the chair she'd put him in. He pulled his phone out of his pocket and opened Twitter.

Grady Benson needs to learn the art of knowing when to quit.

Benson chokes again. Time to hang up the skis, buddy.

Kiss the Olympics good-bye, GB. You'll be lucky to land a job training little kids with a run like that. #crashandburn

He clicked the screen off and flicked it on the table with a clunk.

The race in Vermont would follow him all the way to Colorado with Twitter comments echoing in his head. He should've just gotten on a plane like everyone else. A solo road trip to clear his head suddenly seemed like a ridiculous idea.

Betsy returned with his milk shake, half of it in a tall glass with whipped cream and a cherry on top, the other half still in the metal mixing container. He ate healthy most of the time—it was one of the few rules he actually followed—but he didn't feel like making wise choices right now.

He wanted to do whatever he wanted to do.

Grady glanced up as the door opened and a pretty blonde woman walked in. She wore ripped jeans rolled at the ankles, slouchy and a little too big for her, along with a gray T-shirt underneath an army-green jacket that cinched in at the waist. Like him, she looked out of place, like she didn't belong here, but judging by the welcome she received when she walked in the door, she absolutely did.

He couldn't tell, but it seemed the crowd at the front of the diner was congratulating her about something. Not his business. He went back to his milk shake, and a few seconds later his food arrived.

Betsy stood beside the table for an awkward beat. "Need anything else?" she finally asked.

"I'm good, I think," he said. "Thanks."

She nodded, then skittered away, leaving him to eat in peace. He took a bite of his burger and washed it down with a swig of the shake. While so many of the people around him still seemed on high alert that he was sitting there, several had gone back to their own meals, their own food, their own company.

"Hey, aren't you Grady Benson?"

Grady turned in the direction of the voice and found a booth of three guys, early twenties, off to his left. He swallowed his bite and gave them a nod.

"I remember watching you at the last Olympics, man," one of the guys said. "Tough loss."

"He didn't lose, you idiot; he came in fourth," another guy said.

He didn't need the reminder. The first guy was right. He'd lost. Fourth place had never been good enough, not when he was favored to win the gold. Not when he only had himself to blame.

"Don't beat yourself up, man. Hard to come back after something like that."

"I'm fine." Grady set his burger down.

The guy laughed. "Dude, you're done."

"Jimmy," one of the other guys warned.

Grady gritted his teeth.

Jimmy laughed again. "What? You saw what happened in Vermont. He didn't even finish. Washed-up at thirty, that's gotta suck."

He should stand up and walk away. He should pay the waitress, get in his SUV, and keep driving to Colorado, where he could get ready for the next race. He should . . . but he didn't.

He'd been listening to commentators talk about his skiing, his messy technique, his disregard for the rules for years—but now they'd started using terms like *washed-up* and *retirement*, and whenever he heard them, something inside him snapped.

Grady turned toward the table. "You got a problem with me?"

Jimmy's expression turned smug. "I'm just not a fan, is all. You're not as great as you think you are."

Grady reminded himself he didn't know this guy, didn't care what he thought. And yet something about Jimmy was really getting under his skin. He looked around for Betsy so he could get his check and leave.

But Jimmy didn't let up. "We all watched the races the other day. Guy choked. He choked, man."

"Dude, shut up," his friend said.

"Supposed to be the fastest guy on the slopes, but my Aunt Frieda could've skied better than him. In her sleep."

"You don't even have an Aunt Frieda." The other guy sounded as irritated with his friend as Grady was. Grady's knuckles had gone white around the edge of the table.

"Heard he got his girlfriend pregnant and then tried to pay her to keep quiet. Not like he's got a squeaky-clean image to protect or anything."

That was it. How that lie had ever picked up steam, Grady didn't know, but he was sick of hearing it. Grady spun out of his chair and lunged at Jimmy, pulling him out of the booth by his jacket. A plate crashed to the floor, but Grady barely noticed.

Jimmy tried to fight him off, but he was several inches shorter and not half as strong as Grady. Still, he managed to squirm from Grady's grasp, falling into a table and knocking over more dishes.

The guy didn't know when to quit. He smirked at Grady. "I forgot you've got a temper, too. Is that why nobody wants you on the team?"

Who did this punk kid think he was? Grady didn't hold back as he hauled off and punched Jimmy square in the jaw. Jimmy's body shot backward into a wall of framed photos, which shattered when they hit the floor.

Grady stepped back to catch his breath when out of nowhere, Jimmy lunged toward him, catching him off guard and ramming Grady's body into the long counter on the other side of the diner. He was scrappy, Grady would give him that, but this kid didn't have nearly the fighting experience Grady did. He'd grown up fighting. He practically enjoyed it. He knew how to handle himself.

Grady wrestled him to the ground, his only focus to keep him there. Jimmy yanked himself from Grady's grasp and landed a punch across his left eye. Anger welled up inside him as the sting of pain zipped through his body. Grady's mind spun; long-buried grief demanded to be felt. He had Jimmy's comments to thank for that.

Washed-up at thirty.

Injuries beyond repair.

Sloppy technique.

Embarrassed. Frustrated. Ashamed.

Someone grabbed him from behind and pulled him off Jimmy. Only then did Grady realize he'd unleashed the full force of his rage on the man, who now lay beneath him, bloody and moaning.

He shrugged from the grasp of the person who'd pulled him away and wiped his face on his sleeve. He scanned the diner and found pairs of eyes darting away from him. All but one. The blonde's. She stood off to the side, unmoving, watching him.

He looked away.

He didn't need to be judged by Little Miss Goody Two-Shoes.

Jimmy's friends pulled him to his feet as two officers in uniform yanked the front door open. Grady glanced at Betsy, who wouldn't meet his eyes. He should apologize. He'd made a huge mess of the place. Tables were overturned, at least one of them broken. The glass from the shattered picture frames crunched underneath his feet, and there was at least one place where they'd put a hole in the wall. Oh no, make it two.

He didn't even remember doing that.

Before he could say anything to the wild-haired waitress (or anyone else), one of the cops—an older man with a wrinkled face—grabbed him by the arm. "You'll have to come with me, son."

The other officer did the same to Jimmy, who immediately launched into his side of the story, spouting about how Grady "freaked out for no reason" and "I'm the victim here, man."

Grady let the older cop lead him through the small crowd, avoiding the stares of the people who'd just witnessed yet another of his colossal mistakes. The blonde stood near the door, arms crossed over her chest. She said nothing, but her eyes never left his as the officer pushed him through the door and into the street.

"Do I need to cuff you, or have you calmed down?" the cop asked.

"You don't need to cuff me," Grady said, wishing he'd never stopped in this ridiculous town in the first place. What was it that made him pull off at the Harbor Pointe exit? He wasn't particularly hungry—he was just tired of driving. He should've kept going. If only he could rewind the last hour.

Who was he kidding? He'd have to rewind a lot further back than that to undo the mess he'd made.

The second officer was shoving Jimmy into the back of a squad car parked at the curb.

"Look, Officer—" Grady turned toward the older man—"I'm sorry I lost my temper back there. I'll pay for the damages to the diner."

"I'm sure you will." He opened the other back door of the car and motioned for Grady to get in.

"There's really no need for this," Grady said. "I screwed up. I get it. But I'm fine now, and I'll make it right."

"Well, your version of 'making it right' might not be the judge's version of 'making it right.'" He eyed Grady. "There's still time for the cuffs."

Grady let out a stream of hot air, anger prickling the back of his neck as he leaned down and got into the car. Jimmy sat on the opposite side, sulking. At least he'd shut up. For now, anyway.

Through the windows of Hazel's Kitchen, Grady saw the people who'd witnessed the fight picking up overturned tables and chairs and sweeping broken plates into a dustpan. What a mess he'd made.

The main stretch of Harbor Pointe was made up of cotton candy–colored buildings neatly stacked together on either side of the street. As they drove, he saw a bakery, a flower shop, a couple more diners, antique stores. Old-fashioned lampposts shone on alternating sides of the street, casting a warm yellow hue over the brick road in front of them.

They drove in silence for several seconds until finally the older officer turned around and looked at Grady.

"I know you're not from here. What kind of beef could you possibly have with Jimmy?"

"He's crazy," Jimmy said.

"I'm not talking to you," the cop said.

"No beef. Just don't like people with smart mouths."

The cop laughed. "That I understand."

"It's not funny, Sheriff," Jimmy protested. "I'm pressing charges. Assault and battery. And I want a lawyer because I didn't do anything here." Jimmy was still riled up, and normally Grady would be too, but he'd been here before. He knew exactly what would happen next. He'd be arrested. Booked. Pay a fine and be on his way.

Though, sadly, this time, he wasn't even sure where he was on his way to.

CHAPTER

2

"WELL, THAT WAS . . . EXCITING." Quinn Collins picked up an over-turned chair and put it back on its feet. She straightened the table and surveyed the rest of the damage.

Betsy Tanner, the owner of Hazel's Kitchen, let out a substantial sigh. "What am I gonna do?"

"You're going to make that guy pay for the mess he caused," someone said from the other side of the restaurant.

Nate Kelley appeared in the doorway, and Betsy's whole demeanor changed. "Nate."

"What happened?" He walked toward her. "Got a text saying a fight broke out?"

"It'll be okay," Betsy said. "Maybe Lane can help me redecorate. Maybe it was time for a face-lift." Never mind that the current decor wasn't all that old. Quinn knew Betsy was trying to make herself feel better.

Quinn picked up a few more castoffs from the fight as the crowd continued to recount what they'd just seen—two grown men acting like imbeciles and ruining poor Betsy's business.

Quinn had admired Betsy for a long time. She'd taken Hazel's and turned it into something even better than it had been before. Her pies put the place on the map, and she'd even been profiled in national magazines. Someone said they were going to get that spiky-haired blond guy to come out and feature her on the Food Network. After all, this place was a local favorite and definitely deserved the recognition.

What Betsy had done with Hazel's was exactly what Quinn had been longing to do with the Forget-Me-Not Flower Shop for years. Her hand slid to her back pocket, where she felt the keys, still safe where she put them after her closing just an hour before.

She was officially a business owner.

Somehow seeing Betsy in this state of disarray did nothing to squelch her excitement. This was what Quinn had been praying for, dreaming of. Even knowing there would be difficult times like the one Betsy was going through at that moment didn't dissuade her.

She was ready.

Finally, her life could begin.

She walked out of Hazel's Kitchen and into the cold evening air. Harbor Pointe was smack in the middle of winter, and the evenings were brisk and cold. She pulled her jacket a little tighter around her.

Lane Kelley. Lane had moved back here not too long ago to start her own interior design business. Quinn hadn't thought of calling in a professional, but if she could fit it in her budget, it might be worth it. After all, she wanted to completely overhaul the flower shop. Mimi Hudson had wonderful taste twenty years ago, but nothing much had changed since. Quinn knew because she'd tried, more than once, to update the displays, to paint the walls, to bring Forget-Me-Not into this century. But Mimi was a creature of habit.

And she was cheap.

Quinn walked a few doors down to Forget-Me-Not, and a swell of memories rushed through her. How many times had she come here after school, setting up her own little station for creating adorable bouquets from the cuttings her mother couldn't use?

It still amazed her how easily her mind transported her back. She'd done her best to box up all the feelings (and there was a mix of them) and stuff them away, but sometimes, when she wasn't careful, one would sneak through, like light underneath a door in a dark room.

She was seconds from inserting her key when a glow at the back of the shop caught her eye. *What in the world . . . ?*

When she tugged the door, it opened, and the big bell Mimi had installed overhead jangled. Loudly.

Shoot. What if it was a thief?

Well, that was a ridiculous thought. What kind of thief would rob a flower shop?

No sense pretending she wasn't standing here now. "Hello?"

After a few seconds, she heard a noise in the back room. A moment later, Mimi's face, wearing a sheepish expression, appeared in the doorway.

"Mimi, you scared me to death," Quinn said.

"I'm sorry, hon," Mimi said. "I was just coming to say good-bye." She was smiling, but there was sadness in her eyes.

Quinn shifted her purse from one shoulder to the other. "Don't tell me you're regretting your decision to travel the world with Barry."

"Of course not," Mimi said. "I'm thrilled we get to go on these adventures while we're still young and limber enough to enjoy them." She stilled. "But this place was my whole world for so many years."

Quinn nodded. Hers too. For as long as she could remember, the Forget-Me-Not Flower Shop had been a part of her life. And she'd been waiting for the day she could officially call it hers.

Not that she didn't love Mimi. After all, the older woman had done so much for her—treated her, in many ways, like a daughter when Quinn so desperately needed a mother. Mimi had made her the most beautiful corsage for her senior prom and explained to her how important it was to protect her purity even though boys were often very persistent. Mimi had hugged her through several low, low days, the kind of days Quinn hoped were behind her now.

But in the back of her mind, Quinn had never viewed the flower shop as Mimi's. It was as if Mimi were just taking care of it until Quinn was ready.

As caretakers went, Mimi was certainly a good one. The best. But Forget-Me-Not was a Collins legacy, and Quinn was ready to take the lead.

"You're going to do a fantastic job, Quinn," Mimi said.

Quinn smiled. "I hope so. I want to make you proud."

I want to make my mother proud.

Mimi stepped out of the back room and into the shop. She stood behind the counter, where Quinn was accustomed to seeing her. "You've already made me proud, hon." She smiled and slung her large purse over her shoulder. "Now, one little piece of advice from an old bird who learned the hard way?"

"Of course." Quinn took a few steps closer, the faint light from the back room and the streetlamps outside filling the shop just enough that Quinn could make out the older woman's familiar features. Mimi's red hair framed her face and offset her bright-green eyes. She'd looked that way as long as Quinn could remember—further proof the older woman resisted change.

Still, Quinn knew there was much to learn from her. Mimi was whip-smart and kind to boot. It made for good business in their small town, especially once tourist season was over. This business depended on the locals, not the passersby.

Mimi reached across the counter for Quinn's hands. "Do your work. Be good at it. But don't let it consume you."

"I won't," Quinn said.

"No, really." Mimi squeezed her hands. "It's so easy when you run your own business, especially one that means so much to you, to get lost in it all. To forget that there's more to life than just this place. I worry about you, Quinn. You work here. You live upstairs. You never go anywhere else."

Quinn pressed her lips together. What was she supposed to say? It was true—by design. Didn't Mimi understand why she couldn't leave Harbor Pointe?

"I'll do better, Mimi," Quinn said. "I promise."

"Book a vacation," Mimi said. "Do it tonight. Come visit Barry and me in Italy this summer."

Quinn laughed. "I think I might need to start a little smaller than Italy."

Mimi waved her off. "Go big or go home, sweetheart."

"I'll think about it," Quinn said, knowing it was a lie.

Mimi knew it too, but she didn't say so. She just studied Quinn for several seconds, then finally let go of her hands and joined her in front of the counter. "I don't want to see you get your hopes up, Quinn."

She frowned. "What do you mean?"

"Just that it's been twenty years. I want you to move on. Make this a fresh start—maybe accept the fact that she's not coming back."

Quinn knew it was true; why did the words still sting after all these years?

Mimi pulled her into a tight hug, patted her twice on the back, then let her go. "I'm going to be praying for you every single day. You know that, don't you?"

"I know, Mimi."

"Ask him to take that pain away, honey." Mimi's smile was warm. Maternal. "He's the only one who can."

Quinn shook her head. "I'm fine. You don't need to worry about me. I promise."

"Well, that's no comfort. I'm going to be worrying about you till the day I die." She stepped away. "That's what I do."

"And I'm grateful for it," Quinn said. "How about instead of worrying, you just send me postcards from all the places you see on your crazy European adventure."

Mimi giggled. "I will. I can't believe I'm doing this. I don't know *what* we're going to see over there—Stella Jones told me they have topless beaches. I sure hope we don't stumble onto one of those."

Quinn laughed. "I hope not either. I'd hate to see Barry topless."

Mimi swatted her arm. "I sure am going to miss you."

"Me too." Quinn reached out for one more hug, blinked back fresh tears, and watched as Mimi turned around and walked out the door.

Maybe for the last time.

Standing there, in the middle of the flower shop, surrounded by the old displays, she was suddenly overwhelmed with emotion.

This was it. She was on her own. No more Mimi to take care of her or make sure she was okay. Sure, she still had her dad and his friends, but business-wise, Forget-Me-Not was her responsibility.

And she was determined not to mess that up.

She pulled her notebook from her purse and sat down on the floor in the center of the space. The flower shop was old and run-down, so she'd been collecting ideas on how to improve it for years. She scooted the elastic band holding the book together off to the side and opened the pages. Even in the near dark, she knew what the sketches and scraps of magazine clippings were. She remembered every idea, every plan as if she'd just saved them yesterday.

She was excited, but she knew that as much fun as she'd had collecting ideas, it was going to take a lot of work and money to whip this place into shape. That thought overwhelmed her.

The floors needed to be refinished and the walls needed to be painted. There was a whole shelving system in the back room that still had to be put together. The signs outside hadn't been replaced since the year Mimi bought the shop, and the window displays needed to be rebuilt. She wanted to add some small gift items to their inventory, but she had to get the display shelves put in place, and then, of course, there was the office where Quinn would meet with brides, plan festival displays, place orders, and work on the designs she'd enter into the Michigan Floral Expo, just a few short months away.

Florists from all over the state could enter the Michigan Floral Expo with displays they created for any event—festivals, carnivals, weddings. For Quinn, the Harbor Pointe Winter Carnival would be the locale for her entry. And that carnival was coming up quickly.

She pulled out her phone and swiped over to the Expo website. The entry form nagged at her. She had displays she'd designed throughout the year that would be perfectly fine to enter, but none of them were perfect.

None of them would win.

And this year—after finally becoming the official owner of the Forget-Me-Not Flower Shop, winning was the only possible outcome.

And the only way to get her mother's attention after living twenty invisible years.

CHAPTER

3

GRADY WOKE WITH A START. Where was he? His aching body screamed at him and there was a kink in his neck. He was definitely *not* in a five-star ski resort in Colorado.

He stared up at a blank, gray ceiling. Unfamiliar.

"You're awake."

He turned and saw the bars that surrounded him and wondered if this was how animals at the zoo felt. He sat up. Groaned.

"Wondered how long you'd sleep on that cot." It was the old sheriff from last night.

Grady rubbed the back of his neck, willing away the dull ache around his temples. He wasn't accustomed to sleeping without pillows and a decent mattress, even though this wasn't the first night he'd spent in jail.

His mind spun back to the night before. The annoying guy who'd goaded him until he unleashed the rage of a year of disappointments. "Where's that other guy?"

"Made bail this morning. Pressed charges against you."

"Are you kidding? He's not exactly innocent," Grady said.

"No, he's not. Never is. Jimmy's been known to pick fights around town. It's practically a hobby for him." The man's bushy white mustache moved as he spoke, but that was about the most demonstrative thing on this guy. He leaned in the doorway of an office, thumbs hooked into his gun belt, chewing on a toothpick.

"Did you even go home last night?" Grady asked, though he wasn't sure why. He didn't care how many hours this guy had been on duty.

"I did. Came back this morning when one of my deputies called to tell me something that happened in our little town was trending on Twitter." He said it with disdain.

"What?" Grady sighed. "Great. That's just what I need."

"Figured. I did a little digging. You've been having a heckuva year."

He didn't need the reminder. "Is my manager here? Did he call? Name's Pete Moran. I called him last night."

"Sorry, son. No calls for you unless you count the reporters that have flocked to town." He walked over to the computer sitting on an oversize metal desk just outside the cell. He turned the monitor around to reveal a paused news video, enlarged to fit the entire screen. He hit the space bar, and there was footage taken from inside the diner the night before. Judging by the angle, it was one of Jimmy's friends who shot the video and probably uploaded it to his social media accounts while Grady was standing outside on the sidewalk, the blood on his lip still fresh.

"Turns out, you're kind of a big deal."

The crawl on the bottom of the screen read *Latest in a long line of disasters for Olympic skier Grady Benson.*

Images of Grady's wipeouts from the last three competitions flashed across the screen. He could still feel the pain that screeched through his body as he fell, his dreams of a comeback dashed away in a split second.

He'd been working to get stronger, to fix his mistakes ever since. But after this past weekend's poor showing, he was starting to believe the press. Was he really washed up? Was he done skiing forever? And if so, where did that leave him now?

His thoughts turned to Benji. His brother was counting on him—he owed it to him to do better. So why did he keep messing up?

The computer screen flashed to a newscaster on the sidewalk outside the turquoise-colored restaurant, Hazel's Kitchen. She was standing next to the wild-haired waitress from last night.

The bottom of the screen read *Betsy Tanner, owner, Hazel's Kitchen.* She was the owner? He'd send her a check. A big one.

The reporter held a microphone and turned toward Betsy. "Miss Tanner, I understand this was a lot of excitement for Harbor Pointe last night. I suppose you don't often have fights like that break out—with Olympic athletes, no less."

Betsy pushed her glasses up and looked into the camera—uncomfortably. "I waited on Mr. Benson and he was perfectly kind. I think there must've been some kind of misunderstanding."

"And the damage to your property?"

"We'll get it fixed." Betsy smiled. "I just hope Mr. Benson recovers so he can get back to doing what he does best. We'd sure miss seeing him on the slopes at the Winter Games."

That woman should be furious with him; why was she defending him—to a reporter no less?

"Would you mind turning it off?"

The sheriff paused the video. Grady sat back down on the cold metal bench in his cell. "So, what now?"

"Wait to see a judge, I suppose. Sounds like they're going to bring you over yet this morning."

Grady reached up and felt his swollen, cracked lip. He probably had a black eye to go along with it. Oh yeah, he'd make a great impression on a judge.

The door of the station opened, drawing the sheriff's attention.

"Is that Pete?" Grady stood, hands on his hips, ready to lay into his manager for taking his sweet time getting there.

"No, son, that's just Quinn."

His eyes followed the sheriff's toward the front of the space, where he saw the pretty blonde from the night before setting a tall vase of flowers on the front desk.

"Arlene loves daisies," she said with a smile. "Thought this place could use a little brightening up."

"Your face does that," the old man said.

She started toward him, carrying a small bag with a logo on the side that said *Hazel's Kitchen* and a cup of coffee. "You're not biased or anything." Her glance at Grady was a passing one, barely a footnote in her mind—like she had no idea who he was, nor did she seem to care.

The sheriff pulled the girl into a hug. "I heard congratulations are in order."

She squeezed him tightly, then moved from his grasp. "It's finally mine."

"So proud of you, honey. I knew you could do it."

"Well, there's still a ton of work." She offered the bag and coffee to the old man. "Cheese danish. Black coffee."

"How'd you get into Hazel's this morning? Looked like they were closed."

"Betsy let a few of her regulars in through the back door. Nate and his brothers and Ryan Brooks are all in there cleaning the place up. She'll be back up and running in no time." Now a sideways glance at Grady, who quickly looked away.

The front door swung open and another officer walked in. He was tall and thick, and didn't appear to be in any kind of hurry. Grady supposed that was the difference between this small town in Michigan and every other place he was used to spending time.

Except home. Home had that same relaxed feel—a certain kind of nonchalance he hadn't felt anywhere else. At least it used to. But that was years ago. Mostly, the thought of going back was about as appealing as a root canal.

What he needed was to get out of here so he could go back to training, competing, and proving to the rest of the world that he wasn't what they said he was—a disappointment.

"Quinn Collins." The deputy eyed the blonde as he approached. She straightened. "Hey, Deputy Jones."

"How's it looking outside?" The sheriff stepped in front of Quinn, protectively, almost like he didn't want his deputy anywhere around her. And who could blame him? Grady had spent ten seconds in the same room with this guy, and already he could tell he was a pig.

"It's a mess." He turned to Grady. "Quite a disaster you've caused out there."

Grady glared at the guy but said nothing.

"Quinn, why don't you wait for me in my office?" the sheriff asked.

She glanced at Grady, barely, avoided the deputy's gaze, and did as she was told.

Once she'd gone, the deputy pulled his handcuffs out. "Judge wants to see him now. Should I parade him out front so the press can get a great shot of their former hero in all his glory?"

"You do that and you don't need to bother coming in tomorrow. That's not how we do things around here, Deputy Jones."

"Lighten up, Sheriff. I was just kidding."

The sheriff looked at Grady. "Walker here will take you through the back way. Probably still going to be press in that courtroom, but something tells me you're used to that."

Grady gave a slight nod. "Can I call my manager again?"

The sheriff glanced at Walker, who didn't move, but then pulled a cordless phone off the desk and handed it to Grady. He dialed Pete's number and turned away, willing his manager to pick up.

No luck. At the sound of the tone, Grady sighed. "Pete. Where are you, man? I'm in some trouble. I need you to get here and handle this mess. Harbor Pointe, Michigan. I have to be in Colorado tomorrow. There's another race this weekend and I need the points. . . . I'm running out of time, man, and I've got to get back on that team. Get out here, Pete. Today."

He clicked the phone off and handed it back to the sheriff.

Walker stuck a key in the cell door and pulled it open, motioning for Grady to turn around so he could cuff him.

"Is that really necessary?" Grady asked.

"I saw the video," the deputy said. "Don't want you taking a swing at me."

The sheriff stepped away. "I'll be over in a few minutes. Just need to finish talking with my daughter."

His daughter. That made sense. Grady glanced up and saw the girl sitting on the desk in the office where her father had been when Grady first woke up. She had absolutely no expression on her face, as if she didn't have a single thought about the mess he'd caused. That or she didn't have a single thought about him.

Either way, what did it matter? He was on his way to finding out how much he had to pay so he could get out of this place, and it wasn't likely he'd be coming back anytime soon.

Walker must've caught him staring at the blonde—Quinn—because he gave his arm a jerk. "She's off-limits."

Grady looked away but said nothing. Usually with guys like this—guys who had something to prove—Grady did better when he kept his mouth shut.

Which he almost never did. Today he would, but only because he was already in trouble and couldn't afford to tick anyone else off.

Walker pulled him through a back door of the station and out into a parking lot. "Nobody comes back here. Not even those reporters you brought with you."

"I didn't bring them with me," Grady muttered. "I'd love nothing more than for all of them to lose interest in talking about my every move."

Walker pulled him through another door, just a few yards away from the one they'd just exited. "Maybe if you'd stop making such stupid choices, they would."

At that point, even Grady thought the handcuffs were a good idea.

Walker led him down a hallway and through a few doors until finally they were in front of a door labeled *Courtroom*.

A small woman with her hair piled on top of her head appeared in the hallway. "This him?"

Walker glanced at her. "Janice. You're looking radiant this morning."

"Save it, Walker." She eyed Grady. "My kid idolizes you. Wish you'd clean yourself up, so he doesn't have to watch another one of his heroes crash and burn." She pulled the courtroom door open, and Walker gave Grady a tug.

They followed her into the courtroom, her words heaving themselves onto his shoulders. It wasn't the first time a parent had chastised his way of life, but he was an adult. He could live however he saw fit. It wasn't his job to make sure his choices were kid-appropriate.

Even as the thought entered his mind, he knew it was crap. His coaches had drilled it into their heads that the world was watching and they had a responsibility not to let them down.

Maybe that worked for the rest of the team, but Grady didn't appreciate being told how to live his life. His coaches were there to help get him stronger and faster on the slopes—not to make sure he didn't get in a fight in a bar or spend the night with the wrong kind of woman.

The courtroom was small, but it was filled with reporters and cameramen who were clearly camped out and waiting for any juicy bit of gossip about their favorite bad-boy athlete.

Walker led him over to a table and took off his handcuffs, then motioned for him to sit down next to a small man wearing an ugly brown suit and an even uglier red tie.

"This is Stuart Landen," Walker said. "Your lawyer."

"This guy is not my lawyer." Grady sat.

"All attempts to reach the people whose names you gave us failed. Since you don't have a lawyer, one has been appointed to you."

Stuart turned toward him. There was only one way to describe the expression on his face: fearful. The man's dark hair had been slicked down and combed off to the side, and he looked like a pubescent teen who couldn't quite grow facial hair but who desperately needed to shave, just to keep from looking ridiculous.

He pushed his glasses up on his nose. "I'm a huge fan, Mr. Benson."

Grady drew in a deep breath. "Shouldn't we have met before now?"

Stuart shrugged. "I came into work this morning, and they handed me your file. I haven't even had time to look it over."

"Well, that's reassuring."

The door behind the judge's bench opened and the sheriff appeared, followed by a large African American man with a gray beard and a matching ring of hair outlining a bald head. He wore a white dress shirt and tie under a long black robe. Stuart tapped Grady's arm, motioning for him to stand. The nameplate in front of the bench introduced the man as Judge Harrison, and by the looks of it, he and the sheriff were pretty chummy. Grady wasn't sure that was a good thing.

He watched as the sheriff stepped down and sat in the row behind him.

The judge smacked his gavel down. "No cameras."

A low hum of chatter filled the room as the reporters groaned.

"Keep it up, and I'll kick everyone out."

Everyone with a camera slowly packed up their equipment. The judge didn't move until the last cameraman had exited the room. While Grady was thankful he wouldn't allow cameras, he had the distinct impression Judge Harrison was the kind of guy who might find importance in making an example out of him.

And that was just what he needed to take this year from a huge mess to an absolute disaster.

"You can sit down," Judge Harrison said, looking at Grady.

Stuart took a breath. "Your Honor—"

"Stop talking, Mr. . . . what's your name again?"

"Stuart Landen. Attorney for Grady Benson." He said it like it was something to be proud of. As if he'd been picked first for the dodgeball team in gym class. As if he'd forgotten nobody else was offered as a choice.

"I think we can handle this quite simply, Mr. Landen. Mr. Benson, before I decide on your punishment, do you have anything to say for yourself?"

Grady glanced at Stuart, whose eyes went wide, urging him to speak up. But what could he say? He wasn't sorry for clocking that idiot.

Betsy Tanner's face appeared in his mind. He *was* sorry for messing up her restaurant.

Grady pushed himself up out of the chair as the back door to the courtroom opened. Before Grady could speak, Jimmy stormed into the room and glared at him. A trail of bruises lined the space just underneath his eyes, and he had a bandage on his face.

"That guy broke my nose," Jimmy said. The reporters scrambled to write on their little notepads, and the sheriff sat, stoic, one eyebrow raised as if there might be some part of him, buried deep down, that found this whole thing amusing.

"Mr. Hanner, sit down. You'll get your turn in court." The judge was clearly no fan of Jimmy's. At least he and Grady could agree on that.

Jimmy pointed at Grady. "I want to make sure this guy gets what's coming to him."

"That is not your job, Mr. Hanner. That is my job." The judge peered down at Jimmy, then glanced at Walker. "See him out."

Walker grabbed Jimmy by the arm and dragged him up the aisle and out the door.

The judge turned his attention back to Grady. "You were saying?"

"Your Honor, I'm not from here," Grady said.

"Yes, I know," the judge said.

"I was trying to enjoy a bite to eat after many hours in the car, and this man—a stranger—provoked me."

Beside him, Stuart groaned.

"As you can see, the man is easily worked up," Grady added.

"You did break his nose," Judge Harrison said wryly.

Grady shifted. "Sir, I will write a check to pay for the damage to that restaurant."

"You will, huh?" Judge Harrison didn't look impressed.

"Of course, Your Honor. I'll have my business manager wire the money if that's better."

The judge lifted his chin. "That does seem like an easy way to settle this dispute."

"I'm all about easy." Grady's off-the-cuff comment was met with an elbow to the ribs from Stuart.

"I bet you are," the judge said. "Which is exactly the problem I see with so many young people today."

Grady glanced at his lawyer. "Now you've done it," Stuart whispered under his breath.

"I'd like to make amends for my mistake, Your Honor," Grady said, wondering if there was any way to get back on the man's good side when his mere presence seemed to have put him on his bad side in the first place.

"And you think throwing money at this will do that?" The judge still eyed him, perched several feet above where Grady and his dodgeball buddy of a lawyer stood.

"My client isn't suggesting he would throw money at Ms. Tanner, Your Honor," Stuart said. "He would issue a formal apology and truly make this up to her and the rest of the town."

This was the part when the judge slapped a fine on Grady, he called Pete and had him wire the money, and finally—finally—he could get out of this town, which had proven to be far more trouble than it was worth.

The burger was good, but it wasn't *that* good.

"We're a small community here in Harbor Pointe, Mr. Benson. We aren't accustomed to this kind of attention from the press."

Grady shifted from one foot to the other.

"I don't like it," the judge said. "We believe in our business owners, and we expect their property to be taken care of and our people to be respected."

Grady didn't like how this sounded.

"You did neither of those things last night. I know you have plenty of money to make this little mistake go away, but then you'll probably find yourself back in another courtroom just like this one in a few months' time. From what I understand, this isn't your first run-in with the law."

"I've learned my lesson, Your Honor," Grady said so lamely even he didn't believe it.

"Not yet, Mr. Benson. But you will." The judge leveled his gaze, focused on Grady like a hawk on a wire who'd just spotted a field mouse. "You're going to help clean up the mess you made at Hazel's Kitchen. That means not only will you pay for the repairs, but you will help *make* the repairs. If you don't know how to swing a hammer, son, it's time you learned."

"Your Honor, I'm not sure if you know who I am or what I do, but I've got a competition coming up, and I can't miss it. If I do, I won't have the points to qualify for the Olympic team."

The judge's eyebrows lifted. "Perhaps if you'd had a better weekend, you wouldn't be in this mess."

"But, Your Honor, there are only a few races left before the deadline."

Judge Harrison narrowed his gaze. "I see. Well, you'll have to find a competition that's scheduled for after your five weeks here in Harbor Pointe."

"Five weeks?" Grady's tone turned on the verge of disrespectful. "What about my training?"

"We have a ski lodge just outside of town. I'll allow you to train there. I'm sure the kids up there would love to spend some time with an Olympian."

"Your Honor, this is a little unorthodox," Grady said, despite Stuart's hand that served as a warning on his arm.

"Well, then, I'd say the punishment fits the crime."

"You don't understand." He had to be at that race. He had to win back his spot on the team. If he won, if he was fastest, Coach would have no choice but to take him back—the fans would demand it. It wouldn't matter that his technique was ugly or his attitude was hard. They'd put up with him—like they always had—because he was the best.

If he didn't race, how would he prove it? It would just be that much tougher to fix his mistakes.

"I understand plenty. Which is why you should be thankful I'm offering you community service instead of dragging this out for months with a trial that could end up with you in jail."

Grady lifted his chin as he took the judge's point.

"Once you're finished cleaning up the mess you made at Hazel's, you'll move on to other projects here in town. You'll start with the restaurant, help with our upcoming Winter Carnival, and do whatever else we come up with for you to do. Total number of hours of community service, one hundred and fifty to be completed six hours a day for five days for five weeks. Should put you back on the racing circuit by—" he glanced down at what Grady could only assume was a calendar—"mid-January. I assume there will still be a race or two left."

One. There would be exactly one race weekend left. He'd practically have to win it to get the points. No room for error. "Your Honor, that won't leave me any time to train," Grady blurted.

The judge's eyes darted to Grady, who snapped his jaw shut.

"You'll be released on bond, but if you leave the city limits for any reason other than training at Avalanche Mountain, you will be apprehended and the offer of community service will be off the table." The judge eyed Grady. "So what will it be, Mr. Benson? A long trial that will end in jail time, given all the video proof against you, or community service right here in Harbor Pointe?"

Grady clenched his jaw, forcing himself to stay calm.

"We'll take community service, Your Honor," Stuart said.

"Good," Judge Harrison said. "I think that's the smartest thing you've done in a long, long time." He pounded his gavel, stood, and disappeared through the door where he'd entered.

Stuart turned to Grady. "I'd say that's a win."

If he wasn't already in so much trouble, Grady might've throttled him. "A win? Are you serious?"

"You're staying out of jail. That's a win in my book."

Grady raked a hand through his dark hair, hitting a bruise he'd undoubtedly sustained in his fight the night before.

The sheriff—Gus—strolled over as the reporters clamored toward the front of the room. "Best get you out of here," he said.

Grady stood and followed him out the back door and into the hallway, where he stopped and let out a frustrated stream of hot air. "This is a mess."

Gus turned. "Could be worse."

"I know. I heard." But could it? He might as well be in jail if he couldn't fight for his spot on the team. "There's just no way any of you could understand."

"You're right. We're simple folks. But we do know how to behave in public." Gus turned and flicked his wrist forward, as if to suggest Grady should follow.

Minutes later they were back in the police station. "You look like you could use a hot shower and a good meal," Gus said as he closed the door behind them.

"I'm fine."

Gus's nod was slow and steady as his eyes studied Grady. "Uh-huh."

Grady looked away.

"My daughter Quinn—I think you saw her earlier—she used to hate taking baths at night. It was like torture or something. You know what I always told her?"

Grady responded with a quick, annoyed shake of his head.

"You gotta do it every single day, and complaining about it only makes that part of your day harder."

Grady resisted the urge to roll his eyes. He didn't need the old man's little nuggets of wisdom. He needed a fresh change of clothes and a way out of this dump.

"Well, you get the point. The judge made his ruling, so that's that. No sense complaining about it—you just have to move on. We do have a nice little ski resort, and I'm betting they'd let you train for free."

"Gee, that sounds great." A ski resort in southern Michigan would do him no good. Did anybody here know what kind of skier he was?

Gus smiled and his eyes creased into thin lines. "Well, you don't know anyone, so I'll get you settled in at one of the cottages here in town. You can shower and change and then report to Hazel's for cleanup duty."

"Great."

Gus turned to the plump secretary with short hair and glasses, who now sat behind the desk where Quinn had set the vase of daisies. "Arlene, do you have Mr. Benson's paperwork?"

The woman spun around in her chair, grabbed a manila folder, and slid it across the desk. "Sure do, boss." She looked up at Grady. "It's nice to meet you, Mr. Benson."

Grady nodded. He couldn't get out of here fast enough.

"Just have a few things for you to sign. Then you can be on your way."

"Shouldn't my lawyer be here with me?" Grady asked as Gus spread three sheets of paper out across the desk.

"Probably, but then Stuart Landen has never been the brightest bulb in the bunch. He's probably stuck in the hallway trying to figure out where you ran off to." Gus laughed at his own joke, which Grady did not find amusing.

He huffed, picked up the pen, and signed his name three times. Before he could set the pen down, Arlene stuck a notebook on the desk in front of him. "Can I get an autograph for my daughter? Her name is Madison."

He scribbled, *For Madison. Aim high. Grady Benson* on the paper and threw the pen down.

Arlene picked up the notebook and grinned. "She's going to be so excited. Can we take a quick selfie?"

"Arlene." Gus's tone warned.

"Sorry, boss. Maybe another day. Heard you're going to be in town for a few weeks."

Inside, Grady groaned. Outside, he forced a smile, which he knew looked completely fake, and took a step back.

Gus handed him a plastic bag with his wallet, phone, and keys in it. "Your stuff."

"Thanks." They walked toward the front door.

"And you can follow me out to Cedar Grove," Gus said, peeking out the window. "On second thought, maybe I should drive you. Wouldn't want these vultures finding out where you're staying."

"Isn't that inevitable?"

Gus shrugged. "We can keep them off your scent as long as possible."

Was the man actually trying to help him?

"I'm parked out back. I'll have one of my deputies drive your car." He held out his hand, and Grady put the keys in it. He couldn't believe this was happening. Someone had to be able to get him out of this.

But as he stepped into the squad car—this time in the front seat—and another call to Pete went to voice mail, he wasn't so sure he even had anyone left interested in helping him at all.

CHAPTER

4

QUINN WALKED UP THE SIDEWALK toward the small white cottage where she'd grown up. Nondescript except for the turquoise mailbox she'd insisted on several years ago.

"It gives the house character," Quinn had told her father, who would've much preferred boring old black and not a single pot of flowers on the porch.

"The house has enough character on the inside," he'd said.

At least he had the Christmas lights on.

After Quinn's sister, Carly, and her son, Jaden, moved out, it had been just the two of them—Quinn and Gus. Did Daddy ever miss her now that she was living above the flower shop? Did he miss their late-night chats over hand-popped popcorn or their never-ending games of Scrabble—which she always won?

She should spend more time with him. She'd gotten so busy lately, and sometimes absent-daughter guilt niggled at her, though she knew he was far from alone. Even now, through the window, she could see the living room full of people—Judge Walter

Harrison, Calvin Doyle, and Beverly Sanders, who she was certain had been angling for her father's eye since the day her mother packed her suitcase and drove out of town. These four had become inseparable—and they were always quick to include Quinn in their shenanigans.

In so many ways, it was like she'd been raised by all four of them. After all, it was Beverly who had taken her to buy her prom dress and Judge who had helped her buy her first car. Calvin had tutored her through chemistry—and she'd gotten an A! And of course, her father had been there for everything. Even when she was nursing the grief that sometimes crept in unexpectedly. Grief over a person who wasn't dead but who was gone just the same. Quinn actually found that harder to swallow. At least if her mother had died, she wouldn't have to wonder what she'd done to drive away the woman she thought was supposed to love her unconditionally.

She didn't bother knocking. Instead she walked inside, pushing away the chill of December as she closed the door.

"She's here!" Beverly rushed toward her, pulling her into the living room before Quinn could even take off her coat as Calvin disappeared into the kitchen.

"She's here?" Her father stepped out of the kitchen wearing two oven mitts and a very frilly apron.

"That's a great look for you, Dad."

He waved her off. "No sass tonight, Daughter. This is a celebration."

She felt her brow furrow. "What are we celebrating? I thought it was just dinner."

Judge let out a cackle from his spot in the old recliner in the living room—a spot he didn't appear to have any interest in vacating. "You know us better than that by now, don't you?"

Calvin appeared in the doorway that led to the kitchen. He held a cake covered in flickering candles, highlighted by the backlight of the Christmas tree, which she could only assume Beverly had decorated.

"It's not my birthday," Quinn said as Calvin came into the room and set the cake on the coffee table.

"No, it's your 'Hey, I bought a business' day." Beverly squeezed her arm. "Make a wish."

"I don't think it works this way," Quinn said. She glanced at her father, whose face held the unmistakable look of pride.

"It does tonight," he said. "Blow 'em out."

She sat on the couch with her dad and Beverly on either side of her, almost as if they were both her parents, eyes beaming and everything.

"Make it a good one," Beverly said.

Quinn stared at the tiny flames dotting the white cake with red frosting letters that spelled out *Congratulations, Quinn.* There were flowers all around the border. "Did you get this at Dandy's?"

Calvin sat in the small chair across from them. "Where else?"

"Did you talk to Mary-Margaret, Calvin?" Quinn eyed him from where she sat.

The man—one of the shyest she'd ever met—looked away. "She made your cake, yes."

"And?"

"And didn't she do a nice job?" Beverly tugged on Quinn's arm. "The wax is going to start dripping all over the frosting if you don't hurry up."

"Okay, okay." Quinn closed her eyes. Her wish would be the same as it had been since she'd gotten the idea that she could buy the flower shop in the first place. *Please let me win Best Design at the Michigan Floral Expo. And please let her be there to see it when I do.*

She blew out the candles. She knew it was ridiculous—a childhood fantasy, really—but that wouldn't stop her from hoping.

"Did you wish for some handsome fellow to come sweep you off your feet?" Beverly practically gushed.

"My daughter?" Gus let out a laugh. "You know that's the last thing on her mind. Especially now that her dream has come true."

Quinn sighed. "Well, it hasn't come true yet, Dad. I've still got a ton of work to do before I can reopen the flower shop. You know I love Mimi, but she let everything get so outdated."

"We'll help where we can," Judge said. "And I'm sure we can round up some great volunteers. This town loves to support its local businesses."

"Hey, maybe you should add helping at Quinn's shop to that skier's community service," Beverly joked.

At least Quinn thought she was joking.

"That's not a half-bad idea," Judge said. "Then something good would come out of his little mishap last night."

"No, thank you," Quinn said. "That's about the last thing I need. My plan is to stay as far away from that guy as possible."

"Can we eat?" Her dad stood, tugging his jeans up as he did. His striped button-down was neatly tucked into his pants, and he wore a pair of loafers Quinn had begged him to get rid of for at least the last five years.

"Yes." Beverly also stood, then moved across the room. "The table's already set, so hurry on in. We made spaghetti and meatballs with salad and garlic bread. Hope you're hungry."

Judge's recliner snapped back to an upright position, and he pushed himself out. "You don't have to tell me twice." Quinn had learned a long time ago that he loved to eat. His wife had died ten years prior, leaving a gaping hole in these kinds of gatherings. Eventually, they all settled into a new pattern, though Quinn knew he still thought about her every single day.

The sadness behind his eyes, even when he smiled, gave him away.

She walked into the dining room, the others following behind. "Why are there six places set?"

As she said it, the doorbell rang. "Who else is coming?"

"Your father's big heart strikes again." Beverly glanced at him with those big, round I-love-you eyes. Her father didn't seem to notice.

Instead he walked out of the dining room toward the front door. "Get settled. I'll be right back."

Seconds later, she heard his voice mixing with another male's. She glared toward the door. "Promise me this isn't a setup."

"Oh, nooooo." Judge shook his head. "I can promise you that is not what this is. This is the opposite of that, Miss Quinn, so get that out of your head right now."

"Then who is out there?"

"Another one of your father's charity cases." Beverly sat down in her usual chair, then motioned for Quinn to do the same.

"Like someone from the halfway house?" Quinn kept her voice low as she followed Beverly's unspoken instructions.

"Not this time." Judge took a seat at the end of the table, Calvin at his left, leaving the only open chair at his right, beside Quinn.

Obviously her father had clued everyone in on their mystery guest before she arrived, leaving her hopelessly in the dark.

Gus appeared in the doorway. "Everyone, you remember Grady." Her father scooted to the side and a much taller, broader, stronger-looking man came into view.

Quinn frowned. The guy from the diner? The cocky one with the temper? What on earth was her father thinking inviting this guy to her celebratory dinner? Granted, she didn't know it was a celebratory dinner when she'd arrived, but now that she did, she didn't want him to be a part of it. Grady whatever-his-name-was did *not* deserve cake from Dandy's.

Quinn glanced at Beverly, whose adoring expression appeared to have shifted from her father to the much younger man at his side. *Oh, please.* This guy was not to be admired. Had they all forgotten what he'd done to Betsy's diner?

"Good to see you again, son." Judge was using his judge voice.

Grady glanced over, visibly surprised to see the man who had issued his punishment sitting at the table in a social setting. He'd learn. This was how things worked in Harbor Pointe.

"Here, have a seat." Gus pointed at the chair next to Quinn, then moved to the end of the table opposite the judge.

Quinn stared straight ahead while Grady found his seat.

"This is Calvin sitting across from you, and Beverly next to him. You already know Judge Harrison."

Another glance toward Judge's end of the table. Quinn almost smiled at the serious expression on the man's face. How anyone could find Judge—a big, soft teddy bear—intimidating was beyond her. But people did. He was one of the most well-liked men in Harbor Pointe, but he was also one of the most feared. He was known for being fair and honest, but nobody ever had to wonder what the man was thinking.

She hoped some of that had rubbed off on her after all these years.

"Sir." Grady gave him a quick nod, then turned his attention back to Gus.

"And this is my daughter Quinn." Gus gave her a warm smile. She didn't smile back. She'd let out a groan, but it would be too obvious.

"You were at the police station." Grady was turned in her direction.

Quinn took a sip of water. "So were you."

Judge let out a laugh. Quinn could sense her father's eyes on her. He'd want her to behave, but she couldn't help it. She knew Grady's type. Not all the tourists understood or appreciated their way of life in Harbor Pointe. Maybe Quinn wasn't being fair, but she didn't feel the need to welcome this guy into their family.

"Beverly made the meatballs by hand. You've never tasted anything so good." Gus nodded at the woman sitting next to him.

"Thanks for having me," Grady said.

"Let's pray."

Oh no. Quinn forgot about the prayer. And the hand-holding.

What was she, twelve? It was no big deal. She watched as they all joined hands and felt a prodding squeeze from her father on her right. Slowly, she held out an upturned hand and Grady looked at it, confusion on his face. His eyes scanned the table, and when he realized they were *that* kind of family, he reached over and slid his strong hand around hers.

"Lord, we thank you for this meal and for every person around this table. We thank you for bringing us together . . ."

Quinn's eyes fluttered open, and even with her head still bowed she could feel Grady shifting at her side. Prayer must make him uncomfortable.

"And thank you for bringing our new friend, Grady, into our lives. We pray his time here in Harbor Pointe is fruitful."

A nearly undetectable scoff at her left pulled her eyes open again. She glanced over, but he was staring at his lap.

"Amen."

In unison, everyone grabbed the dish closest to them and started passing.

Quinn picked up the salad and served a spoonful onto her plate. Calvin started the bread around the table. And nobody said a word.

Quinn could appreciate her father's charity—he had a heart as big as his head, but it often misled him. Look at his marriage, after all. How did he keep from letting it all make him angry? He'd been taken advantage of over and over again, yet Gus Collins was still one of the kindest, most generous people she knew.

"Where are Carly and Jaden?" Quinn asked. "Shouldn't they be here?"

"Yes, they absolutely should," Gus said. "But Carly had to work and Jaden had some school project due. They were sad to miss."

She could use her sister's company about now. At least then she'd have someone to commiserate with.

"We were just talking about you before you arrived, Grady." Gus passed the serving bowl of spaghetti and meatballs to Quinn. "How you could help Quinn here as part of your community service."

Grady handed off the salad to Judge and looked up. She couldn't be sure, but he appeared to be about as surprised as she was. "Me?"

Quinn's desire to groan had turned into a desire to scream. Her father's charity had gone too far! She didn't want this guy in her flower shop.

"We weren't serious, of course," Gus said. "Though she could use all the help she can get."

Quinn held the big bowl of pasta with both hands, trying to find a way to express herself without being rude to their guest before Judge actually considered this.

"Do you need help?" Grady was staring at her now, and while she couldn't be sure, he almost looked . . . genuine.

"What?" She glanced down at the giant bowl. "No. I'm fine." She set it on the table and scooped some spaghetti out, though she'd pretty much lost her appetite.

She didn't want reporters camped outside her flower shop while she worked on the most important design of her life. She needed to stay focused. And she had a feeling Grady Benson came with a long list of distractions, not the least of which were his icy-blue eyes.

Quinn didn't pick the bowl up to pass it to him, deciding instead to give it a little push in his direction when she was finished.

"Quinn, you hardly took any food." Beverly sounded surprised. After all, Quinn was a healthy eater.

"Dad, can I talk to you in the kitchen for a minute?"

Her father's eyebrows shot up, like they sometimes did when one of his little plans went awry. She could appreciate his heart, but even kidding about the shop renovations had her on edge.

Or maybe it was all she had riding on getting this right.

Once they were alone in the small cottage kitchen, Quinn closed the swinging door, reminding herself to stay calm so none of her anger was overheard by anyone in the next room.

"Dad. What are you doing?" she hissed.

He put on his best I'm-innocent-and-don't-know-what-you're-talking-about face.

"Don't do that. Was this your plan all along—to figure out a way to get this guy sentenced to *my* flower shop?"

"Quinn, I'm not even the one who brought the idea up," he said.

She wasn't buying it. "And you knew this wouldn't be okay with me, which is why you waited until he was sitting at our table—" she whispered those last four words—"to tell me."

"That's not true. It was just an off-the-cuff idea. We can drop it."

Quinn let out a heavy sigh. "I don't want him at the shop, Dad."

"I understand," her father paused. "Though you do need help. I work all day. Judge works all day. Calvin—God love him—doesn't know the first thing about building repairs."

"And what makes you think this guy does?"

Her dad shrugged. "Just a hunch."

"Well, I disagree."

He leaned against the counter and crossed his arms over his chest. "You seem stressed out. You might be overreacting a little."

She pinched the bridge of her nose and inhaled. Her exhale was slow and steady. Her dad was right. She probably *was* overreacting.

But for some reason, she just went right on doing so.

"Did you see what he did at Hazel's? I was there. I definitely don't need *that* in my shop. He can help somewhere else." She turned away from him.

"Fine by me," Dad said. "But he is helping at the Winter Carnival, which means he might end up moving some things around for your display. Can you at least handle that?"

She sighed.

"He's just one guy, Quinn."

She shook her head. "It's not him, Dad." An admission her father had probably been waiting for. Quinn had a knack for getting upset about one thing when what really bothered her was something else entirely.

He looked at her like he'd already guessed as much. "Then what is it?"

Should she explain how important her design for the Winter Carnival was? How it was the ticket to the Floral Expo and . . . *her*?

She looked up at her father, with his deep-set wrinkles and ruddy skin. Strong as he was, it would hurt him to know how much she still pined for the parent who walked away.

"I have to stay focused, Dad. This guy is a huge distraction, and I can't deal with that right now."

It was a non-answer, and they both knew it. It said, *I'm not willing to confide in you.* There was unmistakable hurt behind her father's eyes.

"That's fine, Q," he said. "But I didn't raise you to be rude."

She'd behaved badly. She'd been unwelcoming, and that embarrassed her father. "I'm sorry, Dad."

He looked away, but he had something else to say, she could tell. "What is it?"

"About this contest, Q." He picked up one of her hands. "You're putting an awful lot of pressure on yourself."

"This is what I've been working toward, Dad. This is my dream."

"I know, I know." He squeezed her hand. "I just don't want you to hang too many hopes on this festival or this expo or this prize."

"You don't think I can win?"

"No, I know you can win." He met her eyes. "I just don't know that it'll change anything." He paused. He knew she wanted to win—but did he know why? For a moment, it almost seemed like he did, though she'd never discussed it with him.

Quinn pressed her lips together and swallowed, working hard to maintain her resolve. He was wrong. This was her only chance—it had to work.

It had to.

Her father walked away, leaving her standing alone in the kitchen inhaling the pungent aroma of garlic and tomato sauce and trying desperately not to entertain the one question that kept racing through her mind: If it *didn't* work . . . what was she going to do?

CHAPTER

5

ONCE AGAIN Grady was sitting at a table and feeling like he shouldn't be here. When the sheriff invited him to dinner, of course his first thought was *No. Way.* But then Gus mentioned that the judge would be there, and Grady hoped he might be able to reason with the man—maybe he'd be more lenient outside the courtroom.

So far, though, Grady had simply endured long, rambling stories of fishing expeditions and high school pranks, as if his presence gave the men a chance to relive their glory days.

And then there was the matter of the ice radiating off of the woman sitting in the chair next to him. Quinn Collins had already made up her mind about him, and whatever she was thinking, it wasn't good.

She'd probably seen the footage of his wipeout at last week's race, followed by his subsequent fight with Brian Murphy, his longtime coach and now one of the coaches of the US ski team. Not his finest hour.

He had to figure out a way to get to Colorado—even if the coach and his former teammates had made it very clear they'd rather he just retire.

He needed the sponsorships. Needed the distraction. Needed the gold. He owed it to Benji.

After they'd finished eating, Beverly, a short woman with a round face and dark hair who he assumed was Quinn's mother even though the two looked nothing alike, stood. "I'll clear away the dishes and be right back with the cake."

"We're celebrating, Grady," Gus said from the other end of the table.

"Celebrating?" Grady should at least pretend to care. Who knows? Maybe playing nice with this group would earn him credit with the judge.

"Quinn bought the flower shop downtown." Beverly reached for his plate. He handed it over and glanced at Quinn, who sat with her hands in her lap, unmoving.

"It's not that big of a deal," she said.

"It is too." Gus leaned toward her. "It's what you've been waiting for."

"I'll help you, Beverly." Quinn grabbed the stack of plates from across the table and disappeared into the kitchen.

"She's very modest." Beverly smiled at Grady.

"Well, we're all proud of her," the judge said. "We can't help it if we want to brag on our girl."

"That's right," Gus said, then called out—this time louder—"You hear that, Quinn? We're all proud of you!"

"That's great, Dad," she called back.

She returned a few seconds later, following Beverly, who carried a cake that looked like it had, at one point, had candles in it. It was an odd way to celebrate something that wasn't a birthday, but then, nothing about this town seemed normal to him.

Quinn set a stack of small plates on the table, and Beverly began slicing the cake. She handed Grady the first piece.

"Bev, he probably doesn't eat cake," the man sitting across from him said.

"Of course he does, Calvin," Beverly said.

Calvin. Grady would try to remember.

Pete always told him he was terrible with names. *"It offends people, you know, that you can't remember any of their names. I mean, Jerrica has worked for you for two years and you still call her Jennifer."*

"Jerrica is a weird name," Grady had said. *"It's hard to remember."*

"Not the point. These people work tirelessly for you. A little gratitude goes a long way."

"I show my gratitude in their paychecks," Grady told him, but judging by the look on Pete's face, his manager disagreed.

Why hadn't Pete called him back?

"You do eat cake, don't you?" Beverly's question pulled Grady back to the present.

"He probably does." The judge leaned back in his chair. "He's not the kind of athlete who buys into that whole 'my body is a temple' thing. This one puts whatever he wants in his body." He let out a laugh, the kind of laugh that got right under Grady's skin.

Grady reached over and took the cake from Beverly. "My body is a well-oiled machine, ma'am. But it doesn't mind a little sugar now and then."

"Good, because it'd be a shame to miss out on Dandy's cake." She went back to cutting. "You probably don't know Dandy's since you're not from here, but it's a local bakery, just across the street from Quinn's flower shop." She flashed Quinn a smile and handed her a plate. "Oh, you'll find it when you're downtown this week. Judge told us about your community service."

Nothing like calling out the elephant in the room. Again.

"About that." Grady turned his attention to the judge. "Wondering if I could have a word with you later about my, uh . . . sentence?"

Could he call it a sentence? It was unlike any court proceeding he'd ever had.

The judge stuck his fork in the cake and broke off a good chunk.

"I don't see that we have much to talk about, Mr. Benson. And I don't talk business at family dinner."

Family dinner? This was the strangest "family" he'd ever seen.

"Judge, give the kid a break." Gus swallowed his bite and tossed a pointed look across the table.

"You don't like to talk shop when you're eating cake any more than I do." The judge pointed at Gus with his fork.

"What's your question, Grady?" Beverly asked. "You just ask me, and if Judge overhears, he won't be able to keep himself from responding."

The judge set his fork down with a clink. "Is that right?"

Beverly shot him a knowing look. She focused on Grady. "Go on."

Beside him, Quinn shifted in her seat, pushing the cake around on her plate. Why did he suddenly feel like he'd been put on the spot? He hadn't intended to make this proposal in front of everyone.

"Well?" Gus glanced up at him.

"December and January are big competition months." He forced himself not to think about his last competition. If he hadn't wiped out, the pressure would be so much less, but he'd lost focus. Stupid mistakes cost him that peace of mind.

How did he explain that to a table of people who could never understand the kind of pressure he was under?

"They going to let you race again after that little stunt you pulled last week?" The judge eyed him. "Most coaches I know don't appreciate it when their players take off, especially not when they're trying to talk to them."

Did the judge know *all* of his business?

Harbor Pointe might be a small town, but they still had the Internet. The clip of him arguing with his coach, then leaving with a dismissive wave, had unfortunately made the social media rounds. There was no screwing up in private anymore.

Grady drew in a deep breath. "I'm going to get my spot back."

"Oh, you are?" The judge leveled his gaze. "How do you plan to do that?"

Was he serious? Same way he'd always done it—brute strength, fearless skiing, and a whole lot of raw talent that made him one of the fastest downhill skiers in the country. "I've got it under control."

The judge laughed again, then glanced at Gus. "Do you hear this guy?"

Gus didn't respond. None of them did. "I'd like to propose that if I pay a fine and make a donation to that restaurant, you let me off without community service. The money will come in a lot handier than my physical labor."

"The boy might have a point there," the man across from him—Calvin—said.

"I'm not the handiest guy," Grady added.

"That right?" The judge took his last bite of cake. "What do you all think? Does this boy deserve to be let off with a slap on the wrist and a fine?"

"Sounds like that's what he's used to," Gus said.

"But does that make it the best choice?" Judge asked. "Say you're me. You see a talented, accomplished guy enter your courtroom. A little bit of digging and you learn this isn't his first offense."

"I can explain—"

The judge held up a hand that silenced Grady. "You have a choice. You can fine him, which will really cost him nothing, or you can help him learn the value of hard work."

"He's an Olympic athlete, Judge. I think he knows about hard work." Calvin seemed to be his only ally at the table.

The judge eyed him. "Do you, son?"

"Do I what?" About now Grady was regretting ever bringing this up in the first place. What he needed was for Pete to call him back, flex some of those monetary muscles, and make this go away.

"Do you know the value of hard work?"

"Of course I do."

The judge looked skeptical.

"These races are important, sir."

"I don't doubt it."

"I need to get out there." Did he sound desperate? He felt desperate. And he hated that.

"You have a rare chance to learn something here, Mr. Benson. I suggest you stop trying to figure out a way out of it and get on board."

"You want me to get on board with giving up five weeks of my life to live in this good-for-nothing town, wasting my time on some stupid festival and parading around your little rinky-dink ski lodge like I'm a circus act?"

The judge folded his hands on the table in front of him but didn't respond.

Grady couldn't believe this. "You know what I think, Your Honor?"

"Can't wait to hear."

"I think you just want to stick it to guys like me. You live for it. Makes you feel important in this tiny little town you live in."

A tense hush filled the room as Grady pushed his chair away from the table. "Thank you, Sheriff, for inviting me over for dinner. It was nice to meet you all." Then he turned to the judge. "You'll be hearing from my lawyer. My real one."

He turned to go, but before he reached the front door, he overheard the judge say, "That one has a lot to learn."

Grady snatched his coat off of a hook and pulled it on as he walked out onto the porch, a memory rushing back so fast it almost knocked him down.

"He's reckless, Randall."

Thirteen-year-old Grady stood between his father and his ski coach—Benji just a few feet away.

"He's fearless," Grady's dad said. "Isn't that something you can work with in a young skier?"

The coach shook his head. "Look, your son has more natural ability and raw talent than anyone I've ever trained."

Grady remembered how that comment had buoyed him, made him feel special somehow.

The coach glanced at Grady. "But he doesn't listen. Raw talent will only take you so far, kid. You've still got a lot to learn."

They left the slopes that day and his dad gave him an earful, but even his father's insistence that Grady listen to his coach and make the necessary adjustments didn't change anything. Grady was fast—faster than anyone his age—and that was what mattered. He didn't care if he had the proper technique. He just wanted to win.

His phone buzzed in his pocket. He pulled it out as he opened the door to his car and got inside.

Pete. Finally.

Grady started the car and answered the call. "You better have a great explanation for going radio silent the last two days."

"Grady. Sorry I've been out of touch."

"Are you seeing what's going on here?"

"I saw the news, yes." Sometimes Grady hated how level-headed Pete was. Shouldn't the man be outraged that his biggest client was stuck in some podunk tourist town? Shouldn't he be on the first plane to Michigan to take care of this for him?

"And?"

"And what?"

"And what are we going to do to get me out of here?"

There was a pause on Pete's end.

"Pete?"

"I don't see that there's much we can do, Grady."

Now it was Grady's turn to pause—mostly because he was trying to process exactly what his manager had said. He had to be kidding. Where was plan B?

"These small towns are particular. I spoke with your lawyer, and he said it's the judge's decision. We can appeal it, but by the time we got any movement on the case, your community service would be finished."

"I can't believe what I'm hearing."

"I know it's not ideal."

"Not ideal? I don't have that many chances left to qualify, Pete." He hoped his manager didn't hear the subtext of that sentence: *I need every chance I can get.*

"You're going to miss a few key races, yes, but there are still a few left in January."

"There's one, Pete. Five weeks go by, and I'm left with exactly one shot."

That shut his manager up.

"How am I going to train here? Do you know where I am?" Grady looked out the window, quaint little cottages dotting either side of the quiet street.

"There's a ski lodge just outside of town. The lawyer said the judge is allowing you to go there."

"This is the Midwest. I can't ski in a cornfield."

Pete sighed. "Look, I hate this as much as you do, but you might not have a choice."

"I expect you to take care of this kind of thing for me. Come out here, pay the judge off, whatever it takes—"

"I can't do that, Grady."

"You can't or you won't?"

"I can't. You don't have the funds."

Grady's heart dropped. "What are you talking about?"

"I've been looking at your statements. Looks like you were pretty busy last month."

"It's almost Christmas."

"You spent more money than some people make in a year. The endorsement offers aren't coming in like they used to. You can't live your life the way you have been—if you do, you're not going to have anything left. And Benji—"

"What about Benji?"

"He's covered for this month. Maybe next month. But that's it, Grady. You've got to make some changes."

Grady rubbed his temples. This could not be happening.

The door of Gus's cottage opened, and Quinn stepped out onto the porch. She hugged her dad, waved good-bye, and turned toward a black Volkswagen Jetta parked across the street. He watched as she set a box (probably leftover cake?) on the backseat of the car, then got in and started the engine. She stared at the cottage for several seconds before finally pulling away, thankfully oblivious that he hadn't left yet.

"Do you hear me, Grady?"

"Yeah, I hear you." He hung up the phone and tossed it on the seat next to him.

How the heck was he going to get out of this one?

CHAPTER

6

THE MORNING SUN POURED THROUGH THE WINDOWS in the loft above the flower shop, drawing Quinn from sleep.

She lay in bed, savoring the warmth of her two old quilts, staring up at the eleven-foot ceiling with exposed ductwork. She rolled to her side. It was Tuesday. There was so much to do. The Winter Carnival was scheduled, as usual, to begin with a ball the day before New Year's Eve, and she hadn't even started on her design for the opening ceremonies stage. The display—and the mixing of snow with flowers—was one of those traditions her mother had started so many years ago in Harbor Pointe. And this year, it was up to Quinn to make it the very best it had ever been.

But for some reason, her creativity was completely blocked. For days she'd sat with an empty sketchbook, trying to summon that fleeting inspiration. So far, it eluded her.

She drew in a deep breath, wishing away the pressure that seemed to follow her around. At least here, in her loft, she felt a modicum of peace.

She'd painted the brick walls white and added long, flowing curtains on each of the three windows that looked out over the street. It might've made more sense to buy a little cottage (though they didn't go on the market very often), but Quinn loved living above the flower shop. She loved the way the old-fashioned streetlights shone through her windows every night, and how, in the summer, she could watch the tourists strolling down the sidewalk, stopping at Dandy's Bakery or the Old Time Ice Cream Parlor for a post-beach treat. She could hear the bells from the trolley cars that took people from the boardwalk to the shopping or dining spot of their choice.

In short, she loved Harbor Pointe, and she couldn't imagine living anywhere else, partly because she never had. Even in college, Quinn had commuted and lived at home.

She'd said it was to save money, but she knew the real reason. Leaving wasn't an option.

She pulled herself out of bed and stepped into her fuzzy raccoon slippers—a gift from Beverly two Christmases ago. She made a mental note to talk to her dad about Beverly. The poor woman had to be in agony trying to win his attention after all these years. Was her father really that clueless?

She stood in the shower and let the hot water run down her back. Winters in Michigan were long and often dreary, and Quinn was always cold. Maybe that's why she couldn't find her inspiration. She leaned against the wall of the shower and prayed it would find her—that suddenly, out of nowhere, she'd fall into a vat of it and emerge with the best design ideas she'd ever had.

"Lord, you know how important this is to me."

He did, didn't he? He was God, after all. Had she been clear enough in explaining it to him?

Just in case, it wouldn't hurt to reiterate.

"Everything depends on this. I've been waiting years—twenty years—for this moment. I can't let it slip through my fingers." She spoke the words aloud, as if that made them matter more.

She finished up in the shower and got dressed for the day—jeans and her favorite gray sweater. Once she'd dried her long blonde hair and put on a tiny bit of makeup (mascara was a necessity thanks to the blonde eyelashes), she pulled on her cozy gray Ugg boots, stuck her planner, sketchbook, and laptop in her bag, and walked out the door.

There was a light dusting of snow on the ground and the air was chilly—surprisingly so because the sun was shining, making someone inside think perhaps they were going to get a little bit of a heat wave.

No such luck.

The streetlamps were decorated with wreaths, and at night the huge Christmas tree at the center of downtown would sparkle with its twinkly white lights. The Harbor Pointe tree lighting was held on the Saturday after Thanksgiving, and Quinn was thankful for the extended period of time in which to enjoy it. When she looked out the windows of her loft, she almost felt as if she were standing in the middle of a snowglobe.

She walked a few doors down to Hazel's, thinking of last night's dinner and Grady Benson trying to buy his way out of his punishment. He obviously didn't know Judge.

Part of her should feel sorry for the man. He was in quite the predicament. But she found it difficult to muster sympathy for someone whose troubles were self-made.

Didn't he feel even a little bit sorry for what he'd done to the diner? Betsy had worked so hard building her business—and now what? She had to spend money and time fixing everything he'd destroyed just because someone insulted his ego?

Another reason Quinn was glad she was single. She didn't understand men. Even Marcus, as predictable as he was, had never made sense to her—and they'd dated for five full years.

She pushed the thought aside as she waved to Juniper Jones, the town's most eccentric resident. Quinn couldn't be sure, but she thought perhaps Juniper was responsible for the cotton-candy paint treatment the storefronts of Harbor Pointe's downtown had gotten long ago. She was, after all, the one always talking about how charming it was—and how unique.

"Cottage towns in Michigan are all the same. Quaint. Brick build-ings. Striped awnings. I'm glad Harbor Pointe is as colorful as the personalities of the people who live here."

Quinn always nodded in agreement, though she couldn't think of anyone quite as colorful as Juniper. She was a perfect example of why Quinn loved this town. She may never have traveled any-where else, but she had to guess if she did, she'd never stumble upon another Juniper Jones.

Quinn pulled open the door to Hazel's and beelined for her usual booth. With any luck, Ryan Brooks would be at his usual table, and Quinn could pick his brain about some of the changes she wanted to make in the flower shop.

Hailey Brooks, Ryan's sister and one of Quinn's best friends, spotted her from across the restaurant. Quinn's eyes scanned the damage. They'd cleaned up the shards of glass and removed the broken tables, but Betsy had lost a number of seats, and Hazel's felt more crowded for it.

She glanced at Ryan, who sat, as usual, at the booth kitty-corner from her, drinking coffee and looking at a menu she happened to know he did not need.

This was his ritual—to come into this diner, order the same thing every morning, and then go off to work. Lately, Ryan's fian-cée, Lane Kelley, joined him, and Quinn swore if she walked in the door right about now, she'd take it as a sign from heaven that she should go ahead and ask them all her questions, even though she was pretty sure she couldn't afford their services.

After all, the two of them worked together to restore cottages throughout Harbor Pointe and all the way into Summers Bay. She'd seen their work. It was exquisite. And while she could use the pro-fessional help, it likely came with a professional price tag.

Hailey brought Quinn her usual skinny vanilla latte and sat down across from her. "You're late today."

Quinn took a drink and let its warmth settle inside her empty belly for a few seconds before talking. "I overslept."

Hailey's eyes widened. "You? My everything-has-to-be-just-so friend? That doesn't sound like you."

Quinn sighed. "I know. I'm usually out cold by eleven. I think it was at least 2 a.m. before I finally drifted off to sleep."

"What's wrong?"

She shook her head. "It's nothing."

"It's obviously not nothing. You're the most regimented person I know. Something's off."

"I'll be fine. It's just been a busy week." Shouldn't she confide in her? Hailey knew all about the Winter Carnival and why her display had to be perfect. Hailey was one of the few people who understood what was at stake here.

The door swung open and Lucy Fitzgerald strolled in. While she was one of Quinn's oldest friends, Lucy was cut from a completely different cloth than Hailey or Quinn. Two married parents who still loved each other. A brother, a sister, an impressive career as a freelance writer and journalist, a boyfriend who was hopelessly devoted to her—not to mention that ridiculous, jealousy-inducing figure she seemed to come by naturally. Plus, she was tan. In December. How was that possible?

But in spite of the fact that both Hailey's and Quinn's lives were the polar opposite of Lucy's, she was impossible to hate. Lucy Fitzgerald was "a friend to all." It said so underneath her senior photo in the high school yearbook. And it was true.

Besides, Quinn knew more about Lucy than the average person, and while it was easy to forget with Lucy's sunny disposition, life hadn't always been perfect for her red-haired friend. Lucy was no stranger to tragedy.

"Girls, I need coffee."

Hailey stood. "I'll be right back."

"Mocha with extra whip," Lucy called out after her.

Whole milk and extra whip? Only Lucy!

Quinn pushed the thought out of her mind and took a sip of her own latte, hoping *it* wasn't accidentally made with whole milk.

"Is it official?" Lucy's face beamed.

Quinn, tired though she was, felt her face warm into a smile. "It's official."

"You're the owner?" Her eyes went wide.

Hailey returned with two drinks, one for Lucy and one for herself. "It's official?"

"I signed the paperwork yesterday. Got the keys and everything."

"How do you feel? You're a business owner! Are you freaking out?" Hailey and Lucy oozed enthusiasm, their questions overlapping each other.

"I feel excited—relieved. Like, finally my life can begin." She glanced up to see that both their faces had fallen. "What?"

Hailey and Lucy exchanged a quick but pointed glance. "It's nothing," Hailey said. "We're really happy for you."

"You can't do that. I know you two. What was that look about?"

Lucy pressed her lips together, then smiled—a genuine smile, not one of those phony, meant-to-make-you-feel-better kind of smiles. "We just hope you're right. That now your life can begin."

"You've just been so stuck, Q. You have to admit it." Hailey turned her mug around in her hand. "Maybe now you'll move on."

Quinn frowned. "I'm moving on toward the Floral Expo—that's been my goal for years. To buy the shop and design a display worthy of recognition."

Lucy reached across the table and laid her hand over Quinn's. "What if it doesn't go the way you want it to?"

"Like, if my display doesn't make it?" Quinn couldn't think about that.

"Like, if she's not there. Or she doesn't react the way you imagine she will?" Lucy's question hung overhead, begging her attention.

Quinn's nervous laugh didn't hide her inner pain—not from her two closest friends. "I don't imagine anything, you guys. I know what I'm getting myself into. I just . . ."

"You just what?" Hailey asked, her eyes kind.

"I just want to prove that I'm good enough."

Lucy's shoulders sank. "You don't need this contest—or your mother—to tell you that, Quinn."

Of course she would say that. *She* had a mother who'd at least bothered to stick around.

"You don't have to prove anything to anyone," Hailey said.

But they were wrong.

"I think you should plan a trip," Lucy said. "On an airplane. There's a whole world outside Harbor Pointe, and you haven't seen any of it."

Quinn waved her off. "Maybe once I get my bearings at the shop." But there were reasons Quinn didn't travel. She had to stay put—just in case.

"Hailey, I need to talk to your brother," Quinn said.

Hailey hooked a thumb toward Ryan's table. "He's right there."

"I know, but do you think he'd mind if I picked his brain about some renovations I want to do?"

"Ryan?" Hailey spun around and faced him.

He stopped mid-bite on his hash browns.

"Would you mind if Quinn picked your brain about some renovations she wants to do?"

He set his fork down. "No."

Hailey turned back to Quinn. "He doesn't mind." She stood. "I'll go get our breakfast."

Ryan sat looking at Quinn, who suddenly felt on the spot. She'd first met Hailey and Ryan Brooks down at the beach one summer when they were growing up, and while the Brooks kids didn't live in Harbor Pointe, they spent plenty of time there. Ryan had always been that charming, good-looking older brother who made Quinn feel like a doting little sister.

Even now.

"Quinn?" Lucy whispered.

"Right. Well, I'm the new owner of the Forget-Me-Not Flower Shop, and I'm wanting to make some changes."

Ryan nodded.

"I just wondered if you might be able to point me in the right direction."

Lane Kelley—gorgeous Lane—appeared in the doorway. She carried a sleek black bag over her shoulder and two big binders in her arms. She sat down across from Ryan, leaned toward him, and kissed him a quick hello.

Lane had spent enough time in Chicago to look a little out of place back in Harbor Pointe, and the beautiful ring on her left hand made her look even more so.

Ryan smiled at Lane, the kind of smile that made Quinn swoon. It was obvious in the way he looked at her how much he loved her. And for the first time in years, Quinn wondered what it would be like if someone looked at her that way.

It was a stupid thought. She knew better than to romanticize romance. It was always fleeting and never—never—lasted. It was one recipe for heartache she didn't need.

Besides, in the five years she and Marcus were together, he'd never once looked at her that way.

Perhaps she should've realized it sooner.

Still, she didn't wish her cynicism on the newly engaged couple—she hoped they'd be the ones to beat the odds.

He turned his attention back to Quinn. "I'd be happy to stop by later."

Lane glanced at her.

"Quinn just bought the Forget-Me-Not Flower Shop down the block," Ryan said.

Lane's face lit up. "You did? I love that place. It would be so gorgeous if you exposed more of the brick—maybe even painted it white—and brought out the natural color of the wood floors. It's such a great old building and—" She stopped. "I'm sorry. You didn't ask for my opinion."

"Actually, I'd love your opinion. I just don't know if I can afford it." Quinn had looked at Lane's website every day since she found out Mimi was retiring. Her business, Memory Lane Designs, was so successful—Quinn could only imagine what Lane's rates were.

"I'll give you the friends and family deal," Lane said with a wink. "I have a vested interest in downtown Harbor Pointe. If it looks good and the businesses do well, we all benefit."

Quinn smiled. "I would love that."

"We'll come by later today."

The front door of the restaurant opened, and a collective silence settled on the whole place. It was as if they sensed Grady Benson before he even set foot inside. Quinn's eyes scanned the other patrons, expecting to see glares and grimaces given the damage he'd caused to this very diner.

But apparently she was the only one who remembered—even Betsy almost looked happy to see him. The owner of Hazel's moved out from behind the counter and over to where Grady stood, looking like a child on his first day of kindergarten. They talked for a few seconds, and then Betsy pointed back to their corner, probably to Ryan, who would most likely be handling whatever help Grady had been sentenced to offer.

Lucy leaned in. "He might have a temper, but he sure is good-looking." She nudged Quinn with her elbow.

"I hadn't noticed," Quinn said.

"What are you, dead?" Lucy rested her chin on her hand, propped up on the table by her elbow.

"I'm sure *Derek* would love to hear you think so," Quinn said.

Hailey sauntered over with wide eyes and three plates of food. "How crazy is it we have an *Olympian* in Harbor Pointe?"

"And a hot one at that."

Quinn took her plate and rolled her eyes. "I don't see what the big deal is about this guy. He's like a walking disaster."

Lucy and Hailey exchanged one of their knowing glances across the table—the kind that said, *We know something you don't know.*

Quinn stabbed her scrambled eggs with her fork and shook her head. "Di-sas-ter."

But as Betsy led Grady Benson past Quinn's table, her eyes met his for a split second, and Quinn quickly glanced away. Lucy was right. He was good-looking. But good-looking meant nothing to her—not when it came to troubled souls and entitled athletes.

And that's all Grady Benson was, as far as she was concerned.

CHAPTER

7

COMING BACK TO HAZEL'S KITCHEN was an exercise in humility, for sure. Grady didn't expect the wild-haired owner to be kind to him. He expected her to throw him out, despite the judge's orders. But apparently that's not how Betsy Tanner operated.

She greeted him at the front door, which was good since he was dreading the prying eyes of every one of her customers—people who definitely knew what he'd done. The proof was all around them.

Thankfully, the news had died down, and as far as he could tell, there were only a few straggling reporters sticking around Harbor Pointe. The others had moved on to chase the underbelly of someone else's life.

"You're right on time," Betsy said, tucking a small notebook into the pocket of her apron.

"You can say a lot of things about me, but you can't say I'm not punctual." Grady forced a smile. He'd been ordered to report to Hazel's at 8 a.m., and while he still had every intention of figuring a way out of this mess, for today, this is where he had to be. Off to the side, one part of the restaurant—the unusable side—had been sectioned off. There was a gaping hole in the wall where he'd shoved Jimmy into it, his shoulder doing the brunt of the damage.

He really had made a wreck of things.

"You hungry? I can get you something before you start. I'll take you over to meet Ryan Brooks—he's the guy in charge of most of the repairs." She pointed to a table near the back of the diner, but the man's back was all he saw. Kitty-corner from him, though, were the sheriff's daughter and her friends.

She didn't like him—but he couldn't blame her.

Grady turned back to Betsy. "I could eat."

"Great. I'll introduce you to Ryan, and then you can take a look at the menu."

Seconds later, they were standing beside the table where Ryan and a dark-haired woman sat across from each other.

"Brooks, this is Grady Benson," Betsy said. "Grady, this is Ryan Brooks and Lane Kelley. They're the ones responsible for the cottage you're staying in."

Ryan stood and extended a hand. "How's your cottage? I think we put you in Lois?"

Grady shook his hand. "It's great. If I have to be stranded somewhere, I'm glad it's with Lois." Each of the cottages at Cedar Grove had been given a woman's name. Lois, as his was called, was a small white house with a cherry-red mailbox and a large, dark-gray porch with two Adirondack chairs off to one side. He'd later discovered that the back of the cottage faced the lake, and in the distance he could see a lighthouse the same color as the mailbox. Some people might find the place charming. To him, it felt like a prison.

He'd spent the evening flipping through the same four channels on TV, catching hints of terribly produced local news, reruns of old sitcoms he hadn't watched the first time around, and the clear knowledge that he wasn't going to last five seconds in this town, let alone five weeks.

Qualifying races were going to go on without him, making

it harder and harder for him to secure his spot on the Olympic team—especially since training here was going to be impossible. He'd looked up the nearby ski lodge, and while he couldn't be sure, judging by its website, they weren't even close to the kind of slopes he needed. A knot tied itself in the center of his stomach.

How was he going to get through this?

Grady reminded himself to be polite. It wasn't this guy's fault he was there. It was that pompous judge's.

"Sorry for the mess," Grady mumbled.

"I imagine you are." Ryan's eyes flickered. "Getting stuck in a place like this—for someone like you? Has to be tricky."

"I'll be fine." Grady wasn't here to make friends. He'd do what he was told—for today—and then he'd get back on the phone with Pete.

"We've made some great progress already." Ryan glanced off to the damaged side. "Course we left some of it just for you."

"Great."

"Once we finish here, I'll sign off on your paperwork, and you can get your next assignment. Do you know what else they've got you doing?"

Grady shook his head. He hadn't really been listening that closely when the judge handed out his laundry list of community service tasks. Mostly he'd been certain it would never come down to him actually reporting to any of them . . . but here he was.

Grady felt someone at his side, turned, and found a young, lanky kid staring at him.

"Jaden," Betsy said, "aren't you supposed to be at school?"

The kid either didn't hear her or had no problem ignoring her. He didn't respond. Instead, he continued staring.

"Seriously, Jaden, you're going to be late for school." Betsy gave him a push.

"Mr. Benson." Jaden reached for Grady's hand. "I'm a huge fan." The kid stood there for an awkward second, looking at Grady, waiting for a response.

"Do you ski?"

"Yes. Every chance I get. I have a pass at Avalanche Mountain—was just there last weekend. But the best skiing is up north a little ways. Even an hour makes a huge difference."

Good to know. "Do you get up there often?"

"Nah, not really. I can get to Avalanche on the bus, but I've only got a local pass. It's okay, though. I'm getting myself in shape. Took some lessons and everything. My dream's to compete—like you."

"That right?"

"I like how you do things your own way. You don't let anyone tell you what to do." Jaden grinned. "I've already got that part down."

"That's not going to get you very far." The voice was familiar, but not one he'd expected. They all turned and found Quinn standing beside her table, purse slung over her shoulder and a scowl on her face.

"Got *him* this far, didn't it?" Jaden lifted his chin.

Quinn glanced at Grady, then back at Jaden. "If by 'this far' you mean stuck doing community service in Harbor Pointe, Michigan, then yes, it did. But it's not going to work for you. Let's go."

Jaden rolled his eyes.

"School starts in ten minutes. Come on."

"Grady, maybe we can ski together sometime while you're here. If you could help me shave even a few seconds off my time—maybe take a look at my form."

"Jaden. Now." Quinn stood behind him like an annoyed babysitter, and it was Grady's presence that annoyed her, he could tell.

"Let's do it, kid," Grady said, mostly to get a rise out of Quinn.

It worked. He couldn't be sure, but it was entirely possible there was steam coming out of her ears.

"For real?" The kid's eyes lit up like a fireworks display.

"Course. You can show me the slopes—I gotta stay in shape anyway."

"For the qualifying races."

"That's right." Or *race*, singular, as the case may be.

"How many will be left when you finish your sentence here?"

Grady felt his shoulders slump. "One."

"Whoa, dude. That's gonna be a killer race." Quinn tugged on his arm. "Gotta go to school, but this weekend?"

"You got it."

"Bets, will you give him my number?" Jaden backed toward the door, Quinn still pulling his arm.

Betsy nodded and gave him a little wave. "You got it, kiddo."

Quinn glared at Grady one last time before walking out the door.

"Seems like a good kid," Grady said once they'd gone.

Betsy let out a little groan. "He's a handful, to say the least."

Hmm. Like someone else Grady knew.

What was the deal with the sheriff's daughter? Why had she whipped out her bossy mom voice? Whatever it was, he had the fleeting thought that getting under her skin could be a fun pastime while he was trapped here in Mayberry-by-the-lake.

Might just make the ridiculousness of his situation a little more bearable.

"He is not someone to idolize, Jaden."

"Give him a break." Quinn's nephew slumped down in the passenger seat of her Volkswagen.

"Did you or did you not see the giant hole in the wall at Hazel's?"

"He's there to fix it. Sheesh."

"He's there because Judge ordered him to be there."

Jaden's shrug was meant to dismiss her. But she wasn't so easy to shut up.

"Is that really the kind of person you want to look up to? A guy who can't control his temper when someone hurts his feelings?"

Jaden shoved his backpack on the floor. "Do you even know who he is, Aunt Quinn? Have you seen what he can do?"

Quinn unintentionally slammed her hand on the steering wheel. "Why is everyone so enamored with this guy?" She'd never been prone to hero worship, and when it came to Grady Benson, she definitely didn't get the appeal.

"How many people do you know who've been to the Olympics? It's kind of a big deal."

"I don't care. I know enough to know that he's bad news. He's arrogant and entitled and—" she stopped before adding *too attractive for his own good.*

"And what?"

"And you should find yourself a better role model."

Jaden stared out the window, a sudden stillness settling over him. "I think God brought him here."

It was a good thing they were at a stoplight because Quinn couldn't keep from eyeballing Jaden. *Jaden,* the kid who hated going to church, thought God was a "big bully," and whose rebellion had his mother literally praying without ceasing every single day.

Tread lightly.

The thought surprised her. She didn't want to dissuade Jaden in any way from thinking or talking about God, but he was terribly mistaken if he believed Grady's stay in Harbor Pointe was divine intervention.

"I know that sounds stupid . . ." He must've sensed her hesitation.

Way to go, Quinn.

"No, it doesn't sound stupid." *Misguided.* That's the word she'd use.

The light turned and she drove the last block toward Harbor Pointe High School.

"I asked for a sign." Jaden still stared out the window.

"A sign?" She kept her voice light, upbeat.

"A sign. About skiing. My mom wants me to give it up. Says I need to get serious about school and quit spending time daydreaming about skiing. I had to stop taking lessons for a while."

That sounded like Carly.

Quinn's older sister only wanted what was best for her son, but discouraging him in the one thing he'd shown any interest in since his model train kick at the age of eight didn't seem like the most prudent move. Still, she understood. Carly had raised Jaden on her own—and she'd been really young when she had him. She was determined to make sure he had a good life, no matter what. To her, that meant a sensible path, which Jaden unfortunately did not want to travel.

If she knew he was out chasing down Grady Benson, her sister would flip.

"So you prayed about it?" She kept every trace of shock out of her voice, but it still spooked him.

They were sitting at the curb in front of his school, and he couldn't have opened the door faster. "Thanks for the ride."

Her sigh was nearly undetectable. "See you later, Jay."

She watched Jaden walk up the sidewalk, wearing nothing warmer than a flannel shirt and a lightweight jacket. To look at him, you'd think he was a kid who'd just transferred to Harbor Pointe, not someone who'd lived here his whole life.

He walked past several groups of kids, head down, backpack over one shoulder, and made no acknowledgment of anyone. It was almost like he was invisible.

He'd grown so withdrawn, yet he loved to ski. It was the one thing that could still make him smile. Did Carly really want him to quit?

Regardless, his worship of Grady Benson was a serious problem. Grady Benson was starting to become a serious problem.

And Quinn felt helpless to do anything about it.

CHAPTER

8

THE PLANNING MEETINGS for the Winter Carnival were always held on Tuesday nights, and Quinn had gotten so busy at the flower shop, she'd almost forgotten. As promised, Ryan Brooks and Lane Kelley had stopped by late that morning, and she explained what she had in mind—a shop that was charming and welcoming, one where people stopped in even if they weren't looking for flowers.

She wanted lots of white, galvanized metal light fixtures, a new Forget-Me-Not logo painted on the back wall, and displays that invited people to lean in and smell, touch, and eventually purchase their favorite flowers.

"Well, it doesn't sound like you need me at all," Lane had told her. "You've got some great ideas here." She'd been flipping through Quinn's book of sketches and torn-out magazine pages, all the designs she'd been storing for years. The styles had changed, but Quinn's vision hadn't. She wanted classic. Traditional. Light and airy.

Ryan had agreed to help her with the built-in displays as well as installing some of the light fixtures and refinishing the floors.

Quinn would add a fresh coat of white paint to the entire space, including the brick wall behind the counter, and of course, she'd decorate for Christmas—white, evergreen, and burlap brown. It would be perfectly classy.

Lane gave her the instructions she needed to add her logo to the back wall (hand-painted, no less), and as they stood there, Ryan got an idea for a brand-new, custom-built checkout counter.

In fact, he and Lane disappeared into their own lingo for a minute, talking about a supplier they knew, some old barn wood they'd found, and a sheet of galvanized metal they could use to face the entire thing.

While Quinn had no idea what most of it meant, she went along with it because she trusted Lane and because they'd practically begged her to let them make it.

"Who am I to argue with a creative idea?" she'd said, praying their help was within her budget.

Now, she walked toward the offices of the convention and visitors' bureau, just down two blocks and across the street from the flower shop. As she did, she passed by Hazel's and noticed that the holes in the wall had been patched up and the place already looked a lot better.

Up ahead, she could see people beginning to arrive for their meeting. The committee was small for such a large event, with only about fifteen key volunteers and leaders. In the summer, it was easy for Harbor Pointe to draw in the tourists, but years ago, someone realized the little town on Lake Michigan could become a winter draw if they wanted to make it one. Since local businesses depended on tourism, it had always seemed like a worthy cause, even before she was a business owner.

Plus, as a single almost-thirtysomething, Quinn had plenty of time to be involved.

She walked up the sidewalk and toward the front door, where Danny Carver waited for her.

"Evening, Quinn." He grinned at her—a little bit dorky, but endearing just the same. Danny was a good guy, just not her type.

That's the way you like it, remember?

While loneliness sometimes nagged her—mostly in the evenings when she was eating dinner alone on the sofa—Quinn had no interest in romance. She'd spare herself the heartache and maintain a safe distance at all times.

Even from someone as harmless as Danny Carver.

Danny pulled the door open for her. "You look beautiful as always." He stood almost eye level with Quinn.

"Thanks." She took off her coat and tucked it in the crook of her arm, switching her purse from one shoulder to the other.

"So, congratulations." Danny shoved his hands in his pockets. "I heard you're Harbor Pointe's newest business owner."

Quinn smiled. "Yeah, I am. Still feels like a dream, really."

"I bet. I remember in high school you went there every afternoon."

She'd had early release their senior year and spent most of her days helping Mimi. The flower shop had been part of their community, though Quinn still believed that had less to do with Mimi Hudson and more to do with her own mother. When her mother had owned it, it had been even more special, almost magical. Quinn and Carly would dance around behind the counter while their mother picked out the most beautiful blooms for her customers.

"Remember, every single person in our shop is coming for a very special reason. Whether they're celebrating or mourning or simply looking to cheer someone up, we get to be a part of that." Sometimes her mother said she could see what a person needed as soon as they walked in the door. And she was right. Quinn had seen it time and time again.

Laura Danvers? A bouquet of poppies. Because her perky, bubbly daughter was about to turn sweet sixteen.

Steve Putnam? Red roses. Because he was in the doghouse with Mrs. Putnam—again.

Morris Davidson? Tulips. Because they were simple, elegant, and beautiful just like his wife, Sadie.

Quinn had always thought it was her mother's superpower, being able to read people like that before they even said a word, when, in fact, she simply paid attention. Jacie Collins had her ears open at all times. Sometimes she'd overhear someone talking at church, and she'd tell them to stop by for a bouquet on the house.

"You look like you need a little pick-me-up," she'd say. "Come by the shop later and I'll have a bouquet of sunshine just for you."

People around town always thought so highly of Quinn's mother, which was, Quinn supposed, why her leaving was such a shock to the system. Not only for the Collins family, but for the entire town. Like a stitch in their fabric had been pulled.

It was ancient history now. Quinn was the new owner of Forget-Me-Not. And she had no intention of leaving.

"It's a special place," Quinn told Danny after too long a pause.

"Special place for a special girl." Danny's face contorted into what looked like a smile. She made him nervous. Either that or he was just awkward. Or both.

"I guess we should head in," she said.

His hand on her arm stopped her. "Before we do, Quinn, there's, uh . . . something I've been wanting to ask you."

No! She was terrible at this sort of thing. Her mind started racing for excuses—anything that would allow her to turn him down easily.

My dad already made plans for our whole family that day. We have a long-standing tradition, I guess you could say.

I'm just too busy at the flower shop—so many demands on my time.

I'm emotionally unavailable.

But before he could get any additional words out, the front door swung open and Grady appeared. By comparison, Danny suddenly looked scrawny and small. Grady, with his height and all those muscles, was indeed a presence, wherever he went—but what was he doing here? At her meeting?

"Whoa, that's him," Danny practically whispered, as if the queen of England had just materialized in front of their very eyes.

Grady looked lost, and he probably was. The polite thing would be to point him toward the meeting room. But of course there was no way she was going to do that. Her father would be embarrassed by her lack of hospitality.

Danny, on the other hand, couldn't seem to stop staring.

"What were you saying, Danny?" Why was she prodding the man to ask her out when only seconds ago she was spinning through her mental Rolodex for an acceptable reason to say no without hurting his feelings?

"Huh?" Danny was still staring at Grady, who, in his winter coat, looked exactly like an Olympic skier. She'd never watched Olympic skiing in her life and couldn't care less who medaled or qualified or slipped and fell. But she was starting to feel like the only person in town who felt that way.

"You were about to ask me something." Quinn gave Danny a little shove, hoping that would bring him back to his senses.

Grady took a few steps into the entryway. It was after hours, so there was no receptionist, and it was pretty obvious he wouldn't be here if he hadn't been court ordered.

"You're Grady Benson." Danny sounded like a twelve-year-old girl who'd just met a member of One Direction.

Grady's eyes darted over to Quinn, who crossed her arms over her chest and looked away.

"You're the best, man."

Man? Since when did Danny call people *man?*

"Thanks. It's always nice to meet a fan." He reached out and shook Danny's hand. "Listen, can you tell me where this, uh, winter festival meeting is?"

"Carnival." Quinn practically barked the word.

"What's that?" Grady was looking at her now. And it was unnerving.

"It's a carnival, not a festival."

"Is there a difference?"

Quinn huffed, unsure why she felt so hostile toward him. "We were right in the middle of something here." *What?* Why had she said that? They were in the middle of exactly nothing. If anything, Grady had just saved her from sure humiliation, and this was how she repaid him?

"I can take you back," Danny said.

"Danny." Quinn tried her best not to sound exasperated, but she was pretty sure she failed.

"Quinn, it's Grady Benson."

She glanced at Grady, whose smug smile was enough to make her want to scream, but she stepped aside as the two of them strolled off to the conference area.

Well, this was going to be fun.

❧

Grady followed the short guy through a hallway and into an open space at the Harbor Pointe convention and visitors' bureau. It was a small town, but it was a tourist town, and they had a decent base of operations for whatever festival—*carnival*—they had to plan.

They'd practically finished at Hazel's. One lousy day was all it took to put things right, and he was still sentenced to five weeks in this hole, so his next assignment was to help with this town event.

More than once, he'd almost gotten in his car and taken off, straight down the highway toward Colorado, where he could finally prove himself and get his life back.

But whatever small dose of common sense he had left stopped him. He didn't need more time added to his sentence. As it was, he'd only get one shot to qualify. If he wiped out, if he overshot a curve, if he miscalculated, if he just wasn't fast enough—he wasn't going back to the Olympics, he'd lose his endorsements, and Benji would never see him win the gold.

That couldn't happen.

When they walked into the open space, Grady saw a handful of people situated in armchairs or standing around the room. They were broken off in groups, talking, laughing, doing what he supposed small-town people did on a Tuesday night.

But as was happening a lot lately, everyone stopped and stared as soon as they realized he was there. He didn't know if people were genuinely interested in him, like the short guy, or if they were annoyed with him for starting a fight and damaging their favorite diner, like Quinn. But either way, he didn't mind the attention. He was used to it, and truth be told, he'd kind of missed it.

He'd grown up in some sort of spotlight, and it had grown right along with him. What would he do when no one was shining a light on him anymore?

Ryan Brooks, the only person in the room he recognized besides Quinn and the old guy he'd sat across from at dinner the night before, lifted a hand in greeting. The guy was decent—he'd been patient and helpful in the work they'd done on the diner—but that didn't change Grady's mind about being there. Still, when Ryan told him about this Winter Carnival meeting, it didn't sound like he was mentioning it as a courtesy. Grady understood—he had to be there. It was part of the deal.

"Hey, Grady, you made it," Ryan said.

"I did. Not sure what I'm doing here, but here I am." He'd never been to a town meeting in his life.

Quinn sat down in one of the armchairs with Denny—no, Danny—tagging along beside her. When he saw there wasn't a seat next to her, he turned in a full circle, a dazed expression on his face, and pulled a folding chair up next to her.

"We'll go ahead and call this meeting to order." A bright woman with neatly styled white hair stood at a small podium near the front of the room. The chairs had been positioned to face her, and now, somewhat in the middle of the commotion, Grady felt even more conspicuous than usual.

"Mrs. Trembley, before we start, I just want to introduce everyone to Grady Benson," Ryan said. "He's going to be with us for a few weeks."

"Oh, right. The community-service skier." The white-haired woman straightened the scarf around her neck as she peered at him through thin glasses.

"He's an Olympian, Martha," the man from last night's dinner said. "A genuine Olympic athlete."

Heads turned in his direction—all but one. Quinn Collins was noticeably unwilling to glance his way. Not that he noticed.

"It's good to be here," Grady said, which was, of course, a lie. He'd rather be almost anywhere else, actually. He even thought for a split second he'd rather be back home than stuck here in Harbor Pointe, but he quickly realized that wasn't true either.

So with that one exception, he'd rather be anywhere else.

"I take it you're here to work?" Mrs. Trembley glared at him.

"Yes, ma'am. I think you'll find I'm a big help to your *festival* here." He'd said it on purpose this time—and as he suspected, Miss Collins shot him a look. He raised an eyebrow in her direction and she rolled her eyes, then quickly looked away. Okay, this could be a little bit fun.

"The Winter Carnival is our largest off-season event. It's nothing to take lightly." Trembley again. He didn't know how, but he'd find a way to win that one over.

"I wouldn't dream of that, ma'am."

"Good. Well, listen up." She wagged a bony finger at him. "We have a lot of business to attend to."

"She's harmless," Ryan said. "Just particular. Like pretty much everyone in this room."

Everyone? He glanced at Quinn but swallowed his questions about her. He didn't need to start inquiring about anyone who lived in this awful town, but especially not Quinn Collins.

The meeting droned on. Grady checked out after about ten minutes, choosing instead to browse his social media accounts. Sometimes—out of sheer curiosity—he'd scan Twitter just to see what people were saying. Usually it gave him a nice little boost to see fans talking about his latest run, but not tonight. Tonight it was nothing but negative.

Benson, hang up your skis before you embarrass yourself. #YoureDone

Anyone else feel sorry for Harbor Pointe, MI? Saddled with Grady Benson and all that baggage.

Grady Benson. What a waste. #KissItGoodbye

Then he stumbled on a whole conversation about whether or not he'd make it back on the Olympic team. Most thought not. It wasn't just a general consensus; it was a landslide majority. They didn't think he had the stuff—not anymore.

And Grady didn't like the pit in his stomach that resulted. He should've stayed off his phone.

"We'll split up into our teams now," Trembley was saying when Grady tuned back in.

He glanced at Ryan. "Teams?"

"Committees. Each team is assigned a builder. We're basically glorified servants." Ryan laughed. Grady didn't. "I'm with the ice sculpture team, so I'll be hauling whatever they need me to."

Trembley walked over, her chunky heels clacking on the tile floor as she did. "Mr. Benson, you can join any one of these teams, and you'll just be at their beck and call. Whoever the team leader is will sign off on your hours and turn them back in to me, and I'll turn them in to the judge."

"Boy, you guys have got this all worked out, don't you?"

"Pardon me?"

"Nothing. So, what, I just pick a team?"

Trembley pressed her thin lips together into one straight line and nodded. "Except the ice sculpture team. They've got Mr. Brooks, and he's our best worker."

Ryan waggled his eyebrows. Whatever the key was to getting on this lady's good side, Ryan Brooks had figured it out.

He scanned the room of small huddles of people. Over to the side he saw Quinn, sitting in her armchair, legs pulled up underneath her. On her lap was a clipboard, and she was addressing her team of four, which included the guy who'd walked him in. She was obviously the one in charge.

"You said I'd report to the team leader?"

The old woman eyed him. "Yes, that's what I said."

"What team is that?" He pointed at Quinn's group.

"Floral displays and decorations. They are responsible for making things look pretty. Not sure that's a good fit for you." She quirked one brow, her expression dubious.

"Oh, I don't know," Grady said. "I think it might be perfect." After all, Quinn was the first woman in a long time who'd given him the cold shoulder. He was intrigued.

"If you say so," Trembley said. "Follow me."

He did as he was told, and seconds later they were standing next to Quinn's huddle. She glanced up, and her whole expression changed.

"He's all yours."

Quinn stood. "No, he's not."

Trembley's eyes widened. "Pardon me?"

Quinn smoothed her free hand over her plaid button-down and clung to her clipboard with the other hand. "Mrs. Trembley, our group is solid. We've got a plan laid out, and I think the display is going to be the best one we've ever done."

"Wonderful," the old lady said. "Just make sure Mr. Benson helps. He's got to earn his community service hours. You'll have to sign off on them and give them to me. Maybe it's good to put criminals to work—free labor and all that."

"I'm not a criminal," Grady said, but she was already gone. He faced Quinn. "I guess I'm all yours."

"Yeah. Lucky me."

But he could tell Quinn Collins felt anything but lucky.

CHAPTER

9

"WHAT'S THE BIG DEAL?" Carly stood at her sink filling her coffee carafe with water. "Are you scared of a good-looking man?"

Quinn should've known better than to tell her sister about the meeting last night. Carly would never understand how annoying this guy was. She wouldn't see past the blue eyes.

But seriously? Every time she thought about the meeting, she wanted to scream. The way Grady Benson had hijacked her group. The way Ashley Perkins had mooned over the big pro athlete. The way he'd flirted right back—not only with Ashley but with every woman there. Even Mrs. Trembley! It was like flirting was the only way he knew how to communicate.

Quinn absolutely refused to flirt back. She would not give him the satisfaction, especially when she had so much to do. But with him sitting there, it was like everyone had forgotten the real reason they were meeting at all.

Even steady, even-keeled Calvin Doyle, who helped Mrs. Trembley with the organization of the event, seemed smitten by the star in their midst. He kept checking on their team to make sure they had everything they needed, and twice he offered to run and get Grady something to drink. The world had gone mad!

In the end, they'd left without deadlines or work divvied up, and Quinn was blaming that on Grady Benson.

Carly opened the lid of her coffee pot and poured the water in. "Seriously, you are getting really worked up over a Harbor Pointe Winter Carnival meeting."

"You don't understand." She watched as her sister scooped the coffee out. "You're making enough for me, right?"

"Yes." Carly put another scoop in. "And what don't I understand? This is Harbor Pointe, Quinn. It's not the St. Patrick's Day parade in downtown Chicago."

"Thanks a lot."

"What?"

"You're belittling my work. This is important to me."

Carly turned and leaned against the counter, arms crossed over her chest, sweatshirt hanging loose over her hospital scrubs. "I'm sorry. You're right. Listen, maybe you just need to find a way to use this guy. Make him do all your grunt work. Sounds like you're kind of his boss now."

Quinn rolled her eyes. "He is not going to take orders from me, I can tell you that."

"Who's not?" Jaden walked into the kitchen wearing what looked like the same exact outfit he'd worn yesterday.

"Never mind," Quinn said.

"That skier," Carly said at the same time.

"Grady Benson?" Jaden pulled a box of cereal off the top of the refrigerator. "What about him?"

"Aunt Quinn doesn't like him."

"Is this about me?" Jaden eyed her.

"What about you?" Carly asked.

"No, it's not about you," Quinn said. "Though I still think you need to find someone else to look up to."

"You wouldn't say that if you'd seen him ski." He grabbed a gigantic bowl from the cupboard and the milk from the fridge, then sat down at the table. "Plus, he doesn't take crap from anyone. Just does his own thing. It's cool."

"Yeah, real cool," Quinn huffed.

Jaden's shrug told her he didn't care what she thought. Not about Grady, anyway. What had happened to that sweet, big-eyed boy who used to coo at her and call her "Win"? Why had he gone and grown up? He hadn't even asked their permission.

"That's the biggest cereal bowl I've ever seen." Quinn watched as Jaden poured the Cinnamon Life into what looked like a small mixing bowl.

"I'm a growing boy." Her nephew grinned, and for a split second she saw the funny little kid he'd once been.

"Yeah, and I'm going to have to take a second job just to keep your stomach full." Carly poured two cups of coffee, added cream and sugar, then handed one to Quinn. "Why do you think Jaden needs a new role model?"

"Have you been living under a rock?"

"I've been working. I don't have time to keep up on town gossip."

"It's no big deal," Jaden said. "Some guy was being a jerk and Grady shut him up."

"What does that mean, 'shut him up'?" Carly asked.

"He got in a fight," Quinn said. "At Hazel's. Put a hole in the wall, broke a bunch of stuff. So now he's stuck here doing community service."

"Oh, yeah, they were talking about this at the nurses' station." Carly set her coffee down. "Was that Dad's idea?"

"Dad and Judge. The two of them together are out to teach this guy a lesson, but he doesn't listen to anyone."

Carly stopped, her mouth twitching upward into a nearly undetectable smile. "I've never seen you this worked up about anyone before."

"Knock it off." Quinn walked to the cupboard and pulled out

a travel mug. She could see where this was headed, and she needed to make a quick exit—but she wanted the coffee.

"Good-looking Olympic athlete meets small-town flower shop owner?" Carly raised her eyebrows. "I like it. It has promise."

"You're off your nut if you think I feel anything but utter irritation for this guy."

"Uh-huh."

"I'm serious."

"He said he'd take me skiing," Jaden said.

Carly's eyes darted to her son. "Seriously?"

"Jaden, don't get your hopes up. This is the kind of guy who says whatever he thinks people want to hear. He's probably going to get one of his big, fancy lawyers out here to overturn Judge's decision, and he'll be gone before he ever has a chance to go anywhere with you."

"You don't know that." Jaden's mouth was half-full. He swallowed. "He could totally make good on that promise, take me skiing, fix my turns, correct my form, and send me on my way to the Olympics."

"Jay." Carly frowned.

Jaden shoveled another bite into his mouth, then grabbed his lunch and his backpack. "I gotta go." He didn't wait around for good-byes.

"Should I give him a ride?" Quinn glanced out the window and saw him walking toward the school.

"He likes the walk sometimes. Says it helps him clear his head." Carly took another sip of her coffee. "What am I going to do with that kid?"

"Carly, I'm worried about him putting too much faith in Grady. I know Jaden's been let down in the past, I just don't want to see him get hurt." The thought of it squeezed her heart like a vise. She loved that kid. He might as well have been all of theirs—hers, Carly's, Dad's. Even Beverly, Judge, and Calvin would claim Jaden as their own.

How could she protect her nephew from getting his heart broken again at the hands of a thoughtless man?

Carly tore a banana from the bunch and stuck it in her open lunch bag. Quinn could see that her sister's defenses had gone up. After all, in her mind, it was her own actions that had led to Jaden's heartache. She'd gotten pregnant when she was just seventeen, and her high school boyfriend—Jaden's "dad"—had all but disappeared. Over the years, Josh Dixon had broken promises to his only son, so many that Jaden now refused to see or even speak to the man.

But none of that was Carly's fault—surely she knew that.

"I just don't know what to do with him, Q." Carly's eyes were glassy and she blinked back tears. "He hates school, has very few friends. The only thing he has any interest in is skiing, but it's so impractical. Does he really think he's going to make it to the Olympics?" Carly grabbed a tissue and dabbed the corners of her eyes. "I don't get it, Quinn. The first time he ever skied was with Josh—did you know that?"

Quinn shook her head.

"It might be the only time his dad has actually shown up for him. What if he's holding on to skiing just because it's the one thing that connects him to his dad?" Her tears betrayed her.

"I think you're reading too much into that," Quinn said. "Maybe that's why he started, but I think now he just genuinely loves it."

"Like you genuinely love owning Mom's flower shop?"

Quinn stilled. "That's different."

Carly's nonverbal reply told her that her sister wasn't so sure.

"Anyway, we aren't talking about me here," Quinn said, steering the conversation away from uncharted waters. "Jaden came to the diner yesterday morning. And that's when he met Grady. When I dropped him off at school, honestly, Car, it was weird. He walked in like the Invisible Man. It was—"

A tear streamed down her sister's face.

"I'm sorry."

"No. I understand. It was sad, right? Jaden made you sad."

"No, he didn't make me sad. He just *seemed* sad. Something about the whole scene—yeah, I guess it was sad."

"You have to talk to Grady."

"What? Why?" Quinn felt her face contort. She hoped it was enough to convey her horror at the thought.

"I know it's not fair, but if he said he'd take Jaden skiing, we have to make sure that happens for him."

Quinn shook her head. "I don't want to get in the middle of that. Grady Benson is a thorn in my side that I will only deal with in order to pull off this carnival. I don't want to talk to him otherwise."

"Please, Quinn. For Jaden. Doesn't he deserve one sliver of happiness?"

"I thought you wanted him to focus on school? To let go of these silly skiing dreams?"

"Did he tell you that?"

"Yes."

"He wasn't listening to me." She sighed. "I told him he had to focus on school, but I never said he had to quit skiing. I can't get through to him." Another sigh—this one heavier than the last. "If he's passionate about this, shouldn't I at least try and support him?"

"Of course. But, Car, do you really think Grady Benson is just going to take some fifteen-year-old kid skiing for fun?"

Carly shrugged. "Do you think he has a bunch of better offers while he's here?"

Given how Ashley Perkins was throwing herself at him last night, Quinn would say that was a definite yes.

"I'll pay. I have some money saved up." Carly took a step closer to Quinn. "You're right—Jaden's had his heart broken so many times. Josh hasn't done anything but let that kid down. But I'm losing him, Q. If we can make this happen for him, maybe it'll turn things around?"

Quinn's mind was spinning. How was she going to convince Grady to make good on his promise? She'd have to speak to him, and while that didn't appeal to her at all, asking him for a favor appealed to her even less.

Still, if Quinn couldn't swallow her pride for two of the people she loved most, what kind of person was she?

But as she left her sister's house, a knot had formed in her stomach at the thought of seeing Grady again. Because she'd rather have a root canal than put herself at his mercy.

Cedar Grove was the kind of place Grady imagined people loved to vacation in the summer. The cottage was remarkable, really, and when he and Ryan were working yesterday, he'd learned that Ryan was responsible for renovating the whole thing by himself.

Grady couldn't imagine doing something like that. He'd never been much for manual labor—he'd never had to be. He'd always been a skier, for as long as he could remember.

But Ryan? He never stopped moving. Never sat down. Never took a break. He was always working—and cottages like this one were the result. Lois had wide-planked wood floors, which Ryan had refinished himself. Apparently Lane had decorated the place in her "signature style," which he would call cozy, though he was sure there was an actual name for the white woodwork, distressed white furniture, and neutral colors with the occasional visual grab from a teal pillow or a red vase. The whole place felt a lot more like home than anywhere Grady had stayed the last few years, but it was quiet. And sometimes, quiet was his greatest enemy.

Wednesday morning, he got up, checked his phone—no messages—and decided to get down to Hazel's a little early. Ryan said they only had about a day left of work. But that wouldn't sway the judge when it came to his sentence. Instead, he'd move from helping out at Hazel's to helping out with this Winter Carnival thing.

He showered, then pulled on a pair of jeans and a gray hoodie with the Olympic logo on it. Was it foolish to wear it given that nobody thought he'd make the team this year?

Why had everyone counted him out? Did they all see something he didn't? Was his ego so intertwined with his abilities that he couldn't pull them apart?

It was a ridiculous thought. He was Grady Benson. That meant something where he was from. He was a world champion. He set the standard.

Surely all of that wasn't behind him.

Not the kind of thoughts he wanted to dwell on. The road into town ran parallel with the lake, a view he was pretty sure he could never get tired of. He'd grown up landlocked in Colorado, which is where he started skiing—so he'd never known the benefits of living near the water. He wondered if the people who lived in Harbor Pointe knew what they had in that view or in the peace it seemed to bring to an otherwise turbulent mind.

Not that he minded the internal turbulence. It kept him on his toes. It kept things interesting, including his skiing. It's why his coaches didn't love coaching him, why they called him reckless and unteachable. He had too much going on inside, and going as hard and fast and messy as he could was the only way to silence those demons.

But those were also not thoughts he wanted to dwell on.

Hazel's Kitchen, sandwiched between so many other brightly painted shops with striped awnings, came into view. He should feel like a complete jerk every time he passed this place, but somehow he didn't. It was like the people of Harbor Pointe were intent on bringing him into their fold, as if he could ever fit in a place like this. Sweet of them to try, though, he supposed.

Most of them tried, anyway. There was still that sheriff's daughter.

He'd gotten a kick out of making Quinn squirm the night before at that winter festival meeting—just seeing him join her circle had caused her face to turn red. It was possible that amused him a little more than it should've.

Hazel's in the morning, at least as far as he could tell on his fourth day in town, was busy and bustling. While he didn't know Betsy, it was obvious that she was well loved here.

As soon as she saw him, she beelined his way, her face almost as wild as her hair. "You're early."

"Thought I'd get a head start on the day," Grady said.

Betsy grinned. "Follow me." When they reached the table near the back of the diner, she poured him a cup of coffee. "What do you want this morning?"

Grady handed her the menu. "Pancakes, bacon, eggs, and the coffee."

"You got it." She jotted his order down on her pad of paper and was gone.

Grady's phone buzzed in his pocket. He pulled it out and saw that it was Pete. About time. While his manager made him think this whole situation was hopeless, Grady knew better. Everyone—even a small-town judge—had a price.

"Tell me you've got good news," he said after clicking on the phone.

There was silence on the other end.

"Pete?"

"I'm afraid it's not good news, Grady."

Grady let out a heavy sigh. "I'm stuck here, then?"

"It's not about that." Pete sounded tired. He paused for several seconds.

"Just tell me."

"It's Bowman."

"What about Bowman?"

He'd been the face of Bowman Skis since he first came on the scene. They'd wanted someone who could energize alpine skiing, and they liked Grady's no-nonsense approach to the sport. *"You don't mess around, Benson. You just get out there and do your thing."*

It was the same trait so many coaches had tried to "fix" over the years. And here he had landed a huge endorsement deal because he'd rocked the boat a little and ignored all that advice.

Pete had gone quiet again.

"Pete, hurry up and tell me."

"They dropped you."

Grady's heart sank. "They what?"

"Your contract was up two weeks ago," Pete said.

"Right, we were waiting on the paperwork."

"Turns out there is no paperwork. They're going to sign Matthew Phillips."

"The kid?"

Pete sighed. "They want someone young and fresh."

It hit him like a sucker punch to the gut. That had been him only a few years ago. What had changed?

"They think I'm finished," Grady said. The sting of saying it out loud needled him.

"Doesn't matter what they think. All that matters is getting back up there and crushing your last time."

"But it does matter, Pete. Without that money, how am I going to take care of Benji, let alone myself?"

"We'll figure something out."

"You're a miracle worker, Pete, but if you believe what they're saying online, even *you* are going to have trouble fixing this."

"Don't underestimate me. Or you. You've never gotten caught up in your negative press before."

"Because it was always about my attitude or my ego. I don't care about any of that stuff. When they start talking about my skiing, that's a different story." Made his blood boil, if he was honest. Because he couldn't respond—he'd just look like a spoiled athlete who didn't know his glory days were behind him.

"What are you saying? You want to retire?"

Grady hated that the word had even entered their conversation. "Of course not."

"There's no shame in it. You'll always be one of the best."

"I can't go out like this. I can't go out after failing to get back on the team. Besides, retirement will have a lot more opportunities if I go out on top—isn't that what you've always said?"

Pete sighed. "Yeah, it is. I can't believe you were listening."

"I was listening." The only problem was, he'd never actually considered that the choice might not be his. He'd never thought there would be a sliver of a chance he wouldn't make it on the team. Now? He seemed to be the only one who thought he had a shot.

"I've got a few phone calls to make, but I wanted to give you the update. Keep your head down out there and get through this community service. You gotta get some training in."

"Gonna be pretty hard." Grady looked down at the plate of food in front of him. He had no memory of Betsy bringing it, but suddenly his appetite was gone.

"Do the best you can with what you've got." Pete hung up, leaving Grady reeling from their conversation. Without that endorsement money, he was done. He'd have to get rid of his condo. And Benji—he didn't want to think about what it would do to him.

His text alert went off.

Speaking of Benji . . . He hadn't been back to see his brother in years, but they still kept in touch, which was more than he could say for the rest of his family.

They're saying you're out of the running for the Olympic team. Don't listen to the haters. You've got a few more years left in the tank. How are things in Michigan?

Grady stared at the words on his screen.

A few years left? Benji was being generous.

Why was Grady suddenly unsure? And if he didn't make the team—what then? What did a professional athlete do with his life when the public decided they'd had enough of him? When his body couldn't keep up with the eighteen-year-old up-and-comers? When the people who were supposed to stick by him until the end abandoned ship too soon?

What was left for Grady Benson now?

CHAPTER

10

GRADY TOOK A TWENTY-DOLLAR BILL OUT OF HIS WALLET and threw it on the table next to his plate of untouched food. Betsy rushed over, and he didn't want to be rude, but he really needed to get out of that suffocating diner with the onlookers and the reminder that he was 100 percent stuck here.

Four years ago, one shot would've been all he needed. It was practically a given that if he showed up at any race, he would easily win—and more than that, the team would be thankful they had him. Sure, he had his quirks, but they'd learn to live with them. After all, he was the one who got it done.

It had been bad enough only winning bronze and silver medals at the first two Olympics he'd competed in, but not medaling at the last games had been the crushing blow that started this downward spiral.

"Are you leaving?" Betsy stood off to the side. "Was there something wrong with your food?"

"No, it's great. I just have something I need to take care of. Can you tell Ryan I'll be back in a little bit?"

"Of course." She picked up the cash he'd left. "You don't have to pay for this."

But Grady didn't turn around or respond. Instead, he stormed toward the front door, reaching it just as Quinn Collins was coming in. She stopped as soon as she saw him, but he barreled through. He didn't have time to navigate her irritation with him.

Outside, Grady found his Jeep Grand Cherokee, which he'd purchased to haul ski equipment. Thankfully, it turned out the SUV was surprisingly fast. If there was one thing he needed, it was a fast car. Given that the speed limit everywhere in Harbor Pointe was around thirty miles per hour, however, he was going to have to risk leaving town to get the kind of rush he craved.

He headed back toward Cedar Grove, which was on the outskirts of Harbor Pointe from what he could tell. He was careful to drive the speed limit, though there was something like a bomb ticking off the seconds on the inside of him. A brown Volvo cut him off at the last intersection out of town, going twenty-five.

He inched out over the center line, checking the oncoming traffic. It wasn't a passing zone, but he didn't care. He zipped around the Volvo and sped off down the highway, ten, twenty, thirty miles over the speed limit. He cranked his music as he accelerated.

He replayed his conversation with Pete as he rounded a curve. Bowman wasn't just a company to Grady. They'd been like family. Endorsing their skis, wearing their logo—it was a sign that he was on top.

If Bowman dropped him, that said something. He could only imagine the talk. Everyone cluttering the conversation about his career, everyone who thought he was done—they'd have their proof now.

Without this—without skiing, without his reputation—he didn't belong anywhere.

He flew past Cedar Grove and straight on past a sign that read, *Come back home to Harbor Pointe soon!*

Home. A place he hadn't been since he first went pro. He didn't need the memories or the reminders of who he'd been and what he'd done. It was hard enough just keeping up with Benji every week.

Sometimes his brother would text nothing but a Bible verse. Those texts always annoyed him. How Benji could still believe everything their parents had drilled into their heads when they were kids made no sense to Grady. After all his brother had endured, did he really believe God was merciful?

He zipped around another curve, this one leading to a straight-away that ran right alongside the lake. The road ahead was clear, so Grady pressed down on the accelerator. The engine revved as all parts of the vehicle worked together to throw his adrenaline into high gear.

The back end of the car slipped slightly, and for a split second he imagined losing control—spinning out and ending up in a ditch somewhere, the same way he felt on the slopes. As if at any moment, he could shift an inch in the wrong direction and go down. He'd seen guys carried off on stretchers, retrieved by medical teams, flown off to hospitals. Some had broken bones. Some would never race again. The possibility of those things were always at the forefront of Grady's mind. But it never deterred him. It only pushed him forward.

He lived for those moments, dangling on the precipice of control. The rush, the thrill—it excited him. He'd been cooped up in this sleepy town for too many days with no release, and it was cutting off his oxygen.

The road had eventually taken him away from the lake, and all around him were cold, brown fields. Occasionally, he'd pass a house or a barn—sometimes run-down and dilapidated. Completely forgotten, the way he'd be if he didn't figure out what to do.

In the distance, Grady saw flashing lights—an accident?

As he approached, he slowed down, looking for some sign that a car had crashed, but he saw nothing. Only the squad car, lights flashing, blocking his path on the rural highway.

A heavyset deputy wearing a brown uniform and bulky coat

stood in the middle of the road beside his car, waving his arms in the air. Grady slowed the car to a stop and rolled down his window as the lawman dropped his hands and approached him. But he reached Grady and kept on walking.

Grady glanced in the rearview mirror and saw another squad car, lights flashing, behind him. He turned his music down and heard the last push of a siren as the squad car came to a stop. The door of the car behind him opened.

Was that . . . ? *Gus.*

Unbelievable.

The sheriff exchanged words with the deputy, who glanced back at Grady's car as they spoke.

Was this about him? Were they really keeping such close tabs on him?

Gus must not have anything better to do if this was how he spent his days—chasing after Grady on the highway. He pulled the door handle and got out of the car.

"What's going on?" he demanded.

Gus reached out and shook the other man's hand. "I can take it from here, Andy."

The heavyset deputy tipped his hat (what was this, the Wild West?) and turned toward Grady, giving him a once-over before getting in his barricading vehicle and driving away.

Grady kept his gaze firmly on Gus, who leaned against his car. "You goin' somewhere?"

Grady turned in a circle like a trapped animal, raking a hand through his hair. "I'm going nowhere fast." He'd mumbled the words under his breath, but they surprised even him. It wasn't like Grady Benson to admit defeat—ever. "Just needed to get out of that town for an hour."

"That right?" Gus squinted up at him, the morning sun highlighting his face.

"I was gonna come back."

"I clocked you doing eighty-five back there."

Was that all? Grady thought he'd kicked it up to at least ninety. They must've caught him just before that final acceleration. "So, what, now you're gonna slap a speeding ticket onto my record?"

"I'm thinking about it." Gus eyed him. "Saw the work you did at Hazel's."

"Yeah, so?" Grady didn't have time for this. Any of it. He'd call his lawyer himself as soon as Gus left him alone. He would listen to Grady, even if Pete couldn't get the job done.

"It's good work."

Grady didn't reply. He'd felt worthless working alongside Ryan Brooks. He wasn't used to taking orders, and he wasn't used to feeling helpless.

"Brooks said you were a good help."

Grady looked away. "You're surprised?"

Gus ran a hand over his white mustache. "You don't have a reputation for being a hard worker."

"Would I be where I am if I wasn't a hard worker?"

Gus shrugged. "Well, talent can get some people pretty far—work isn't even a factor."

"I work." Grady resented the implication.

"Level with me, son," Gus said. "What's really going on with you?"

Was he serious? Did he really think Grady was going to open up and lay all his problems out on the table in front of the man who was single-handedly ruining his life?

"Never mind," Gus said, before Grady could tell him off. "I get it."

"You get what?"

The sheriff waved a hand from Grady's head to his feet and back again as if to indicate whatever it was he got.

"What?"

"This thing you're doing. This persona you've created. Rebellious. Annoyed. The tough guy."

"You don't know a thing about me."

"But I know about regret."

"You don't know what you're talking about." Grady walked back toward his car.

"What is it you're running away from?" Gus called out.

Grady ignored him and got in the SUV, started the engine, and sat there, stewing. Then he stuck his head out the window. "I'm not going anywhere and I don't need a babysitter. You can go."

"I'll escort you back to town," Gus called. "It'll be my gift to you."

Was that sarcasm? This guy. Good grief.

He turned the car around and sped off, leaving the squad car without a prayer of catching up, and his mind without a prayer of shaking the old man's question.

What is it you're running away from?

———

Quinn had always loved working late at the flower shop. She'd never minded being alone, which was probably why she'd gone so long without a date. Valentine's Day would be here before she knew it, and that *should* bring her down, since her only plans always included cookie dough ice cream and chick flicks. But there was far too much to do this year.

Now that she owned a local business, she saw the value of bringing tourists to town in the off-season even more clearly than she had before.

But even she knew her bottom line was not her motivator to knock this design out of the park. The opening ceremonies of the Winter Carnival included the ball in the large outdoor pavilion. There, locals and tourists could enjoy the spectacular winter garden, a mixture of snow and ice sculptures and floral designs meant to highlight the work of the artists.

Last year's theme had been Alice in Wonderland. Throughout the pavilion were the most beautiful sculptures of scenes from the classic tale. She'd been so inspired by the quirky, whimsical story, it was almost as if the design poured out of her.

She'd chosen large, less-often-used blooms—red and orange dianthus, bright-orange chrysanthemums, and pops of bright-pink orchids. The combination of her flowers and the sculptures had been the highlight of the whole Winter Carnival.

If only she could've entered her design in the competition last year.

"It's not quite right," Mimi had said, which had bothered her at the time. After all, Quinn might be a creature of habit, but she still had a creative side.

Mimi did not.

And the Alice in Wonderland display had been the talk of the carnival last year.

Could she make it happen again?

This year, she'd work with the sculptors again, but she had also agreed to take on the main display behind the stage where the opening ceremonies would take place, along with the ice princess contest on the second day of festivities. That competition brought in a number of visitors in its own right, and while Quinn didn't hope to understand pageant culture, she could appreciate that they needed lots of flowers.

She'd create something truly unique—remarkable, even—and they wouldn't be able to ignore her.

She wouldn't be able to ignore her.

Quinn had met with the sculptors, and they'd settled on the theme Secret Garden. The ball would be a masquerade, playing on the "secret" part of the theme. It all catered perfectly to her unique talents. Why, then, was her brain so blocked? It was like her creativity had just given up and gone home, leaving her staring at page after mocking blank page.

She sat on the floor of the shop, only a few lights on, sketching the pavilion, strategically placing the twelve ice sculptures in the ideal pattern from the entrance all the way to the pavilion stage.

The stage. It had to be an explosion of color—something to complement the rest of the display, but still its own unique design.

She glanced up at the shelves she'd brought in from The Rustic Farmgirl, a vintage shop with the perfect look for her new and soon-to-be improved version of the Forget-Me-Not Flower Shop. A mix of distressed white and barn wood and vintage pieces with stories of their own to tell would fill her space . . . as soon as she could find time to put it all together.

She lay back on the floor and stared up at the ceiling. Old light fixtures stared back. She'd been eyeing a set of perfect galvanized metal barn lights, but she was holding off on purchasing them until she was certain she could afford them.

Never mind that she had no idea how to install the lights. One problem at a time, right?

And yet her grand reopening was only one week away. If she didn't hurry up, she was going to end up with a not-so-grand reopening where everything looked exactly like it did when Mimi owned the flower shop.

Someone pounded on the glass door and Quinn shot straight up, adrenaline rushing. Her dad had always told her to pull the shades if she was going to work late at night—but this was Harbor Pointe, where nothing ever happened.

Until now.

She glanced out the window, knowing she was fully exposed, under the cover of absolutely nothing.

Outside, she saw the shadow of a man standing on the sidewalk. Her heart kicked up a notch.

She stood and peered outside, trying not to look obvious. She reminded herself she knew everyone in town, and this was very likely just someone checking on her; after all, it was past ten, and she was practically inviting strangers to meddle in her business.

She approached the door cautiously, her hand on her cell phone, as the figure outside turned around. Was that . . . ?

Grady Benson stood on the sidewalk outside *her* flower shop. She stared at him through the glass as the seconds ticked by. Somehow she could see, even under the faint light of the lampposts, that his skin was ruddy and tan, his five o'clock shadow was looking a little more like an actual beard, and his piercing blue eyes were leveled squarely on her.

He leaned an arm on the doorjamb and knocked again, even though there was literally only a double pane of glass between them. "Can I come in?"

"What for?"

He lifted his chin to meet her eyes. "It's cold outside."

She pulled the door open. "I'm only letting you in because you're practically yelling, and my neighbors go to bed early."

He stumbled over the threshold. "All the stores are closed."

"But there are apartments above the stores," she said, stepping away from him.

He righted himself and closed the door behind him. "What are you doing in here alone?"

She rooted her feet to the ground and angled her chin upward. "Are you drunk?"

He waved a hand in the air and let out a puff, dismissing her question. "I had a couple of drinks." He reached over and tugged on the end of her hair. "But I'm not drunk."

She pushed his hand away and walked toward the back of the store, aware—how could she not be?—that he was following her.

"This is your business?" His words were slightly slurred, his balance slightly off. If he wasn't careful, he'd end up falling into one of her new shelves. That was about the last thing she needed.

But what she needed even less was to be alone with Grady Benson after 10 p.m. on a Wednesday night.

"This is it." He must think it was all so small—this town, this business, this life. She'd never been embarrassed about where she came from before, so why did she feel that sudden pang to make it all seem more important than it was? She owned a flower shop in a small town. That was her life. And that was enough.

Except that when she was standing across from Grady Benson, Olympic athlete, it seemed anything but.

"What are you doing here?" she finally asked, deciding that it was better to be rude and get rid of him than shrink under the weight of his stare for one more second.

"You're not so friendly, you know?" He leaned across the counter she stood behind, suddenly very close.

"I'm plenty friendly with my friends," she said, eyeing him. "You're not my friend."

He laughed. "Tell me how you really feel." He pushed himself up and walked over to the wall where the photo gallery hung. Framed images of Forget-Me-Not's history, including two photos of her mother, one with Quinn and Carly, lined the wall. She had plans to reframe—or maybe get rid of—those pictures, though a part of her didn't know if she could ever let the memories go.

Never mind that those same memories kept her frozen. Her mother's long blonde hair, the way the curls bounced when she twirled Quinn around. The way the flower shop had been so full of laughter, so full of *life*.

How long had it been since Quinn had felt truly alive?

What a ridiculous thought. She'd just bought her own business. She was living her dream. Where were these crazy ideas coming from anyway?

"Why flowers?"

Did he really want to have a conversation? With her? Right now?

"Everyone loves flowers."

He shrugged and faced her. "I don't."

She turned away. Everyone *else* loved flowers. Apparently egotistical jocks were immune.

"Tell me," he said. "I want to know."

She avoided his eyes.

"Come on," he said. "When did you first know you wanted to do this?"

"When I was a kid," she said without thinking.

His eyebrows shot up. "Really? I don't know many little girls who grow up wanting to be a florist."

"It sounds so stupid when you say it."

He casually put a hand on her new shelves. He gave them a shake, as if to test their sturdiness. "I don't mean to make you feel stupid. I was just trying to get to know you a little."

She wanted to ask him why, but something stopped her.

"Calvin, I think, is the reason I wanted to do this," she said after a moment of silence.

"Calvin?"

"Calvin Doyle. You met him at dinner."

"Calvin," Grady repeated.

"He used to come in here every Friday afternoon, after work. He was a teacher, and I'd watch him pick out the perfect bouquet of yellow tulips every single time. He was very particular. Before leaving, he'd say to my mother, 'Do you think she'll like them?' And my mother always smiled and said, 'I think she'll love them, Calvin. They're perfect and beautiful, just like your Anne.'" Quinn stopped. Her mother had such kindness in her eyes, every time she sent Calvin out the door with a bouquet. She'd taken such good care of the people of Harbor Pointe. How, then, had she just . . . left?

"That's the whole story?" Grady leaned against the shelves now.

"Sorry, no. I always pictured Mrs. Doyle getting that bouquet every Friday. Tulips were a wonderful choice, and my mother always made sure to have some in the cooler. She'd save them for Calvin. He was like a clock. One day, years later, I was walking home from school and I saw him with his bouquet of yellow tulips. He was standing over Anne's grave, holding them and, I think, talking to her. All that time, he'd been getting flowers to put on her grave. To make sure she wasn't forgotten."

Grady didn't move.

She felt suddenly self-conscious and regretted saying anything at all.

"I can see why you'd like it, I think."

He could? She wouldn't have imagined so. "We do all kinds of weddings and proposals and Valentine's Day flowers, so we're there for people's celebrations—and I love that. But knowing that I have something that can bring a little bit of beauty to somebody's worst day?" She shrugged. "I guess that's why I always wanted to do this."

His eyes held hers for seconds in which her heart thumped like a bass drum.

Why had she told him any of that? He was not someone to try to connect with!

He must've felt her discomfort, because he started walking again. Walking and picking up things he had no business touching.

She moved out from behind the counter just in time to snag a glass vase from Grady's grasp. She gave it a slight tug, but he held firm, and the strength of her pull drew him closer—too close.

"Will you let go, please?"

He reached up and touched her forehead, swiping his finger along the length of it, just above her eyebrows. "Do you feel that?"

"What? You poking me in the head?" She swatted his hand away.

"That's your serious line." His mouth quirked upward in a lopsided smile.

"What are you talking about?"

"You're always so serious." He touched her forehead again, this time rubbing in small circles as if to knead away something that wasn't supposed to be there. "Don't you feel that? Your forehead is always tight."

She glared at him through his fingers. "Are you finished?"

He pulled his hand away and sighed. "Just trying to help."

"I don't need your help."

"You need something." He spun around and walked to the other side of the shop.

"Really? And what would that be?"

His laugh mocked her, but before she could ask for clarification, the front door swung open and Walker Jones strolled in.

"You okay, Quinn?"

Walker sometimes acted like he was her big brother, though she had absolutely never given him a reason to think of himself that way. He seemed to feel like he owed it to her dad to watch out for her. When would both of them learn she could take care of herself? She glanced at Grady—she couldn't be sure, but she thought if it weren't for the shelf he was propped up on, he might fall over. He blinked—slowly—then bobbed his head in her direction.

For the briefest moment, she almost felt sorry for the guy. He was clearly miserable and trying to cover it up with bad behavior and alcohol, and while she couldn't relate because she covered her misery with hard work and a neatly checked-off to-do list, she supposed she could muster a bit of empathy for him. From somewhere down deep. Down very, very deep.

Besides, she had Jaden to think about. She'd made Carly a promise, and she'd never be able to ask Grady for her favor if she got on his bad side now.

"I'm fine, Walker."

The deputy's eyes darted from her to Grady and back again. "You sure?"

"She said she's fine." Grady's slur had gotten more pronounced. For the love. This guy had terrible timing.

"I didn't ask you, Benson." Walker sauntered over to Grady, who didn't move. "Heard you were making quite the commotion at the Lucky Lady a little while ago. Got a call about you disturbing the peace."

"Why do you think I left?" Grady's words were sharp and staccato. A short pause between each one, as if he was working overtime to sound, well, not drunk.

It wasn't helping.

Walker stuck his thumbs in his belt loops and squared off with athletic, intoxicated Grady. "You planning to drive home in that condition? See your car's out on the street."

"I don't plan on going home for a long, long time, for your information," Grady said.

"He wasn't going to drive, Walker," Quinn heard herself say.

"How do you know?" Walker faced her.

"I was just about to get my keys and give him a ride back to Cedar Grove."

Walker watched as she pulled her purse out from behind the counter. "I'll just take him then."

"No," Grady said. "I want her."

Quinn felt her eyes widen, but she quickly recovered. "I've got it, Walker. I'll be fine."

Walker watched Quinn for a long moment, then turned toward Grady. "If you lay a finger on her . . ."

Grady's scoff cut him off. "Her? She can't stand me. She's. Driving. Me. Home. That's. It." Again with the overpronounced words.

"He's not wrong. I can't stand him," Quinn said. "But my dad would want me to run him home." She leaned toward Walker. "I think he might actually need a friend."

She'd made up that last part, though she had no idea why.

"Fine, but you call me if he gets out of line." Walker started for the door.

Grady waved a hand up over his head. "So long, Texas Ranger!"

Walker slowed his pace but didn't turn around.

"You really don't know when to quit, do you?" Quinn asked after Walker had gone.

Grady laughed. "That guy is like a cartoon character."

"Maybe, but he can throw you straight in jail if you're not careful, and I'm pretty sure he can't stand you either, so you should probably knock it off." She slung her purse over her shoulder. "Are you ready?"

"Ready for what?"

"For me to drive you back to Cedar Grove?"

He let out a stream of air. "I can walk."

"Don't be an idiot." She reached into his coat pocket, hoping to find his keys, trying to ignore the close proximity of his ridiculously muscular body.

"What are you doing?"

She reached into the other pocket. "Looking for your keys."

She felt—not saw—his grin. "They're in my pants pocket."

She rolled her eyes and pulled away, holding out an upturned hand. "Give them to me."

The frown he put on was apparently meant to match her own. He dug into the pocket of his jeans and pulled the keys out, then stuck them in her hand, and seconds later that mischievous smirk returned. "I can't figure you out, Quinn Collins."

"Good." She walked toward the back door, but quickly realized he wasn't following her. When she turned around, she saw him standing in the same spot, looking a little disoriented. "What's wrong?"

"My head is spinning."

She felt her frown grow deeper. "Can you walk to the car? Wait. You're not going to throw up, are you?"

His upheld hand said *Wait a minute*, and she stopped moving. After several seconds, he glanced at her. "I'm good." He took one step and stumbled forward, the weight of his tightly toned body landing on her. She tried to hold him up, but his fall had caught her off guard; plus, he was twice her size. She peered out the window toward the SUV he'd parked across the street, just a few doors down from the Lucky Lady, Harbor Pointe's one and only bar.

She could drive that instead of taking her Jetta, but how was she going to get him out there, into the car, and then into his cottage at Cedar Grove? The drive to the edge of town could lull him right to sleep, or worse, he could pass out—and then what was she going to do? She couldn't leave an unconscious Grady Benson in the car overnight.

Against her better judgment, she wrapped an arm around him and tried to maneuver his bulk through the flower shop and into the back room.

"Where are we going?"

"Will you just try not to pass out? Walk." She sounded bossy—even she could hear that.

He did as he was told and they made it to the back room, where she pulled open the door that led upstairs to her apartment.

"What's this? A secret passageway?" Grady sounded equal parts intrigued and sleepy.

"It's the stairway to my apartment," she said. "Can you make it?"

He stopped and looked at her, his face perilously close to hers. "Are you going to try to take advantage of me, Quinn Collins?"

She let out a purposeful huff. "You wish."

"I do wish," he said, laughing.

She ignored his drunk comment, reminding herself that it absolutely did not qualify as a compliment, and tried to push him up the stairs. "Let's go, lover boy."

He laughed again. "I wonder what Quinn Collins's apartment looks like on the inside. Gotta say, Q, I never thought I'd find out."

"Well, extenuating circumstances and all that." This had to be the worst idea she'd ever had. She should've shoved him out on the street and gone to bed. But that's not who she was, not even with someone whose charms she was intent on resisting.

They'd reached the top, and she made sure he was somewhat stable leaning in the corner of the stairway before letting him go. "Don't move."

"You got it." He picked up a strand of her hair and twirled it around his finger while she hurried to get the door open.

She didn't bother telling him to knock it off—he likely wouldn't remember any of this tomorrow anyway.

She pushed open the door and took a couple of steps inside, waiting for him to do the same. He was slow and methodical as he moved, as if there was a slight—or not-so-slight—chance he might collapse at any moment.

"Why don't you sit down and I'll make you some coffee?"

"You don't have any beer?"

"Seriously?"

"It was a joke. Sheesh." He plopped down on the sofa as she flipped a few lights on. She was aware that he was watching her, but she was the only other person in the room. What else was he supposed to look at?

She moved to the kitchen and filled her coffee carafe with water. "Do you take your coffee black?" She'd called out so he'd hear her from the living area, but when she turned around, she found him standing at her kitchen counter. "What are you doing?"

"You're being nice to me," he said. "That's not like you."

She had no idea why, but the comment amused her, and she had to look away before he saw the smile on her face. "Go back and sit down. I'll bring you some coffee when it's ready."

He tipped his head to the side and shrugged. "Whatever you say."

But he didn't go back and sit down. Instead, he started walking around the loft, looking at her decorations, touching knickknacks, making her nervous. He held up a framed photo that was on a shelf of her entertainment center. "This is the same picture on the wall downstairs."

He remembered that?

"Who is it?"

She moved into the living room, took the photo from him, and put it back on the shelf where it belonged. "It's nothing."

"Obviously it's something or you wouldn't have two copies of it."

She didn't want to talk about her mother—not with anyone, but especially not with Grady. Somehow she thought it would make her horribly unattractive, admitting that her own mother didn't want her.

Not that she wanted Grady to find her attractive. It just wasn't a subject she discussed.

"Sit down." She gave him a push and he fell onto the couch.

"You're bossy."

"Yes, I am. You'd be smart to start listening to me." She walked back into the kitchen and poured him a cup of coffee, struggling not to feel off-kilter about the turn this night had taken. She knew herself. She liked rules and thrived on routine. Having Grady Benson in her loft was against the rules and certainly not in her routine, which was quite possibly why the whole situation had her on edge.

She'd only made him coffee because it's what people in the movies made for drunk people when they were attempting to sober them up. At this point, however, she might be better off to let him pass out on her couch and call it a night.

She handed him the mug, and he set it on the table beside the couch without taking a drink.

"I'm curious about you," he said. "You're not like most girls."

She should probably be enough of a modern woman to take that as a compliment, but somehow it nicked a nerve—the I'm-not-pretty-enough nerve. But she had a feeling he wasn't talking about the way she looked.

"You're different."

"Why, because I don't throw myself at you?" She had no idea where that came from, and she regretted it as soon as she said it.

He, however, found it amusing and laughed. "That's part of it." He leaned his head back on the sofa, forearm resting on it. "My sponsor dropped me."

She quietly sat down on the other end of the couch.

"Been with them ten years and they cut me off—" he snapped his fingers—"just like that."

"I'm sorry," she said quietly, realizing she actually meant it.

He shook his head. "It's my own fault. I've got a temper. I don't listen to my coaches. I'm always trying to do it my own way."

"Sounds like a bunch of stuff you've heard other people say about you."

He moved his arm and looked at her, sinking a little bit lower in his seat. "It's true, though, isn't it?"

She gave a soft shrug. "I don't know."

He shifted. "That's right. Because you think skiing is stupid."

She laughed. "I do not."

He stopped, then leaned in closer. "Did you just laugh?"

"It does happen on occasion," she said.

"It should happen more."

There was a soft lull, and for a moment, she wasn't sure what to do next. Should she say good night? Try again to drive him home? Get him a blanket?

"You've got everything all figured out—like a grown-up," he said.

"I am a grown-up."

"Yeah, I'm supposed to be one too, and look at me."

"You are kind of a mess."

He laughed and shook his head. "I know. And I'm going to get worse if I don't get back on the team."

She could see it in his eyes—a quiet desperation for something just out of reach. She recognized it because she saw it in her own eyes every single day. Odd as it was, she thought she and Grady Benson might actually have something in common.

"So, what, am I spending the night or are you going to let me walk?"

"You are not walking all the way to Cedar Grove."

He raised his eyebrows. "Fine with me."

"You can sleep on the couch." She stood. "I'll go get you a pillow and blanket."

This is a very bad idea.

She disappeared into the bathroom, the only room in her whole loft with an actual door on it, and drew in three deep breaths. What was happening? Why was she suddenly feeling sorry for him?

Get a grip, Quinn. He's just a guy who needs a couch to crash on. That's it.

But as the thought left her mind, she wondered how on earth she was going to sleep knowing there was only a thin partition at the foot of her bed separating the two of them.

A knock on the door startled her, but she pulled it open, again doing her best to look nonchalant.

Grady stood on the other side. He'd taken off his coat and now wore only a gray T-shirt and jeans. Unfortunately for her, she could see the definition of his muscles under the shirt, and that did nothing to calm her jumpy nerves.

He leaned against the doorframe and stared at her.

She met his eyes, wishing she didn't feel as unsteady as he looked.

"Can I get a glass of water?"

She clung to the doorknob more tightly than necessary. "Of course."

"Thanks." He walked off, leaving her standing there, reminding herself that this man was a terrible dose of really bad news.

He was the kind of guy her father had always warned her about, and she knew it.

Remember that, Quinn.

She grabbed sheets, a blanket, and an extra pillow from the linen closet and went back into the living room. She set the blanket and pillow on the end of the couch and unfolded the sheet, then spread it across the cushions.

Grady shut the light off in the kitchen and came up beside her. "What are you doing?"

She let the sheet fall to the ground. "I'm making your bed—what does it look like I'm doing?" She kept her tone light, feeling a surprising kindness toward him.

He set his water down and she went back to spreading the sheet. Seconds later, his hand was on her shoulder. "You don't have to do that."

She turned—slightly—toward him. "I don't mind. I'd rather have you on my couch than walking home—or worse, driving—in your current state." She glanced up and found his eyes on her, an oddly serious expression on his face.

"Thanks," he said.

"My father thinks you're redeemable."

He watched her, still touching her arm, his large hand making her feel small. "What do you think?"

His eyes held sadness, maybe even deep pain, the kind she was sure he rarely let show through. She held his gaze for several seconds but didn't respond.

"Never mind," he said. "Don't answer that." He let his hand slide down toward hers, then picked up the sheet she was holding. He slung it sloppily over the couch, then picked up the pillow and threw it down. "There. Perfect."

"You can't sleep on it like that."

"Does it bother you that it's not neatly tucked?"

Maybe.

She said nothing, but bent over and tugged at the corners, making the makeshift bed a little neater.

Behind her, he laughed. "I really can't figure you out."

She stood upright and faced him. "You said that already."

"You can't figure me out either. Don't pretend you can."

She narrowed her gaze and stepped forward. "You're not that hard to figure out, Grady." Though she had to admit, tonight had her rethinking a few of her perceptions of him. "You like fast cars, fast women, and anything that puts you in danger."

He looked like he was about to say something but snapped his jaw shut.

"You're such a cliché." She shook her head and turned to go back to the sheets, but he moved between her and the couch.

"Don't get mean again on me now." His smile was lazy, his eyes flashing mischief. Whatever serious moment they'd almost had a minute ago was long gone, and the slightly drunk, not remotely serious version of Grady Benson had returned.

"I'm not mean," she said, picking up the pillow.

"You get all flustered and your cheeks turn pink." He grabbed the end of the pillow and tugged on it, pulling her closer to him, still wearing that smirk. "It's kind of cute."

She tugged back, but his grip was solid, and instead of putting the desired distance between them, she stumbled forward and straight into his brick wall of a body. As if it was what he expected all along, his hand steadied her, but before she could pull away, he leaned in closer and kissed her.

The kiss only lasted a few seconds, but it was long enough to elevate her heart rate and plenty of time for her to notice how soft and full Grady's lips were.

And that he knew how to kiss a woman.

She pulled back, pillow still in her hand, scanning him for any sign of regret. She found none.

Instead, he looked perfectly comfortable with what had just happened even though it was highly inappropriate and had sent her insides tumbling around in ways she would never admit out loud.

"You need to sleep whatever this is off." She tossed the pillow onto the couch. "I'll see you in the morning."

But as she lay in her bed on the other side of the partition, she couldn't help but touch her lips, the memory of his kiss still playing at the corners of her mind.

CHAPTER

11

THE POUNDING IN GRADY'S HEAD pulled him from sleep. He forced his eyes open, though his eyelids still felt heavy, like he'd slept in fits and starts. He stared up at unfamiliar wooden beams on a high ceiling. Slowly, he turned, trying to piece together the events of the previous night.

He'd been upset about losing Bowman—really upset. He'd gone into town and found what seemed to be the only place in all of Harbor Pointe to get a drink. Never mind that there were three churches just on his drive in from the cottage. Three. Wasn't that a little excessive? How many churches did one tiny town need?

He didn't like that he noticed them at all. He'd stopped paying attention to church a long time ago. Just another way he'd disappointed his parents.

He'd had too much to drink. His throbbing head told him that. The guy next to him said something about skiing, about his career being over—because for some reason that was the only thing people were talking about when it came to Grady Benson.

Grady didn't want to hear it. Not last night. Especially not after losing Bowman. He'd gotten in the guy's face—rammed him into the bar, threatened him. And he would've made good on the threat too if someone hadn't pulled him off.

He'd ended up walking around downtown. He couldn't drive, not in his condition, so what was he going to do? Fall asleep on a park bench like someone who'd really hit rock bottom?

And then he'd seen it. The light in the flower shop. And he'd seen her. Sitting on the floor, completely oblivious to the outside world. She was like a beacon of light—something about her was special.

He knew it in the way she *didn't* fall all over herself to get his attention. In the way she'd never be caught dead in that bar. In the way she'd told him that story about the old man buying flowers for his dead wife.

A clang in the kitchen roused him from his thoughts. He sat up and looked in the direction of the noise.

This morning Quinn wasn't so much a beacon of light. More like a warning flare—a loud one. She glanced up from her spot behind the counter.

"Sorry," she said, her eyes wide. "I'm clumsy in the morning."

He ran his hand through his hair, then over his face, which was in need of a shave, and watched her for a minute. He was in Quinn's apartment—a loft that was smaller than most hotel rooms he stayed in. He couldn't place the details of getting here.

She wasn't looking at him anymore. "I'll be out of here as soon as I get my coffee." Her head was down and she was fishing around in a drawer that sounded like it was loaded with metal kitchen utensils.

He pulled himself up off the couch and stood still for a moment, righting himself as his head spun. How much had he had to drink? He had to stop doing that—it only ever led to mistakes.

How many mistakes had he made last night?

After a few seconds, he walked into the kitchen, still wearing jeans and one of his old gray T-shirts, but no shoes or socks. "I slept here."

She stopped what she was doing—organizing silverware?—and looked at him, eyes wide again. "Yes. You came to the flower shop. You don't remember?"

He looked away, still trying to piece together the details. He glanced back and found her staring at him, and in a flash he remembered. He'd told her about Bowman. She'd listened—no one ever listened to stuff like that—but then he'd closed up. Because Grady Benson didn't talk about his pain. Not about Bowman. Not about Benji. Not about his past.

But she would've kept listening if he had. And he supposed that meant something.

"Do you remember . . . anything about last night?" She screwed the lid onto her travel mug, still avoiding his eyes.

"Was I rude?"

"I think you were rude at the bar," she said. "Walker said someone called the cops and told them you were disturbing the peace."

"Great, that's just what I need." He sat on a tall barstool on the opposite side of the counter.

She poured a cup of coffee and slid it across the counter, still not looking at him.

"Thanks." He took a sip. "You're being nicer than usual."

Now the trademark furrow in her brow had returned. "I'm always nice."

"Not to me." He grinned. Pushing her buttons was quickly becoming one of his favorite pastimes.

"I have to go. I have work to do." She picked up a small notebook held together by a flimsy piece of attached elastic, her travel mug, and her phone.

"Am I working with you today? Festival stuff?" He took another drink. She might be cranky, but Quinn made good coffee.

"It's a carnival, for the twelfth time, and I hope not."

He pulled his phone out of his back pocket and opened his e-mail. "Think I am, chief. You're going to have to put me to work."

She groaned. "What am I going to do with you tagging along all day?"

He shrugged. "We could start with breakfast."

"No."

"Why not?"

She frowned. "I'm meeting my friends for breakfast."

"Let me come along. I promise I'll be polite."

She eyed him. "No. I have to go. I'm going to be late."

"Suit yourself. I'll see you at nine, boss."

She came out from behind the counter and started for the door, but stopped abruptly and turned around. "You really don't remember anything else about last night?"

Grady shook his head. "Do you want to tell me something I'm forgetting?"

Her eyes widened and she shook her head—quickly, like a guilty child. "I gotta go."

"Do you mind if I take a quick shower?" he called out as she reached the door.

"Whatever!" She didn't turn around, and seconds later, she was gone, leaving him wondering exactly what it was he'd forgotten about last night.

~

Quinn raced down the stairs and out onto the street. He didn't remember that he'd kissed her. That was a good thing. That was a great thing. Now she could just pretend it had never happened, because in his mind, it never had.

So why did she feel that slight twinge of disappointment?

Really, he was doing her a favor not remembering. It would be so awkward to navigate that one.

Still, how was she supposed to spend the day working alongside this man? Because as much as she wished she didn't, she *did* remember that kiss.

She clomped her way over to Hazel's and found Hailey and Lucy already sitting in their usual booth. Lucy's eyes lit up when she spotted Quinn. Or maybe that was just how Lucy's eyes always looked—bright and expectant, as if something good were bound to happen at any moment.

How did she always stay so positive? Was it an act?

Lucy tossed her long auburn hair away from her shoulder and scooted over.

"Sit by me today."

Sometimes it was like they were still in junior high school. Quinn slid in next to her.

Hailey pulled her phone out and looked at the screen. "Sorry, Jack wasn't feeling great this morning, so I'm trying to pay extra attention in case the school calls."

The image of Hailey's little boy popped in Quinn's mind. "How is Jack?"

"Don't change the subject," Lucy said.

"There's a subject?"

"You're late." Hailey propped her chin up with her fist and stared at her.

"I know. I'm sorry."

Hailey's eyes narrowed. "You're never late."

"I am sometimes."

"Never."

Quinn looked away. Hailey knew something about her was different this morning. Hailey always knew.

"We could set our watches by you, Quinn," Lucy said. "What's going on?"

Quinn opened her menu, but Hailey snatched it away from her. "Spill it."

"Nothing. I was up late working on my designs for the carnival; that's all. It's a lot harder than I thought it would be."

"You haven't finished your designs yet?" Hailey's face fell. "It's only a few weeks away."

"I know." *Don't remind me.*

"Don't you have to, like, order flowers and stuff?" Lucy took a drink of her mocha.

"Yes," Quinn said. "As soon as I figure out what to order."

"Maybe this is just too much all at once," Hailey said. "Buying the shop, renovating it, building the display for the carnival. You're putting a lot of pressure on yourself."

Quinn didn't respond. She didn't want to hear that she'd taken on too much. As overwhelmed as she was, there was nothing she could take off her plate.

A waitress named Shannon brought Quinn her usual latte. She thanked her and took a quick drink even though she still had a whole travel mug of coffee—which she'd made solely for the purpose of busying herself while Grady Benson awoke on her couch this morning. She didn't feel right about leaving him asleep in her apartment, but figuring out how to wake him hadn't been easy. Did she throw things at him? Shake him? Set an alarm?

In the end she'd opted for the make-a-lot-of-noise option. It had worked.

"I'm serious," Hailey said. "You can enter your design next year. Why are you in such a hurry?"

Quinn leveled her gaze. "You know why."

Hailey sighed. "Maybe this isn't the best way to get her attention."

"You're saying this to me now? This is all I've ever talked about doing since I saw her at the Expo three years ago." Quinn tried not to think about that moment, but somehow it always came back to haunt her.

She and Mimi had been walking the floor. They didn't have a display in the finals—no surprise there. Mimi had been submitting the same old tired displays for at least ten years, and she wasn't open to any new or creative ideas.

The image of her Alice in Wonderland display raced through her mind. It had turned out even better than she'd imagined. If only Mimi would've agreed. If only she'd entered it, this whole thing would be behind her now.

They'd been at the Expo all day, and the crowd was beginning to thin out when they rounded a corner at the end of one aisle where a company showcasing new, environment-friendly flowerpots was situated. That's when Quinn saw her. An older version of her mother—same slight build, her hair cut shorter than it had been when she'd left all those years before.

Mimi had gasped then, just a quick, shallow intake of air, and Quinn had frozen to the spot.

"Mom." Quinn had whispered the word, and even as she did, it felt wrong. How many years had it been since she'd heard a word from the woman who had practically hung the moon for her as a girl? She'd been waiting for so long to see her again, and now, here she was.

She'd played the moment over and over in her mind for years. She practically had a script of what she would say if ever given the chance. But here, on the Expo floor, she realized there were no words. She ran off before her mother ever saw her.

It was one of her greatest regrets.

Mimi told her later that her mother hadn't given up everything about her old life. Only her family. Her career in the floral industry was still going strong. In fact, she wasn't just an exhibitor at the Expo—she was a board member and a judge of the design competition, which was, perhaps, the true reason why the old woman had never allowed Quinn's designs on their entry form. She was worried about more than Quinn's career—she was worried about her heart.

Jacie Collins was at the top of their industry, and while that was about all the information Quinn had amassed on the woman, it was enough for an idea to hatch.

She'd create a design that deserved her mother's attention, a design that would remind her mother that what she'd given up— *who* she'd given up—was worthy of a blue ribbon.

To prove that her mother had made a mistake.

It had been three years of praying for some shift in Mimi's stubbornness, and now, finally, here she was. Armed with a warning from the old woman not to let her work consume her and the memory of an absent mother who'd given Quinn her first heartbreak.

Her design *had* to win. Surely Lucy and Hailey understood that. They were two of the only people in the world who knew her plan. She'd even kept it hidden from Dad and Carly. She couldn't break her father's heart all over again—he'd be devastated if he thought for a second that Quinn sensed something in her life was missing, especially after he'd spent every waking hour trying to take care of her and Carly, to make sure they had all they needed.

And they did, of course, except for one thing.

Their mother.

Shannon brought their food and set it on the table in front of each of them.

"You know we're going to support you no matter what," Lucy said, pouring syrup on her pile of pancakes.

Quinn thought it was wholly unfair that her friend could eat that way. She turned her attention to her two scrambled eggs, turkey bacon, and side of fruit. Some people weren't so lucky. "I know. I'm just stressed, is all. There's so much riding on this—I have to get it right."

Quinn stabbed at the eggs with her fork but stopped mid-bite when she spotted Grady just outside the door.

"Oh no."

Lucy followed Quinn's gaze as the bell above the front door signaled Grady's arrival. It might as well have been a siren the way he pulled the attention of everyone in the restaurant.

"Oh, I heard he was out causing trouble again last night," Hailey said. "Someone said he almost got in another fight at the Lucky Lady."

"Who cares? As far as I'm concerned, a man who looks like that can do whatever he wants." Lucy took a bite of pancakes.

"I know you don't mean that," Hailey said. "That's just not a smart thing to say."

Lucy waved her off. "Oh, you know what I mean." She set her fork down. "Is he coming over here?"

Quinn, who at this point was staring at her food as if it were the most interesting thing in the world, could feel her friends staring at her.

"He's looking at you," Lucy practically hissed the words. "Oh my heck . . ."

Grady was now standing beside their table—Quinn could see his shoes. Shoes she recognized because they'd been on the floor of her living room that very morning.

"Morning, Mr. Benson. I'm Lucy Fitzgerald." Lucy stuck a hand out across the table, in front of Quinn, and waited for Grady to shake it. He did, and Quinn scooted back in her seat, daring a glance at Hailey, whose wide, curious eyes were asking Quinn all kinds of questions. Namely, *What is he doing at our table and why does he seem to know you?*

Grady dropped Lucy's hand.

"Do you already know Hailey and Quinn?"

"We've met," Hailey said. "I obviously work here." She glanced down at her Hazel's uniform—a brightly colored turquoise T-shirt with yellow lettering.

"And Quinn?" Lucy was digging now, Quinn could tell.

"We've met," Grady repeated. Quinn didn't have to look at him to know he was wearing that trademark Grady Benson go-ahead-and-fall-in-love-with-me smile. She'd spent the better part of her morning shoving the memory of that exact expression out of her mind.

Because no matter what, she was absolutely *not* going to succumb to his charm. She could only imagine the number of women who'd fallen for it over the years. He clearly knew what he was doing when it came to making women swoon. Even her friends seemed smitten by him, for Pete's sake.

"Hey, I just wanted to come by and say thanks," Grady said, attention now firmly on Quinn.

"Thanks for what?" That was Lucy. Always inquisitive, that one. Today inquisitive felt a lot like nosy.

"Don't mention it," Quinn said.

No, really, please don't mention it.

"What are you thanking Quinn for?" Lucy asked, her tone a little more serious this time.

"For last night. She was a saint. Guess she's good at keeping secrets too." He tapped on the table twice. "I'll see you in a little bit." He started off but turned back only a few steps away from the table. "Oh, and you're out of shampoo. I'll pick more up for you since I used the last of it."

She shot him what she hoped was a very dirty look, but was met only with his lopsided smile before he walked out, the bell clanging as the door closed behind him.

"*What* was that?" Hailey asked.

Both she and Lucy started talking at the same time, demanding explanations and "the scoop" and "the whole story." Comments like "super hot guy" and "why was he using your shampoo?" were being thrown around at mach speed until finally Quinn held up a hand to silence them both.

She told them everything—the way he'd shown up outside her flower shop, drunk; the way she'd planned to take him back to Cedar Grove, but had to improvise thanks to his level of intoxication.

"He slept on my couch. That's it."

Both Lucy and Hailey eyed her suspiciously.

"What?" Quinn didn't like when the attention was on her.

"That's it?" Hailey asked.

"You had *that* man on your couch and that's it?" Lucy looked incredulous.

"He's hardly my type, you guys," Quinn said, pulling a chunk of cantaloupe off of her fork with her teeth.

"Who cares?" Lucy sighed. "He's such a beautiful man."

"I care. I'm not interested in dating anyone right now—didn't you just tell me I'm taking on a little too much at once? A relationship would be nothing more than a distraction. Besides, that man is not relationship material. He doesn't even remember half of last night."

As soon as she said the words, she regretted it.

"What doesn't he remember?" Hailey asked.

Betsy strolled over at that exact moment—lifesaver!—and glanced at Hailey. "You clocking in, girl? I need you."

"Oh, yes," Hailey said, dropping her napkin on top of her empty plate. "Be right there."

"Two minutes," Betsy said.

"She really means five," Hailey said. "Which is more than enough time for you to tell us what he doesn't remember."

Quinn rubbed her forehead, willing this whole conversation away. "It's not a big deal, really."

"It obviously *is*," Lucy said. "Did he try something with you?"

"No, it wasn't like that," Quinn said. "He's not a bad guy; he's just full of himself."

"And?" They were both looking at her like wide-eyed toddlers waiting for a giant piece of birthday cake.

"He kissed me, okay?" Quinn whispered.

They gasped. Loudly. In unison. "He what?"

"Would you both be quiet?" She hated every second of this conversation. "It was so quick it barely counted as a kiss."

One-one-thousand, two-one-thousand, three-one . . . Did that count as a kiss?

"And you kissed him back?" Lucy was not going to let this go until she had all the details.

Quinn scrunched her face, meaning *I'm not really sure. It's all a blur.* But all her friends saw was . . .

"Oh my gosh. You kissed him back." Lucy sounded a lot like a thirteen-year-old girl.

"Seriously. It was nothing, and like I said, he doesn't even remember." Quinn wished she didn't. "And I was only nice to him because, one: I didn't want him driving home; and two: I need him to do Jaden a skiing favor." She pulled her billfold from her purse, left enough cash on the table to cover her meal and the tip, and stood up. "Don't make a big thing out of this, okay? This is a man who has kissed dozens of women."

"Try hundreds," Lucy said.

Quinn groaned.

"Sorry. We won't say anything." Lucy held up a hand as if that somehow solidified her promise.

"We won't," Hailey said. "But if anything else happens, you better come tell us about it immediately."

"Nothing else is going to happen. Nothing but planning the Winter Carnival and hopefully convincing him to take Jaden skiing. Beyond that, I have no use at all for Grady Benson."

No matter how good-looking *everyone else* thought he was.

CHAPTER

12

AFTER STOPPING OUT AT CEDAR GROVE to change his clothes and take some Advil, Grady made his way back to town. Ryan had signed off on the diner, content that the work was finished, though he told Grady he reserved the right to call him back in if it turned out more needed to be done.

Which meant today, he had to work with Quinn, his "boss" for all things Winter Carnival.

His phone buzzed, and when he picked it up, he saw Benji's name on the screen. Benji, the guy he'd always looked up to, probably since the day he was born. *It should be you competing for the gold, Big Brother.* After all, Benji wouldn't have messed things up so badly. Bowman wouldn't have dropped Benji. And to be honest, the Olympics had always been Benji's dream, not Grady's.

He stared at the phone until the vibrating stopped.

Seconds later, the voice mail notification dinged. He listened, the sound of his brother's voice pulling him back to places he was usually unwilling—or unable—to go.

"Hey, Gray, it's me." Benji sounded—what? Worried? "I just got off the phone with the physical therapist's office. They said the payment for the month didn't go through. Look, man, I know you've hit some rough stuff lately, and I don't expect you to always pay what the insurance doesn't cover with these medical bills. Just let me know and I'll get it worked out on my end. Love ya, man."

Typical Benji, letting him off the hook.

"Don't worry about winning the gold, man. You're a world champion. You've got plenty of medals."

But none of those medals were the ones Benji had wanted. Benji had wanted Olympic gold. It was the thing that meant the most to him right up until the day he learned he'd never walk again.

Grady threw the phone on the passenger seat. Pete said he had another month at least before his money ran out. What was the deal?

He let out a heavy sigh. He was headed nowhere fast. Between losing Bowman, his trouble with the law, and his screaming headache after the poor way he dealt with his frustration last night, Grady's life was quickly spinning out of control.

Worse, it had been almost a week since he'd been on the slopes. Little by little, he could see his chances at getting back on the team slipping away, but he felt utterly helpless to stop it.

And helpless wasn't something he was accustomed to feeling.

He picked his phone back up and called Pete. His manager was doing a poor job of taking care of him, that was for sure.

As the phone rang, he parked his car in front of the Forget-Me-Not Flower Shop, where Quinn and her cold shoulder were probably waiting for him.

"Grady, hey."

"I just got a call from Benji. Said his last PT payment was denied. What's going on, Pete? You told me we had at least a month. Maybe two."

Pete sighed. "I guess I miscalculated."

"Are you kidding? This isn't a grocery bill here—this is my brother's life."

"I know, Grady. Let me see if I can move some things around."

From where he sat on the street, he could see movement inside the flower shop. Quinn was pushing a large shelf from the middle of the store against the wall, and his first thought was *She shouldn't be doing that by herself.*

"Just call me when you get it figured out, will you? I don't want my brother worrying, and right now, he is. That's the last thing he needs."

"I know, Grady. I'll take care of it. How are things there?"

"You're kidding, right? How do you think things are?"

"Sorry. I am trying. I called your lawyer again—had him review your contract with Bowman."

"And?"

"They'll owe you some money—you won't see it for a little while—but it's in their right to cut you loose as they see fit. But I do have one piece of good news."

Well, that was a change.

"Spectre called. They heard about Bowman. Wanted to know if you'd be interested in repping them instead."

"Spectre?"

"I know it's not ideal, Grady, but they're making a name for themselves. It's a young company—you could help brand them."

It was a young company without much money and a whole lot less prestige than what Grady was used to. Bowman had treated him like a prince. Private jets to competitions, suites he could easily live in. Cars. Parties. Women.

Grady could still remember one summer just a few years ago when Brent Bowman, grandson of the company's founder, showed up at his condo after one particularly wild night of partying. Brent wore an expensive gray suit with a blue tie. Grady wore last night's jeans and nothing else.

At the sight of him, Brent held up a ring of keys, jingling them around as if they meant something.

Grady squinted, the light of the morning sun doing a number on his hangover. "What's that?"

"Get dressed and come find out." Brent grinned. Grady had gotten to know the man over the years—he was a good guy, and he understood Grady's affection for speed. Maybe he'd rented a particularly unique sports car and had a joyride planned?

Grady let him in, though he wasn't proud of the condition of his condo. People—mostly strangers, really—had come over the night before, and they'd done a number on the place.

Brent pretended not to notice.

"Do I have to dress like you to go wherever it is we're going?"

Brent laughed. "I wouldn't know who you were if you did."

Grady brushed his teeth and pulled on fresh clothes—jeans and a well-worn Chicago Bulls T-shirt. "You wanna tell me where we're going now?"

"Rather show you." Brent's BMW was the only car parked outside. They got in, and for the next ten minutes, the man talked to Grady about his value to their company.

"Having an athlete of your caliber wearing our logo—it's something we've strived for at Bowman," he'd said. "We're all feeling pretty lucky you're on our team."

"I've been on your team for years, man," Grady said, feeling oddly uncomfortable with the praise.

"But it's only been the last few years we could give you the perks you deserve." They were pulling into the parking lot of the speedway—a large racetrack just outside of town.

"What are we doing here?"

"You're the fastest skier competing right now—you obviously love fast things."

"No way." Grady glanced up at the speedway as Brent put the car in park.

"Time to see what you're made of, man."

As a rule, Grady drove fast, but he'd never topped 150. That was all about to change.

The Bowman race car was on the track and a crew of men in

jumpsuits moved around it, making sure it was ready for him. He stared at it for a minute before moving toward it.

"You sure?" He glanced up at Brent, who nodded, his own grin matching Grady's. "This is awesome."

He suited up, got behind the wheel, and waited for the all clear. He took off like a shot, pushing the car toward its limits on his first lap. He loved the way it felt to control something so fast, so powerful, and as he accelerated, the background noise drifted away, leaving only the track in front of him and the concentration needed to take the car around the curve without crashing. He zipped around for another lap, pushing the car even harder—faster—still focused only on the speed and the accuracy necessary to stay on the course.

As he finished the final lap, Grady's heart pounded, adrenaline simmering through his veins, and for a split second, he thought maybe he'd found something even more exciting than downhill skiing.

Bowman had arranged other events for thrill seekers like Grady— snowmobiles during training, skydiving in the off-season. Pete complained about it every time—"Our job is to keep these guys safe," he'd said. "What they do for a living is dangerous enough."

But Brent Bowman was an extreme sports fanatic. He craved the fast life as much as Grady—which was, he supposed, why they'd become friends.

Maybe that's why Bowman's dumping him stung a little more than it should have. Brent hadn't even called to break the news himself. He'd had Pete do it. On the phone. Hadn't their partnership over all these years warranted more than that?

"Grady?" Pete was still on the phone, probably wondering where Grady had disappeared to in the quiet on his end.

"Yeah, no thanks," Grady said, remembering the question.

"Just think about it."

"I did. And I gave you my answer."

"Grady, nobody else is calling. This might be your best bet."

It was like a sucker punch to the gut. If his best bet was Spectre, then Grady's skiing career was in a whole lot worse shape than he'd realized.

And the hits just kept on coming.

—————

When Quinn saw Grady's SUV pull up outside the flower shop, the nerves kicked up in her belly.

Knock it off, Quinn. He doesn't even remember.

He was out there—on the phone? Waiting for him to come to the door was unnerving. She tried to busy herself—moving shelves to places she knew they did not go, recopying the list she'd made of things he'd have to do before he could clock out that night, checking her hair—again—in the reflection of the glass in the door to the back room.

That last one? That's what she was doing when Grady finally decided to stroll through the front door.

Naturally.

"You really don't need to make yourself pretty for me," he said. "I've seen you in your pajamas."

She spun around and faced him, certain her cheeks were flushed. "You have not. You were passed out by the time I changed."

"I might've peeked."

She rolled her eyes. "Right, because that would be terribly exciting, me in my black-and-white flannel pajamas."

"The red shirt really pulled the whole look together."

She wanted to respond, but she had no words. He'd actually seen her in her pajamas. It wasn't a big deal, really. After all, she'd been known to make an emergency Ben and Jerry's run late at night wearing pajamas. Only on special occasions, of course, or in moments of desperation. Like the anniversary of the day her mom left. April 25. Still, something about knowing he'd been paying attention—it flustered her. And she absolutely could not be flustered. There was too much to do.

"I don't believe you remember a thing about last night." She picked her notebook up off the counter as she walked toward him. "You were drunk."

He waited until she glanced up into those disastrously attractive eyes before responding. Then he smirked—barely—and said, "I wasn't that drunk."

Her pulse quickened. Did that mean what she thought it meant? Was he only pretending not to remember the hardly-kiss?

But it wasn't a hardly-kiss, was it? It was the kind of kiss she'd been thinking about since the second it happened, and she could kick herself for it.

"Well, against my wishes, you're here to work on preparations for the Winter Carnival." Why couldn't the rest of her committee have community service hours to work off? This would be so much easier if it weren't just the two of them. "I'm in charge of decorating the pavilion, which is, unfortunately for you, a lot of work. It's a big responsibility." She gave him a once-over. "Are you familiar with that concept?"

He sauntered over to the stool behind the counter and sat down. "You sound very judgmental right now."

"Hey, I call it like I see it."

"You're doing it again." He was looking at her. Just sitting there, looking at her. How was she going to get anything done with him here taking up way too much room behind her counter?

"Doing what?"

He wagged his finger in her general direction. "That thing with your forehead. The I'm-serious-all-the-time furrow."

She set the notebook down and stuck her hands on her hips. "I am not serious all the time."

His eyebrows shot up. "Really?"

"Really."

"Prove it."

She shook her head, her level of annoyance skyrocketing. "I don't have time for this. Do you know the carnival is only three weeks away? We have so much to do to get ready."

"I'm sorry. Is that you being serious again?"

"You're the worst," she muttered under her breath as she walked over to the shelving unit she'd pushed out of the center of the store only moments before he strolled in. She used her hip to push it to the other side of the store, aware that Grady was watching her the whole time.

Once it was in place, she moved some of the small gift items she had in stock onto the shelves. This would be a brand-new display with some of the wall art and home decor items she'd been waiting to exhibit.

"So you own this place, but you're not open?" He was leaning up on the counter now, the side of his head on his fist like a child.

"I just bought it," she said. "I have some work to do before I can reopen."

"Like what?"

She drew in a deep breath. She didn't really want to get into it with him. She didn't want to explain her plans or hear how silly they sounded to the famous Olympic athlete when she knew the only thing Grady Benson really wanted to talk about was Grady Benson.

But that wasn't fair, was it? He'd asked her more questions about herself than she'd wanted to answer.

"What do you have to do?" He stood up, still watching her.

Was he just bored or genuinely interested?

"Well, I'm going to paint the walls and refinish the floors. I've got new valances for the smaller windows, and I'm going to paint our new logo on the back wall behind where you're standing. I've got a few more shelves like this one for all the displays and the gifts I'm selling. Mimi—she was the previous owner—never really sold gifts. Just flowers."

"When does that all have to be done by?"

She hated that question. It was like a quiet reminder that she wasn't going to make her deadline. When Ryan and Lane had come in with so many "simple, easy-to-do" ideas, she'd been so certain she could get it all done. Now? Now she was pretty sure she'd reopen with nothing but a few new shelves.

And maybe that was okay.

"I wanted to reopen next Wednesday."

He whistled, as if saying, *Whoa, you've bitten off more than you can chew.* As if she didn't already know that.

"That and the Winter Carnival? You've got your hands full."

"I'm very efficient," she said. "I have a plan."

"Seems like you could use some help." His eyes were wide—as if meant to communicate something she couldn't read.

"What are you saying?"

"I'm saying I'll help you. It's the least I can do since you gave me a place to crash last night. I was going to sleep in my car."

"You can't be serious." Could he?

"No, I really was going to sleep in my car."

"Not about that. About helping me."

"Why not? We'll take care of the carnival stuff, but mostly that's work we're going to do the week of, isn't it? I'll help you paint. I've never refinished a floor, but how hard can it be?"

"I think it's very hard, actually."

He laughed, shaking his head: "I'm offering you my help, Collins. Do you want it or not?"

She wasn't so sure. Somehow she felt like she was walking into a trap. "What's the catch?"

"No catch."

She watched him through narrow eyes.

"Okay, I was hoping maybe you could put in a good word for me? With your dad and the judge?"

She felt her shoulders slump. So he wasn't offering just to be nice. That shouldn't surprise her. Of course he had an ulterior motive. What did she expect? He wasn't going to fall in love with Harbor Pointe in a few days' time.

"I help you out, you tell them how much extra work I did.

Maybe I get out of here early on good behavior. Catch a couple more races."

"You're really worried about these races you're missing." Quinn studied him.

He looked away. "Just trying to give myself the best possible chance."

Maybe you should've thought of that before you got in a stupid fight.

She looked away. "Well, I don't think the good behavior thing works like that."

"I think that's exactly how it works. That judge makes up the rules as he goes."

She straightened two small, hand-poured soy candles on the shelf. They didn't need to be straightened; she just needed something to do with her hands.

"What do you say?"

She faced him. "I'll think about it."

"What's to think about? I mean, I know you can't stand me, but I'm a strong guy. I can move shelves and use a paintbrush."

"I never said I can't stand you."

"You did, actually. Last night. When you were talking to that cop."

"I don't remember that. I don't even know you."

"That's what I'm saying," he said. "Get to know me. Give me a shot. And then tell your dad I'm a good guy, and I don't need to learn some great lesson about life by being trapped in your charming little town."

He said "charming little town" as if it were a swear.

She pressed her lips together, fully aware that her brow was both serious and furrowed. "I'll consider it on one condition."

"You want me to tell people we're dating?"

"Are you insane?"

His face lit into a cocky grin. "I'm just kidding. What is it?"

"Do you remember that kid Jaden? From the diner a few days ago?"

"Vaguely."

"He's my nephew, and he's got it in his head he wants to ski." She looked away. "Professionally." She said the word cautiously, as if Grady's laughing would injure her even though it was her nephew's dream.

But he didn't laugh. He only stared. "And?"

"And you told him you'd think about skiing with him, and now he's got it in his head that you're going to."

"You want me to take the kid skiing?"

"Yes."

"And in return you'll tell your dad I'm a good guy and try to get me out of here early?"

"Yes." She drew a deep breath. This was very much against her better judgment, so the word came out quietly and through clenched teeth. "If you actually help out around here."

"Done." He stuck his hand out. "Shake on it."

She hesitated before taking his hand.

"So it's a deal." He wore a mischievous expression, like a cat with a bird in its mouth.

"What?"

His eyes widened. "What?"

She recognized phony innocence when she saw it. "Why do you look like that?" She pulled her hand away, crossing her arms.

He mirrored her stance. "I might've already bumped into Jaden, and it's possible I already made plans to take him skiing this weekend."

She glared at him.

"But hey, a deal's a deal." He grinned.

She started to protest but quickly snapped her jaw shut. A deal was, in fact, a deal, though she'd never agreed to a timetable and figured she could put a good word in for Grady whenever she felt like it.

Which might be tomorrow if it meant he'd be out of her hair. After all, having him underfoot while she tried to reopen the shop and finish her designs for the Winter Carnival suddenly seemed like the worst possible idea in the world.

CHAPTER

13

AFTER OUTLINING A LIST OF TASKS FOR GRADY TO DO, Quinn sent him to the hardware store to pick up supplies. When he returned with three gallons of paint, rollers, and brushes, he found her sitting in the middle of the shop, staring at the wall behind the cash register.

He stood outside for a brief moment, not sure if he wanted to risk scaring her. After all, it didn't take much to set her off. He tapped the door with one of the paint cans, and she spun around, jumped up, and let him in. She reached out to take something from him, but he pulled it away.

"I can help you," she said.

"I'm the guy. I've got it."

She gave the door a push and glared at him. "Could you be any more sexist?"

"It's not sexist. It's chivalrous." But as he took a step toward the counter where he'd planned to set everything down, one of the paint cans slipped. Seconds later, everything he'd been carrying was on the floor in front of him. The blue tape escaped the plastic bag and rolled across the floor, spinning in an annoyingly loud circle before finally coming to rest.

"Well," she said. "It's good to know you've got this under control."

His eyes scanned the floor in front of him, settling on the large sheets of sketch paper she'd spread out in front of where she'd been sitting, a few feet from the mess he'd made.

"What's all this?" He picked up one of the sheets.

She hurried across the room and snatched up the other pieces of paper, tucking them back inside a large sketchpad. "Can I have that?" She held her hand out toward him, expecting him to turn over the sheet he held.

"You're still working on the designs," he said.

"Yes." She sounded exasperated. "I'm behind. I know."

"I didn't mean—"

"Creativity doesn't just happen." She gave him a once-over. "Never mind. You wouldn't understand."

He glanced back down at the images she'd drawn on the paper he held in his hand. "It's supposed to be a secret garden, right?"

"It's inspired by *The Secret Garden*," she said.

"So that's a yes?"

"It's a book."

He didn't have to tell her he'd never read it.

"Can I have that back, please?"

He ignored her, choosing instead to walk over to the counter and set the page down, studying it intently for effect. "It all looks pretty boring to me."

He felt her irritation. "You have no idea what you're talking about."

"Maybe that's a good thing?"

She glared at him. "How could that possibly be a good thing? You don't see me over here telling you how to ski."

"You get worked up a lot," he said. "It must be exhausting."

"I have a lot to do." She slammed her sketchpad down on the other end of the counter. "And so do you if you want me to put in a good word for you. How about you pick up all the stuff you dropped in the middle of my floor?"

"I think a secret garden should have a wild side."

"You think everything should have a wild side."

"Think about it. If it's a secret, maybe it's left alone a lot. And it kind of does its own thing whenever it can. Maybe it can't really be tamed."

She drew in a slow breath and glanced down at the paper in his hand. He expected her to tell him to shut up, but when she said nothing, he took it as a sign he could continue. He didn't get many creative ideas—but there was such rigidity in her drawing, it seemed almost the opposite of the effect she was going for.

Should he tell her so?

"You seem to like things in their place."

She stiffened. Everything he said must come across as an insult to her.

"But think about it—if a garden was just growing somewhere, wouldn't it be sort of haphazard? I don't know anything about flowers, but I know about nature, and nothing ever really seems to stay in its place out there."

The image of the wildflowers that grew in the woods around the house where he'd grown up sprang to mind. He'd never paid them much attention, but he did know they were relentless in the way they grew. Chaotic, even.

He glanced up, seeing that familiar furrowed brow he'd come to expect from her.

"Never mind. I don't really know what I'm talking about." He turned away, reminding himself he really didn't care about this Winter Carnival and he should keep his uneducated opinions to himself. No sense giving Quinn yet another reason to be annoyed with him.

Quinn drew in a slow breath that was meant to calm her down, but her imagination had started swimming. She could kick herself, but she wanted Grady to keep talking. As he spoke about wildflowers, about untamed nature, images started forming in her head. And they weren't standard Quinn images. They were different, as if something new had been sparked, and she couldn't keep the ideas from rolling in.

Grady stared at her, clearly finished with his thoughts. "It was just an idea." He slid the sheet of paper across the counter toward her.

She glanced down and saw boring, safe, uninspired designs. Embarrassed, she tucked the page in her sketchpad, itching for a new sheet to mark on. It was as if something had been unlocked within and she needed to record it before it all oozed out of her, washing away like a paper sailboat in an angry river.

"You can get started here, right?" she asked, not wanting to admit to him that it was what he'd said that had finally—finally—triggered the creative spark she'd been missing.

"Sure. Paint the walls and the ceiling. I think even I can handle that."

"I'll be in my office." And with that, she disappeared. Off to the small office in the back, where she could be alone with her thoughts—and the ideas that spiraled so quickly through her mind that she could hardly get her notebook open fast enough.

Why hadn't she thought of that? Wild, untamed—flowers that grew with reckless abandon? She could wrap them in a seemingly arbitrary fashion around the snow and ice sculptures, tying the two elements together perfectly. It was brilliant, really. But she'd never admit out loud that it was Grady who'd given her the idea.

She sat down and opened her sketchpad. She was no artist—not on paper, anyway. Her tools were always flowers, never graphite or paint. But she needed a plan if she had any hope of accomplishing what was necessary in the next three weeks. Deciding which blooms to order would be her first task; finding a supplier that would come through would be her second.

As she flipped through catalogs, she noted which flowers seemed to have a mind of their own, which ones were whimsical and almost overgrown. She began to envision large antique mirrors and white lights strewn throughout the pavilion. She'd find a way to rig vintage chandeliers along the walkways and turn the entire area into a garden that almost seemed to have invaded an old English mansion.

Finally she had the perfect plan, and the excitement that bubbled up inside her would propel her past any overwhelmed feelings. She put in a few calls to her committee, who all agreed to meet her at the flower shop later that evening.

She spent the entire morning working, and probably would've kept going if it weren't for the loud crash. She shot out of her office and found Grady standing near the wall that once held all the picture frames, most of them now on the ground in many, many pieces. He held a paint roller attached to an extender and had paint all over his shirt and jeans. An overturned ladder lay at his feet.

"What happened?" She scanned the mess before finally meeting his eyes.

He held up a hand as if to calm her down. "It's nothing to worry about."

She came around to the other side of the counter and saw the tipped-over bucket of paint, which was now all over her wood floor. "Nothing to worry about? You ruined the floor."

"I'm sure there's a way to clean it up."

"Yeah, paint the whole thing gray." She frowned. "Wait. Why is this gray? I ordered creamy white." She picked up the lid to the paint can, which read *Moonlight Gray*. "What is this?"

Grady shrugged. "It's what the guy gave me."

Quinn groaned. She didn't have time to check up on every little detail, but if Grady couldn't get one thing right, what choice did she have? "Can you go get some rags from the back room?"

He started toward the door.

"Stop!"

"What?"

"You have paint on your shoes. Did you even put down a tarp?" She glanced at the supplies he'd spread out on the counter and saw the two large canvas tarps she'd purchased still wrapped up in their packaging.

"I didn't know I needed a tarp."

Another groan. "You made a huge mess."

"I know. I'm trying to clean it up. Can I get the rags?"

"Don't. Move." She practically growled the words. He may have unlocked her creativity, but he'd single-handedly set her way back in the flower shop renovation.

"What can I do?" He did look sorry, at least.

"You can start taking some of this stuff seriously," she said, a little angrier than she'd intended. "It's all just some awful punishment for you, but this is my life. I'm not in the habit of slopping stuff together and calling it good."

"I didn't mean to—"

"Maybe you should just go."

"No, let me clean it up," Grady said.

"No, just go. You've done enough." Broken glass crunched underfoot. She glanced down and saw the image of her happy smile, standing next to Carly and holding on to her mother's hand.

Grady stood there in silence for too many seconds, then took off his shoes and started for the door. She'd been mean, and it had been an accident, but she didn't care. She didn't want his help—not on the carnival and not in her shop—and one way or another, that was what she planned to tell Judge.

CHAPTER

14

WHATEVER CREATIVE EXCITEMENT Quinn had felt that morning was now long gone. The mess Grady had caused had taken her two hours to clean up, and when she called the hardware store, Bob told her that her "deliveryman" had picked up someone else's order.

To make it worse, while she sat on the phone making arrangements to pick up her original paint order, she discovered paint splatters in the corner and along the baseboards. Had Grady ever painted anything in his life?

Sloppy, sloppy, sloppy! How had he ever made it to the Olympics? Was he was one of those natural talents who had everything handed to him?

Whatever the case, it was annoying, and as she unpacked the paint she was supposed to get in the first place, she ran through a mental list of all the things she was going to say to her father in an effort to get Grady on the next bus out of town.

She'd only managed to cover one wall with the creamy white when there was a knock on her door. She turned and saw Danny standing on the sidewalk, peering in. Was it already five? She must've lost track of time.

She set the roller down and opened the door. "Hey, Danny."

Danny shoved his hands in his pockets and stared at her, but said nothing.

"Come in. Is it already time for our meeting?" She'd planned to have her presentation a little more put together by the time everyone arrived. So much for that.

"I'm a few minutes early," Danny said.

She forced a smile. This was going to be awkward.

"Quinn, I've been meaning to talk to you about something."

Not again. Her heart raced. She didn't want to lead Danny on, but she also didn't want to reject him and make things even *more* awkward—if that were possible. He was a nice guy. Sweet. Maybe she should give him a chance. After all, if her heart didn't get tangled up in the romance of a relationship, she'd be safe—protected. And wasn't that what she really wanted?

Maybe someone like Danny would be good for her.

But before he could continue, Ashley and the others showed up at the door, followed by . . . Grady? What was he doing back?

They came in, Ashley laughing that loud, flirtatious laugh of hers and Grady with his sparkling eyes that seemed to say, *That's right, you can admire me.*

"What are you doing here?" She didn't mean to say it. The words just kind of came out.

Grady met her eyes and his smile faded. "Heard our team was meeting tonight. Thought I should be here."

She leveled her gaze and lowered her voice. "Haven't you done enough today?"

He raised one eyebrow, his tone matching hers. "Apparently not."

She shook her head. "You really don't have to be here, Grady. We all know you have much more important things to do."

He shrugged. "I actually have nothing else to do. Seems to be the way things work in this town."

"Hey now, Mr. Benson, don't pretend this isn't the most charming place you've ever been." That was Mona Deery, who'd seemed skeptical of Grady at their last meeting but now seemed to have a twinkle in her own eye when she looked at their adopted Olympian.

"Oh, it is charming, Mona," he said. "I'll give you that. But there's not a lot going on in the evenings. Not for a guy like me, anyway."

A guy like you? Meaning—a reptile?

"I think you just haven't found the right people to hang out with," Ashley said. "If you're not busy later, we could go out."

"On a Thursday?" Quinn practically spit the words.

Grady's lazy smile hung there, taunting her. She knew what he was thinking. That only a boring, small-town girl with no life would say something like that. He probably spent every night of the week out at bars or parties. She, on the other hand, hadn't gone out on a weeknight since she was in college, and even then, it was rare.

"Fun things happen on Thursdays too, Quinn," Ashley said. Quinn couldn't be sure, but it sounded like she was implying something.

"Some of us work early on Friday mornings," Quinn said.

"Some of us don't need a lot of sleep," Grady said.

"Maybe we should get started." Mona, the voice of reason, set her purse on the counter. "As much as I'd like to have a fun Thursday night, the only thing waiting for me is a house of small children who are all going to be hungry and need baths. I know you're all jealous."

Quinn *was* a little jealous, but she didn't say so. She glanced up and found Grady watching her. Was he trying to bug her?

"You said you had the designs?" Mona prompted Quinn, who definitely did not want to show her designs to the rest of them when Grady was there.

But as she glanced around the small circle, she knew she had no choice. They were already behind, and that was her fault. She couldn't put them off any longer. The five of them huddled around the counter, where Quinn spread out the designs she'd been working on that morning before Grady's accident with the ladder. She'd added color and stapled images of the flowers she was planning to use along the sides of the pages.

"Wow," Mona said. "These are beautiful."

"It reminds me of a fairy tale," Ashley said.

Grady waited until he had her eyes, then smiled. "Looks kind of wild. Sort of . . . untamed."

She ignored him. At least she pretended to ignore him, but she knew he absolutely did not have to search for that word. Oh, it irritated her that she'd been found out. "I've ordered all the flowers, but we will need to build a few structures." She filled them in on her plan to find large, ornate mirrors, chandeliers, and white lights, and turn the pavilion into a beautiful secret garden.

"I think you've really outdone yourself this time, Quinn," Mona said after volunteering to pick up white lights—they'd need tons— and shop for antiques.

"I hope you're right," Quinn said. "There's a lot riding on this one."

Of course none of the others knew just how much.

They figured out their timetable and divvied up their tasks, and while Grady was very quiet for the entire meeting, Quinn was keenly aware of his presence, more so than she would've liked.

"Okay, if that's it, I've got to run," Mona said. "Duty calls." She scurried out the door, leaving the rest of them standing there awkwardly.

"We should all go out," Ashley said in her much-too-chipper voice.

Did Quinn need to remind them again that it was Thursday?

"I'm up for it," Grady said, then turned to Danny. "How about you, Donny?"

Danny flinched. "It's Danny."

"Oh, sorry. Danny."

"Sure, I'll go."

Both men looked at Quinn.

She frowned. She was still wearing paint clothes, hands and fingernails covered with dried creamy white. She hadn't eaten anything all day, and while she couldn't be sure, she had a strong suspicion she didn't smell very good.

"I can't, guys, but thanks," she said. "You all go ahead."

"You've been working all day," Grady said. "You deserve a break."

She did, didn't she? But that didn't mean she could take one. She had so much left to do, and thanks to him, she was even farther behind. Should she remind him of that?

Ashley leaned in toward Grady. "Quinn's always been kind of a downer. We can head over to the Lucky Lady? Grab a drink or two?"

Danny's cheeks reddened as he began to put together the kind of evening Ashley had in mind. "I'm just going to head home," he said.

Quinn lifted her hand in a lame wave as Danny scooted out the door. Grady stood still, like a brick wall in the middle of her shop. He exuded strength, and even though he wasn't a wide man, he was sturdy. And so far, he hadn't moved.

She picked up her paint roller and dared a glance in their direction. Ashley's shirt was low cut and revealing, her body near perfect. She had gorgeous hair that fell into loose waves past her shoulders.

By comparison, Quinn was wearing ripped jeans that had paint splatters on them along with a too-big gray sweatshirt that hung off one shoulder because she'd cut the collar off. Her hair was pulled up into a ponytail, and she likely had paint on her face.

She had no delusions about who she was, and she'd never been one to try to impress people. Really, there was only one person whose attention she'd been striving for, and that person was nowhere near Harbor Pointe.

Why then did she suddenly feel like a slug?

"Grady, let's go." Ashley tugged on his arm.

"Do you want me to stay and help you?" he asked, probably out of guilt.

"And keep you from your fun Thursday night? I wouldn't dream of it." She didn't look at him when she responded, but she could feel him watching her. He lingered for several more seconds until finally he followed Ashley out the door. Quinn turned around just before they disappeared from her view through the front windows, and for the briefest moment she met his eyes.

It was none of her business how he spent his evening, but somehow she wished he was smart enough not to spend it at the bar with Ashley Perkins.

What did she expect? This was the life he was used to.

And it was certainly not a life that she belonged in.

Grady sat at the table across from Ashley, nursing the same beer he'd been drinking since they first sat down. Somehow it had lost its appeal. Ashley, on the other hand, had plowed her way through three fruity cocktails and had just ordered her fourth.

"Don't you want another drink?" she asked, her words starting to slur.

His mind flashed back to yesterday when he'd wound up at Quinn's, too drunk to drive home. He did not need a repeat of that. In hindsight, the whole scenario made him feel like an idiot, especially since he had a vague memory of kissing her. She'd been too polite to mention it, but he was pretty sure it had happened. And he knew that was no way to impress someone like her.

Ashley reminded him of most of the girls he dated. They liked to go out, drink too much, throw themselves at him. At first, of course, that had been one of the biggest perks of his fame, but now—tonight—for some reason it didn't appeal to him.

Maybe he *was* getting old.

"Grady?"

He realized he hadn't responded to her question. "Oh, no. I'm fine, thanks."

Ashley laughed. "Maybe you should've stayed back at the flower shop with boring Quinn."

"So, what's her story, anyway?"

Ashley shrugged. "Who knows?"

"Doesn't everyone in this town know everything about everyone else?" He kept his tone light—so she didn't think he was prying.

"I only keep up with the interesting people," Ashley said. "And Quinn Collins is not interesting."

Grady disagreed, but he wouldn't say so. Not out loud. She certainly wasn't the kind of girl he was supposed to find interesting. She was infuriating and rude. But maybe those were things that made her more—not less—intriguing.

"She's always been more of a church girl than a bar girl," Ashley said.

"A church girl?"

"Never misses a Sunday. She's practically a fixture at The Pointe—that's the name of that church up on the hill. Guess that gives her the right to look down her nose at the rest of us. You know the type."

He did, actually. But he didn't know Quinn. "Enlighten me."

"Thinks she's better than everyone else. Can't loosen up. Plus, she's never even left Harbor Pointe."

"Never?"

Ashley shrugged. "I mean, she commuted for college, about forty-five minutes away, but she lived at home." She laughed. "How lame is that?"

"And that flower shop—she just bought it?"

Ashley took a sip of her drink through a straw that was meant to stir the concoction. "Her mother used to own it. Before she left her family for some other guy or something."

Grady frowned. "Her mother left?" Wasn't that older lady at dinner—Beverly?—Quinn's mother?

She shrugged again. "Guess she thought her kids were lame too." Her laugh was too loud. "Can we dance now?"

Grady nodded toward the small dance floor, which was empty. "You go ahead."

Ashley made a pouty face. "It won't be any fun without you."

"I think you'll be okay." He was starting to get annoyed.

She reached across the table and took his hand. "Last chance. I'm a really good dancer."

"I'm sure you are," he said. "But I'm not. So I'm going to stay here and finish my drink."

"Fine." She giggled. "But you don't know what you're missing."

He did, actually. The scenario was so familiar he could easily outline what came next. She'd drink a little bit more. They'd leave. He'd drive her home. She'd insist he come upstairs with her. He'd weigh that option against going home alone, and the next thing he knew, he'd be waking up next to a woman he hardly knew with scattered memories that would make his mother cry.

It wasn't like he didn't know better. He'd been brought up more of a church boy himself, but he'd abandoned that way of thinking long ago. Everyone thought he was careless in the way he lived his life, but nobody ever bothered to ask him if his choices impacted him. Sadly, the answer was yes.

Why, then, did he seem helpless to escape the cycle?

He watched Ashley for a few seconds as she slinked her way over to the dance floor. Her movements were meant to arouse him, but somehow they left him cold, his thoughts straying out the door and down the block to a girl who'd gotten stuck in his head. It was stupid, really. Quinn Collins was all wrong for him, and she wouldn't give him the time of day. He glanced at Ashley, who had laser-focused her gaze on him. That was a girl he understood. One who wanted very little from him. No strings. No attachments. No responsibilities.

But that night, as he loaded Ashley into his car, his gaze drifted across the street and a few doors down to the sunshiny-yellow building with white trim. The light was on in the flower shop. Quinn must still be working, probably cleaning up the mess he'd made. He should've done a better job. The years when he was supposed to be learning responsibility were spent on the slopes training, and he'd been too proud to ask for her help.

It didn't seem right to leave her there alone when he was the one who'd doubled her workload. And yet he was pretty sure he wasn't welcome. Maybe he could drive Ashley home and come back. At least offer to stay and paint over his mistakes.

The passenger-side window rolled down and Ashley hung her head out. She reached over and grabbed his hand. "Come on, Grady, take me home."

He looked up at the flower shop just in time to see the light go off.

And he wondered if anything in his life would ever change.

CHAPTER

15

FRIDAY MORNING, QUINN WOKE UP SLOWLY. It was one of those days when the warmth of her bed was far more enticing than anything on the other side of her covers. Her body ached from the late-night painting she'd done. She snoozed the alarm twice—unheard of!—but finally dragged herself up. Her courtesy text to tell Hailey and Lucy that she was running late was met with snarky replies: Did you have an Olympic athlete on your couch again last night? and This is getting serious ;)

Quinn wasn't sure she wanted to meet them at Hazel's today. They'd ask questions about working with Grady and she'd have to tell them how awful it was—how he wasted the whole morning making a mess and painting her space the wrong color. They'd pry and prod until they finally got out of her that he came back for the team meeting after she kicked him out—and then he left with Ashley.

They might even find a way to get her to admit to staying up far past her Thursday-night bedtime watching the door of the Lucky

Lady for any sign of Grady and Ashley—which, it turned out, was a faulty plan, given the way it made her feel when they finally did emerge from the bar.

It wasn't that she was pining over Grady—not really—but that she was a little bit jealous she would never be the kind of girl Ashley was. Fun-loving and carefree, the kind who dropped everything to spend an evening out.

That just wasn't Quinn. Hailey and Lucy would tell her who she was was just fine, thank you very much, and they may even remind her that being alone was better than being with the wrong guy, which she really did believe. But as she gave her loft apartment a once-over before closing the door behind her, she realized that none of those platitudes would take away the loneliness she often felt at night.

Of course, her friends might misunderstand that loneliness as a crush on a certain downhill skier, which was absolutely not the case. Even if he was different than she'd originally thought. Even if he'd asked her questions about herself—and then listened to the answers. Even if he'd told her about that ski sponsor who dropped him and given her—for the briefest moment—a peek behind that tough-guy facade.

But it was none of that, not even paired with bright-blue eyes, that had her attention. It was seeing him and the way he lived—as if risks were something to be faced and not avoided—that stirred something in her, whether she liked it or not.

As Quinn descended the stairs, she heard movement in the flower shop. She'd been exhausted when she finally went to bed last night, but she was sure she'd locked the door. She paused at the bottom of the stairs and listened. Maybe she'd imagined it. Seconds later, the sound of footsteps left her frozen where she stood.

She peeked around the corner carefully to avoid being seen by whoever the intruder was, but she saw nothing. Had she imagined it?

Slowly she inched out a little farther, and when she did, she fell forward off the bottom step with a thud. She righted herself and took a step into the shop, aware that her attempt to stay hidden had failed. Light streamed through the two large front windows and glass door, filling the space with the promise of a new morning. But she couldn't focus on the beauty of sunlight when she was certain she'd heard someone.

Quietly, she took a step over the threshold of the back room and farther into her shop.

"Morning."

She gasped, clutched her chest, and turned to face Grady.

She wouldn't delude herself by thinking it was kindness that brought him here. He probably hadn't even gone to sleep last night. Besides, he was still angling for her good word with Judge and her dad.

"What are you doing in here?" She willed her pulse to calm down.

He stared at her for several uncomfortable seconds, then finally cleared his throat. "I came to help you. Isn't that what I'm supposed to do?"

"But how did you get in?"

He knelt down over the can of paint she'd been using last night. She'd almost finished painting the first coat on the walls, but in the morning light, it was obvious that wouldn't be enough. He pulled the lid off and began stirring with the stick.

"Whoa, I don't know if this is a good idea."

"I'll be careful—I promise," he said. "Tarps and everything. I watched a YouTube video on painting walls last night."

She pretended not to be surprised by that. "You didn't answer my question." She stared down at him—probably the only time she'd get to see him from this angle, given that he had several inches on her.

"Your dad let me in." He stirred the paint. "Said he thought you'd appreciate the help."

"Did you tell him I spent half the day cleaning up after your 'help' yesterday?"

He glanced up at her, then stood. "Left that part out."

"Convenient." She walked to the other side of the counter and glanced down at the photos she'd stacked there. When the frames had broken, she'd pulled the pictures out and made a list of sizes so she could buy new homes for all of them, even though part of her thought maybe it was time to put them all back in a drawer somewhere.

"Looked like you were working pretty late last night," he said.

Her eyes met his. "How would you know that?"

He shrugged. "Saw the light on."

"Oh, that's right," she said. "Because you and Ashley had your impromptu date." It had come off snarkier (jealous, even?) than she'd wanted it to. She turned away so he wouldn't see the red in her cheeks.

"What's that tone for?"

She could practically hear the amusement in his voice. She wouldn't give him the satisfaction of thinking for one second that she cared who he spent his evenings with. Because she didn't. Obviously.

"I have to go," she said. "I'm late to meet my friends."

"I'm taking Jaden skiing tomorrow," he said, clearly ignoring her attempt to leave.

"Yeah, I heard," she said. Carly had texted her to thank her for giving him the day off. Her reply had been simple: You owe me.

"Come with us."

She faced him. "Why would I do that?"

"Well, Ryan is refinishing the floors tomorrow, so you won't be able to work much in here."

"There's still plenty to do. I have to finish my application for the design competition and—"

He cut her off before she finished her laundry list, which seemed to play on repeat in her own mind. "And I heard a rumor you don't have much fun."

"What? Who would say that?"

He shrugged.

"Oh, Ashley? Ashley Perkins doesn't think I have fun, so you feel like you have to intervene?" She shook her head and switched her purse from one shoulder to the other. "She and I don't exactly have the same idea of what fun is. Maybe work is fun for me. Maybe I like what I do so much that I can't get enough of it."

"Well, that's not true."

"How do you know?"

"Because skiing is fun, but some days it still feels like work. You have to have a break from that once in a while. Besides, from what I can tell, Q, you're not much of a risk taker. What's the most dangerous thing you've ever done?"

That was the second time he'd called her Q. It felt familiar. She was surprised how it endeared her to him. Still, she scoffed. "Just because I don't purposely put myself in danger does not mean that I've never taken a risk. I bought this business, didn't I?"

He squinted at her. "Betting you had the business plan all laid out before stepping into that one."

Shoot. He was right. She'd crunched those numbers so many times—just to be sure she wouldn't lose money. Barring natural disaster, there was nothing risky about buying Forget-Me-Not.

"This is ridiculous. I really don't need some thrill-seeking Olympic athlete telling me my life is boring. Of course to you it seems boring, but this is normal life. I live a normal life. Maybe you should try it sometime."

He shook his head. "Why would I want to be normal?"

She groaned and started for the door.

"Are you afraid to try something new?"

Yes. I am. Especially something that requires athletic ability, which I do not have.

"I try new things all the time." Just last week the grocery store was out of cookie dough ice cream and she bought chunky monkey instead. Not bad, though cookie dough was still much preferred.

"Great, then meet us down here at six." He poured some of the creamy white paint into a tray.

"In the morning?"

"Gotta get an early start."

"That's not going to work for me. I'm going to be up late again."

"Hot date?"

She gave him a yeah-right look.

"I don't know, that Danny guy seems pretty into you."

She ignored his comment and opened the front door.

"If you don't show up tomorrow, I'm going to know they're right about you."

She turned back. "What makes you think I care?" Oh, if only she didn't . . .

"Just a hunch."

"You're going to bug me about this all day, aren't you?"

He shrugged. Thanks to their annoying agreement, she was stuck with him today, whether she liked it or not.

"I'll think about it," she said.

He grinned. "You won't regret it."

"Well, that remains to be seen. Now, how about you get to work?"

She walked away, her heart pounding and her head reeling. She couldn't go skiing with an Olympic athlete! She'd never come close to doing something so dangerous. She'd fall and make a fool of herself. She'd have to figure a way out of it.

But the insecure teenager buried somewhere inside her didn't want anyone—especially Grady—thinking she was a boring girl who refused to take risks.

Even if she was.

So how was she going to get out of this ski trip without seeming exactly like that?

～

Grady couldn't be sure, but he thought it was possible Quinn had avoided him for the better part of Friday. She set him on a variety of tasks, and he managed not to mess anything up, but she kept her distance.

Before he went home that night, he reminded her he'd meet her in the morning for their impromptu ski trip. He could see her searching for an excuse to get out of it, but she must've come up empty because she simply nodded and ushered him out the door.

Truth was, a part of him was nervous too. He hadn't skied since his last competition—the one that had everyone talking. Normally he'd be up for the challenge of proving everyone wrong, but lately he felt more frustrated than inspired. Maybe he could figure out another way to stay afloat—and pay for his portion of Benji's medical bills at the same time.

Pete had sent him the details of Spectre's offer. Better than he'd expected, but not nearly what he was used to. Shouldn't he be insulted they'd assume he'd take such a deal?

"It may be your only option," Pete had said. "Think about it, Grady. What's more important—your pride or your brother?"

Had Pete given up the idea that he could come back?

His stomach knotted at the thought. He'd know if he was done, wouldn't he? When he heard it or read it online, it didn't resonate with him. But nothing about the sport was coming as easily to him as it used to, and he supposed that was what bothered him the most.

He arrived at the flower shop early and found the lights on. He could see Quinn inside. Her hair was pulled up into a ponytail and she wore a purple headband. Maybe if he taught her to ski—helped her overcome this fear she seemed to have of taking risks—he'd earn her respect.

Why he wanted it, he didn't know. Perhaps because she hadn't given it to him automatically.

He parked his SUV out front and walked toward the door just as another car pulled up. Jaden practically jumped out, decked out in full ski gear. His goggles were on top of his head and his coat practically swallowed him up.

"Grady, hey!" he said, as if they were old buddies. Why did he have the feeling this was a side of Jaden most people didn't see? With Grady, Jaden was in full-on fan mode.

A young woman who sort of resembled Quinn but with darker hair got out from the driver's side.

"You must be Grady Benson," she said.

"That's me."

"I'm Carly Collins, Jaden's mom."

"Quinn's sister," he said.

Her eyebrows pulled down, but a look of amusement crossed her face. "That's right. I didn't think you and Quinn were that close."

"Oh, she can't stand me," he said with a smile.

"Sounds about right." Carly gave him a quick once-over. "You don't look like you're really dressed for skiing."

He shrugged. "I've got my gear in the car."

"See, Mom?" Jaden said. "You should've let me get dressed when we got there."

"Nah, you look great," Grady said.

"Thanks for doing this." Carly didn't look him in the eye. "I want you to know it means a lot."

"Course. I'm happy to. Gets me back out on the slopes anyway." If you could call them that. Grady knew the manufactured snow and so-called mountain were going to be borderline comical, but he supposed they were better than nothing.

He pushed the thoughts away and turned toward the flower shop door.

As he did, Quinn opened it and walked outside.

"You look like a marshmallow," Carly said.

Grady stifled a laugh, but Carly was right. Quinn wore a bulky pair of white ski pants and a puffy white winter coat, the kind with fur in the hood.

She glared at her sister. "I had to borrow it from Lucy. It's not like I have ski clothes in my closet."

"You're going with?" Carly frowned.

"Yes, and you should come too so I don't have to suffer through this day by myself."

"It'll be fun, Aunt Quinn," Jaden said. "Promise."

"You'll have fun watching me make a fool of myself," she said. "I, however, plan to have no fun."

"That's a great plan, Q." Carly folded her arms. "Why are you going? Did you lose a bet?"

Another glare from Quinn, this time directed at Grady. She almost looked cute with the scowl on her face and in her ridiculous getup.

"I have Hailey's ski clothes inside, so you won't even have to go home and dig yours out of the closet." Quinn turned toward Carly.

"I don't ski, Quinn. This is Jaden's thing."

"I don't ski either, but here I am."

Carly groaned. "I was supposed to work today, and then I traded shifts with someone else and I was really looking forward to being home by myself and catching up on laundry."

"Gee, you two really know how to have a good time," Grady said. "I'm going to Hazel's to get some coffee. When I get back we're leaving. All of us."

Carly groaned again. "I don't want to go skiing."

"Come on, Mom, it'll be fun. You haven't seen me up there in months. Maybe I can teach you a thing or two. Show you that you didn't waste your money on those lessons."

Grady wandered across the street to Hazel's. He told Betsy who he was ordering for and she knew their drinks, as if she had them saved in some mental database or something. She stuck the cups in a cardboard carrier and handed them across the counter.

"It's nice to see you acclimating to our small-town life," she said.

Grady laughed. "This isn't acclimation," he said. "This is just passing the time until I can get out of here."

"Well, that's too bad."

The voice came from behind him, and while he'd only heard it a few times, he recognized it immediately. He turned and found Judge Harrison, looking a little more irritated than Grady remembered.

He gritted his teeth to keep from saying something he'd regret.

"I was hoping our way of life might rub off on you," the judge said.

"Don't hold your breath." Grady picked up the drinks and nodded at Betsy, who gave him a slight smile.

"Son, maybe there's something here for you that you haven't even thought of yet," the judge said as Grady turned around.

"I can tell you with absolute certainty, Judge, there is nothing here for me." He held the man's gaze for a moment, then slipped out the front door and into the icy Michigan air.

If the judge thought keeping him here was going to teach him some kind of lesson, he was crazy. A familiar anger flared up inside him. His dad said this happened when things didn't go his way.

"You can't just quit because it doesn't come the first time," his father had told him after one particularly frustrating run years ago. "You get so mad and you give up."

"Because I should be able to do that in my sleep."

"Who says? You've never done it before." His dad was firm, and they'd always butted heads. Grady didn't like to be told what to do.

"I should just know," Grady had shouted then. He took off his goggles and his gloves and threw them on the ground as he stormed away. The jump made sense in his head—why couldn't he land it?

His dad let him go, probably shook his head as he watched Grady storm off. So many of their practice sessions ended this way, and it wasn't too many months later that his father found him a real coach.

"Someone you're not related to is going to have better luck teaching you," he'd said.

But Brian only reminded him of his father. It was like suddenly he had two dads, and he didn't want to listen to either one of them.

Once, about a year after Benji's accident, Grady left practice in a huff. He'd wanted to quit. The jumps weren't coming, and Brian was insistent that he needed to change his form.

But Grady was fifteen. What did he care about sloppy or safe so long as he was fast? Benji watched his brother practice—a constant reminder of how Grady's need for speed played out in the real world—and while he never said much, Grady knew Benji had opinions.

For months, Benji said nothing. Not *This is all your fault!* Not *If you weren't so reckless, I'd still be out there.* And never *It should be me competing—not you!*

Why didn't he just lay into him? If he did, maybe then the shame of it all would start to go away.

As it was, his brother was nothing but gracious, Grady's biggest fan. Didn't Benji know how hard it was to do it all without him?

When Benji finally did break his silence, Grady knew he had to listen. He owed him at least that.

"There will come a day when you will realize that everything isn't just handed to you, Grady," Benji had said. "And on that day, you call me. Because you're going to need someone to work through it with."

"Okay, Benj," Grady had said, pretending there were no tears welling in his eyes. He'd started to walk away, but Benji grabbed his arm.

"You don't work for anything," Benji said. "And still you have everything you could ever want—and more. You act like it's owed to you, like you should never have to try, like nothing about it should be hard."

Grady had stared off in the distance, looking out across a mountain he'd just conquered.

"But one day it will be hard." Benji squeezed his arm. "And I know a little something about that."

Now, as Grady walked back toward the flower shop, he had to wonder if he'd finally reached the day Benji spoke of—the day it all stopped being easy.

And if he had, he had no idea what to do next.

CHAPTER

16

NOTHING ABOUT THE DRIVE TO THE SKI LODGE was what Quinn expected it to be.

Jaden didn't stop talking the entire way. More than once, Quinn and Carly exchanged glances as if to ask, *Who is this kid, and what has he done with our moody, introverted Jaden?*

Grady did not give annoyed one-word answers to Jaden's constant barrage of ski questions, as she thought he might. Oddly, the opposite happened. He almost seemed happy to have someone to talk to and carried on a lively conversation with her nephew in a way that an older brother might.

Huh. She certainly hadn't seen that coming. So far, most of what she'd assumed about this man had been wrong. Not that it changed anything—and yet, she could practically feel her heart softening toward him.

But just a little.

Grady and Jaden's conversation might as well have been in Chinese for as much as Quinn understood, but did it matter? It was the most alive she'd seen her nephew in years—ever since he got wise to the fact that his own father didn't seem to care about him.

Quinn knew a little something about being abandoned by someone who was supposed to love you unconditionally. Maybe that's why she felt extra-protective of her nephew. She hoped he wasn't looking at Grady as a replacement for his own father. That would only lead to heartache.

Grady would leave Harbor Pointe as soon as was humanly possible. Jaden had to realize that. Should she remind him?

They arrived at the Avalanche Mountain Ski Resort and a wave of nausea rolled through Quinn's stomach. Why had she agreed to this?

She'd never been athletic, and she had scars to prove it. In tenth grade, Sara Camp talked her into going rollerblading after school. She'd never been rollerblading, but she and her sister spent their fair share of time at the Good Times Roller Rink growing up, so how much harder could it be?

Turns out, a lot harder.

Sara was an athlete, so rollerblading and every other sport came easily to her. Quinn supposed that was why she took off down a hill like it was no big deal.

"Come on, Quinn!" she yelled over her shoulder.

In retrospect, Quinn should've probably gotten down on all fours and crawled to the bottom of the hill. Or maybe taken the skates off and met Sara on flat ground. Neither of those things were what she did, of course. In a rare moment of bravery, she inched over the top of the hill and started racing down.

Somewhere in the middle of the slope, she picked up speed. Seconds later, she realized she had no idea how to stop and the end of the incline would put her right in the middle of oncoming traffic. She panicked. Arms flailing, scream escaping, she practically dove to the ground, skinning not just her knee but her entire leg, her hands, and her elbow on the cement underneath her.

Most of those wounds had healed, but she still had a scar on her elbow to remind her what happened when she stepped outside her comfort zone.

Skiing felt a lot like that, and suddenly, looking at the lodge in front of her, Quinn thought perhaps a day inside by the fire was a better idea than trying her luck, even on the bunny hills.

Grady parked, and they all got out. Of course, Grady and Jaden both had skis and boots and goggles and helmets, while Quinn and Carly had borrowed coats, ski pants, and little else.

"Are those the only gloves you brought?" Grady squinted down at her.

"These are perfectly acceptable for my usual outdoor activities." Quinn glanced down at her puffy pink gloves. Underneath, she had a thin cotton pair on. She thought that would be fine.

"Yeah, they're not acceptable for skiing." Grady sounded so put out, Quinn wanted to roll her eyes and walk away.

"Well, it's not like I had a ton of time to plan for this little excursion. If you'll remember, I didn't want to come in the first place."

"Oh, I remember."

Smug. That's how she'd describe him right now. Like a school principal who couldn't wait to issue detentions.

"Guess I'll have to stay inside," she said. "I brought some work, so that's just fine with me."

Grady opened his trunk and pulled out a giant bag. "I have an extra pair."

"Of course you do." Her sarcasm was in full effect.

He handed her a pair of big black gloves with a tag that read *Bowman*.

Her mind raced back to the night in her apartment when he'd confessed the truth about his sponsor. A Google search told her he'd been exclusively working with Bowman practically since the beginning of his career. Amazing how that simple memory could warm her toward him, even for a moment. Despite how it seemed, she knew even professional athletes had their share of troubles.

He slammed the hatch and slung the bag over his shoulder.

When they turned, they found Jaden and Carly both staring at them.

"You two good?" Carly asked, that miserable smirk on her face.

Quinn straightened. "Fine."

"Good; let's go." Jaden started off in the direction of the lodge, where the ski rental was located. Grady fell into step beside Jaden, and while Quinn was a few steps behind, she swore she heard her nephew say, "I can't believe I'm going skiing with Grady Benson."

"I don't know if I've seen Jaden this excited since he got all the Ninja Turtle figures in fourth grade," Carly said, coming up alongside her sister.

"It's something, isn't it?"

Carly groaned. "You have that look."

"What look?"

"You get this line in your forehead when you're worried." Carly mirrored Quinn's furrowed brow with one of her own, but put on an extra-grumpy expression to prove a point.

"I'm shocked by how much insight can be gained by looking at my forehead," Quinn said.

"You're not hard to figure out," Carly said. "Plus, you're worried 90 percent of the time."

"No, I'm not."

"I can't believe he got you out here." Carly shook her head. "Must have cast some kind of spell over you. I've never known you to do anything as crazy as downhill skiing, and I've known you your entire life."

"*He* didn't get me out here," Quinn argued, but judging by the skeptical look on her sister's face, she wasn't fooling her. "I think he brings out the worst in me."

Carly gazed in front of them to where Grady and Jaden were walking. "He brings out *something* in you, that's for sure."

"I don't even want to know what that means," Quinn said.

Walking into a ski lodge, even one as small as Avalanche Mountain, with Grady Benson must've been a little like walking into an LA nightclub with Beyoncé. This was his world now, and entering it made her realize that he was still at the center, despite whatever bad press he'd gotten lately.

People gawked—literally gawked—as soon as they realized who he was, and the way the conversation picked up was uncanny. The whispers passed from one person to the next, like a row of dominoes in a game she didn't know they were playing.

Over and over, she heard his name whispered, and while he didn't outright acknowledge it, she had to believe Grady heard it too. And if she had to guess, she thought he might like the attention.

The attendant working at the rental counter stopped mid-sentence when he spotted Grady. Jaden straightened a little, clearly relishing the privilege of being at Grady's side. As if this man needed *more* of an ego boost. His head was already practically too big to get through a regular-size door.

Though once she saw him interact with the staff at Avalanche Mountain, she thought maybe that wasn't a fair assessment. While they practically fell all over themselves to give him whatever he wanted, he graciously signed autographs, gave bits of advice, and even lifted a small boy up on his shoulders to pose for a picture that the boy's father said they would "treasure for the rest of their lives."

Seriously? Was this real life for this guy?

After a few minutes that seemed like an eternity, they all finally walked out of the lodge toward the back of the resort with skis, boots, goggles, and helmets—all things that were given to Grady as a "thank you for skiing with us today."

Grady said he'd be back to give youth lessons, and Quinn tried not to laugh as the entire staff, made up mostly of twentysomething snowboarding types who said "dude" a lot and probably indulged in the kind of partying that was only legal in certain states, fell all over themselves to find out when that was happening.

Of course, Grady didn't know. She doubted he was used to keeping his own schedule.

"I'll keep you all posted," he'd said.

Now, standing in the back of the resort, decked out in ski garb that made her feel like she was wearing an inflatable sumo wrestler costume, Quinn peered up at Grady, who she decided was only pretending to be wholly unfazed by the scene they'd just witnessed.

She could see it on his face. He missed it. Missed the attention, the affirmation that he was the best. She supposed it made sense—he was human, after all. But she wasn't prone to hero worship, so he'd get none of that from her.

Jaden, on the other hand, was completely taken. "That was awesome! Does that happen to you every time you go somewhere to ski?"

Grady laughed. "No, not everywhere. Where I train, I'm just another skier." Quinn couldn't tell if his humility was false or genuine.

She'd guess false, but she'd been wrong about him so many times before.

"We know that's not true," Jaden said. "You're the world champion. I'm sure that's how it is—even where you train."

Quinn pulled her goggles down over her eyes to shield herself from the sun—and the scene in front of her.

"You look like you're ready to go." Grady turned toward her.

"Looks can be deceiving." Her nerves were like Mexican jumping beans in her belly.

"Maybe Mom and Aunt Quinn should go take a lesson or something?" Jaden clearly didn't want them holding him up, and Quinn couldn't blame him.

"Why would we go take a lesson when we have a *world champion* skier right here with us?" Quinn was just being mean now. It was as if her mouth had a mind of its own. A mean, childish mind that needed a time-out in the corner.

"I've actually been skiing before," Carly said. "It's just Quinn who doesn't know how to put her boots in her skis."

Quinn groaned. "Like I said, I would happily stay inside."

"Nah," Grady said. "I'll teach you. You'll be upright in no time."

You haven't seen me rollerblade.

Disappointment skittered across Jaden's face, and Quinn hated that she was the cause of it. She would hold them up all day long if they waited on her.

"Maybe go ski with Jaden for a while first, and then you can teach me later?" she asked, softening her tone. As annoyed as she was to be there, this day wasn't about her. She should've remembered that sooner.

"What will you guys do?" Grady asked. Was he actually concerned about her?

"We'll be fine," Quinn said. "I'd rather Jaden get the benefits of your expertise. It would be wasted on me."

So off they went. Jaden and Grady, the student and the master. And Carly let out an unmistakable sigh as they did.

Quinn shot her what she hoped was a quizzical look. "What was that for?"

"Come on, Q," Carly said. "You can't pretend you don't think that guy is beautiful."

"Beautiful?" Quinn picked up her skis and headed toward a bench. A bench would be safe. Perfect for the nonathletic people in the crowd.

"Not to mention kind. Look at him with Jaden. He's smart and attentive and—"

"Egotistical and frustrating," Quinn cut in. "Don't make him out to be what he's not, Carly. He has one goal—suck up to whoever he can to help get him out of town sooner."

"So?"

"So?" Quinn plopped down on the bench, dropping her skis on the ground beside her. "He's using us. That's it. He's not some do-gooder with a heart of gold."

"He didn't have to take Jaden," Carly said. "And he doesn't have to teach him now." She shook her head and looked away. "When will you ever stop seeing everyone through that lens, Quinn?"

"What lens?" She could feel herself bristling.

Carly turned toward her. "That lens of brokenness."

Quinn frowned.

"You believe the worst about everyone. It's like you dismiss them out of hand, you decide right off the bat that they're going to let you down. You think you're protecting yourself, but I think you miss out on a lot of great people that way."

"That's not true."

Carly pressed her lips together the way she did when she was debating whether or not she should say something.

"It's not true, Car."

"When was the last time you had a relationship?"

"I have all kinds of relationships."

"I'm not talking about your relationship with Bob at the hardware store or your friends from the diner. I mean an actual, put-yourself-out-there relationship?"

Quinn looked away.

"I can't remember when you've ever risked your heart. Not even with Marcus, and how long did you date that man? Five years?"

She didn't respond.

"Look, I know you're still hoping that one day Mom is going to come back, but she's not. She left us. We may never know why or how she's lived with herself, but, Quinn, she's gone. It might be time to accept that."

Quinn stared off in the direction of the ski lift. "Why are you bringing up Mom? She has nothing to do with whether or not I've had a serious boyfriend."

"I think she has everything to do with it."

Quinn longed to run. She didn't want to talk about her mother. Especially not with Carly, because she'd never understood how Carly had so easily gotten over their mother's choice to leave. "That's ridiculous."

"You've been in Harbor Pointe your whole life," Carly said, as if that were proof of something.

"So have you!" The words came out a little more heated than

she meant, drawing the attention of a couple a few yards away. "So have you," she hissed, much more quietly this time.

"But I've also traveled. I've been on an airplane. I've gone on job interviews in other states. You bought Mom's flower shop. It's like you're still nine years old, sitting on the front steps, waiting for her to come home." Carly reached over and put a hand on Quinn's. She resisted the urge to yank it away. "What are you so afraid of?"

This was not how she'd planned to spend the day. This was not what she'd expected when she asked Carly to come along. Not when she had so much to do, so much to think about—when she was so close to confronting their mother once and for all. She was weeks away from proving that she didn't need Jacie Collins anyway—why was Carly saying all of this now?

"I'm sorry, Quinn. I just don't want you to spend your whole life watching everyone else from the second-story window. You deserve better than that."

"So, what? You want me to risk my heart on the first guy who tells me I'm pretty? That didn't work out so great for you."

Too far, Quinn.

Throwing Josh back in Carly's face was just about the worst thing she could've done. Carly had never openly wondered what her life would've been like if she hadn't gotten pregnant so young, and suggesting it was a mistake was like saying Jaden shouldn't be a part of their lives.

And that wasn't something they would ever wish for.

"I'm sorry, Car—"

But her sister's upheld hand silenced her. Her eyes were glassy. "I know you didn't mean it. I know you get like this when you feel backed into a corner, which means something I said must've hit a nerve." Carly stood. "I'm not trying to be mean. I just hate seeing you in this perpetual holding pattern. You never do anything that you don't already know how to do."

"Do you see where we are?"

"On a bench. At a ski lodge."

"I'm going to try it," Quinn said, hating that now she'd have to try it.

"Okay," Carly said. "Then I'll see you up there." She pulled her goggles down over her eyes and started off toward the ski lift. Carly didn't love skiing, but at least she knew how to do it. Quinn didn't even have that going for her.

She sat, watching people mill about, hearing the occasional mention of Grady Benson, and wishing that she could deny what Carly had just said.

But sadly, she had the worst feeling all of it was true.

17

THEY'D BEEN SKIING FOR AN HOUR when Jaden finally stopped talking. The kid was excited—passionate about skiing in a way Grady wondered if he'd ever been. In some ways, he reminded Grady of himself—he was strong and agile and seemed to come by the sport naturally. What he wasn't, though, was stubborn. Jaden was eager to learn, and very obviously eager to please his coach for the day.

Jaden listened intently to everything Grady said, made corrections, and improved right there in front of his eyes. Things that had taken Grady years of trial and error, Jaden learned simply by listening to someone who'd been there.

They were standing at the top of the hill when Carly skied over, noticeably alone.

"How's it going?" she asked.

"It's awesome, Mom. Grady is the *best* teacher. You've gotta see how much faster I am now."

Carly moved her goggles to the top of her head. "He's not giving you any trouble, is he? He doesn't always respond well to coaching."

Grady frowned. "Really?"

Jaden looked away.

"Sometimes he thinks he knows more than the coaches he's worked with," Carly said. "I've tried to tell him he's never going to get anywhere that way."

"He's been really receptive," Grady said. "I was just thinking what a quick study he is."

"So you think I'm ready to compete?" Jaden's eyes brightened.

"We've talked about that, Jay," Carly said, her voice a warning.

"Yeah, but if Grady thinks I'm ready . . ." Jaden looked at Grady with those pleading eyes, as if waiting for his okay.

"Oh no."

Grady followed Carly's gaze toward the bottom of the hill until his eyes landed on a white blob—Quinn. She obviously had no idea how to even move forward on her skis.

"I can't believe she's standing upright," Jaden said. "Should we go help her?"

Grady couldn't help but smile. "Nah, let's see what she does."

They all watched for several seconds while Quinn, who'd somehow figured out how to hook her boots into her skis, struggled to navigate the flat terrain beneath them. At one point, she almost toppled over, but righted herself, only to be thrown off balance by a small child who zipped past her on the way to the ski lift.

Her arms circled in the air as she wobbled back and forth, finally landing in a heap in the snow. Grady could practically feel her anger, even from up here.

"We should go help her," Jaden said.

"I don't know," Carly said. "This might be good for her."

"Why don't you go show your mom what we worked on, Jaden?" Grady offered. "I'll help your aunt."

Carly and Jaden started off toward a more advanced hill, and Grady watched Quinn for several more seconds, convinced she had no idea how to get up. Worse, not a single person had stopped to help her.

In order to reach her, he'd have to ski down the hill to the much flatter stretch of land that led to the bunny hills. He wouldn't say so, but every hill there felt like a bunny hill to him. Still, even coasting down Avalanche Mountain, which he could do in his sleep, brought back an unfamiliar fear—that his skiing career was over.

He'd never worried about that before, but then, when you had sports commentators and fans doing nothing but singing your praises, it was difficult to ever imagine a day when you wouldn't be on top. Now, though, he was searching for something—anything—to rely on. Something that would give him the strength to believe he still had what it would take to win.

But as deep as he dug, he came up empty.

And for the first time in his life, that scared him.

"There will come a day when you will realize that everything isn't just handed to you. . . . And on that day, you call me. Because you're going to need someone to work through it with." Benji's words were back, flashing through his mind like a neon sign. But what was he going to say? He'd sound so ungrateful whining about his career being over to a man who would never walk again.

He watched Quinn struggle for a few more seconds, then started down and around the small incline until he reached her. Standing at her side, he cast a long shadow across her, and she scowled up at him. At least he thought she was scowling—it was hard to tell behind the goggles, which were too big and looked borderline ridiculous on her.

"Need some help?"

"I'm fine," she snarled.

"Right. You've obviously got this under control."

"If that kid would've watched where he was going, I wouldn't have fallen down," she said.

He dropped his skis. "Oh, I think you probably would've fallen down eventually."

She tugged at the ski on her right foot. "It's stuck."

He knelt down next to her and unhooked the ski, popping it off the boot in one quick motion. She was clearly not amused.

"Ready for your lesson?" He stood and reached a hand out in her direction to help her up.

She looked at it, as if she wasn't sure what the ramifications of accepting his help were.

"Come on, I don't bite."

"I think maybe I should just call it a day. They're probably finished with my floors. I should get back and get the shop set up."

"They're not finished with your floors."

"Then I should work on the designs for the Winter Carnival."

"The ones you already finished?"

She groaned. Finally, she stuck a gloved hand in his and he pulled her up. Their eyes were hardly level, given that she was about a foot shorter than he was, but her big attitude made up for her small stature. "I'll go easy on you. I promise," he said. "We'll start really slow."

"This from the fastest skier in the country." She stuck her hands on her hips and looked up in the direction of the very small, barely-an-incline hill where a group of tiny children were having a lesson.

"Have you been reading up on me?"

She rolled her eyes. "Hardly."

He straightened his skis. "Well, I'm pretty sure I'm not the fastest anymore."

She glanced at him, and before she could pity him, he started off for the bunny hill. "You coming?"

Quinn stood there for a few seconds, then finally grabbed her skis and poles and followed him. He knew because her shadow gave her away. He had a feeling she would rather be cleaning out sewers.

They stopped at the bottom of the chair lift, and she stood there, shaking her head. "This is a bad idea."

"You're going to have to put the skis back on." He motioned for her to put them on the ground, then knelt down and set the skis on either side of her feet. "Step in."

She did as she was told and he clicked her boots in.

He led her over to the chair lift and waited until the guy operating it waved them over. Her face had practically turned the color of the snow.

"I'm not going to let you fall off," he said.

She glanced at him but didn't respond. They stood at the loading spot as the chair came behind them, and Grady reached back to steady it as they both got on.

"There," he said, once they were moving. "Not so bad, right?"

She nodded, but he could see there was still fear on her face. Their feet hung over the ground as it moved them up and over toward the bunny hill. This was usually the point when Grady would get in the zone—clear out his mind and focus on what needed to be done.

But his mind was too cluttered for that.

He helped Quinn off the chair lift and moved her out of the way, stopping when they reached a small clearing near the top of the bunny hill. She stuck her poles into the snow beside her and continued with her scowling.

"First of all, you're going to have to change your attitude," he said.

Her eyes widened in full-on irritation, but he gave her a little shrug as if to say, *I'm serious about this.*

She drew in a breath, one that was undoubtedly meant to calm her down, and the expression on her face softened. Barely.

"There," he said. "That's better. Now you're ready to learn."

"Are you going to spend the entire time talking to me like I'm seven?"

"If you act like a seven-year-old, I'm going to treat you like one," he said, doing his very best not to crack a smile. He failed. After all, the whole scene in front of him—her in her marshmallow ski gear, at the top of a hill next to six very small humans who seemed to be catching on at an alarming rate—was amusing.

"I'm an adult," she muttered. "Why am I putting up with this?"

"Because you're an adult who hasn't done anything fun in—how old are you?"

"Twenty-eight."

"Twenty-eight years."

"Very funny."

"Am I wrong?"

"Yes," she said. "You are. I've had plenty of fun."

"What's the most fun thing you've ever done?"

Her face fell and she shook her head, as if to let him know she wasn't going to tell him.

"What was it? Something shocking? Skinny-dipping in Lake Michigan, maybe?"

She shot him a look.

"Come on. You thought of something."

She surveyed his face for a moment, then looked away. "Honestly, going to the flower market with my mom when I was little. We used to go every Saturday, and she'd pick out the most gorgeous flowers—different ones that we couldn't get just anywhere. I told her that one day I was going to have a flower truck. Sell flowers right out of the back of it—the kind of flowers we got at the market." She looked away. "She laughed and said it was the craziest and best idea she'd ever heard of, and when I was old enough, she'd buy me an old Volkswagen and we'd turn it into a flower truck together."

Grady watched her as she quietly shut down, realizing, as he knew she would, that she'd just shared something she hadn't meant to share. With him.

"Sorry," she said. "I don't know why I just told you that."

"Why didn't you buy the truck?" he asked.

She shrugged. "Seemed like a stupid idea once I grew up. And besides, my mom was long gone."

"Here," he tugged the zipper of her coat up to the top. "The wind can be brutal." He found her eyes, but he didn't know what else to say. He didn't have much advice when it came to relationships or forgotten dreams. After all, he was trying to dig his own out from the rubble of the mess he'd made.

He shook the moment away. "Well, if that's the most fun thing you can remember, you're in for something awesome," he said. "Because once you get the hang of this, you're going to know how it feels to be free. You'll be hooked."

"I'm just hoping I'll still be in one piece," she said.

"I'll make sure you are."

And he vowed to keep that promise, on the slopes and off. He suddenly had the inexplicable desire to protect feisty, maddening Quinn Collins.

And that was a desire he wasn't accustomed to at all.

CHAPTER

18

"FIRST YOU NEED TO LEARN TO MOVE FORWARD IN YOUR SKIS," Grady said, thankfully changing the subject after her embarrassing outburst about her mother.

She was starting to make a habit of revealing too much of herself to this man. Her only solace was that he'd likely forget all about it in an hour.

Still, she had not meant to broach that subject with him or anyone else. Her mother was on her mind—and some things she couldn't keep from spilling over.

Slowly, patiently, he taught her how to move in her skis. They skied to a clearing where she could simply use her poles to propel herself forward across the flat land.

"See, that's not so bad," he said as she managed to stay upright for longer than five minutes.

Quinn didn't pretend she'd accomplished anything remotely impressive, though she had to say, it felt good not to be stuck in a snowdrift with small children pointing and laughing.

She'd expected Grady to give up on her almost immediately, but once again, she was wrong about him. He walked her through a number of basic, beginner-type things she was sure he hadn't thought of in years. Skiing, for him, was clearly second nature—she could see it in the way he moved. Still, that didn't stop him from breaking things down in a way she understood. He was a good teacher.

Three times, their lesson was interrupted—twice by kids who wanted pictures and autographs and once by a tall, thin blonde who wanted something else entirely. She wore a bright-pink ski outfit with perfectly coordinated boots, gloves, and goggles, her long, curly ponytail so perfect it could've been drawn on, like Betty's in the old Archie comics.

After the woman took a selfie with Grady—who looked unusually uncomfortable—she leaned over and whispered something to him, then sashayed away.

Quinn shook her head.

"What?" His eyes widened.

"I don't even want to know what she said to you." Quinn dug her poles into the snow.

He didn't respond.

"I won't be offended if you want to go with her." *But I will be really, really annoyed.*

"No way," he said. "We're learning to ski here."

Why did she feel relieved by his response?

The lesson continued. He taught her about proper posture, about not leaning backward, and how to stop—in theory. She felt comfortable on the flat ground, but when he suggested they try one of the bunny hills, she bristled.

"I don't think I'm ready for that," she said.

He watched her for a few seconds. "You are."

Going down a bunny hill with a bunch of very small people shouldn't be that big of a deal. It seemed like a silly thing, really. She was a grown-up. Twenty-eight was practically thirty. That was a real adult age. The bunny hill should not scare her.

But then, neither should leaving Harbor Pointe or getting on an airplane or doing anything outside of her comfort zone. Grady really did have her pegged, didn't he?

"Come on, killer," Grady said. "You've got this."

Somehow, Quinn felt like she was standing on one side of a line and Grady was on the other, coaxing her forward. She knew she had a choice. She could stay warm in her comfortable little cocoon, this world she'd built for herself—or she could take one small step toward the unknown.

And who knew what would come after that? It was the not knowing that gave her pause. And it was likely the not knowing that excited Grady.

He stood in front of her, motioning for her to move toward him. "Come on." He started skiing backward—show-off—and gradually, she started in his direction.

A kid in a green snowsuit zipped past her. Her arms swung around in a circle as she struggled to keep her balance, and remarkably, this time she didn't fall.

"Look at you," Grady said. "You're getting the hang of it."

She started to move a little more confidently than she had when she'd been pulled away from the chair lift. Beside them, a group of small children giggled. Were they laughing at her? Before she could decide for sure, they all took off down the hill like pro skiers.

They weren't even afraid of falling.

She wanted to find that inspiring, but instead Quinn's mind started in with a barrage of fear-invoking thoughts. They could collide with someone else or slide headfirst into a tree. They could tumble head over feet and break multiple bones. But children didn't think of those things, did they?

"Come on. It's time," Grady said. "You've got the basics. All that's left is for you to actually do it."

She stuck her poles into the ground. "I think maybe this was a bad idea. Have I made it clear that I'm not very coordinated?"

"Oh, you didn't have to make it clear." He laughed.

"See? It's obvious. I shouldn't be up here. I'm going to end up breaking my arm. Or worse, my neck. Who will win top prize at the Floral Expo then?"

He frowned. "Top prize?"

She snapped the goggles back down on her face. "Never mind."

"Are you entering a competition?"

"It's stupid. Forget it." She eyed the hill. If she weren't such a chicken, she'd push herself off just to get away from him. What was with her telling Grady all her secrets today?

"Why do you do that?" He was looking at her—she could feel it.

She kept her gaze ahead at the seemingly insurmountable task in front of her.

"You downplay the things that mean something to you."

"I do not," she said. He hardly knew her well enough to make such a broad claim. And why was everyone ganging up on her today? First Carly, now him?

"Is it your design for the carnival?"

She nodded. "Florists all over the state enter their best designs. Judges go around to score them. The Winter Carnival design will be my entry." There. Nothing but the details. He didn't have to know all the reasons why it mattered.

"Well, I think it's great the contest is so important to you, and I think your design is going to win."

He said it with such assurance, she almost believed him. She would've thought he'd make fun of her. Her little flower contest seemed so small next to his Olympic tryout.

"But right now, we need to conquer this hill," he said.

"I'm going to fall."

"That's the spirit." His sarcasm wasn't lost on her. "Just remember what I taught you. Don't lean backward, and let your legs do the work."

"And at the end? What if I can't stop?"

"We worked on stopping," he said.

"Going down a hill and stopping is way different than moving across the flat land and stopping."

"Will you quit stalling?"

She groaned. Her heart was racing, her stomach knotted. She wasn't sure what made her more uneasy—the thought of getting hurt or the knowledge that she was about to make a fool of herself in front of Grady and everyone else out there.

"You gonna go, Aunt Quinn?" Jaden skied up behind her, turning to stop like it was the easiest thing in the world. Seconds later, Carly appeared at his side. Even she seemed comfortable on her skis.

"She's gonna go!" Grady called out, then leaned closer to her. "I'll be right beside you."

Was that supposed to make her feel better?

"All right," she finally said. "I'm gonna go." Her nerves kicked up instantly. "This must seem so silly to you."

"Why?"

She kept her eyes forward. "The bunny hill? How stupid to be scared of the bunny hill."

"Hey, we all start somewhere," he said.

He had no idea how true that was.

"We'll go together," he said. "On the count of three."

"Oh my gosh." The anticipation of it was getting unbearable now. "Okay, fine. But hurry up before I lose my nerve."

"Okay, one—" he pulled the goggles over his eyes—"two—" one more look at her—"and three!"

Almost without thinking, she pushed herself over the edge, the sounds of Jaden and Carly cheering behind her. At her side, Grady coasted along as easily as if he were walking across the street. Quinn floundered for a second, glancing at Grady, who reminded her of her posture, which was definitely *not* what he'd taught her. She leaned forward and picked up a bit of speed, and she turned back and forth to keep from going too fast. He stayed right beside her the whole time.

She coasted along, and for a brief few seconds, she didn't feel like she was going to crash to the ground. She was staying upright, moving well, even. In fact, she felt almost giddy, like the laugh that bubbled up from inside her wasn't going to stay inside. The cool wind blew across her face, and while she couldn't believe it, she actually thought this might be a little bit fun.

But she started to panic when she realized she had two options: 1. Stop or 2. Crash. Stopping, her old nemesis, laughed at her now.

Grady must've sensed her fear because he inched closer. "Just turn your toes in," he reminded her. She knew this wasn't the way he would stop—he'd do something fancy that would flick snow up at whoever was standing nearby. But she had to stick with the basics, so as they cruised to the bottom of the hill, she did as she was told, and somehow, remarkably, she started to slow down until she wasn't moving anymore.

Her eyes widened as she stared down at her skis. She'd made it all the way down the hill without falling. Now the laughter escaped. "I did it."

"You seem surprised." Grady ignored the looks from the other skiers, who all seemed to be gawking at him.

"I am surprised." Quinn laughed again. "I'd prepared to somersault all the way down the hill."

Now he laughed.

Her heart was racing—she wasn't sure if it was adrenaline or if she was just really out of shape. Either way, she tried to steady her breathing as she pulled off her goggles.

She glanced up at him. "You know, you're a pretty good teacher." "Yeah?"

"If you can get me to ski without breaking a limb, you must be."

"Well, the day is still young," he said with a smile.

"Have you thought about it?" she asked. "Coaching, I mean."

He shrugged. "Not really. Always thought, 'Those who can't do, teach.'"

She looked away. "I disagree. I honestly thought you'd get really irritated with me, but you were surprisingly patient. It's always something to keep in your back pocket—you know, if you need a change down the road or something."

"Are you giving me a compliment?"

She glanced back and found him goggle-less and grinning. "Oh, please, don't let it go to your head. It's not like you don't have enough people singing your praises out here."

They headed off, and Quinn handled her skis quite well if she did say so herself.

"I'm just glad you had fun," Grady said. "You did have fun, didn't you?"

She smiled. "I did. I can't believe it, but I did."

He seemed genuinely happy to hear it.

As they neared the chair lift, Quinn slowed and stared. She'd managed to get herself onto it once before, so she could do it again, right? Because she really wanted to go again.

"You probably want to go with Jaden. I know this place is so boring compared to what you're used to," Quinn said.

"Nah, it's fine. Let's get up there and do it again."

"Really?" She tried not to let on how grateful she was, but she wasn't sure she could find the courage again on her own.

They arrived at the lift at the same time as a rowdy group of young guys. They were laughing, which always made Quinn self-conscious. Maybe they were laughing at her—a grown woman scared of the bunny hill.

Remarkably, she found a way onto the ski lift without Grady's help, and he took the seat next to her, the rowdy bunch in pairs after them.

When it came time to jump off, Quinn's heart dropped. She wasn't good at this part. She slowly edged toward the front of the seat, then slipped off, landing with a thud on her backside. The operator stopped the lift, and instantly, Grady was next to her, hand extended to help her up. Once she was upright, he pulled her out of the way of the lift.

Seconds later, one of the guys behind them started laughing. "I knew Grady Benson was off his game, but dude has been demoted to the bunny hill."

The sounds of their laughter started to fade as the guys got off the lift and headed in the opposite direction.

She glanced down and realized Grady was still holding on to her hand. She squinted up at him in the late-morning sunshine.

He watched the guys for several seconds, then looked back at her. He let go of her hand but didn't say a word.

"You okay?"

He laughed. "I'm fine. I don't need to prove myself to those morons."

She eyed him for a second but eventually accepted it. Were professional athletes as used to trash talk as they were to the endless gaping? And why was Grady suddenly able to brush it off?

"Besides," he said, "those guys are just jealous."

"Jealous?"

"Because I get to spend the day with the prettiest girl here."

She could feel her surprise register on her face. Was he talking about *her*? He didn't even like her. And she was probably blushing over the compliment too. *Shoot!*

He was just trying to get on her good side. She reminded herself he needed her to speak with the judge if he had any hope of getting what he really wanted—a quick ticket out of Harbor Pointe.

And yet, as she stood at the top of the hill, ready to ski down again, her knees turned to Jell-O and she became hopelessly aware of the attention of the man at her side.

CHAPTER

19

GRADY SPENT THE BETTER PART OF HIS DAY giving advice to Jaden and Quinn, and while he was happy to do it, being on the slopes—but not really—was hard for him. He hadn't trained in a week, and as someone who was used to being out there every day, he missed it.

Still, Quinn's comment about keeping the idea of coaching in his back pocket suddenly felt less like an insult to his abilities and more like a viable option. Down the road, after he won gold at the Winter Games.

He never would've considered it if she hadn't made it sound so . . . admirable.

He shoved the thought aside now as he skied slowly alongside her, marveling at the fact that she'd smiled more this morning than she had the entire time he'd known her—which, admittedly wasn't very long. Had he really only been in Harbor Pointe for a week?

When Quinn decided she'd had enough, she told Grady to go find Jaden. "I'll head back to the lodge and turn in my skis."

"You sure?"

She smiled again. "I'm sure. I should probably quit while I'm ahead. There's still the danger of me breaking something if I get too cocky."

He lingered—probably for too long—then headed toward the lift. While he was with Quinn, Jaden had come around more than once, updating him on his progress. Hinting that he wanted him to come back to slopes that weren't made for children. Grady had a suspicion Quinn was feeling bad for monopolizing him when her nephew's happiness was so important to her.

He liked the way she looked out for the kid.

A few hours later, after several trips down the most challenging slope Avalanche Mountain had to offer, Jaden and Grady walked toward the lodge. Jaden was replaying their entire day, as if it were a distant memory he wanted to relive over and over again.

They spotted Carly and Quinn at a table in the Avalanche Café. Quinn had surprised him, the way she'd eventually let herself enjoy her trips down the hill.

"It's like second nature to you—and the way you move, " Jaden was saying when they came up on the table, "it's not like anyone else. I can't believe your coaches tried to get you to change your form."

Grady met Quinn's eyes. He should probably give Jaden some sort of safe advice about listening to his coaches, but he didn't regret his choice to buck the system, and he wouldn't tell the kid otherwise.

"And then the way you smoked those idiots up there." Jaden's voice grew louder, his eyes wider, replaying the incident. The same kids he and Quinn had seen on the chair lift seemed intent on provoking him, but it only took one run to shut them up. "You guys should've seen it—these guys were giving Grady a hard time, saying he didn't have a shot at the Olympics this year, and Grady was awesome. They looked so stupid, like kids on the bunny hill trying to keep up with him. No offense, Aunt Quinn."

She was looking at Grady incredulously, the slightest trace of a smirk on her face.

"Hey, at least I didn't punch the guy," Grady said.

"Yeah, at least there's that, or you'd never get out of Harbor Pointe." Quinn shook her head. "What happened to not having to prove yourself to guys like that?"

Grady shrugged. She may never understand it, but he knew as soon as that guy mouthed off to him again, he wasn't going to be able to let it go. But yeah, up here he could put him in his place without putting him on the ground. It was a good trade-off, he thought, though Quinn seemed unimpressed by the whole thing.

"Can we get dinner?" Jaden asked. "I'm starving."

"Did you stop for food at all today?" Carly asked.

Jaden shook his head.

"Why don't we all go out?" Grady asked. "We can celebrate."

"Celebrate what?" Jaden asked.

"Quinn trying something new for the first time in decades," Carly said.

Quinn stiffened, annoyance on her face.

"I was going to say, 'Quinn learning how to ski.'"

"Yeah," Jaden said. "And we can talk about that competition I want to enter next month."

Carly shot him a look.

"You said we could talk about it. And I've kept my grades up."

"What competition?" Quinn asked.

"Some competition Jaden's been talking about for a month," Carly said, putting her phone and her sunglasses in her purse.

"It's at a ski club up north. They have way better runs," Jaden said, that trademark excitement on his face. "We should go up there—maybe Grady can come up and give me some pointers before the race."

Quinn frowned. "I'm sure Grady has other things to do, Jaden."

"Not really," Grady said. "I'll go. If the judge will let me."

Instinctively, all eyes found Quinn. She bristled. "Why are you looking at me?"

"You've got an in with Judge, Aunt Q," Jaden said. "He loves you like you're his own kid."

"He loves Carly, too," Quinn said.

"Not like he loves you." Carly was very matter-of-fact. "You've never faced him in the courtroom."

Grady felt his eyes widen.

"It was a misunderstanding," Carly said with a wave.

"Will you talk to him, Aunt Quinn? Grady needs to ski somewhere other than here to get ready for his race anyway."

"Wait." That wrinkled line was back in her forehead. "Did you put him up to this?"

"No, we didn't even talk about any of this," Jaden said. "I wanted him to see me ski, then ask him if he thought I was ready." The kid almost looked embarrassed.

Quinn's eyebrows drew together in a familiar motion. "What kind of skiing is this?"

"Alpine skiing. Like what Grady does."

Quinn's head moved back and forth, as if the action were involuntary. "No way, Jaden. You're not ready for that."

"I am so. Ask Grady."

Uh-oh.

She shot him a look and his hands went up in surrender—that action was involuntary. "Let's go grab some food and we can talk more about it."

"It's too dangerous, Jaden," Quinn said. "Carly, you're not on board with this, are you?"

Concern washed over Quinn's sister's face. "How dangerous are we talking here? Jaden skis all the time."

"Have you seen the way Grady skis?"

"Have *you* seen the way I ski?"

Quinn looked caught.

He tried—really hard—not to smile. Had she looked him up?

"I'm ready, Aunt Quinn. I swear."

"I need to head back to the shop," Quinn said.

"Aren't they redoing your floor?" Carly asked. "You won't even be able to get in."

"There's still a lot I can do." Quinn grabbed her bag and stood.

"Well, I'm starving." Grady purposely blocked her way, and she didn't look happy about it.

"You can drop me off and go grab something to eat." Quinn planted herself right in front of where he stood and glared up at him. "Hazel's is right down the street."

"I don't really want diner food tonight. Do you have another suggestion?" He was just being difficult and he knew it. She knew it too, but he didn't mind making her squirm.

"We can go get pizza at Dockside," Jaden said.

"Sounds great," Grady said, eyes still fixed on Quinn.

"Dockside is in Summers Bay, Jaden," Quinn said.

"So?"

"Grady isn't allowed to go anywhere but the ski slope." *She* was just being difficult now, and she knew it. She locked her eyes on his in an intoxicating battle of wills.

She had no idea whom she was challenging. Grady didn't back down from anything.

"I'll call Dad, Quinn," Carly said. "I haven't had pizza in weeks. I might eat a whole one by myself."

Grady opened his mouth as if to challenge her back, and Carly and Jaden walked off.

"I really need to get back," Quinn said.

"As soon as we're done eating, I'll take you home."

He could see the irritation work its way through her as she straightened her shoulders and glared at him.

"Come on, it'll be fun." He grinned at her, but she continued to glare. "I was so hopeful I wasn't going to see that anymore after today." He pointed at her forehead, but before he touched her, she swatted his hand away.

"Just because I agreed to go skiing doesn't mean I'm going to shirk all my responsibilities to eat pizza with you."

"It's Saturday night, Q." Grady picked up his bag. "And we haven't eaten any real food all day. Give yourself a break."

She groaned. "Fine. But we aren't staying out late."

"Wouldn't dream of it."

She stormed past him and he turned to follow her, catching the eye of a blonde sitting at the next table. Grady couldn't be sure, but he thought maybe he'd taken a picture with her earlier. She lifted a hand and waved at him. He waved back and started toward the door. Time was, he would've slid into that booth across from her and let nature take its course, but as he caught sight of Quinn, Carly, and Jaden waiting for him, he found he had no desire to waste time on a casual acquaintance who would never be anything more.

———— ~ ————

"Wow, you weren't kidding," Grady said when they pulled up in front of the restaurant. "It really *is* a hole-in-the-wall."

On the drive to Summers Bay, Quinn had listened to her sister and nephew go on and on about Dockside, the tiny pizza joint they'd adopted as the Collins family favorite. With a single father, she and Carly had grown up eating pizza at least once—sometimes twice—a week, and after they'd tried every restaurant within a twenty-mile radius, Dockside had won out.

"You're setting the bar a little too high, you guys," Quinn said from the backseat. "The lower the expectations, the better it will be."

Carly elbowed her in reprimand.

Quinn was grumpy, and it showed. It was all she could do not to call a cab to come get her and take her back to the flower shop.

Facing the lake, Dockside Pizza was a nondescript gray building with a hand-painted sign out front. There was a closed-up window with a red awning on the side of the building.

"In the summer, you can get pizza by the slice at the window, so lots of people come up from the beach," Jaden said.

Grady parked and looked out over the water.

"It's usually nicer here. Winter isn't the greatest weather," Jaden said.

"I disagree," Grady said. "I live for winter."

Jaden grinned. "Right. I live for winter too."

Quinn shot Carly a look. Her sister smiled. Had Carly forgotten? Grady was *not* a good role model for her son.

Grady's phone buzzed.

"You need to take that?" Quinn asked.

He stared at the image of a man's face on the screen, then quickly hit the Decline button. "Nah, I'll call him back."

They walked into Dockside, and Terrance, a round man with a sliver of a mustache, greeted them. He stood behind a small podium next to a rack of menus. Behind him, the wood slats on the walls were painted white. The red, white, and gray theme carried throughout the small space. Not a traditional pizza joint, for sure, yet it fit here on the beach. The smell of tomato sauce and baking dough wafted through the small space, and Quinn's stomach growled.

Fine. She was hungry, but she wasn't about to admit that to any of them.

"Ah, the Collins family is back," Terrance said. "It's been too long."

"It's gotten busy, but we needed our Dockside fix," Carly said. "Terrance, this is Grady Benson."

Terrance's eyes widened. "The skier?"

Great. A fan.

Grady flashed him that trademark smile—she'd seen it online in nearly every single posed photo that had popped up when she made the mistake of googling *Grady Benson*.

It wasn't like she wanted to dig up every little bit of information on the man. She was simply trying to figure out what he was like—for Jaden's sake.

Still, she'd closed the door of her office at the flower shop and looked over her shoulder—twice—before actually typing in his name.

Hundreds of thousands of pages popped up.

Her eyes scanned the top results. A Wikipedia page, a Twitter account—she clicked on that one but quickly learned someone else was likely managing it for him—a link to his profile on the US Alpine Ski Team website.

She clicked on each one, then on an article titled "Grady Benson's Olympic Dreams Slip through His Fingers."

As her eyes danced across the screen, the picture of what was at stake for Grady came into focus.

She had no idea—and was almost a little embarrassed by it—that he was such a big deal. He wasn't just a skier, or even just an Olympian. He was supposedly some kind of legend in his sport. If he didn't make it back on the team, it would be a huge upset.

This whole time she'd been so focused on his faults, she hadn't given a single thought to the pain he could possibly be feeling over his current situation.

She clicked on a video embedded in the article. Then another and another. Races, interviews, profiles—she watched it all, even found herself getting caught up in the excitement as he keenly maneuvered his way down impossibly challenging slopes.

At one point she'd let out an audible gasp as he tumbled, head over feet, then slid humiliatingly down the side of the mountain. She'd checked the shop again after that, for fear of someone—Grady—walking in on her. He seemed to have a way of showing up unannounced.

This pro athlete business was beyond the realm of anything she could imagine. Understanding that made a lot of what he did make a little more sense, yet so many things about him remained a mystery.

Why he didn't get along with his coaches, for instance. Why they all said he had more natural talent than anyone they'd ever seen, but when it came to working through the stuff that didn't come easily to him, he faltered. Why he hadn't been back home in over fifteen years.

The Internet gave her only so much information. If she wanted the details to fill in those blanks, she knew she'd have to go straight to the source.

And that wasn't going to happen.

Terrance was flat-out gushing by this point, so much so that even Grady had started to look uncomfortable.

"Terrance, is it okay if we sit at our usual table?" She interrupted him, but her tone was kind.

Terrance's bushy eyebrows lifted, and his eyes widened with excitement. "Of course. Head back there, and I'll send someone over."

He walked away, muttering, "Grady Benson, as I live and breathe . . ."

Grady glanced at her. "Thanks for that."

"I didn't do it for you," she said. "I'm starving." It slipped out before she could catch herself.

His face lit up. "Huh. I guess it's a good thing we stopped, then."

She ignored him and led the way to a table near a window that faced the beach. She'd always loved this spot at Dockside, even when she was a kid and even in the winter. It was as if sitting there, in this little hole-in-the-wall pizza joint, the rest of the world faded away and all she could see for miles was the beach, the lake, and endless possibilities.

A familiar leggy blonde showed up at their table with a pitcher of water.

"Well, look who it is." Ashley Perkins was eyeing Grady unashamedly. When he met her eyes, surprise registered on his face.

"Hey." He shifted in his seat as if it were suddenly covered with bristles.

Ashley filled their glasses with water, moving around the table but focusing solely on Grady as though the rest of them weren't there. She stopped when she reached his glass. "You never called me."

Quinn had the distinct impression he did not remember Ashley's name—and she wasn't about to help him.

If Ashley lingered too long, Quinn's memory would betray her, flashing images of the two of them exiting the Lucky Lady that night.

More than once she'd wondered how that night had ended, though she'd tried and tried not to fill in the blanks.

There it was again—that sense of inferiority, which, if she was honest, felt a lot like jealousy.

"Sorry," Grady mumbled.

Ashley let her hand rest on his shoulder. "You're forgiven." She laughed. "You look good, Grady."

She sauntered off.

"Man," Jaden said. "Is that what it's always like for you?"

Quinn could see admiration in Jaden's face, and it twisted her stomach in a knot. The Internet had also been quite forthcoming with information about Grady's many, *many* romantic entanglements. At one point, he'd even had to get a restraining order against someone who kept breaking into his condo because she was convinced they were married.

What kind of world did he live in that something like that was normal?

"Jaden," Carly scolded him.

"What? It's awesome." Jaden laughed and Quinn drew in a deep breath to keep herself from exploding.

"This is just what I said would happen," Quinn said.

Carly glared at her.

"What did you say would happen?" Grady sat there, looking a little too comfortable, as if he was perfectly fine with all of it. But Quinn wasn't fine.

"Nothing," Carly said.

"This. You and Jaden." Quinn should stop talking. She heard a tiny voice inside her tell her so, but she swatted it away. "The way he idolizes you. You are not the kind of man a fifteen-year-old boy should be looking up to."

Grady's face fell.

"Quinn, stop," Carly said.

Quinn pressed her lips together, as if that could keep the words from spilling out.

"No, don't stop," Grady said. "What kind of man do you think I am?"

"One who takes drunk girls he hardly knows home with him and then doesn't call them the next day," Quinn said, her voice a loud whisper. "I'm betting you don't even remember her name."

Grady started to respond but quickly snapped his jaw shut.

She made sure her expression appropriately conveyed her satisfaction.

Grady leaned across the table, toward her. "I didn't sleep with her if that's what you think."

Quinn's eyes widened. "You expect me to believe that?"

"Why wouldn't you believe that? It's the truth."

"Because I read all about your love life, Grady. You've got a new girl on your arm in almost every non-skiing photo there is of you on the Internet."

Did I just say that out loud?

"So what? That doesn't mean I'm sleeping with all of them," he said.

"Aren't you?"

"No!" He straightened, something like anger flashing across his face.

His response took her aback. Wasn't he? That's the way every website made it sound—Grady Benson was a playboy, a womanizer, and he'd left a trail of lovers in his wake.

"Why do you care anyway?" he asked.

"I don't." But even she knew it was a lie.

And the fact that she did care was every bit as maddening as the man himself.

CHAPTER

20

SUNDAY MORNING, Quinn awoke early. She didn't want to get out of her bed, go to church, or do any of the things she normally did on Sundays.

She wanted to crawl into a hole. She'd made such a fool of herself last night she could hardly stand it, and knowing that both Jaden and Carly had been there to witness it made everything that much worse.

After her childish outburst and public argument with Grady, everyone around the table had grown tense. Jaden had tried to lighten the mood with talk of skiing, but Grady looked like he'd rather be chewing on nails than sitting there one more minute. She was lucky he didn't drive off without all of them, and honestly, she was kind of surprised he didn't.

Now, lying in her warm bed, her body ached from putting it through the task of skiing, using muscles she didn't even know she had, and she thought she might die from humiliation.

Sunday. Church at The Pointe, Harbor Pointe's largest small

church, and then brunch at her dad's. Hopefully Carly had a conflict. She did not want to rehash last night's disaster.

After she showered, she sat down with a bowl of oatmeal and flipped open her laptop. Her Facebook newsfeed was lame on all counts, but she tried to keep up on the latest with her friends and her community. Plus, it was a great distraction.

She was mid-bite when Grady's face showed up on a video someone had posted that linked to the Facebook page of the local news. Instinctively, she enlarged the video and turned up the volume.

A blonde reporter proceeded to recount the details of Grady's "fall from the top," which she called "more of a crash and burn." They replayed images of his wipeout last weekend, followed by the mug shot Quinn's father had taken and someone had released to the press. Quinn's money was on Walker.

"Matthew Phillips, who has taken Benson's spot as the next face of Bowman Skis, had this to say about the fallen Olympian."

The image of a rugged-looking, not-quite-attractive man with sandy hair popped on the screen. "You know, Grady has given a lot to the sport, and we all thank him for that, but I think there's a general consensus that, you know, when it's time to go, it's time to go."

Back to the reporter. "The Olympic ski coaches all seem to agree with Phillips that, yes, it is time for Benson to hang up his skis and—"

Quinn clicked the video off, minimizing it so her newsfeed showed up again. She couldn't help it—she felt sorry for Grady. How awful would it be to have your every move critiqued for the masses?

She kept scrolling and came across another video. This one, posted by someone whose name was vaguely familiar, was homemade—filmed on an iPhone. She watched as the video panned to a familiar spot at the top of the bunny hill at Avalanche Mountain, where the image of Grady standing next to Quinn in her puffy white marshmallow coat appeared on the screen.

She gasped.

"What do we have here?" A man's voice, stifling a laugh, impersonated a reporter. "Looks like Grady Benson is trading in the Olympics to teach private ski lessons. Leave it to this would-be womanizer to find a way to pass the time."

A close-up of a look between Quinn and Grady—a private moment, just after she'd finished her first run. Quinn's heart clenched. There had been people filming them on and off all day. She hadn't thought anything of it.

Quinn continued to stare at the screen as the video stopped. She felt so . . . violated. They'd twisted everything. They'd gotten it all wrong. Made Grady look like a laughingstock and Quinn like his latest conquest. She stood and paced across the living room floor. Now she felt even more terrible for the way she'd acted yesterday—she'd had no idea Grady was up against this kind of negativity.

Her phone buzzed. When she picked it up, she saw a text from her sister:

You're coming to church today, right?

Quinn wasn't fooled into thinking Carly was concerned for her salvation—she simply didn't want to sit there with their father and Beverly without Quinn as a buffer. While Gus was the kind of guy everyone in the world seemed to be able to get along with, Carly was the exception.

She texted back a quick Yes, then rinsed out her bowl.

She didn't expect her sister to have any more to say, but another text came through seconds later.

Jaden invited Grady.

Quinn's heart dropped. She wasn't sure she could face him yet, not after this humiliating turn of events.

But then she remembered the odds of Grady Benson showing up at church were very, very slim.

~

"Did I see you in a Facebook video this morning?"

It was Lucy, dressed like she'd just stepped out of an Anthropologie catalog and wearing that you-never-tell-me-anything expression on her face. Quinn cringed. Was she really recognizable in that video?

"Don't deny it. I'd know my Stay Puft ski clothes anywhere."

Quinn groaned. She was the first of her family to arrive at church, which meant she was sitting in the second pew, where her father had sat for nearly twenty years, ever since the first Sunday after her mother took off. He'd told them later he knew he needed help—and not the kind any human being could bring. She supposed the good Lord had heard his prayers because his daughters had made it to adulthood in one piece.

Never mind the trouble Carly had been in or the fact that she had had a baby at seventeen.

Gus had done well. It was their mother who'd messed everything up.

"Pretty harsh comments, I thought," Lucy said.

"I thought so too, and I don't even like the guy."

Lucy gave her a quizzical look. "The video of the two of you says otherwise."

"No, it doesn't."

Hailey slid into the pew behind Quinn, next to Lucy. "You've been keeping secrets."

Quinn huffed. "I have not."

"You said you were going skiing for Jaden. I did not see Jaden anywhere on that video."

"Seriously? You guys cannot tell me you actually watch Facebook videos."

"I watch them when I'm fixing my hair," Hailey said. "They're a nice break from Jack's cartoons."

"I never saw anyone filming me, only adoring fans with phones pointed at Grady," Quinn said. "I think I should sue someone."

"Right, you go out in public with Grady Benson, and you don't expect someone to snap a picture or take a video?" Lucy looked away. "Just wish *I'd* been the one to get the whole story."

"That was not the whole story," Quinn said. "It was fiction! They made it look like Grady has been relegated to teaching beginners how to ski when really he was just trying to do something nice."

Both Hailey and Lucy stared at her with those wide-open eyes that told Quinn they were reading way too much into her defense of him. Thankfully, Gus and Beverly showed up, and Lucy and Hailey gave it a rest.

For now.

Carly and Jaden walked in two minutes after the service started, and Quinn found herself relieved Grady wasn't with them, no matter how disappointed Jaden would be.

Her nephew sat on the other side of Carly, sulking as usual, every trace of that vibrant, excited kid she'd spent the day with yesterday completely gone. What would it be like to have something in your life that made you feel alive like skiing did for Jaden?

For a fleeting moment, she wondered if Grady felt that way about skiing too, or if it had just become a job for him. He had said it sometimes felt like work. Regardless, the threat of losing it had to hit him hard.

He'd been going through something legitimately distressing, and she'd been nothing but awful to him.

As the music started, Quinn closed her eyes and asked for forgiveness. She hadn't been welcoming or kind, and despite what she thought she knew, she didn't have the whole story. What if much of what she'd read about him—the very articles she'd used to form her opinion of him—were as fictitious as the story and video she'd seen this morning?

The thought shamed her.

I'm sorry, Lord. She knew better.

But as the music swelled, she had the distinct impression that God wasn't the only one who deserved an apology.

<hr />

Sunday brunch at her father's house was something Quinn almost never missed. She'd always told herself her commitment to it was because she didn't want her father to feel lonely, but as she sat in the car across the street watching Beverly, Judge, and Calvin all filter in through the front door, she had to wonder if maybe she was the one threatened by loneliness.

Throughout the meal, she admired the way they all interacted, with their familiar, comfortable rapport. And when she caught a knowing smile between her father and Beverly, Quinn began to wonder if she'd been too busy to notice something had changed between the two of them.

When her father went to the kitchen to fetch dessert, Quinn followed him.

"What was that about?"

"What?" His expression was guilty and innocent at the same time. She had a hunch the guilty part was real and the innocence was a put-on.

"Are you and Beverly . . . ?"

He stuck his head in the refrigerator and hunted around for something. "What if we are?"

"Dad, it's great," she said. "And it's about time."

He popped back out, holding a can of Reddi-Wip. "You think so?"

She closed the refrigerator and faced him. "Absolutely. You two are perfect together."

"Well, don't make a big thing about it," he said. "Nothing has to change."

She smiled in agreement, but she knew it wasn't true. Things would change—and they should. Her father had moved on with his life. He'd made room for love in his heart.

She was happy for him—so happy . . . So why did her heart feel alone?

For a moment, her mind wandered back. She could practically see her nine-year-old self sitting on the porch of their small bungalow, a house her father had bought for her mother because "she loved the porch and the swing and the way it made her feel cozy."

Before her mother had left, Quinn had spent her afternoons at the flower shop, but the first few years after they'd sold it to Mimi, she spent them in the other place she thought maybe her mother would miss—their front porch.

One Saturday, she put on her very best church dress, brought her dolls outside along with her pink floral lunchbox, and stared across the street at the neighbors' house. After about half an hour, when all her snacks were gone, her resolve started to waver. That's when her father showed up.

He sat down next to her, and even though she hadn't told him what she was doing, Quinn was pretty sure he knew.

"Nice day out here." He nudged her shoulder with his.

"I'm a little cold," she said.

"Maybe you should come in."

Quinn shrugged.

"You don't want to?"

Another shrug.

He wrapped his arm around her. "Maybe I'll just hang out with you for a little while, then."

They'd sat there for at least another hour, and while he never said so, she was sure he was giving her space to miss her mom without ever saying a word.

Carly was right. Some days Quinn still felt like she was sitting on that porch. Stuck in time because the pain of her past had wrapped itself around her ankles and kept her from moving on. And while she wasn't an angry person, she was angry about this. Because it wasn't fair. It wasn't fair that her mother left when she needed her most. It wasn't fair that while other girls and their mothers went shopping for school clothes, Quinn had opted for Carly's hand-me-downs because it was easier than admitting she needed someone to teach her how to put an outfit together or go shopping for a bra.

It wasn't fair that the woman she'd spent the first eight years of her life idolizing cared so little about her that she could simply walk away and never look back. Did her mother ever think about what she'd done—about the daughters she'd left behind? Or was she so engrossed in a new family and a fancy new life that she'd convinced herself her choice had been warranted?

Quinn needed to know. She deserved to know. It was like a giant puzzle had been set in front of her, but she hadn't been given all the pieces.

How would she ever feel truly whole again?

CHAPTER

21

GRADY NEVER SHOULD'VE LOOKED AT HIS SOCIAL MEDIA. Hadn't he learned this by now? He recognized the reporter almost immediately. She'd been at the lodge the day before, and while he'd noticed her staring at him, he'd assumed she was just another fan.

He should've known better. Lately, he had to wonder if, outside of Harbor Pointe, he had any fans left at all. Funny how quickly people turned on you when things looked bleak. Did he have a single real relationship in his life?

His phone buzzed against the white coffee table. Probably Pete. Again. He'd already called twice, but he could sweat this one out. Grady didn't like being his last priority, and he really didn't like being blindsided by all this social media stuff his manager hadn't bothered to tell him about.

But what really had him on edge were the sound bites from his old teammates, dismissing him as if he were yesterday's news. Everyone had made up their mind about him—they'd all but moved him out, like a scorned woman throwing his belongings on the front lawn.

He stood up and padded his way into the kitchen. It was almost noon, and he was unshowered and still in the sweatpants he'd worn to bed. He poured his third cup of coffee and opened the refrigerator, even though he knew if he wanted to eat, he was going to have to leave the cottage.

Was it laziness or humiliation that made that idea so unappealing?

He'd just settled back onto the couch when the doorbell rang. In the week he'd been here, he'd had no visitors, and honestly he preferred it that way. Maybe if he didn't make a sound they'd go away.

But then the knocking started.

He set the coffee mug down on the table and pulled his Captain America T-shirt on as he walked toward the door.

Through the window, he could see blonde hair and long legs on the porch waiting for him. *Amber? No, Ashley.* Ashley something-or-other from the bar. And the pizza joint. She certainly was persistent.

He pulled open the door and she gave him a once-over. "I bet you just woke up."

"I've been up for a while," Grady said. "What are you doing here?"

She made a pouty face. "I thought you could use some company. You've got the day off, right?"

He stood, blocking the entry, but she quickly pushed him aside and let herself into the cottage. "I've always wondered what these little houses look like on the inside."

Grady drew in a deep breath and closed the door. Apparently he had company. Too bad she didn't bring lunch.

She walked around the living room, eyeing the space. "I heard all about Ryan and Lane turning Cedar Grove into a real town treasure, but I guess now I'm seeing it with my own two eyes."

"Yeah, they did a nice job," Grady said. And they had. Maybe it had felt a little like a prison at first, but he realized now Cedar Grove was the kind of place he would *choose* to stay even if he weren't sequestered in this small town.

"You should've seen them before." Ashley stopped near the fireplace. "They were so run-down. Ryan saw something in them nobody else saw."

She faced him then. "Kind of like me with you."

"How's that?"

"You know, everyone else has kind of given up on you." She moved toward him.

Wait a minute . . . He took a step back, but she kept coming forward.

"I see something in you nobody else can see." She was close now—too close. His mind flashed back to the night he'd driven her home after they hung out at the bar. She had been drunk—really drunk—and he'd practically carried her upstairs to her apartment, where he laid her on the couch. Her arms had been wrapped around his neck, and she pulled him close, *that* smile on her face. "Stay with me," she'd said.

But despite his reputation, Grady wasn't a creep. She was drunk and it was wrong—so he pulled a blanket over her and walked out the door.

But nobody would ever see that side of him online. Even Quinn assumed the worst of him.

Now, as she slid her arm up his, underneath the sleeve of his shirt, he straightened. She was very sober—and so was he—but it was still wrong.

She was wrong.

He took her by the arms firmly. "I think you should go."

Confusion filled her eyes. "What?"

"You should go."

She scoffed. "You don't mean that."

He held her gaze. "I do."

"So maybe everyone was right about you." She took a step back. "You are a disappointment."

The doorbell rang again.

What the . . . ? He just wanted to be left alone for a day—didn't the people in this awful little town understand that? He groaned, walked back through the entryway, and pulled the front door open. And as soon as he did, everything within him wished he hadn't.

Quinn stood on the porch with a bag of what he could only assume was food, a rare, kind smile on her face. His heart sank. He knew how this would look—Ashley in his house on a Sunday morning when he was still in his pajamas. He raked a hand through his hair.

"Wow, you look worse than I thought you would," Quinn said.

"Well, I feel worse than that."

He studied her. Jeans. Boots. Jacket. Scarf. Real.

Everything about her was real.

He wanted to invite her in. He wanted to tell her the way that stupid video had made him feel. He wanted to tell her that deep down, he was terrified what they were saying was right—he was done.

And he wasn't sure who he was without skiing. Maybe nobody worth knowing.

Quinn wasn't caught up in the flash and sizzle of who he was. It grounded him.

And he was about to lose it—about to lose her—before he'd ever had a chance to prove to her that she was wrong about him.

He stepped out on the porch and closed the door, praying that somehow Ashley had the good sense to stay put, but hating that he couldn't invite Quinn inside. He drew in a breath, then moved toward the porch swing and sat down.

"Aren't you cold?"

He was, but he shook his head. As a man with few options, enduring the weather seemed like his best choice.

She faced him. "We always do Sunday brunch after church."

"Church." He sighed. "I forgot about that."

"It's okay. Jaden was fine." She held up the bag in her hand. "I thought you might be hungry, and we had lots of leftovers."

He watched her for a long moment. Somehow he thought it was difficult for her to be there—like holding on to her dislike of him was easier. But there she was, offering kindness anyway. He hated knowing what she must think of him. Why hadn't he made better choices?

"Thanks for that. I actually am starving."

She didn't look at him as she set the bag near his feet. "I saw the video."

He should reassure her that it meant nothing to him, but the desire to pretend wasn't there. He'd never been completely open with anyone—what was so different about her? She was exasperating. Absolutely drove him up the wall. She was stubborn and not usually all that nice to him—and yet, seeing her standing there, he had to wonder if it was all just a front. He'd seen her kindness toward other people, the way she protected her nephew, the way she brought flowers to the police station because that receptionist lady liked them.

Maybe the standoffish Quinn was not who she was at all.

Would he ever get the chance to find out?

"I'm really sorry if spending the day with me out there hurt your street cred or whatever."

"My street cred?" He laughed.

Her cheeks flushed. "Whatever it's called."

"It's fine."

"No, I thought it was awful. Those videos were so wrong—they made it look like teaching beginning skiers was the only thing you can do."

He shrugged. "Maybe they're right."

She frowned. "I know you don't believe that."

He didn't. Not really. But that fire in his belly to prove everyone wrong was flickering. How did he get here? So unsure of himself? That's not who he was.

"Maybe you just need to get back out there." She sat down next to him. "You need to actually ski—and not in Harbor Pointe."

When she had his eyes, she smiled. "I talked to Judge this morning at brunch. Well, Jaden and I did. I told him how you're helping

217

at the shop and how you helped Jaden yesterday. He said you can go up north this weekend. Jaden said it's better skiing up there and that maybe it'll help get you back in the swing."

"He thinks I'm not in the swing?" Grady stared off across the street at the row of cottages, all similar in structure but different in design. One was painted gray with a red mailbox and white trim. One was white with black trim and a turquoise mailbox. One was a subtle shade of green with a pink mailbox. Oddly, they all looked like they belonged together—a neatly stacked row of houses that had been restored. All because one man thought they still had something to offer.

"He thinks you've forgotten how to love it," Quinn said.

Grady eyed the perfectly manicured yards. The pristine landscaping. The simple details that made these houses new again.

He needed someone to do the same for him.

"I'm not sure I ever loved it."

Quinn stilled.

"It was my brother, Benji. It was something we used to do together. We skied. A lot. And it was a competition between us at first, but then . . ." How much of this did he want to tell her? "It just became this thing I had to do for him—because he couldn't do it for himself."

"Is he still skiing?"

Grady closed his eyes, aware that this pleasant conversation could be interrupted at any moment by an unwanted visitor who was doing who knows what inside his house. "No. He's not."

"Maybe you should talk to him?"

"Listen, Quinn, there's something I need to tell you—"

But naturally, before he could get the words out—words that might've exonerated him from this horrible scene—the front door opened and Ashley walked onto the porch.

Grady's eyes found the floor as he let out the subtlest sigh.

"Oh. My . . ." Quinn's voice was barely audible.

"Hey, Quinn. Did you bring our boy some lunch?" Ashley asked.

"Why didn't you say something?" Quinn whispered as she stood.

"It's not what you think, Quinn." Grady stood too.

"Oh, don't try to explain. I don't care about any of this." She waved her hands back and forth between Grady and Ashley. "My dad made me bring you lunch. Thought you might not have much in the fridge, and most places around here are closed on Sundays. At least during the off season."

"It was real sweet of your dad to think of Grady like that." Ashley smiled as if she belonged here, on his porch, in his house.

Quinn smoothed her hands over her jeans, avoiding his eyes. "I have to get back to the shop."

And as he stood there, feet away from Ashley, one thing was clear: the only person who belonged there with him was hightailing it in the other direction.

22

I'M SUCH AN IDIOT!

Quinn could count on one hand the number of times she'd done something impulsive, and she didn't even need all her fingers to do it. She hadn't completely lied—her dad did encourage her to bring Grady something to eat, but only after she'd said she wanted to visit him. Quietly in the kitchen, so nobody else could hear.

"I kind of want to tell him Judge said he could go up north. I think that's going to be a big deal for him. And after those Facebook videos, he might need some good news."

"Then you should go over there," her dad said. "Bring him lunch."

"Yeah, that's a good idea," Quinn had said. Because it had sounded like a good idea.

When really it was the most horrible, terrible, awful idea she'd ever had.

Ashley Perkins? Seriously?

Her groan filled the car, and she followed it up with three slams on her steering wheel accompanied by "Stupid, stupid, stupid!"

She took a breath. "It's fine. It's not like I liked him or something. That was pity food. A pity visit. It's good to know he doesn't need my help. It's great that he's got a *friend* here in Harbor Pointe." She said the words aloud, but she could hear the lie in her voice.

This man! He was the *worst* kind of man. He was far too experienced for someone like her, someone whose only real relationship had been practically platonic and beyond that had only ever casually dated anyone her whole entire life. That meant she was . . . well . . . not experienced. And she valued that. It meant something to her.

It meant nothing to Grady. That was a big difference. Plus, he was an athlete. Well-traveled. Well-off. She was none of those things. They were nothing alike. And perhaps most important, she was sure they didn't share the same faith. Just look at the way he lived his life. His choices told her all she needed to know.

And yet her heart was tender toward him. Why?

She pulled into her parking space behind the flower shop and let her forehead rest on the steering wheel. "What is wrong with you, Quinn? Pull yourself together."

So much for apologizing for her behavior.

She sighed. She knew it didn't work that way. His decisions didn't give her the right to treat him badly.

She'd be smart to remember that.

She got out of the car and walked toward the back door. She hadn't even seen her refinished floor, and she had shelves to move and displays to finish. She'd spend the next two days painting her new logo behind the front counter, hanging the hand-lettered chalkboards on the walls, and setting up the new displays.

Her big flower delivery would come Wednesday morning and then she'd be open for business. Her plan was to stay open late on Wednesday and host a daylong open house with refreshments and door prizes. Lucy had interviewed her for a story that had run in the Sunday morning edition of the *Harbor Pointe Gazette*, encouraging people to come out and support the new endeavor.

Her father had three copies of the paper at brunch.

There was a lot to finish before Wednesday, and she did not have time to waste thinking about Grady and Ashley. Once she got through this week, she'd focus all of her attention on the Winter Carnival. She'd been dreaming about her Secret Garden designs, and she practically had the entire pavilion decorated already in her mind.

If she couldn't win first place at the Floral Expo with what she had planned, then she may never have any hope of winning anything at all. She was convinced it was her very best work.

Inspired by Grady.

She knocked the thought aside. He might've said a few things that helped her out of her creative slump, but the work was hers.

She unlocked the back door and let herself in, the scent of fresh paint filling her nostrils. It smelled clean, which was exactly what she wanted—a new start for her and for Forget-Me-Not. She hung her bag on the hook by the back door.

With the natural light pouring in from all the windows, she didn't even need to turn on the lights to see how gorgeous her floors were. They were original to the building, and they hadn't been refinished the entire time Mimi owned the shop. Now, looking at the thin boards, freshly sanded and polished, Quinn would've thought they were just installed yesterday.

Before she could forget, she took out her phone and texted Ryan Brooks.

You did an amazing job on my floors—thank you! And she knew his invoice wasn't his full price—he called it the "friends and family discount." When he and Lane Kelley got married, she'd extend the same discount on their flowers as a thank-you.

She flipped the lights on and walked to the center of the space. This was *her* shop now. She could do whatever she wanted with it. The creamy white walls practically begged for her attention, the perfect neutral palette for whatever she wanted to put on them. She had all kinds of new inventory to add to the shop—it had been arriving almost daily even before she was the official owner.

In all the craziness, she'd almost forgotten to stop and take in these small moments. She pulled out the photo of her, Carly, and their mother and stared at it as the clock ticked off the seconds. "I did it, Mom," she said aloud. "All by myself."

She heard the defiance in her own voice, even though she knew the words weren't completely true. She'd had so much help along the way. She had Carly and her father and, of course, Beverly and Judge. Even Calvin, in his own way, had been a help to her. She had good friends in Lucy and Hailey, and while she didn't have her own kids, she had Jaden. God had given her so many wonderful people to love and be loved by—why didn't it ever seem like it was enough?

Was it because she was still single? Or was Carly right? Was she holding on to a false image of a mother who never really existed?

She shook the thoughts away and set the photo down. This was supposed to be a time for soaking up an accomplishment. She was a business owner, and that was a big deal.

So why did everything feel so hollow?

Outside, a lone car on the road caught her attention.

"Oh no."

Grady's black Jeep parked in front of the flower shop. What was he doing here? It wasn't like he owed her an explanation. Besides, she didn't want to see him. At all.

She made a mental note to have blinds installed so she could at least pretend she wasn't there when she wanted to be alone. She watched as he got out of the car. He'd showered and changed, which was great for him, but not so great for her. A gray hoodie and warm-up pants somehow made him even more attractive.

"Get it together, Q," she said, hoping the self-scolding would be enough to get her brain back on track.

He spotted her through the window and raised a hand in a subtle wave. She held his gaze for several long seconds, then finally walked over to the door, drew in a deep breath, and pulled it open.

"Hey."

Well, that was just great. Not only did he look like this, he also smelled *really* good. The unfairness of it all didn't escape her. "Hey."

Play it cool, Collins. He's just a guy. A very, very good-looking guy. Who, for all the aforementioned reasons, was a terrible fit for her. She chose safe guys. Guys whose pasts were as boring and mundane as hers. She had never in her life dated "the bad boy." It wasn't in her nature.

"I thought you might need some help."

She stood in the doorway, scowl on her face, willing him to go away.

"Can I come in?"

"Why would you want to help me on a Sunday?"

He shrugged.

She narrowed her eyes. "Oh, you want me to sweet-talk Judge and get you out of here early; I forgot."

"That's not it," he said.

She met his eyes. "Then what?"

He pressed his lips together. "Just thought you could use some help. You reopen in a couple days. Saw this—" he reached in the pocket of his hoodie and pulled out a torn page of the newspaper and handed it to her. "I didn't know if you had a copy."

She stared at the front page of the paper, her photo staring back at her. He brought her a copy of the article? Never mind that she had a stack of papers on the front seat of her car.

"Anyway," he said, "I knew you'd be freaking out about how much work you had to do. Especially since you took yesterday off."

She stood there, mind teeter-tottering back and forth. She was irritated with him, but she had no right to be. She'd been nothing but rude to him since he first came to town—and he had no reason *not* to spend time with Ashley. Even if that time was in the middle of the night.

The thought of it turned her stomach.

She stepped away from the door and let him through. "You really don't have to help me. I've got a plan for the day."

"You do?"

She closed the door and nodded. "Get my shelves back out. Set the inventory up. Paint my logo on the back wall." She wasn't sure if it would all actually happen today, but it made her sound busy, and that's exactly what she needed Grady to believe. Maybe then he'd leave her alone. Maybe then the somersaulting in her belly would subside.

"Sounds like a lot." He stood in the middle of her shop, hands shoved in the pocket of his hoodie.

"I'll get it done." She walked over to the counter and pulled out her planner. She had all kinds of notes inside, along with the list of all the tasks she needed to complete. Thankfully, she'd made that list at a time when Grady was not in the room, so it was clear and made sense.

"What can I do?" He took a few steps toward her.

She glanced up. She'd be stupid to turn him down, but having him here was unnerving, especially after their brief encounter only a half hour before. She sighed. "You really want to help?"

"Yes, and I can tell by your enthusiastic reaction you're excited about it." He was trying to win her over, but it wouldn't work. She'd let him help if that eased his conscience, but that was it. They weren't friends.

"You can get the shelves, I guess. They had to move them out to do the floor."

"Great. Point me in the right direction."

She showed him to the back room, where she'd stashed almost everything that wasn't on the walls. She walked over to a shelf and stood on one side, then glanced up to find Grady staring at her.

"What are you doing?" he asked.

"Helping you move shelves."

"Don't you have other stuff to work on?" He looked genuinely confused.

"They're heavy," she said.

He reached over, picked the shelf up with both hands, and walked out of the storage room.

Well, okay then.

He continued to haul heavy things out of storage, and she turned her attention to the back wall. She'd borrowed an old overhead projector from the elementary school and had just figured out how to project her logo onto the back wall so she could trace it before painting it in bold black. In her head, it would tie the whole space together. In reality, she found herself paralyzed to start.

"What's wrong?"

She turned and found him looking at her. "Just thinking through the steps. I want to make sure I get it right." Back to focusing on the wall, head tilted, imagining the way it would look once it was finished.

He leaned across the counter from the opposite side, still watching her.

After too many unnerving seconds, she dared a glance in his direction. "What?"

"Is this normal for you?" He folded his hands, and leaning on his elbows, he looked relaxed.

"Is what normal for me?"

"All of this second-guessing. Making sure things are perfect. It's no wonder you never try anything new."

She spun around and faced him. "I went skiing yesterday."

"Practically on a dare."

"Can we not talk about this again?"

"Because you know I'm right."

She turned back around. "Well, is it normal for you to wake up with women you hardly know?"

Quinn had the sensation of watching the words spiral away from her as she tried to throw a lasso over them and pull them back in. What was wrong with her?

He pushed himself upright—thankfully, because now he was behind her and couldn't see how red her cheeks must be. "You're talking about Ashley."

She waved her hand dismissively. "No, it's none of my business. Forget I said anything."

"She bothers you, doesn't she?"

For the love. Why couldn't she just have kept her mouth shut? "No, she's fine. Ashley is a perfectly lovely girl. I hope you guys are very happy."

Sarcasm did not become her.

He moved to the other side of the counter, the side where she was standing. *No, no, no.* She didn't trust the way it felt when he was close—edgy and out of sorts.

"I don't know what you read about me," he said.

She stared at the wall. "Grady, really, forget I said anything. This is not my business. I mean, we aren't even friends." She glanced at him just in time to see his face fall.

"We aren't?"

She had a choice and she knew it. She could continue to be cruel and feel terrible about it tomorrow, or she could swallow her pride and extend the man even a little bit of kindness. That wouldn't hurt, would it?

"I mean, we haven't known each other long," she said.

"Ashley came to the house this morning. I didn't invite her—she just showed up."

Why did the tightness inside her soften when he said that? She didn't even know if it was the truth. "What did she want?"

He looked away, but his expression told her what she needed to know.

"Oh," she said quietly.

Ashley was willing to give Grady things a man wants—things Quinn wasn't willing to give. Not without a ring on her finger. And if that made her old-fashioned, so be it, but it was a decision she'd made a long time ago when Carly announced she was pregnant, later confirmed when Hailey found out she was pregnant too.

And it had cost her many second dates.

She'd always comforted herself with the typical "I guess he wasn't the one . . ." and "God has someone better for me." But sometimes they felt like things people told you because they didn't know what else to say. Sometimes they felt like lies.

Regardless, one thing was certain: if plain, old, regular guys had lost interest because she wouldn't sleep with them, there was no way Grady Benson was going to be okay with waiting. Not when he had girls like Ashley throwing themselves at him.

Grady propped himself up on the stool next to her, half-sitting on it, but with his feet still on the ground. "Have you ever done the same thing your whole life, and then you wake up and one day it just feels all wrong?"

He was looking past her, out the window.

"I never really thought about it until recently," she said. "Because of you."

His eyes found hers, and in that moment she chose to be kind. Guarded, of course, but still kind.

"I've done the same thing every day of my adult life. My friends set their clocks by me. I never thought I wanted anything more until this past week. What you said before about me being scared—it's true. Sometimes I think I'm scared of everything."

"Everything?"

She smiled. "Most things."

"Like . . . ?"

"Like spiders." She looked up at the ceiling. "And mice. And squirrels."

"Squirrels?"

"They're crazy." She laughed. "And . . . other things too."

His silence encouraged her to go on.

"Like never seeing my mother again. Like never proving to her that I did just fine without her." *Like showing her she made a huge mistake when she left.* "Like leaving Harbor Pointe." *Like falling in love.*

"That scares you?"

Her eyes found the floor. "Stupid, right?"

"No. Not stupid." There was a lull then, but not the kind that made her uncomfortable. Just a quiet stillness while they both gathered their thoughts.

He reached over and took her hand. "I have no idea why, but I want to be the person who helps you get over all of that."

She looked at their two hands, his wrapped around hers, as if they formed some sort of hard shell—a casing meant to protect her—and for the briefest moment, she wondered what it would feel like if she let herself believe that's what he could be for her. Someone who showed her that there was a whole big world waiting to be explored. And it wasn't scary at all. Or at least the scary parts could be conquered.

She just had to stop waiting and step off that front porch. Why was it so hard to take that first step?

"What about you?"

His eyes searched hers. "What about me?"

"What are you afraid of? And don't say nothing because I'll know it's a lie."

He half laughed.

"I mean, I know you're not afraid to put yourself in danger. You kind of seem to thrive on it."

"Does that bother you?" He shifted, then pushed himself off the stool, pulling his hand away. She missed the warmth of his skin on hers.

"Of course not." It didn't *bother* her—it scared her. Did he have a death wish or something?

He stood directly across from her now, only about a foot away. He was so close, and she felt herself wanting to retreat. Why was he asking so many questions? Why was he standing so near? Why had he held her hand?

"Not even a little?"

She looked up at his face and found a small scar just above his right eyebrow. She hadn't noticed it before, but then, she'd never really taken the time to actually study him. His eyes were the perfect shade of blue, and he had just the right amount of stubble on his chin. When he smiled—if he smiled—she might buckle at the knees, because she already knew the effect it had on her, though she'd done a stellar job of denying it up until this point.

"You don't like me very much, do you?" he asked, a lazy smirk dancing across his face.

"Why would you say that?" Her heart raced as he placed his hands on the counter on either side of hers.

"I get on your nerves."

"You do."

"You think I'm selfish."

She nodded.

"And you believe all that stuff you read on the Internet."

"Most of it."

His eyes fell to her lips, then met her gaze. "I'm not all bad, Quinn. And right now, the only thing that scares me is the thought of leaving this awful little town without ever properly kissing you."

Say what?

She felt her jaw go slack as she searched his eyes for some indication that he was joking. She found none. Quite the opposite, really—he looked deadly serious.

"I tried to send Ashley away before you ever showed up at my door this morning."

"You did?"

"Yes—I promise. That's not what I'm looking for."

"What are you looking for?" she whispered.

He edged even closer, studying her eyes for a few painstakingly long moments in which she realized she *wanted* to kiss him.

She wanted to kiss Grady Benson.

One simple little kiss. And technically he'd already kissed her once, so it wouldn't even be like a first kiss that carried all kinds of questions and hidden meanings.

"You're overthinking this," he said quietly, his mouth turning up in the slightest smile.

She drew in a breath. He was right. She was overthinking it. She'd made up her mind already that Grady was not good for her. Decided it in a moment of clarity without even a hint of emotion involved. Had she done that in anticipation of a moment like this, when she couldn't be trusted? She couldn't go back on that decision now.

"I—I've got to get this painted."

His face fell as he searched her eyes, but she'd severed their connection. She shrank out from under his arm and turned her back to him. Never mind what she wanted. She wasn't accustomed to choosing her heart over her head, no matter how intoxicating the idea was.

CHAPTER

23

GRADY HAD STRUCK OUT BEFORE, but not like this. He'd met his match in Quinn Collins. She shut him down, and he knew when to walk away. Still, he was good at reading people, and he could've sworn that underneath her Brillo Pad exterior was a girl who actually kind of liked him.

Why else would she have shown up at his cottage that morning? Why else would she have talked to the judge about getting him permission to go skiing up north? Why else would she have looked at him the way she was looking at him only moments ago, before pulling herself away and sticking in her earbuds?

They weren't even going to talk now?

All right, Quinn Collins. If that's how you want to play it.

He'd give her space if that's what she needed. But he wasn't going to give up. That wasn't in his nature. She'd given him plenty of work to do, and if he tried hard enough, maybe the mindless chores would be good for him.

"Oh. No." Quinn's voice behind him pulled his attention.

From where he was, up on a ladder in the opposite corner of the store, he turned toward her. She was sitting on the counter, staring at her phone. She tugged the earbuds out of her ears.

"No, no, no."

"Is something wrong?"

No response. Only the slow headshake of a woman who looked devastated.

"Quinn?"

He balanced the tools on the ladder and stepped down, though he was unsure how she'd respond, given that he was likely the last person in the world she wanted to talk to.

"What's the matter?"

She sat on the back counter, which sat flush with the wall and parallel with the checkout counter, legs crossed in front of her, pencil stuck in her ponytail, scrolling on her phone. She looked like she might cry.

"Is everyone okay?" Grady asked. "Your dad—Jaden?"

"They're fine," she finally said. "I just got an e-mail from Kitty Moore."

Grady frowned. "Who's that?"

"She's from the Floral Expo." She met his eyes for the briefest second.

"And . . . ?" She certainly wasn't making this easy for him.

Quinn slipped down off the counter and stood in front of him, then focused on her phone and read out loud: "'Dear Miss Collins, we tried reaching you by phone, but had no luck. I wanted to let you know we received your application for the Best Design competition, but we are unable to process it due to the missing information. As per the rules listed on our website, each applicant is required to submit a copy of their business license and tax info for our records. Of course we hate for you to be disqualified over a technicality, but rules are rules. Hope you'll try again next year with all required documents. Have a wonderful weekend.'"

Quinn's voice had grown progressively more staccato as she read, punctuated finally with the cell phone dropped onto the counter. She covered her face with her hands and stayed hauntingly still.

"Are you okay?"

"My only chance." The words were barely audible. She picked up the phone and dialed what he could only assume was the number listed at the bottom of the e-mail. He watched as she stood there, one arm wrapped around her midsection, eyes fixed on the ceiling as if she were trying to keep from crying.

She shook her head. "I can't believe this. No answer."

"Try again?"

"It's Sunday," she said. "Whoever Kitty Moore is, she's not going to pick up. The e-mail came in yesterday. I should've checked it sooner."

The outgoing voicemail message came on and Quinn put the phone on speaker.

"Thank you for calling the Michigan Floral Expo. We're sorry we missed your call. If you're calling about tickets for the Expo, please visit our website or try back during normal business hours. If you're calling about a design entry, please hang up and call our new president, Jacie Whitman, as all entries have been forwarded to her."

"Jacie Whitman," Quinn said, clicking the phone off.

"Who's Jacie Whitman?"

She turned and faced him, eyes clearly filled with tears. "My mother."

⌒∼⌒

Quinn's throat swelled, and she struggled to get a deep breath.

This couldn't be happening.

"This is what happens when I make stupid, rash decisions," she said, tossing the phone onto the counter.

"What are you talking about?"

"I should've been here yesterday. All day."

"You wouldn't even have been able to get in," Grady said pointedly. "Ryan had to clear the whole shop—that includes people, too."

"I would've heard the phone ringing." Did she sound as hysterical as she felt?

"From upstairs?"

She should've sent the calls to her cell. Why hadn't she thought of that?

Quinn had never given it a second thought—never dreamed for a single moment that her application for the contest was anything but completely thorough. She'd worked for days putting it together. Her hand-drawn designs of this year's Secret Garden event. Her portfolio of past work. Her details—name, address, age, phone numbers—how had she forgotten to include the business license and tax information?

"Call them tomorrow," Grady said, still sounding uselessly hopeful.

"What's the point?"

"Is it important to you?"

She glanced up at his quizzical face. "Of course it is."

"Well . . . ?"

"Well, what?"

He searched the air. "Well, don't just throw in the towel."

She watched him for a second. "Do you hear what you just said?"

His mouth tightened into a line, but his expression was blank.

"You said, 'Don't just throw in the towel.'"

"So?" he gave her an exasperated shrug.

She narrowed her gaze, fixing it on him. She was angry, but she wasn't going to let this opportunity pass her by. "So, I could say the same thing to you. About skiing. If you love it—if it really matters to you—why would you give up without a fight?"

"I'm not giving up."

"You're not training. You're eating garbage food. You're not working out. Do you really think everything is going to be handed to you for the rest of your life?"

He shook his head and turned around. "We're not talking about me."

She followed him as he walked back to the ladder where he was . . . What *was* he doing over here? "You're older now. Your body doesn't work the way it used to. So what? Stop wallowing and start fighting. You might have to actually listen to your coaches instead of doing everything your own way for once."

"You don't know anything about that."

She knew plenty. She was embarrassed to admit how much. She'd read everything she could find on Grady Benson, and the articles were always the same. *Most talented skier we've seen in years. Doesn't listen to instruction. Wants to do things his own way. Faster than everyone else. Natural talent. Reckless and rebellious.*

It all left Quinn wondering—what happened when natural talent wasn't enough? What happened when the demigod he was on the slopes suddenly discovered his own mortality?

"I know you haven't said a single word about anything personal since you got here today. You wouldn't even tell me what you were scared of."

He started up the ladder. "I told you plenty. You just didn't want to hear it."

"That's not even true."

He stepped back down, meeting her gaze. "Then why'd you walk away? What are *you* so scared of?"

"I'm not afraid of you, if that's what you think." She steeled her jaw, refusing to back down.

"I think you are."

"Well, you're wrong." Heat rushed to her cheeks as she practically spat the angry words.

In one quick motion, his hands were at her face, his lips on hers. He kissed her like he meant it—pointed but not forceful—and she began to feel her anger disintegrate as she closed her eyes and gave in to the kiss.

The unwanted—yet so wanted—kiss.

She would allow herself a moment, but she would *not* melt in his arms.

But they were strong arms, and they made their way around her body, pulling her toward him as if he couldn't get close enough. Slowly, she moved her hands, resting them on his solid back. He deepened the kiss, and her stomach turned itself into a knot. For a moment, her mind went completely blank.

There was nothing but Grady, his lips, and her wobbly knees.

And then reality smacked her upside the head. She pulled herself from his grasp, hands going up as if to say, "Whoa. Hold on a minute." Because in her mind, all she could think was, *Whoa. Hold on a minute.*

"This is a bad idea."

"Why?" He took a step toward her and she took a step back.

She turned away and walked to the counter, letting out an ironic laugh as she did. "So many reasons."

"Tell me."

"We're really, really different people, Grady," she said. "And that—what just happened—"

"Me kissing you?" He supplied the answer in the most amused tone, and she could only attribute his nonchalance to his prior experience. A huge problem she had but would never say aloud.

"Yeah, that. That was a big mistake."

"I don't think so," he said.

She paced the width of the floor, thankful for the counter between them. "No, you're wrong. And you're all wrong for me." She laughed. "Anyone who knows us can see that."

"I know us, and I don't see it."

She stopped moving and looked at him. "This is what you do, isn't it? You draw women in and then you break their hearts. You're so comfortable doing it. You're so comfortable knowing that you're going to have to leave. It doesn't even matter that this could never work."

"Maybe I haven't decided that it can never work."

"I'm telling you. It can never work. And casual romance is not my thing." She pressed her lips together, still a bit dazed from the spell his kiss seemed to cast over her.

His eyes turned serious. "It's not my thing either."

"Grady, please. I know how to use Google."

He shoved a hand through his hair. "What if I don't want it to be my thing anymore? What if I want something real? Something different?"

She searched his eyes. This was what guys like him did with girls like her. They pretended to be something they weren't. But she wasn't going to fall for it.

He faced her, standing completely still. "I've never met anybody who makes me think that what I have isn't enough. But you do. And I don't have the right to say this, but I want more."

The unexpected words spiraled toward her, landing squarely on her shoulders, and there they sat, threatening her resolve.

She wanted to believe him. *Oh no. She wanted to believe him.* When had she turned into the kind of woman who wanted to take a man at his word when she knew she absolutely could not? He would leave, just like everyone else had left—just like her mother had left.

And she couldn't bear that pain again.

"I'm sorry, Grady."

He moved around the counter and stood right in front of her, clearly unfazed by her nearness. "Tell me you didn't feel that between us. Tell me that wasn't real."

She forced herself to look at him. "It wasn't real."

He searched her eyes but she held her ground, refusing to allow even the hurt look on his face to sway her.

But when he broke away from her and walked off, instant, painful regret wound its way through her belly.

And she couldn't shake the idea that the only mistake she'd made was letting him walk away.

CHAPTER

24

GRADY STORMED OUT of the Forget-Me-Not Flower Shop and marched toward his SUV. That woman was infuriating! For all his faults, at least he was up-front with people.

It wasn't real, my eye.

He'd never felt anything more real than the connection between them. As soon as his lips touched hers . . . it was more than just attraction; it was so much more. How did she not feel that?

Before he got in the car, he cast one last, longing gaze at the flower shop, hoping to see her standing in the window, watching him. At least then he would know she cared.

But she wasn't there.

The only thing that lingered were her pointed words.

"You're not training. . . . You're not working out. Do you really think everything is going to be handed to you for the rest of your life? . . . Stop wallowing and start fighting. You might have to actually listen to your coaches instead of doing everything your own way for once."

He'd lied when he said she didn't know anything about it. It seemed like she knew everything. What's more, she wasn't afraid to say what she thought about all of it.

He'd surrounded himself with friends who told him only what he wanted to hear, and at the first sign of trouble, they'd all disappeared.

He sat behind the steering wheel, key in the ignition, eyes fixed on the empty street and sidewalks in front of him. An Open sign shone in the window of the bar across the street. He tapped the steering wheel with his thumb, knowing that getting lost in a bottle might help him forget all of this—the social media mess, Quinn, the realization that he was, in fact, not the skier he used to be. But those things would all still be there when he woke up, wouldn't they?

Which left him with one question: If he didn't drown his sorrows in a Jack and Coke, where would he drown them?

He started the car and drove away, certain of only one thing: the answers weren't anywhere he'd ever looked before.

~

The cottage was quiet. Too quiet. It left him too much time in his own head, and Grady knew from experience, that wasn't a good thing. The television blared in the background—white noise to drown out the loneliness.

Loneliness. What was he—an old, retired widower putzing around the house aimlessly?

His heart dropped. Wasn't *that* what he was really afraid of?

That and the thought of never making amends for what had happened to his brother.

He'd been dreaming again the past few nights. He'd wake up fitful and sweating, his mind straining to piece together the fragments of a nightmare that put him straight back on that mountain the day he thought Benji had died.

His heart raced as he tried to shove the unwanted memories from his mind.

He clutched a Nerf football he'd found in the garage—good stress reliever in a pinch, though right now, it wasn't doing its job. He willed away the guilt, the shame. Not just what had happened on the slopes, but everything that had come next.

The ego. The women. The alcohol. The fights.

Was this all there was to him without the accolades of skiing? If so, he didn't like it.

Thoughts of Benji only stoked the fire Quinn's words had lit earlier in the day.

He'd struggled. He'd faltered, made so many mistakes. Somehow, this past year, they'd begun to mess with his head. He'd never had that problem before. Chose not to listen to the negative press—or anyone, for that matter.

He stood and paced the length of the living room, clasping the football between his hands.

Quinn had challenged him, maybe without even knowing it. What was he going to do? Run away because more was required of him? He owed it to Benji to at least go down swinging.

He owed it to himself.

He pulled out his laptop and muted the TV. He scoured the bottom of his duffel bag for a notebook and pen, then did what Brian and his other coaches had tried to get him to do for years—watched videos of his mistakes.

"What's the point of reliving my worst moments?" he'd demanded.

"You can learn from your mistakes, Grady," Brian had said. "This is part of every athlete's process."

"Not mine."

He'd been so stubborn, so pigheaded. Full of excuses and unwilling to admit that he might've been wrong, that the mistakes might've been his. Instead, he'd only watched the replays of the races where he'd triumphed.

But if he was going to try a new approach, it started here. Would it be easy? No. But it was necessary, and he knew it.

He sat on the couch as day turned to night, watching, studying, rewinding and rewatching to catch what had caused each stumble, each fall. Eventually, he became detached from the process, critiquing it like a spectator would, forgetting that it was his own race, his own mistakes, he was watching.

He stood up, right there in the living room, and pretended he was on the slopes, getting the movement in his body, correcting the missteps.

And it started to click.

Still, he knew—and it was hard for him to admit—that he wasn't going to be able to come back strong enough by himself.

For the first time in his life, Grady felt like he actually needed someone else.

He'd all but destroyed his relationship with Brian, who'd been with him practically since the beginning. Brian's career had taken off, and he was now the head coach of the US Olympic ski team. It was a relationship Grady would have to salvage, but not today.

Today, there was only one person he thought might still be in his corner.

He pulled his phone out and dialed his trainer, a solidly built black guy everyone called Happy because of his sunny disposition and endless optimism, something Grady had always endured but now desperately needed. Happy had always been committed to Grady's training, considered himself part of Team Benson. Grady hoped that hadn't changed.

Their partnership hadn't ended poorly; it had just ended. Grady hadn't even meant for it to happen—one day he just stopped showing up. Maybe because he didn't like what his trainer had to say? How arrogant he'd been.

"Grady, my man. Where you been?" Happy actually sounded, well, happy to hear from him.

"You don't wanna know, Hap." Grady plopped down on the sofa. "Listen, I need some help. I've got a race in a couple weeks and I have to get back in shape—fast."

"Have you been keeping up with your training?"

Grady's eyes found the ceiling. He could picture his trainer's earnest eyes, and he knew he owed the man the truth. No sense sugarcoating it. "No. I got sloppy, but I'm committed now. More than ever."

Happy let out a sigh. Probably frustrated his expertise had been disregarded. "You know what this is going to take, right?"

Grady knew. It was going to take everything he had. And then some. "I'm ready."

"You know my rules," Happy said. "No booze. No late nights. Lots of early mornings."

"You have my word."

"And you're ready to change it up a little?"

Grady thought back to the last time they'd worked together. Happy had tried to convince him to make some changes then to compensate for physical limitations Grady wasn't willing to admit. If only he'd listened, maybe he would've already qualified.

"Listen, Hap," Grady said. "About our last session—"

"Forget it," Happy said. "I'm just glad you're coming around now."

"Yeah," Grady said. "You were right. I'm not twenty anymore."

Happy laughed. "You're not even twenty-five."

Grady listened as Happy outlined the new plan—one that would work best for his body. The eating plan would be difficult to follow in Harbor Pointe, but he'd get help if he had to, no matter how hard it was for him to ask.

"I'm going to work you hard, Grady," Happy told him. "Because you can handle it and because you don't have a lot of time."

"I can take it," Grady said. "But my resources are limited. We gotta go bare bones on this one." He'd explained his situation, being stuck in Harbor Pointe, the poor skiing options.

"Bare bones is my specialty," Happy said. "Listen, if we're gonna do this, we're gonna do it right. No shortcuts."

We. That's what he needed. Someone on his team.

"You'll check in with me every day," Happy said. "At least twice."

"I will."

"And I'll know if you're slacking."

"How?"

"Because you'll still be able to walk." Happy laughed. "Aw, man, I've missed you. It's going to be fun putting you through the paces again."

"I think we have different ideas of what fun is," Grady said.

"I'll e-mail you. I already had a plan written up for you from before. It's going to be the same as what we talked about, only now we're doing it long-distance. You get stuck, you call me. You get discouraged, you call me. Got it?"

"I'll be fine," Grady said.

"Listen, Grady, from what I've seen, you haven't been fine," Happy said. "But you've got to let that all go now."

What if I can't?

"All those jokers out there running their mouths, they don't know you like I do. I see nothing but gas left in your tank."

Grady's eyes clouded over at the words. *Seriously?* What was he now, a little sissy?

And yet, he'd been hearing nothing but negativity for weeks. Only words that tore him down—and he'd believed them. Finally, someone to offer some hope.

Grady composed himself, then cleared his throat. "Thanks for taking my call, man."

"You kidding? I'm in this for the long haul. No matter what happens."

And somehow, Grady knew he meant it.

"Check your in-box," Happy said. "And call me in the morning."

Grady hung up and opened his e-mail. The plan came complete with personal notes like *Don't go to the bar on the weekends—you'll undo five days of solid training.*

Happy knew him too well.

Grady wasn't out of shape, but he'd have to commit in ways he never had before if he had any chance at getting back on that team.

But it would be worth it.

Four thirty a.m. came fast. His alarm went off at the same time a text came in.

You up?

Happy.

Grady texted him back: I'm up, drill sergeant.

Good. Don't phone it in. Visualize the moment you're back on that team.

Grady tapped out the words: I'll do you one better. I'm visualizing that gold medal around my neck.

LOL. One thing at a time, my man, but I like your enthusiasm. Go get 'em and call me later. I'm going back to bed.

He pulled on his gray hoodie, brushed his teeth, and splashed some water on his face, making a mental note to go to bed earlier tonight. He couldn't stay up late watching old race videos if he was going to get up at this hour.

He trudged downstairs, the smell of coffee a welcome distraction. He'd set the automatic timer to start brewing so he could have at least half a cup before heading out.

A few minutes later, the doorbell rang. One glance at the clock—5 a.m.—told him his training partner was right on time.

Impressive.

He pulled the door open and found a sleepy Jaden standing on the porch. "I don't think I've ever been up this early."

Grady laughed. "This is the life, kid. This is what it really takes."

How had Grady forgotten? How had he gotten so sidetracked—so arrogant—that he let himself believe he didn't need the same hard-core training his competitors were putting in?

"I'm not goin' easy on you, either. You said you wanted to compete, so you're gonna get the real picture," Grady said as he grabbed his phone and keys. "Wait. How did you get over here?"

"I jogged," Jaden said.

Grady gave the kid a nod. "Wow."

"I'm tired."

"Yeah, yeah, let's hit the weight room." They started off in the direction of the Cedar Grove clubhouse, which Ryan had told him offered a state-of-the-art gym that was open twenty-four hours a day.

"We're gonna do this every day?" Jaden asked.

"If you wanna be the best, you have to work for it," Grady said, sounding like every coach he'd ever had.

"Wow, you're like a fortune cookie." Jaden tossed him a quick grin.

"Some overused advice is actually helpful," Grady said. "Listen, I've been way off track since I got here. Since before I got here, really. So don't go throwing what I do back in my face. Everything changes as of this moment right here. You got it?"

"I got it, old man," Jaden said. "But I've got my eye on you."

Grady frowned. "What's that supposed to mean?"

"It means you can train me, but if you're not working hard enough, I'm calling you out on it."

Grady stuck his hands on his hips and watched the kid's reaction. When Jaden didn't back down, he shook his head. "Fine, but if you get too annoying, I'm kicking you out."

He laid out the plan for the kid—the basic training plan Happy had given him back when his body worked a little more like Jaden's.

"That's a lot." Jaden groaned.

"I told you it's not going to be easy." Grady pulled out his phone and found the workout plan Happy had given him. It was designed to build power in his legs, something he'd always come by naturally.

"You expect me to do all this yoga stuff?" Jaden stared at the paper Grady had handed him.

"Skiing is about more than speed and power, dude," Grady said, hopping on the treadmill. "It's about balance and agility. At least I'm not making you take a ballet class."

Jaden rolled his eyes. "Yeah, that's where I draw the line, though I'm betting it'd be pretty fun to see you in a tutu."

Grady shook his head. "Get to work."

After ten minutes, sweat dotted his brow. He tried to pace himself because he knew he'd have to go on a trail run later. Happy had a theory that working out in the great outdoors was somehow better for people like Grady, who had to compete outside.

Jaden sat on a weight bench and stared at him. "This sucks, Grady. I just want to get up there and ski. Can't we just meet out at Avalanche after school?"

For a moment Grady felt like he was looking in a mirror, but not one that reflected who he was today.

"Look, Jaden, I'm going to tell you something that you're not going to want to hear," Grady said.

The kid used his shirt to wipe his face dry.

"Do you want to compete?"

"Course I do," Jaden said. "Which is why I don't get why we're here. I already went for a run this morning—isn't that enough?"

"No, it's not," Grady said. "This is where you separate yourself from everyone else—not out on the slopes, but right here in the gym or out there on the trails. You've got so much natural talent, but unlike me, you'll actually take correction up there."

"But that's not enough either?" Jaden asked.

"Not even close." Grady might not have any business talking to Jaden about a lesson he'd only just learned, but suddenly the desire to spare him the wasted time seemed worth possible hypocrisy. "So are you ready?"

"To be the best?" Jaden grinned. "You know I am."

Funny, Grady felt exactly the same way.

CHAPTER

25

GRADY ARRIVED AT FORGET-ME-NOT ten minutes after 9 a.m. on Tuesday.

Great, he thought as he pulled up. *Show up late—way to let her know you've changed.*

He'd received a call from Ryan on Monday after his workout, asking if he could report to him that day. He claimed to need his help building foundations for the Winter Carnival statues, but the timing made Grady wonder if maybe Quinn had requested the change.

Today, though, she'd have to face him. He'd asked Ryan if he could spend the day here, helping her get ready for her big day tomorrow.

From the sidewalk, he saw a flurry of activity inside. Who was he kidding? Quinn was probably grateful he wasn't there, in the middle of all the people she actually cared about. He'd only be in the way.

But he'd given her his word. And he wasn't going to go back on it, no matter how wounded his ego was. Bad enough he'd let her run him off the other day.

He pulled the front door open, and everyone seemed to shift into slow motion. Heads turned, eyes fixed on him.

He lifted a hand in a lame greeting, searching the only slightly familiar faces for Quinn, who was nowhere to be seen.

Beverly sat on the floor just in front of him. She glanced up. "Grady, we didn't know you'd be here today. Calvin, did you see? Grady's here."

The wiry man popped out from behind a display on the ground.

"Grady, good to see you, son." Calvin stood.

Grady's eyes landed on the logo Quinn had been painting the last time he was here. She'd finished it—and it looked perfect behind the counter.

"It's looking good," he said. "Is Quinn around?"

The older woman's eyes danced. "You and Quinn have been spending a lot of time together, haven't you?"

Uh-oh.

"Gus said she brought you leftovers on Sunday." She grinned.

"Beverly, hush," Calvin said.

"She's around here somewhere, Grady. I'm sure she'll be happy to see you."

Grady doubted it.

A peppy girl with a red ponytail made her way over to him. "You came." She smiled up at him, her eyes big and blue. "I'm Lucy," she said, probably sensing his inability to place her. "Quinn's friend. Best friend, really. We've known each other our whole lives."

He nodded.

"She likes you," Lucy said.

Grady was pretty sure his face went blank. "No. She doesn't." He tried not to remember the way she'd felt in his arms, the way he'd inhaled her, the scent of her shampoo—strawberries—filling him with a feeling he'd never experienced before.

He'd been trying to erase the whole thing from his head since he walked out of here Sunday. So far, he was doing a pretty crummy job.

"Quinn's prickly," Lucy said. "But she's worth the fight."

What was this—a running theme? Was he going to have to fight for everything now?

"She made it pretty clear where I stand," Grady said. "I'm just here to work."

Lucy's face fell. "I never pegged you for a quitter, Grady Benson."

He looked away. "Do you have a job for me?"

"Quinn's in the back. I think she might have a job for you. I'll go check." And with that, Lucy walked away.

Grady made his way through the maze of people who'd come out to help Harbor Pointe's favorite daughter—the woman everyone seemed to love. He couldn't blame them. Quinn might be prickly, but she was the best person he'd ever known.

And while a part of him wanted to fight for her, like Lucy said, another part of him knew the truth: no matter how much he changed, he would never be good enough. Not for her.

❧

Quinn had slipped away to the back room as soon as she saw Grady's SUV pull up in front of her shop.

He came?

She was sure he'd go see Judge about having his community service assignment changed. He'd ask to wash dishes at Hazel's or clean gutters around town. Anything would be better than being here, with her.

But here he was, walking up to her door.

She turned a circle now, trying—failing—to regain her composure.

It was just a kiss.

A mind-blowing, knee buckling, when-can-we-do-it-again kiss.

And the answer was, of course, never. They could never do it again.

Lucy's face appeared in her doorway. "You've got a new helper."

Quinn turned away. The combination of Lucy's incredible perception and Quinn's inability to lie made this all a very bad scenario.

"What is wrong with you?" Lucy hissed. "What are you doing back here?"

"I'm just tidying up," Quinn said, wondering when she became the kind of person who used the word *tidying*.

"What is *really* going on with you?"

Quinn groaned. "Don't do that, Lucy."

"Do what? I'm your friend. You're obviously not telling me something."

Quinn faced her. "There's nothing to tell. Can you have Grady unload the two boxes out there and just set everything on the counter? We'll arrange it all once it's unpackaged."

Lucy stood in the doorway for too many seconds. "You're hiding something. You know how I know?"

Quinn assumed the question was rhetorical.

"Because you're terrible at it." She took a step closer. "Did something happen with you two?" Thankfully, she kept her voice low.

Quinn pinched the bridge of her nose and closed her eyes. "It was nothing."

Lucy gasped. "I cannot believe you didn't say anything at breakfast."

"Well, I was a little preoccupied, what with losing my chance to see my mother and all."

Lucy's face softened. "I know, and I'm sorry about that, though if you really want to see your mom, there are other ways."

Quinn dropped into the chair behind her desk. "I don't want to see her. I want her to see me."

The realization nestled itself inside of her. She didn't even want to talk to her mother. She just wanted to prove to the woman that she made a mistake in leaving them behind.

And now she couldn't.

"We can figure all that out later, but right now, you've got an incredibly good-looking Olympic skier in your shop. And he's not here for me."

Quinn looked up sadly. "He's here because the court ordered him to be here." It was true, more or less, though helping with the shop wasn't exactly part of his community service.

Lucy squeezed her shoulder, then slipped out of the back room, leaving Quinn alone, in hiding, and wondering how everything in her perfectly comfortable life had been turned upside down so quickly.

~~~~~

The day wore on and Quinn did a really good job of avoiding Grady. There was the time they'd both reached for the same box, but that had been easily remedied because at almost the exact same time, the FedEx guy showed up.

She'd never been so thankful for a FedEx delivery in her life.

More than once, Lucy had prodded her about whatever it was that had happened between the two of them. Hailey had shown up with lunch from Hazel's for all of the workers, though Quinn noticed Grady chose his packed lunch instead.

He packed his own lunch?

By late afternoon, her help had thinned out, but the shop was beginning to look exactly like it had in her mind. How would she ever repay these people for donating their time to make this all happen?

Even Grady, though his time wasn't exactly a donation, had been a huge help. She could be angry with him and grateful to him at the same time, couldn't she?

A few times, she'd caught him looking at her, but she would not be swayed by his piercing eyes or that perpetual smirk that played at the corner of his mouth.

Quinn spent the entire day hyperaware of where he was, of whom he was talking to, of what he was doing. She made general announcements to give him tasks instead of instructing him directly. She was being childish, and she knew it.

She forced herself to stop thinking about Grady and start

thinking about tomorrow. Her grand reopening. It was a big day for Forget-Me-Not, and for her.

Why couldn't she keep her mind focused on that?

Around 4 p.m., Judge wandered in. His face brightened when he met Quinn's eyes. "Look at this place."

She pulled her hands away from the display she was styling and met him at the center of the store, so much more put together than it had been that morning. They'd fashioned the gifts into the most beautiful displays, making it easy for shoppers to see all the possibilities.

"We aren't done yet, but it's almost there." Quinn let him pull her into one of his usual fatherly hugs.

"I love it. Love how you've put your own spin on it. The place has never looked better."

Quinn smiled. "Never?"

Judge's eyebrow winched up slightly. "Never."

The compliment made her feel better than it probably should've. "Did you just stop by to say hi?"

"And to check up on our favorite Olympian." Judge's deep baritone had only ever been warm and inviting to Quinn, but she could see how the man might be intimidating if he were sitting on the other side of the bench. "Where is Mr. Benson?"

Quinn was surprised she couldn't pinpoint his exact location—she'd known it practically all day—but when she scanned her little shop, she couldn't find Grady.

"He was just here," she said.

Judge looked around, then half shrugged. "Don't see him now."

"Is he in trouble?"

He eyed her. "Depends. Is he keeping up with his community service?"

"Yes, Judge," Quinn said. "He's actually been an exceptional worker."

"That so?"

"I haven't seen the boy take a single break today," Beverly chimed in. "He must really like our girl." She slid an arm around Quinn, who suddenly felt claustrophobic.

The last thing she needed was their matchmaking. She shrugged herself out of Beverly's grasp. "Let me see if he's in the back."

Judge nodded, then turned toward one of the displays. Outdoor garden decorations. That wouldn't keep him occupied for long—Judge wasn't exactly the gardening type.

She slipped into the back room, checking the bathroom and her office, but Grady wasn't back there.

Why had Judge chosen that exact moment to come in? Why couldn't he have stopped by earlier when the man was hauling old shelves and bookcases up from her filthy basement?

More importantly, why did she care? If Grady had skipped out early, he'd pay the consequences. That wasn't her fault.

And yet, despite everything, it wasn't what she wanted.

She pulled out her phone. She'd text him quick, see if she could find him. But before she could get a word typed, she spotted him in the alley out back, behind the shop, phone to his ear, pacing back and forth.

She made her way through the back door, pulse racing because she knew she couldn't avoid him for another minute, not if she wanted to keep him from making things worse for himself.

As soon as she opened the door, she heard him, though his back was to her.

"I can't even believe you'd bring that up, Pete," he said. "I'm telling you what I want. What I need. If you can't get on board with that, then I'll find someone who can. It's not like you're doing a whole lot for my career right now anyway."

There was a pause.

"That was true, when I was on top. Now that I have to fight my way back, you've all but disappeared. You've already quit on me." Another pause. "I don't care what the reporters are saying—listen to what I'm saying. I'm not done yet. And I'm getting back on that team." He spun around and saw her standing there.

Why hadn't she slammed the door or cleared her throat or something? Now she looked like she was eavesdropping.

"I gotta go." Grady held her gaze as he pulled the phone away from his ear.

"I'm sorry. I didn't mean to . . ."

He looked angry. Or maybe something else—hurt?

"Everything okay?"

"Just taking a short break, boss." He moved past her, toward the door.

"Judge is in there." She stopped him just before he pulled the door open.

Grady turned. "Why?"

"Checking up on you, I think."

He let out a heavy sigh. "Great."

She followed him inside, the echo of his phone call playing on repeat in the back of her mind. He wasn't giving up. He was going to fight?

That was good, right?

"There you both are," Judge said when they reappeared.

"Sorry, sir," Grady said. "I had to take a phone call. Thought it would be best to go outside."

"I see." Judge eyed the younger man for several unnerving seconds. "Miss Collins tells me you've been an exceptional worker."

Grady shot her a sideways glance, which she did her best to ignore. "She did, did she?"

"High praise from Quinn," Judge said. "Our girl isn't known to color the truth."

"No, she's certainly not," he said.

Quinn took a step closer. "Grady's helped out a lot, Judge. We started with the Winter Carnival, but he also volunteered to help me get the shop ready for my reopening."

"Just trying to be useful, sir," Grady said.

Judge looked skeptical, but he didn't get a chance to say anything because the front door opened and a flush-faced Jaden walked in. "Sorry I'm late."

"Late for what?" Quinn asked. "I didn't expect you here."

"Not for you, Aunt Quinn," Jaden said. "For Grady. He's training me."

"He's what?"

"I needed a training partner," Grady said. "Someone to keep me accountable. It's hard to wake up at four thirty."

"I wake up at four thirty every day," Judge said.

"Of course you do." Grady laughed. "I am not so disciplined, sir."

"But this is what it takes to compete. Hard work and not quitting when it gets harder." Jaden punctuated his revelation with a nod.

"Is that right?" Judge looked impressed.

"He said he wanted to learn. He wants to compete, and I thought maybe I could help him," Grady said.

Quinn tried not to let that quell her anger, and yet, just looking at Jaden standing there, eyes all wide with expectation, she knew this was no small deal. Her nephew was training with an Olympian—for free—and it had nothing to do with community service.

Well, darn it. She'd wanted to stay mad at him forever. How was she supposed to do that now?

"He's welcome to take a break anytime he wants to," Grady said. "But I can't. I've wasted too much time already." His eyes found Quinn's.

"No way. We're doing this," Jaden said. "Why aren't you dressed?"

"I can't leave yet," Grady said.

What was he saying? That it was up to *her*? Shouldn't he be eyeballing Judge?

"So, let me get this straight," Judge said. "You took this young skier under your wing with no coaxing or prodding from anyone else?"

Grady glanced at Quinn. Had she coaxed him? If she had, she

hadn't meant to. *"Take my nephew skiing"* was not the same as *"Become Jaden's personal trainer."*

"I prodded him," Jaden said. "I've never had a real coach before."

"I'm not a coach," Grady corrected. "Just an older skier."

Judge and that eyebrow again. Looking at Grady with something Quinn almost thought resembled admiration. "Say what you want, son, but you are a coach."

"Right now, he's just a slacker," Jaden said. "We've got a trail run."

"Only if the boss says it's okay," Grady said. "I can come back after dark—make sure everything is set up and ready for tomorrow."

Quinn was still trying to make sense of the way this whole scenario had turned what she thought she knew on its ear. "Uh, sure. Go ahead."

"Thanks, Aunt Quinn."

She and Judge watched as the two of them disappeared out the front door.

"Well, that's interesting," Judge said. "It would seem Harbor Pointe has had a good effect on him after all."

She glanced up and found the older man's eyes tender.

"Why'd you make him stay, Judge?" she asked. "I mean, there's a chance he won't make the Olympic team now."

Judge put a hand on her shoulder. "Sometimes, Quinn, we have to get out of our comfort zone in order to see what else God has for us."

The words hung there, heavy like a cloud thick with rain too stubborn to fall.

"Grady was used to doing things a certain way. I felt like shaking that up a little might knock some sense into his head. We only find out what we're really made of when our backs are up against the wall, you know."

She looked away.

"Sometimes our biggest setbacks turn out to be our greatest blessings." Judge gave her shoulder a slight squeeze. "Looks great in here, kiddo. I'm mighty proud of you. We'll all be here to help you celebrate tomorrow."

She nodded and watched him go, but his words lingered.

Was it time to see what she was made of?

26

THE HELPERS HAD ALL GONE, and the shop was quiet, leaving Quinn alone for a few minutes with thoughts she wished wouldn't come.

She stood in the middle of the neatly packed, perfectly styled shop and snapped a photo. She wanted to remember this day, to mark it fresh in her mind. Maybe even to allow it to replace her old memories of Forget-Me-Not and the woman whose buoyant laugh often invaded her mind.

She was ready. The shop was ready. Why did she still feel so unsure?

She gathered her sketches, her portfolio, her laptop, and stuffed them all in her bag, whispering a gentle prayer that felt more like making a wish on a star.

"Please let this be a success."

She walked over to the Forget-Me-Not wall of memories. Mimi's gold and clashing wooden frames had all been replaced, along with their previously haphazard arrangement on the wall. Now the photos were encased in brand-new white frames with thick white mats and hung with great care.

There was one empty frame, which she would fill after tomorrow's festivities with an image to commemorate her grand reopening.

The image of her with her mom and Carly caught her eye. Maybe she shouldn't have included it on the wall. Maybe it was time to put it away and accept the fact that she wasn't coming back.

Maybe being disqualified from the design competition was confirmation of that.

She touched the face of the little girl in the picture, looking up at a mother who'd made her world come alive. Why did everything have to go so terribly sideways?

Before the knot in her throat manifested itself in tears she absolutely did not want to cry, she heaved her bag up onto her shoulder, turned off the light, and walked out the back door.

She'd do better with a little space between her and the flower shop.

She parked her car in front of Carly's small bungalow and turned off the engine. She'd barely had time to check in with her sister since the ski trip, but she was curious about Jaden's "training." Was Carly aware he was getting up so early and spending so much time with Grady?

She had to admit, it had surprised her, almost endeared her to him a little bit, but her practical side argued with that emotion. What if Grady filled Jaden's mind with Olympic dreams—or worse, stories of his own escapades?

Quinn headed up the walk and knocked on the door, pushing it open as she called out her sister's name.

"Back here!" Carly must be baking.

"I smell something delicious," Quinn called out. She moved toward the kitchen, the smell of cinnamon and banana filling her nostrils.

"Banana bread," Carly said.

"The kind with the crumblies on top?" Quinn exaggerated her inhale as she moved into the kitchen.

"Is there any other kind?"

"Not any kind worth eating," Quinn said. "I didn't come for dinner, but if you're cooking, I'll stay."

Carly packed together a nice-sized meatball and eyed her sister. "There will be plenty, but this isn't all for us."

Quinn walked over to the empty bowl where Carly had mixed together the banana bread. "I love when you don't rinse the bowl out." She slid her finger along the inside of the bowl, scooping out a good amount of the batter, then licked it off. "Even the batter is good."

"I know. That recipe was a good find." Carly rolled another meatball.

"Who's all this for?"

"I thought it would be nice to take a meal to Grady," Carly said.

Quinn only stared.

"Look, I know you don't like the guy, but he's been really great to Jaden. Got him up before dawn the past two days to work out, Quinn. This is Jaden we're talking about here."

"Jaden, the fifteen-year-old who still has schoolwork?"

Carly sighed. "Don't be like that."

"That's actually why I came over here. I'm surprised you're okay with this whole arrangement." Quinn dropped her bag on one of the kitchen chairs and plopped herself in another.

Carly shrugged. "All I know is my kid is happier than I've seen him in a really long time. And his grades have actually gone up the last few weeks." She glanced up at Quinn. "You know how hard things have been with him, Q. I was really starting to worry about him."

"And what? You think Grady is going to cure all of that? What happens when he leaves?"

Carly's forehead wrinkled in what could only be described as maternal concern. "Is this about Jaden? Or you?"

Quinn scoffed. "This is about Jaden. How can you even ask me that?"

"Because I think you like him." Carly raised a brow.

"Grady Benson is not my type, Car; you know that."

Carly walked over to the stove and turned on the burner. "I hate to be the one to break it to you, but you haven't really dated enough to have a type. Marcus doesn't count. You might as well have been dating a piece of lint."

"Gee, thanks."

Carly scrunched her face. "That guy had no personality."

Quinn groaned. "Give me something to eat. A brownie. A cookie. Anything."

"There's Dove chocolate in the drawer," Carly said. "But that's not going to make him go away."

Quinn walked across the kitchen to Carly's stash drawer, where she kept every good and wonderful thing that would make Quinn feel better. At least for a minute. "That's exactly the problem. Well, part of it anyway."

"What is? That chocolate won't make Grady go away?"

"That I don't have . . . experience."

Carly watched her for too many seconds—it made Quinn uncomfortable. "What do you mean?"

"I did an Internet search," Quinn said. "Grady—he's had a lot of girlfriends."

"So?"

"So, I'm not like that, Carly. I should be with someone who . . ."

Carly's face fell. "Someone who hasn't slept around?"

"It's different," Quinn said to the back of her sister's head. "It's different with you and Josh and—"

"Q, by your logic, I don't deserve to be with someone unless he's got a questionable past." Quinn could hear the hurt in her sister's tone as her voice kicked up a notch. "Should I just give up trying to find a decent guy now?"

"That's not what I meant."

"Then what?" Carly spun around. "What is it, Quinn? Because all it sounds like to me is that you're up there on your high horse judging the rest of us for the mistakes we've made because you haven't made any. Admit it: you think you're too good for him."

"That's not true!"

"Then what?"

"I'm scared of him!" The words were out and she could do nothing to reel them back in. She sank back onto the chair. "He scares me to death. He's infuriating and impulsive and dangerous. I am none of those things."

Carly turned the burner down and faced her. "A case could be made that you can be infuriating."

"You know what I mean."

"I do."

"We are completely wrong for each other."

"Why do I feel like you're trying to convince yourself?"

"Tell me what about it would make even a bit of sense. He doesn't even like Harbor Pointe."

"So, you leave."

Quinn's gasp was audible. "I can't leave."

"Why not? Because you never have? It might be good for you." She shook her head. "No. I'm meant to stay right here, to run the flower shop. To marry a nice, uncomplicated man and have kids and live happily ever after. I'm not supposed to go off chasing some adrenaline junkie with no concept of what an actual relationship is."

Carly let out a wry laugh and went back to tossing meatballs in the pan of oil. "Oh, you've got it all figured out, don't you?"

Quinn only stared.

"You think you know just how everything is going to go."

"I have plans, Carly. I'm not going to apologize for that."

"Okay, but things don't always work out like your favorite song, little sister." She threw down her spatula and walked over to her. "This is real life. You can't figure everything out before it even happens." She sat down and covered Quinn's hand with her own. "You're going to miss out on . . . everything."

Quinn looked up at her through clouded, tear-filled eyes. "What if I already have?" Her voice broke and a tear streamed down her cheek. "What if that *is* my greatest mistake?"

The back door popped open and Jaden walked in. "You got that food, Ma?"

Quinn turned away, praying Grady wasn't right behind him.

Carly stood. "It's not ready quite yet."

"Okay. I told him he could just eat with us here."

Quinn stood. "I'm going to go." She slung her bag over her shoulder. "Thanks, Car."

She turned around just as Grady walked in, eyes fixed on her, still perfecting that rugged "I should be on a billboard in Times Square" look.

"Stay and eat, Quinn," Carly said. "I know you've probably been too stressed to sit down for a good meal."

"I can't. Too much to do before tomorrow." It was a lie. Truth was, she had no idea what she would do once she left Carly's. She'd gotten every task on her list finished up early, thanks in part to the help of so many other people, including Grady. "Have a good dinner."

As she drove home, her conversation with Carly replayed in her mind. Her sister was right. She'd pinned her goodness to her shirt like a ribbon she'd won at the state fair, turning herself into a judgmental person who could only see the flaws in the people around her.

How had that happened without her even realizing it? It had blinded her to her own flaws—her inability to forgive, to move beyond the past, to let it all go.

She'd been a prisoner to it her whole life.

And she had no idea how to break loose of those chains.

CHAPTER

27

LATE FRIDAY AFTERNOON, as Grady and Jaden packed the car for their trip up north, all he could think about was how good it would be to get out of town for a few days.

The grand reopening of the flower shop had been the buzz of the town for two days straight, and while he was happy for Quinn, it was hard to get her out of his mind when she was all anyone was talking about.

She'd cold-shouldered him Tuesday night at her sister's house, but he'd gone to the shop on Wednesday regardless. He wanted to congratulate her. He wanted to be a part of her happiness.

Worse, he wanted to be the reason for it.

But she was so busy with the crowd of people who'd come out to celebrate with her that he'd left without saying a word.

Thursday, Ryan Brooks caught Grady in the gym to tell him to report to him that day—something about renovating a small cottage on the other side of the lake. Grady had been dog tired by the time he got home, but he put himself through the paces of his workout anyway and even cooked his own meal.

And the icing on the proverbial cake? He'd heard from Benji that he'd pieced together the money for that month's PT, so he must've either dipped into his own savings or gotten it from their parents, which meant once again, Grady was the letdown. Benji had been coaching kids for a while, but Grady knew that job didn't leave Benji with much extra, and the insurance was only paying about half the bills. Grady had promised he'd take care of his brother. He couldn't break that promise.

He called Pete immediately after he hung up with Benji.

"There's still Spectre," Pete had told him. "They're talking about having you design your own line of ski gear, Grady—it could end up being a pretty sweet deal."

Reluctantly, Grady had given Pete the go-ahead to get some facts and figures. They'd talk about it Monday. And Grady would see just how bad things really were financially. Pete was trying to prove he was still on board, but Grady wasn't convinced.

Now, as he and Jaden headed out of town, he tried to think of something—anything—other than Quinn.

Turned out, he had the world's best distraction riding shotgun in the car. Carly had told him at dinner the other night that Jaden wasn't a talker. He was moody and withdrawn. They'd had trouble with him at school.

"That all kind of changed when you showed up," she said.

At first, the idea of it hadn't sat well with him. He'd always balked at the idea of being anyone's role model. But he actually liked Jaden, and if he'd ever been moody and withdrawn, Grady had never seen it.

At this moment, he was prattling on about a World Cup race where Grady had "absolutely crushed it." It seemed like Jaden had every single one of Grady's races memorized.

"What's it like? Being up there with the cameras? Knowing the whole world is watching?"

Grady chuckled. "Well, it's not the whole world. Lots of people don't watch skiing. Even your aunt had no idea who I was."

"Still. It's a lot of people watching. How do you do it without freaking out?"

"You just do it. You tune all of that out, get in the zone, remember your training, and go for it." Though that wasn't exactly his routine, was it? At least not the "remember your training" part.

But he did know how to get in the zone. He tuned out the rest of the world, the voices in his head—all of it. It was as if the soundtrack of his life were suddenly muted, and it was just him and the finish line. Sometimes his body seemed to move on its own, as if it instinctively knew when to lean, when to push, when to let up. He wished his instincts were that good off the slopes.

"Bet the girls fall all over you," Jaden said.

Grady laughed. "Is that important to you?"

The kid shrugged. "Maybe just one girl."

"Oh, so there's a girl? You talk to her?"

Jaden stared straight ahead. "Nah. She doesn't even know I'm alive. Or if she does, she acts like she doesn't."

Grady sighed. "We always want the ones who won't give us the time of day, don't we?"

"Like you and Aunt Quinn?"

Grady shot him a look.

"Come on. I'm young, but I'm not stupid."

"Let's just say your aunt isn't my biggest fan." Grady hated knowing it was true.

"You two are just different is all," Jaden said.

"How do you figure?" Grady was genuinely curious what kind of insight he could gain from a teenager.

"Well, first of all, the religion thing."

"What religion thing?"

"She's kind of really into Jesus, and you're, you know, into partying."

Grady frowned. "Is that what you think?" *Is that what she thinks?*

Jaden let out a mocking laugh. "Do you read the stuff they write about you?"

Unfortunately, yes.

"It's why Aunt Quinn doesn't want me hanging out with you. She thinks I'll pick up your bad habits." Jaden blew out a stream of air.

"She doesn't want you hanging out with me?"

Jaden's pointed expression was his only reply.

That stung a little. "Because you're into partying too? You think the Jesus stuff is a waste of time?"

Jaden faced him. "Heck no. I'm not into partying. I want to keep my body strong, you know, for the slopes. And me and Jesus are tight."

"For real?"

"Ever since my first time up on skis," Jaden said. "Never feel closer to God than when I'm up there, giving up control."

Grady felt a twinge of something at the back of his mind. He wasn't sure he could relate to that. He was always perfectly in control on the slopes. There was nothing spiritual about it. Besides, his memories of church and religion were more a laundry list of all the things he wasn't allowed to do.

Didn't that pretty much sum up who God was?

Underneath the Jeep, the road clicked along at an even pace. Grady stared straight ahead at the horizon. The sunlight had begun to fade, but his eyes were still shielded by a pair of aviators. He was thankful for that; he didn't need Jaden reading anything into what he was—or wasn't—saying.

"Don't tell me you don't at least believe in God," Jaden said.

No, he did. He just chose to ignore God, same way God had ignored him the day of Benji's accident. He'd sat there, holding his brother in his arms, begging—pleading—for divine intervention, but God had stayed silent. How Benji could still spout off about God's goodness the way he did made no sense to Grady.

Maybe that's what his parents could never understand about Grady. They all went back to church like everything was fine. They still did the whole Bible study thing, and Mom still played her worship songs while she cleaned the house.

And the rage pulled itself into a tight ball at Grady's core.

"See, that's a hill Aunt Quinn isn't gonna climb."

Jaden's voice jerked Grady back to reality. "Sorry, I was thinking about something else. I do believe in God. I just haven't spent a lot of time with him these past few years."

Jaden shrugged. "Maybe you should."

He said it like it was the most obvious thing in the world. A heaviness settled on Grady's shoulders.

"Then there's all the other stuff," Jaden said.

"What?" Grady had lost track of their conversation.

"You and Aunt Quinn. All the other things that make you a terrible match."

"We're still talking about that?" Grady tried to play it off like it was nothing, but the truth was, he didn't want to hear it—not really—because all he heard was *You're not good enough for her.* And of course, he already knew it was true.

But Jaden wasn't done talking. "Like, you have sports and she has flowers. You travel all over and she stays here. I don't know if she's ever even been on an airplane."

"Seriously?"

Jaden shrugged. "Even I've been on an airplane. Went out to see my dad once."

Grady focused on the road in front of him. Jaden had never mentioned his dad before, though Grady had gathered they weren't close. "How'd that go?"

"I haven't seen him since, if that gives you an idea."

Grady kept his eyes on the road. "I haven't seen my dad in a while either."

"I'm talking years here," Jaden said, as if he could one-up Grady.

"Yeah," Grady said. "Me too."

Jaden's wounded eyes found Grady's. "Really?"

Back to the highway in front of him—it was safer to look there. No chance of unwanted emotion creeping in. "We had a sort of falling-out. I haven't been back home since I was eighteen."

"Wow," Jaden said. "Does he ever call or anything?"

Grady shook his head. "Not for years."

The kid's shoulders dipped. "Yeah, mine neither."

"I'm sorry, Jaden," Grady said.

Jaden waved him off. "I'm over it."

But Grady recognized the nonchalance of a protective lie.

"Anyway," Jaden said, "how *do* you get the girls to notice you?"

Grady laughed. A much better topic, for sure. "What's her name?"

"Mariah." Jaden sighed. "Mariah Kramer."

Grady glanced over. "Man, you've got it bad."

"She's perfect. Dark hair. Beautiful. And she skis." He dropped his head back on the seat.

"So what are you going to do about it?" The GPS interrupted their conversation with instructions to take the next exit.

"I told you—she doesn't know I'm alive."

"Win the competition, and maybe that'll all change."

Jaden's grin cut through the darkness in the car. "You think?"

"Why not? You've just got to go for it. Push yourself." When had he become a font of wisdom? He wasn't even sure it was good advice.

"You think I've got what it takes to be as good as you?" Jaden wasn't looking at him now. The question likely made him feel vulnerable, something Grady had a hard time relating to. He rarely let anyone see his own insecurities.

And yet, he'd shown that side to Quinn, hadn't he? Almost immediately. Granted, he was intoxicated at the time, but still. Some part of him must've known from the start that he could trust her.

Maybe his instincts weren't all bad after all.

"No way, buddy," Grady said.

Jaden gave him a sideways glance.

"You've got what it takes to be better."

Even in the darkness, Grady could see the hope on Jaden's face, and it struck him how strange it was that he actually meant what he said. He wasn't blowing smoke or stroking the kid's ego. He *wanted* Jaden to be better than he'd been. Maybe because he deserved it more.

And one way or another, Grady wanted to help make it happen.

CHAPTER

28

GRADY STOOD AT THE TOP OF SUNSHINE MOUNTAIN, adrenaline coursing through his veins. Had it really only been a couple of weeks since his last real run? He fixed his goggles onto his face and drew in a deep breath.

Memories spun through his mind—past races, mistakes made, advice from coaches he'd mostly ignored. He latched on to all of it now, determined to extract the wisdom he'd discarded so many times before.

"You praying?" Jaden had come up beside him, but Grady hadn't noticed.

"No. Just getting focused."

Jaden gave him a nod, his expression serious, then closed his eyes. He *was* praying. Grady felt like he should look away—but Jaden didn't seem to mind anyone watching him connect with his Creator.

"Let's do it." Jaden pulled his goggles down with a grin. "Any words of wisdom, Coach?"

"Yeah, don't fall."

And with that, he took off like a shot, certain the kid wouldn't be able to catch him. Jaden might have youth on his side, but he didn't have the power Grady had. That power was what had won world championships.

It was the little mistakes that seemed to cost Grady. Turning too soon. Overcompensating. Wanting it too much.

The thought startled him.

Wanting it too much? Was there such a thing?

He shot around a curve, body as close to the powder as he could get, then up over a rise, and for a brief moment he felt like he was floating. The sun shone behind him, making his visibility nearly perfect. His speed wasn't there yet, but it would be after he knew the slope a little better. One, maybe two times down, and he'd have it.

Jaden's words rushed back at him as the rest of the world fell away. Another jump—air between his skis and the ground.

How would it feel to really give up control? To trust that he could be carried by something greater than him? To believe that there was a God who cared enough to answer when Grady called?

But then, Grady never called. Not since he was fourteen.

He picked up speed as he zipped around to the right. He'd turned seconds too soon, but he corrected the error and kept going. He couldn't afford to make mistakes like that.

Another jump—this one bigger than the others—sent Grady into the air. Weightless. Free.

As he came back down, he realized he'd never been in control up here. Not really. Sure, he could do all the things he knew how to do. He could cut and carve. He could practically fly, but he had no control over what happened. Not winning or losing. Not falling or failing. Why had he spent so many years thinking he did?

He shot through to the end of the run, then came to a stop. He was out of breath—out of practice.

The rest of the day, he worked. Tirelessly and like he never had before. When he wanted to quit, he thought of Quinn, Benji, and that spot on the team. Maybe he did want it too much, but if he could find a way to take that desire and turn it into something positive instead of something crippling, he was going to do it.

By the end of the day, he had a feel for the course. He'd practically memorized it, so now it was time to prove he still had enough gas in his tank to compete with guys ten years younger than him.

He stood at the top of the hill just as he had that morning, and Jaden showed up beside him. "There's a crowd down there."

Grady kept his eyes on the course, still imagining it in his head. *Cut left. Jump. Turn right. Jump.*

"Someone found out it was you up here," Jaden said. "I think they could tell by the way you ski."

Time was, that compliment would've affected Grady. Today, he saw it as a distraction. "Not doing this for them."

Jaden smiled. "Yeah, I get it. You've got something to prove to yourself."

Grady pulled his goggles over his eyes.

"Get it done, man. Give up control."

Grady stood, perched on the precipice not unlike the mountains he'd conquered so many times before, but this one felt different somehow. It felt important.

For the briefest moment, he closed his eyes.

Okay, God. I'll try it your way. You take control.

As his arms propelled him forward and he crouched in the stance he'd been perfecting for years, he heard Jaden's words loud and clear echoing in the back of his mind.

"Give up control."

Cut left. Jump.

With the wind beneath him, he started to feel it, that loss of himself, that surrender to something greater.

Turn right. Jump.

Midair, he did something he never did—he exhaled.

Another turn. Another jump. Another exhale.

Something bigger than him. It was here, on the slopes, every time he went over a hill. He'd always looked at it as cheating death—daring whatever it was that had been out there that day with him and Benji to come back and finish the job. But today, here, it all felt different.

He rushed through to the finish, same way he had so many times that day, but this time, a crowd had gathered, just as Jaden said. They cheered as he streaked by, but he didn't care.

He bent at the waist as he slid to a stop. He'd given everything on that last run, left it all on the slopes, exactly like his coaches had told him to. For years, he thought he'd done that, but he'd always been holding back.

"You gotta ski with your heart, Grady," Happy had told him. *"That's where the good stuff is."*

He got it now. Give up control and just ski. The rest was out of his hands.

He stood up and moved toward the crowd, most of whom were still watching him, some waiting for photos or autographs.

But before he could sign or pose, he heard someone shout, "We need help up here!"

He looked over and saw a guy who'd just barreled past. He called out again. "Can we get some help?"

Grady's heart dropped. *Oh no. Jaden.*

"What's going on?" He rushed over to the guy.

"There's a kid up there. Crashed. I left my buddy up there with him so I could come get help."

"Blue ski coat?"

"You know him?"

"Yeah, let's go."

Quinn had just finished setting the table when Carly's cell phone rang. She'd left it on the table and run outside because she forgot her purse in the car. Quinn thought almost nothing of it until it stopped and her own phone started ringing almost instantly.

She pulled it out and saw Grady's name on her screen.

"Hey." One word and she could tell something was wrong. "What is it?"

"Are you with your sister?"

"Yeah, she's outside. What's going on?"

"Quinn, it's Jaden," he said. "There was an accident."

~⁓~

Bad things always happened around Christmas. Didn't it seem that way? Or maybe accidents simply seemed worse because of the time of year. This one sure did. Tomorrow, they were supposed to celebrate Christmas Eve at her dad's. Instead, they'd be lucky if they were home from the hospital.

The drive up north felt like a nightmare. Their dad drove with Beverly riding up front and Carly and Quinn in the back.

Quinn was feeling downright irate with Grady for taking her nephew skiing in the first place and with Carly for letting him go. She wanted to scream, "I told you so!" like a dutiful (but annoying) little sister, but of course she didn't.

She held her tongue. Because it wasn't the time. And because Grady had given them almost no information as to what happened or how Jaden was doing or if he was going to be okay.

Quinn stared out the window, mind racing with horrifying possibilities.

No. Stop it. He's going to be fine.

Carly sniffed. Quinn reached over and took her hand. "He's going to be okay."

Quinn's phone buzzed in her lap and she answered it before the first full ring ended. "Grady?" She put the phone on speaker.

"Hey," he said. "We're at the hospital now. They're talking about surgery."

"Surgery?" Carly practically shrieked. "On what?"

"Looks like his leg is broken," Grady said. "They're checking into a few other possible injuries."

Carly grabbed the phone. "What kind of injuries?"

Grady paused. "They're concerned about his head. He spun out of control and hit a tree. His helmet came off."

"But you talked to him, right?" Carly asked. "He's awake and everything?"

"Yeah, we talked a little," Grady said.

He sounded exhausted. Worried. And it was in that moment that her anger began to dissipate.

"Where were you when he spun out?" Carly's tone accused.

A brief pause, then, "I was already at the bottom."

Carly scoffed. "So, what? He was trying to keep up with *you*?"

"No, he wasn't. He—"

"I should never have let him go with you," Carly cut in. "I should've listened to Quinn."

"Carly—"

"He wasn't ready. You were right." Carly dropped the phone back in Quinn's lap. "He was probably trying to show off for Grady and he wasn't ready." Her voice broke.

Quinn took the phone off speaker and stuck it against her ear. "You there?"

"I'm here," he said, his voice quiet. "She's right. It's my fault. Jaden was my responsibility."

"Grady, don't say that."

"I gotta go."

"Grady—"

But he was already gone.

"You tried to tell me," Carly said. "I should've listened. He's a terrible role model for Jaden."

"We don't know what happened, Car," Quinn said. "Grady may not have had anything to do with it."

"I can't believe it." Carly faced her. "Are you defending him? My kid is in the hospital, and you're defending the man who put him there?"

"He didn't 'put him there,' Carly. It was an accident." Quinn had clearly lost her mind. If anyone asked her later if she'd defended Grady on this point she would surely deny it.

Carly turned away.

"Your sister is right, Carly," Dad said from the front seat. "You know Grady didn't force Jaden out there. You couldn't keep him off the slopes if you tried."

Carly swiped her hand across her cheek.

"If anything, I have to say I think Grady has been good for Jaden," Dad said.

And Quinn, for all her doubting, agreed. She never would've predicted it, but it was true, even in these circumstances.

Dad tried to catch Carly's eye in the rearview mirror. "This injury—whatever it is—it's a setback, not an ending."

"But we don't know that, Dad," Carly said, voice breaking. "What if he can never ski—or walk—again?"

"No sense dwelling on the what-ifs," Dad said. "Only one thing to do now."

Carly's head dropped, and once again, Quinn reached over and took her hand.

"Let's pray."

⁓

For three hours, Grady sat in the waiting room at the tiny hospital in a town he didn't even know the name of. A paltry Christmas tree strung with popcorn and crocheted ornaments had been propped in the corner. It was hardly festive.

When he got tired, he stood. Paced. Tried hard not to replay the scene out on the slope. Tried even harder to keep his mind from spinning back to the day of Benji's accident.

The visibility had been good that day too. The snow fresh. The trail clear.

If we'd just stayed on the trail . . .

Would Carly ever forgive him? Would Quinn? Maybe he'd

overestimated Jaden's abilities? Gotten too carried away with his own training and taken his eye off the kid? If he'd been paying closer attention, maybe he would've spotted an error in Jaden's form or helped steer him back on track. He could've preempted this disaster.

Grady had reached Jaden just a few minutes before the medical staff.

"Buddy," he'd said. "What happened?"

"Went for it, man, just like you said." He tried to move but grimaced at the pain.

"Just stay still. We're getting help."

"Good. It's all in God's hands now."

"What?" Grady flinched at the words.

"Out of my control." The kid's eyes fluttered shut.

"Jaden, stay awake," Grady said, sure that letting him pass out was about the worst thing he could do.

Now, pacing the floor of the hospital waiting room for the millionth time, when he replayed the words, he balked.

How could he say it was in God's hands? Hadn't it been in God's hands *before* he wiped out? Where was God then?

Where were you?

The doors slid open and Carly rushed through, followed by Gus, Beverly, and Quinn. The very sight of her settled something inside him.

Carly rushed past him to the front desk. "I need to see my son."

"He's still in surgery," Grady said, drawing their attention. The medical staff had called Carly for her consent not long after he had hung up with Quinn.

"Have they given you any updates?" Carly asked.

Grady shook his head. He felt useless.

Carly turned back to the sturdy-looking nurse with tightly curled hair. "I need an update on my son."

"Name?"

"Jaden Collins. He was in a skiing accident."

"Have a seat," the nurse said.

Carly leaned in closer. "You want me to sit down?"

"If you want information, you'll have a seat." The nurse glared.

"I've been sitting in a car for three hours, lady." Carly might come unhinged.

Quinn put a hand on Carly's shoulder as the nurse stared her down. "Let's sit. She'll find out what she can."

Carly hesitated, but finally pulled her gaze away from the nurse. They all moved toward Grady and sat down.

"Did he say anything to you?" Carly asked. "Before they took him away?"

Grady met her eyes. "Yeah, actually. He said, 'It's all in God's hands now.'"

Carly didn't move. "Jaden said that?"

Grady nodded.

She covered her face with her hands and hurried to wipe the tears away as fast as they fell. Quinn slid an arm around her sister and glanced up at Grady, kindness in her dark-brown eyes.

"That's one smart kid," Gus said. "It's all in God's hands now." He took Beverly's hand and bowed his head.

The scene was different from when Benji was the one on the operating table. That day, there had been no prayer—for all of their religious talk, his parents didn't seem to rely on God the way Quinn's family did. Instead, his dad spent that time blaming Grady for the accident.

Maybe that was the day Grady stopped trusting in anything bigger than himself. Maybe he'd never seen genuine faith at work before.

But here it was, in front of him. And he had to wonder if it was the thing that had made Quinn different from the start.

Grady shifted, feeling not only like an outsider but an impostor. Would his own God issues hinder their prayers from reaching the heavens? He didn't want to chance it. "Do you want me to get you some coffee?"

"I'll go with you." Quinn stood.

If she noticed his surprise, she didn't let on. "I think the cafeteria is in the basement."

Under different circumstances, getting coffee with Quinn might've been pleasant, even exciting. But he was wrung out, his emotions raw. This whole day had brought back too many memories, and along with them his old travel buddies, guilt and shame.

She leaned against the wall of the elevator as he pushed the button that would take them to the basement. "What are you thinking about?"

He studied the gray floor of the elevator, maybe with a little too much interest. "My brother, actually."

The elevator doors opened and the empty hospital cafeteria came into view. It was closed at this late hour, but there were vending machines off to the side. Hopefully one of them had coffee.

He fished some change from his coat pocket, thankful she wasn't prodding him to go on. He'd been replaying that day, everything that happened with Benji, for hours. Saying any of it aloud would be nearly impossible.

And yet, she was safe. If there were ever a time to get it all out, this was it.

Wasn't it?

"Do you want something?"

"A mocha would be good," she said.

He nodded, stuck more change in the machine, and waited for it to spit out her drink. She took it from him and met his eyes. The great divide between them seemed to have lessened.

"Are you okay?" he asked.

She nodded. "Jaden was right. It's in God's hands."

He laughed. "You guys and your God talk." He started toward a table in the dimly lit cafeteria. "Mind if we sit here a minute?"

She shook her head and sat across from him. "You don't buy into all this God stuff?"

It was an important question, and he knew it. Not only because Jaden had told him this was one of the greatest differences between them, but because he could see it on her face. He shrugged. He didn't want to lie to her. "I guess my idea of religion is a little skewed. My parents preached a lot, but I'm not sure how much they practiced." But earlier that day—he'd given over control. And he'd felt genuinely free.

How did he keep that feeling once he was back on the ground?

Quinn gave a soft nod.

"I can tell it's important to you and your family," he said.

"It's everything." She looked away. "I can't imagine getting through something like this without my faith. I think I'd end up angry."

"At me?"

"At God." Quinn met his eyes.

Something inside him shifted, and for a split second he felt like she could see straight through him.

"I don't think your sister loves having me here," he said, anxious to change the subject.

"She's just stressed out," Quinn said.

"I actually thought you'd be the one who would be mad at me." She took a drink. "This is kind of terrible."

"You're used to fancy coffee drinks." He took a sip of his own black coffee. "Oh, nope. You're right. It is terrible."

She laughed. "I thought I'd be mad at you too, but I'm sure it wasn't your fault. It was an accident."

He stared past her, willing away the unwanted emotion that balled up in his throat. "Maybe it was my fault."

He didn't have to look at her to know her eyes were fixed on him.

"He trusted me to guide him," Grady said. "I just got so caught up in my own skiing, maybe I didn't give him enough coaching."

"He's not a beginner, Grady. He does know his way around that mountain."

Grady forced another drink down, mostly an attempt to distract himself. He would've changed the subject if he'd been able to think of a single thing to say.

"Jaden told me you didn't want him training with me," Grady said. "Maybe you were right."

She straightened. "I'm sorry I said those things. I was wrong. I actually think you've been good for Jaden."

Grady shook his head. "Obviously not."

"You didn't force him to go with you. Don't beat yourself up over this."

"You don't understand, Quinn. This isn't the first time something like this has happened. And last time . . ." His voice trailed off.

"Last time, what?" He didn't miss the concern in her voice.

He shouldn't tell her about Benji. Not right now, not when her nephew was lying on the operating table somewhere in this very hospital. And yet . . . her eyes pleaded with him for one honest moment.

"Forget it," he said.

"Grady, you can tell me."

He thought about her faith, Jaden's faith—the way God had ignored him up there on those slopes. Grady was the one taunting death—why wasn't he the one getting hurt?

"You were right to push me away, Quinn." The words physically pained him, but he knew they were true. "I'm not good enough for you."

He studied her from across the table. Her long blonde hair was pulled into a loose bun, her eyes centered squarely on him. There was something simple about her. She wasn't fussy and didn't pretend to be. Somehow it made her more beautiful than every woman he'd ever known.

"I'm not good enough yet," he said. "But I want to be."

He braced himself for whatever it was she was about to say, but before she could respond, the elevator just outside the cafeteria dinged and Gus appeared.

"He's out of surgery," the older man said. "And he's asking for you, Grady."

CHAPTER

29

QUINN STOOD OUTSIDE Jaden's fourth-floor post-op room with her dad and Beverly, waiting for Grady to finish talking to Jaden so she could go in and check on him herself.

The hospital had a strict policy allowing only two people in the room at a time, and at that moment, Quinn found rules annoying.

"He's going to be fine," her dad said. "The doctor said the surgery went well, and while he's groggy, he's strong."

She peered through the narrow window in the hospital room door. "Will he ski again?"

Dad looked at Beverly, then back at Quinn. "We don't know yet."

It would crush Jaden if he couldn't ski anymore. And yet, if it was this dangerous, how smart was it to keep going?

She glanced at the nurses' station, then back at her dad. "I'm going in. I don't care about the stupid rule."

She pushed the door open and slid inside like she was some kind of burglar. Carly, Jaden, and Grady all turned toward her.

"You guys are taking too long," Quinn said. "I wanted to see for myself how he's doing." She focused on Jaden. "How are you feeling?"

His eyelids looked heavy, his nod difficult. "I'll be okay."

"The leg is broken in two places," Carly said. "But the head injury was minor. Thank God for that helmet we spent a fortune on." She squeezed Jaden's arm. "Good thing it didn't come off until after you hit the tree."

Quinn glanced at Grady, whose eyes were bloodshot and tired. She'd ached for him to open up to her, wished she could be a person he could trust, but once again, he'd shut down. Changed the subject. What secrets was he keeping buried so deeply inside?

Why had he left so much unspoken?

"I'm not good enough for you." His words had shamed her because she, sitting on her throne of judgment, had once agreed with them. Didn't she believe that God could get ahold of this man and turn his life inside out? Wasn't everyone redeemable?

But Grady had to want that first. She couldn't want it for him.

"Grady's gonna help me get back up there," Jaden mumbled.

He was already talking about skiing again? Shouldn't he let himself heal first?

"When you're ready," Grady said, as if he'd read her mind.

But Quinn knew what Jaden didn't: Grady would be long gone by that time.

"I'm gonna head back to the hotel." Grady stood. "Get some sleep." He picked up his coat, then turned back. "You scared me to death today, kid."

"Sorry," Jaden slurred.

"Just get better, okay?"

"Grady," Carly said. "I'm sorry—for reacting the way I did. I didn't mean—"

He stopped her with an upheld hand. "It's fine. I get it. And I meant what I said—whatever I can do to help him get better, I'll do it."

"Thanks." Carly gave him a soft smile.

He turned, eyes working their way up to Quinn's. "Night." He moved past her quickly, his shoulder brushing against hers before he stole out of the room, leaving an emptiness behind.

Whatever she'd thought about Grady Benson, she'd been wrong. At least partly wrong. There was more to him than she'd ever imagined, and as she recalled the pain behind his eyes, she felt her resolve to stay away from him crumbling.

———

Christmas had been somber, to say the least. With Jaden knocked out on painkillers and Carly a fussing mess, they'd barely even had a chance to eat a complete meal. Quinn tried not to be too disappointed, even though Christmas was her favorite time of year.

The next day, her father asked her to play Santa Claus and deliver a stack of gifts to Grady. She stared at the neatly wrapped presents and wondered how long it had been since someone had hand-wrapped a gift for him. Had anyone ever knit Grady a scarf like Beverly or picked up a box of Harbor Pointe peanut brittle at the old-fashioned candy store like Calvin? Surely nobody but Dad had ever given him a Harbor Pointe key chain with the engraving *Can't wait to get back home.*

The gifts were small potatoes compared to the kind of presents he was probably used to.

She showed up on his doorstep and rang the bell, but there was no answer. She left the gifts on the porch and drove away, wondering if he was inside the cottage, watching her go.

In the days that followed Jaden's accident, Quinn turned her attention back to the flower shop and the Winter Carnival. In the evenings, she'd sit with Jaden while Carly was at work, or meet with her carnival team to make sure things were still on track. Her days were spent pulling together the arrangements that would fill the pavilion.

Disqualified from the Best Design competition, Quinn could breathe a little and even indulge creative ideas that hit her along the way without worrying they would be the wrong choice.

Once she was able to take a step back from the emotional turmoil of Jaden's accident, her sense of logic returned, and she resigned herself to becoming a bystander in Grady's life. Occasionally she ran into Grady, and while she was cordial, she wasn't friendly. His shoulder was cold toward her, as if he now believed what she'd said all along. They weren't a good fit.

Besides, the clock was running out on his time in Harbor Pointe, and while she hadn't resorted to crossing off the days on her calendar, she did know exactly how many were left.

Not many. Not nearly enough.

She'd been perfectly content before she ever knew he existed—she could get back there again. It was just taking a little longer than she thought it would.

On the opening day of the Winter Carnival, December 30, Quinn woke up early, her to-do list fresh in her mind. She pulled on a pair of ripped jeans, a tank top, and a flannel shirt, along with her favorite pair of fur-lined low boots and her coat, and trudged over to the pavilion, where several people had already begun working.

There was a table of coffee and donuts near the wall and volunteers milled around, waiting for their marching orders. She hadn't expected to see Grady out so early, but there he was, off to the side, looking like one of them.

If she didn't know how much he hated this so-called awful town, she might actually think it had grown on him.

He held a disposable coffee cup, and when he spotted her, he lifted it as if to say hello.

She waved, then filled her own cup and picked up a donut.

"You're eating that?" Lucy appeared at her side.

"Don't judge."

"Oh, I'm not judging," Lucy said. "You know me; I eat whatever I want—but you never do. Aren't you worried you won't fit into your dress for the ball?"

Quinn took a bite. "Nope."

"Well, good for you." Lucy grinned. "I'm proud of you."

Quinn raised her eyebrows. "You've taught me well."

"Yet I'm the one without a date."

"Where's Derek?"

"Working. Out of town. As usual." She pouted.

"Well, I don't have a date." Quinn swallowed the bite.

Lucy shot a look across the crowd. "I thought you were going with Grady?"

She frowned. "Why would you think that?"

Lucy shrugged. "I guess I assumed."

"You assumed wrong."

Mrs. Trembley tapped the microphone up on the stage. "Attention. Attention, everyone. Can you hear me?"

The crowd began to settle as they listened to the old woman's instructions, most of which weren't necessary, given that a majority of the volunteers had been working at the event for years. Still, they let her ramble.

While the woman talked, Quinn ran through a mental checklist of what she and her team needed to do to turn this pavilion into the stunning secret garden she had in her head.

Once Mrs. Trembley finished, the crowd began to scatter, and Quinn's team found their way to her. Danny gave her his trademark awkward smile.

"You look nice today, Quinn," he said.

She glanced down at her disaster of an outfit and mumbled a thank-you, looking away just in time to catch Grady's amused grin.

"Okay, people," she said, trying to remember that she was the one in charge of this team. "It's the day we've been planning for. We've got roughly eight hours to pull this thing off."

"I can't stay here for eight hours," Ashley said. "I have to go get ready for the ball."

Quinn pressed her lips together to keep from saying something snarky. "Maybe just stay as long as you can, okay, Ashley?"

"Whatever," she said. She turned to Grady. "You're dancing with me tonight, Mr. Olympian."

Grady shifted, then glanced at Quinn, who did her best not to look flustered.

She was pretty sure she failed.

She laid out the plan. The ice sculptures had been finished yesterday, which meant they could begin assembling the arches and walkways immediately. She had a specific map, which she'd detailed color-by-number style, so there would be no confusion over which flowers went where. When she was finished, guests would feel like they were walking into a garden maze, and the masquerade theme of the ball would be the perfect complement to her designs.

The day wore on. They worked. They made multiple trips to and from the flower shop to gather all the flowers she'd already arranged from the coolers in the back of the store.

Twice Grady had come to her aid, once when she almost dropped two big buckets of flowers and once when she nearly fell off a ladder.

His hands were around her in a split second, lowering her safely to solid ground. It upended her inside, but she managed to thank him before walking away.

All day long, it was like he was there, but just out of her reach. And it left her teetering back and forth between what she'd resigned to do and what her heart wanted to do.

She didn't like the precipice of uncertainty.

By evening, most of the volunteers had gone home to get ready, and Quinn welcomed the quiet. She wanted to walk through the space once without the commotion of so many bodies. Just to be sure it met her standards, lived up to the image in her head.

She stood in front of the main stage, where the band for tonight's ball would play. It looked beautiful. The reflections of the white lights shimmered in the mirrors she'd placed throughout the space, sprays of wild, untamed flowers mixing with the various ice sculptures. The chandeliers were dimly lit, adding a warm glow in spite of the cool weather. Sadness clung to her at the thought of not being able to compete at the Expo. So much had happened over the last week, but it didn't dull the pain of losing her chance to prove herself to her mother.

What if she didn't have another design this good inside of her?

"I'm sorry about the competition thing." It was Grady, standing behind her, reading her mind once again.

She stared straight ahead, eyes fixed on the stage. He'd surprised her today, the way he stuck around and helped. He worked with the fervor of someone who was invested. Like it meant something. But then, he'd surprised her before, hadn't he?

"It's okay," she said, unable to hide the sadness in her voice. "There's always next year, right?"

He took a step forward and stood at her side. "For some of us."

The race. It must be weighing heavily on him now, only three weeks away. She hadn't been following the competition, but she had been following Grady. She'd seen him at the grocery store in the produce aisle, running along the streets of Harbor Pointe, and even sitting across from Jaden while her nephew recuperated.

Was this him trying to become a better man?

"Will you be back tonight?" she asked.

"Course," he said. "Can't let you locals have all the fun."

She smiled and looked away.

"Missed seeing that." He faced her now, his nearness unraveling the knot in her stomach. "Missed you."

She glanced up at him, wishing everything about him made sense to her when nothing—absolutely nothing—did.

"Save me a dance?"

She smiled. "If you can find me."

He groaned. "You're doing that whole mask thing, then?"

"Of course I am." She gave him a slight nudge, and he grabbed hold of her wrist, looking at her with those eyes. She steadied herself.

"Quinn, I've been thinking . . ."

So had she. Nonstop. And she needed to knock it off. "I have to get home."

He released his grip on her and pulled his hand away. "Of course. I'll see you tonight."

She started off, but after only a few steps, she stopped and turned back. "Grady?"

His attention was instant.

"Thank you."

His shoulders dropped. "For what?"

"Everything. Being there for Jaden. Helping with all this." Her eyes found the ground. "Not giving up on me."

What was she saying? Warning bells went off at the back of her mind. Where was her logical side now?

He inched closer and picked up her hand. "I could never."

With her free hand, she reached up and touched the scar just above his brow. "I want to know where you got this scar."

"It's a really stupid story." There was shyness in his smile.

"But it's your story. And I want to know it."

He looked away. "Not all of my stories are good ones, Quinn."

She found his eyes. He had a past—one that he wasn't proud of. Was she going to continue to hold that against him, or was it possible to move beyond it—together? Slowly, she wove her hand up around him, pulling him closer. "I'll save you that dance."

His face warmed into a lopsided smile. "You really drive me crazy, you know it?"

Somehow she didn't think he meant it as an insult.

"See you tonight." She pulled out of his grasp and smiled. And she realized she could hardly wait to get back to him.

CHAPTER

30

IT WAS ALL TOO MUCH. The accident. The memories. *Her.*

Grady was ready to walk away until she turned around and thanked him. Looking at her then—her eyes so earnest and honest, like no one he'd ever known. He knew he didn't deserve her, but oh, he wanted her.

In the week since Jaden's accident, Grady had done a lot of soul-searching. He'd cashed out some stocks and caught up on Benji's medical bills, instructing the hospital to send back the half of the payment his brother had made. It was a Band-Aid, and he knew it, but he'd take the rest as it came. He'd kept up with his training. Made an important phone call that might turn out to be fruitless—but maybe not. And he'd even reached out to Brian, and that conversation had taken a lot of courage.

Brian wasn't convinced anything about Grady had changed, figured it was just a ploy to get back on his good side, and that was okay. Grady wouldn't try to twist his arm—not with words, anyway. He'd let his skiing and his attitude speak for themselves.

His workouts were going well, and though he spent his evenings soaking his weary muscles, he was getting stronger, feeling better and more ready for his race than ever before.

Perhaps the biggest surprise, though, was that he'd started praying—some version of praying, anyway. It wasn't pretty or poetic, but it was honest, and he had to believe it was enough.

He didn't sense a huge change, not yet anyway. But he wasn't playing the short game here, and he wasn't giving up.

The Winter Carnival drew a good-size crowd, considering that Harbor Pointe wasn't a big town. He carried his mask, shocked to see there wasn't a single face that wasn't covered.

"You better put that on," Ryan Brooks said, coming up beside him. "If they see you without one, I think you get sentenced to two more weeks of community service."

Grady laughed. "Don't act like that's so crazy around here." He stuck the mask on his face.

"Good to see you, man. Your big race is coming up. Feeling good?"

"Feeling ready," Grady said, though even thinking about it kicked up the nerves in his belly. "Well, I *will be* ready."

"I'm inviting the whole town out to watch it in the clubhouse. We can't all fly to Colorado, but we can cheer you on from here." Ryan clapped a hand on Grady's shoulder, and he was thankful for the mask covering his eyes. He'd never had a cheering squad, at least not one made up of people he knew.

"Thanks. That means a lot."

A dark-headed woman came up behind Ryan and wrapped her arms around him. "You owe me a dance, Brooks."

"Okay, but hurry up before my fiancée sees me."

"Funny." She swatted him on the shoulder. "Hey, Grady."

"Hey, Lane."

"We'll catch up with you later," Ryan said, letting Lane pull him onto the dance floor.

Grady watched them, something like envy rising up inside. He didn't often envy other people, but Ryan and Lane had something special—it was obvious. He hoped one day he'd have something worth holding on to.

He wandered through the pavilion, captivated by the beauty of the white lights, the ice sculptures, and yes, the flowers. Quinn had cast the vision, and it had turned out perfectly.

He listened to the chatter as people marveled at her artistry. If only he could find her to congratulate her himself.

As he wound his way through the crowd, he maneuvered around the tall, circular tables evenly spaced throughout. Servers zigzagged through the maze carrying trays of champagne and hors d'oeuvres.

He stopped near one of the tall tables and turned a quick circle, hoping to spot Quinn, but in the sea of black tuxes and formal dresses, he came up empty.

"It's quite beautiful, don't you think?" A regal-looking woman stood at the nearest tall table, a program of the night's events splayed in front of her with a few other papers.

He nodded. "It really is."

"Were you involved with—" she waved her hand in the air—"all this?"

"Sort of."

"What's your favorite part?"

Grady reminded himself that people in Harbor Pointe weren't the same kind of nosy as the people he usually encountered. These people actually cared about more than tabloids and headlines.

"The flowers, hands down," he said, still admiring the scene in front of him. White lights had been hung from the rafters of the pavilion, casting light like diamonds on the dance floor. And while the snow statues scattered throughout the space had all been decorated with sprays of Quinn's flowers, it was the display on the stage that was truly magical. One of the sculptors had created the likeness of a little girl peeking behind a giant, ornate door, which revealed the display Quinn had intended to enter in the contest that had been so important to her.

"What do you like about them?" the woman asked, moving closer to him. "If you don't mind my asking."

He glanced down at the papers on the table in front of her and eyed the words *Floral Expo Best Design* at the top of one of them. It looked like an entry form. "May I ask why you're so interested?"

The woman smiled from behind her mask. There was something familiar about that smile. It reminded him of . . .

"I believe art, whether it's floral design or a painting or something else entirely, should make a person *feel* something. It's interesting to hear what other people feel, is all." She folded her program over the other papers and tucked them in her purse.

"It makes me feel—" he looked around—"free, I guess. Like here, none of my mistakes matter. There's just this peaceful existence where I can be who I am."

The woman at his side shifted. "You're the one who called."

He pushed the mask onto the top of his head. "And you're Quinn's mother."

The woman reached into her purse and pulled out a photo identical to the one Quinn had framed on the wall of the flower shop. In it, two laughing girls, dancing alongside a young woman, as if they didn't have a care in the world.

"I didn't think you'd come," Grady said.

"But you called anyway," Jacie said.

"I felt like it was my fault Quinn was disqualified. It was really important to her. And look around—she's crazy talented."

The woman's smile came and went so quickly he almost missed it. "She is."

"And she's really special."

Her head tilted as she studied him. "You're in love with her."

He looked away, still drinking in the beauty of what Quinn had created. The beauty of her soul, which she'd poured out into every bit of this design. Love? He'd never been in love with anybody—not really. But was that what this was?

He turned back. "I don't know why you left, but I know it would mean a lot to her if she could see you."

Jacie shook her head. "That's not a good idea."

Grady frowned. "But you came all this way."

"Against my better judgment, yes. But don't misunderstand, Mr. Benson. I'm here in a professional capacity only."

"Is that why you brought that photograph?"

She tucked the picture back inside her purse. "It's been too long. Too many years—too many mistakes and missed opportunities."

"Too many to be forgiven?"

His own words stunned him for a split second. Were *his* mistakes too many to be forgiven? He'd always felt they were, but what if— just what if—he was wrong? Seeing Jacie standing there, he was sure the mistakes of her past could be redeemed somehow. Why didn't he believe the same thing about himself?

"Those girls are better off without me," she said.

"But are you better off without them?"

She held his gaze for a moment, then looked away. "The design is beautiful. I'm glad I got to see it. Thank you for reaching out."

"Mrs. Whitman, wait." His hand on her arm stopped her from leaving. "You can't come in here and not even see her. She'll be devastated if she finds out."

"Mr. Benson, I have a new family now. They're my priority."

"But what about Quinn? What about Carly? Did you know you have a grandson?"

The woman stiffened, looking suddenly uncomfortable. "This was a mistake. I have to go." She pulled her arm away and started for the door moments before Quinn walked up beside him.

"I knew you'd never find me," she said. "I swear you looked at me twice and didn't even know it was me."

"Wow," Grady said, admiring the way the deep-teal dress fit her curves. "You look amazing." Her honey-colored hair was mostly pulled up, a few purposeful curls decorating her face on either side.

She smiled. "Thanks. You clean up pretty nice yourself. I was saving you that dance."

He drank her in for a long moment, this beautiful woman with so much buried pain. Would telling her about her mother only make that pain worse?

He slipped his hand into Quinn's and led her to the dance floor, pulling her close as they swayed to the music.

Near the exit, he spotted the regal woman in the red dress watching, mask at her side. Eyes fixed on the two of them, Jacie stared longingly, the way a person looks when her mistakes become so immense they're unable to be tamed.

He should go to her, force her to come back and at least give Quinn the closure she so desperately wanted.

But as he held her gaze, the older woman crumpled, covered her face again, and turned away.

And then she was gone.

CHAPTER

31

QUINN STOOD UNDER THE SPOTLIGHTS, trying not to overthink the scenario playing out around her. She tried to tell herself it was just the twinkling lights and not the way he looked in that tuxedo. It was the dreamy, magical snow garden she'd created and not the way he'd sat by her nephew's side every day since they returned from up north. It was the fact that they were standing in a sea of couples and certainly not the way his hands rested on the small of her back, as if he were protecting her from things she didn't even know existed.

She drew in a deep breath as he pulled her closer.

Could she give herself one minute without the barrage of internal questions?

"You did an amazing job," he whispered. "Everything is beautiful."

She relaxed into him ever so slightly. "You know, I can't believe I'm going to say this out loud, but I have you to thank for it."

He inched back so he could see her face, not hiding the incredulous look on his own. "Is that right?"

She pulled her gaze from his. "When you first got here I was so blocked. I had no idea what I was going to do for this design, and it was important. My first time doing this without Mimi. My first time entering the Expo design contest. My only shot at reconnecting with my mother. And it's not in my nature to relax—"

"I never would've guessed that about you."

She smiled at his interruption. "I was pretty worked up."

"I remember."

"Do you remember what you said to me?"

"Something profound, I'm sure."

"You said when you think of a secret garden, you think of something wild and untamed."

"I said that?"

She met his eyes and nodded. "It was a simple thing, really, but it shook something loose in the right side of my brain. I could hardly keep up with the ideas. I sketched and colored and looked up flowers I'd only ever heard of, and this—" her arm whirled around them—"is the end result."

His grin turned lazy. "So, you could say I'm your muse."

"Well, *you* could say that, but I'm not going to." She laughed. "In a lot of ways it doesn't even matter that my mother will never see it or that I'll never win that competition. It's worth it just to know I can do it."

"Quinn—"

"And it's amazing that something wild and untamed could be so beautiful." That's what he was, wasn't he? Wild and untamed. And yet there was something so beautiful about him, even beyond his charming smile.

"Why do I get the feeling you're not talking about flowers anymore?" He stopped swaying, the music still swirling overhead.

"Because I'm not. I don't take risks, Grady." She forced herself not to look away, even though she felt naked and vulnerable. "Letting you in is a huge risk for someone like me."

"I know." He smoothed her hair away from her face, eyes still locked on hers.

"And nothing about it makes sense. You're leaving. I have a business here. You're practically famous and I'm completely unknown. You can ski and I, well, can't. How will we navigate all of that?"

He smiled—that sweet, lopsided smile she'd grown to crave. "Maybe we can figure it out as we go. It's like jumping off the dock into the lake—you don't really know what's out there, but you deal with it as it comes."

"I'm not so great at the 'deal with it as it comes' part."

"Well, it's a good thing you've got me, then. That's what I live for." He took her face in his hands and spent several moments studying her. "I don't want to mess this up, Quinn." His gaze was so earnest, so genuine, she was sure she would get lost in it.

When his lips found hers, the rest of the world seemed to drift away like a sweet-smelling, magical dream. A dream in which she could let herself get carried off without ever once speculating on all the reasons it was a bad idea.

For a moment, it was as if they were floating, as if their differences meant nothing. She clung to that moment, marking it in her memory, wanting to be certain that if she ever needed it again she could recall it with ease.

For the first time in her life, she didn't have a plan. And she was actually okay with that.

The rest of the evening was a success, and as she navigated through the crowd of familiar faces, she relished the way her hand felt firmly tucked inside his. After the ball ended, they joined the locals for a late-night brunch at Hazel's, and while Grady stuck to egg whites and whole-wheat toast, she ate a pile of her favorite pancakes and bacon.

"I've never been on a date with someone who can eat more than me," he teased.

"This is only my first plate," she shot back, as if issuing a challenge. It felt good to set her rules aside for a night.

Sitting there in the diner, surrounded by Hailey and Lucy and Carly and the rest of her friends, Quinn realized that while, yes, she hadn't known Grady long, he'd made his way into her heart. And going back now wasn't an option.

She liked the way he felt next to her, his leg pressed up against hers, as if they were a couple in a group of really good friends. As if he belonged there.

But he didn't belong there, and she knew it. She tried not to think about it, but there it was, lingering at the back of her mind.

"How's your breakfast?" he asked as she popped the last bite in her mouth.

"Gone." She grinned. "Yours?"

"Unsatisfying." He pushed the plate away. "Would've much rather had the cinnamon roll French toast and bacon."

She set her fork down. "You're doing an amazing job sticking to this whole regimen."

"Have to," he said. "I'm not twenty-five anymore."

She squeezed his hand. "Is this how you usually train?"

He took a drink of his water with lemon. "Actually, no. This is how I *should've* trained. I kind of did whatever I wanted up until recently. But I'm making changes. You're not the only one who was inspired."

She set her coffee mug on the table. "What do you mean?"

"I came here miserable and broken, and I watched you and Jaden and, man, just everyone. You all work so hard. When you gave me that suck-it-up-and-deal-with-it speech, I guess I took it to heart."

"Really?"

"Yeah, I needed someone to be straight with me, so thanks."

She smiled. "So, I guess you could say I'm your muse?"

He tucked a wilted curl behind her ear. "Definitely."

"And when you win the whole Olympics, you could say it's all because of me?"

He laughed, but his smile quickly faded and his face turned serious. "Everything good in my life right now is because of you."

Lucy, with her impeccable timing, plopped down in the booth across from them, where her untouched plate of biscuits and gravy still sat. Couldn't her conversation with Betsy have lasted three minutes longer?

Grady and Quinn both watched her as she opened the paper napkin and tucked it on her lap.

"Oh, don't mind me." Lucy smiled. "I'm just here to eat my giant plate of food and whisper 'I told you so' to my oldest friend."

Quinn waved her off. "We have to go. Grady has to train early in the morning."

Grady groaned. "Why'd you have to remind me?"

She scooted out of the booth. "Because I want bragging rights when you bring home that medal."

⁓

Grady paid for their meals, and they walked out into the brisk air. Quinn wrapped her arms around herself, as if that could keep the cold away. Her shawl was obviously doing nothing to keep her warm. He quickly took off his tux jacket and hung it over her shoulders.

Only a few minutes later, they were in front of the flower shop, with her apartment up above. The memory of so many similar nights flashed through his mind, and yet not a single one of them had felt like this one did.

There was no alcohol, no pretense, no promise of something more if he came upstairs with her. And yes, he wanted to go upstairs with her, but Quinn wasn't like other girls. She was special. Pure. Good.

And he'd respect that—no matter how difficult it was.

His hands slid up her arms, underneath the jacket around her shoulders. "You're amazing—you know that?"

Her eyes flashed, a smile skittering across her face. "Just don't break my heart, okay, Grady?"

He wanted to tell her about her mother. In that moment, he didn't want a single thing between them. Secrets would only cause them pain, and he wanted to start this—whatever it was—the right way. But as he peered down at her face, full of hope, her fear exposed like a raw nerve, the only thing he could do was close the gap between them. How would he ever tell her that her mother had not only seen her design, but seen *her*? And she'd still chosen to walk away. He knew it would break her heart.

And standing there, under the awning of the Forget-Me-Not Flower Shop, breaking her heart was the last thing in the world he wanted to do.

CHAPTER

32

THE DAYS FOLLOWING THE BALL were filled with Winter Carnival activities. In true Harbor Pointe fashion, the event lasted a full week. Every day and most evenings, there were activities throughout town, which meant tourists, which meant more business, which meant Quinn had a very busy week.

Grady had been a great sport about attending all of their small-town events—they'd played Moonlight Bingo on New Year's Eve, attended the downtown winter art walk, which was one of Quinn's favorite events, closely rivaled by the snowman building contest, which was almost always won by the Kelley family. If any of it bothered him, he didn't let on.

Most of the press about him had died down, giving him time to continue his training in peace, and he was serious about it. He got up before dawn every morning for his early workout, and then he checked in for community service. This week, his duties were all centered on the carnival, ranging from hauling garbage to cleaning the sidewalks. She hadn't heard him complain once.

In the evenings, another training session, usually via FaceTime, with a guy called Happy. Grady's commitment was impressive, and while Quinn tried to stay out of his way, she also didn't want to be away from him.

She'd turned into *that* girl. Giddy when her friends mentioned his name. Blushing when his photo lit up her phone screen. Counting the hours until she would see him again.

At the moment, she stood in the window of Forget-Me-Not while he signed autographs and posed for photos across the street at Dandy's Bakery. To her knowledge, Dandy's had never hosted an Olympic athlete, or any other celebrity for that matter, and even though Grady had become something of a fixture in their little community, he still brought out quite the crowd.

"Looks like your boyfriend is pretty popular."

Quinn found Geraldine Byers standing at the center of her shop, mailbag strapped crossways over her shoulder, stack of letters in her hand. Geraldine had been delivering mail to the flower shop for as long as Quinn could remember, and though she was slower than she used to be, the old bird still had a lot of juice left. And she used at least some of that juice for whatever town gossip she could soak up.

"You two set a date yet?"

Quinn could feel her cheeks flush. "We're just getting to know each other, Gerry."

The old lady lifted her eyebrows. "Look at him. What do you need to get to know?"

Quinn laughed. "Do you have mail for me?"

"Saw you two all lip-locked at the ball the other night." This woman always said exactly what she thought. It was terrifying and refreshing at the same time. "Along with half the town."

"Sorry about that. I guess we got caught up in the moment."

She grinned as she peered up at Quinn. "You don't have to apologize to me. There's nothing like young love. I still remember the day I met my Charlie. That was a fine-looking man."

Quinn laughed. "I'm sure you were a real catch yourself."

"Oh, I was." She chuckled. "Though it's been a little while since then."

Quinn watched as she tugged her gray uniform pants up, her ample belly tucked in behind a thick black belt. She handed Quinn the stack of mail and gave her a loose salute. "You take care of yourself—and that good-looking man."

"Thanks, Gerry."

Quinn smiled at a customer who passed Gerry on her way out the door. "Let me know if you need any help."

The woman gave her a nod and Quinn slid behind the counter, a place she couldn't be without thinking of Grady. His kisses had grown more frequent now, but they weren't familiar enough for her to stop savoring them.

Actually, she hoped she never stopped savoring them, even when they were familiar.

She flipped through the envelopes Geraldine had just handed her when a logo that read *Michigan Floral Expo* in pink letters caught her eye. It stung to see the words, a reminder that she'd missed her chance. She still remembered when her mother brought home her first Best Design award all those years ago. She'd been so proud, so excited. It had validated her somehow, given her confidence.

Maybe Quinn craved that validation too.

She tore the envelope open and pulled out the letter inside.

Dear Miss Collins,

We are pleased to inform you that your design, "Secret Garden," has been accepted to the Michigan Floral Expo this spring. "Secret Garden" will be showcased along with the two other top designs. Please prepare to bring a piece of your display that highlights the overall design for the rest of our judges to see. The attendees always find these displays so inspiring.

On a personal note, I'm thrilled to hear you were able to send in your required documents after all. I apologize for my mistake. It would've been a shame if the rest of the world wasn't able to see your beautiful work. Our president spoke very highly of the entire Harbor Pointe Winter Carnival ball, but especially of your display. Judging this year's preliminary competition was her last order of business before retiring to Florida with her husband, and she said she was thankful she had the chance to do it one more time.

I look forward to meeting you in person at the Expo, as I'll be stepping up as the acting president until a new one is voted in this summer. Additional information and details about your display will arrive within the next week.

Don't hesitate to reach out if you have any questions.

Sincerely,
Kitty Moore

The paper fluttered from her fingers to the counter, the words barely registering. What was this woman saying? There must be some mistake. Her mother couldn't have been at the ball—if she was, surely Quinn would've known.

Wouldn't she?

"Miss, could you help me?" The customer from earlier stood on the opposite side of the counter, holding two containers of flowers and a small garden gnome. "Miss?"

Quinn stared at her blankly. It didn't make sense. She hadn't included a copy of her business license or tax information—she'd found it on the desk in her office. And to imply that her mother had been here, had seen her designs . . . Kitty Moore must not have all the facts.

Why would they still judge her design if her entry was incomplete?

She picked up the phone and dialed the number on the letterhead, but of course it went to voice mail. Quinn was beginning to wonder if Kitty Moore ever answered her phone.

"Miss, I'm ready to go." The customer again, this time in a tone that was thinly laced with impatience.

"I'm sorry. Of course." Quinn rushed through the process of

ringing her up, going through none of her usual chitchat. Instead, she said nothing but the woman's total, made her change, and sent her on her way.

Once she'd gone, Quinn turned the sign in her door over to Closed and shut off the lights. She dialed Kitty's number one more time, but again, voice mail.

If what the letter said was true, then her mother had been here in Harbor Pointe. She'd been at *her* event in the midst of *her* designs.

And she hadn't even bothered to say hello.

CHAPTER

33

QUINN SAT AS STILL AS A SIGNPOST in the middle of her sofa, the letter from the Expo open on her coffee table. She'd found her way upstairs, where she paced the floor for a solid half hour, trying to piece together how any of this could've happened.

She called Carly but hung up before she answered. Carly had enough to deal with. Besides, it was embarrassing to admit that the mother she hadn't seen in twenty years passed through town without a single word.

Carly would pretend she didn't care, but somehow Quinn thought even she would be sad if she knew.

The sun had dipped behind the horizon, spilling a haze of gold and orange across the loft. Quinn pulled her legs up underneath her and willed herself not to cry.

She jumped at the sound of a knock on the door. She didn't want to see anyone—not like this.

"Quinn?"

Grady.

Why would this man—this beautiful, successful man—ever want to be with her when her own mother didn't even want her?

She padded over to the door and opened it.

He sprang forward at the sight of her. "Are you okay? You're not sick, are you?"

She didn't want to lie to him. He'd promised to be honest with her, and she should do the same—let him know now what he was getting into.

But the shame of it—it was too much.

"I'm fine. Not sick. Just needed a mental-health afternoon."

"Can I come in?" He held up two brown paper bags. "I got Chinese. It's my cheat meal."

She moved away from the door, allowing him room to pass through.

"You sure you're okay?"

She closed the door and let out a heavy sigh.

"All right, I know something is wrong." He set the bags down on the counter and enveloped her in one of those hugs that said *It's okay to cry*. So she did. He held her like that, quietly allowing her to soak his shirt with her tears. When she finally regained her composure, she pulled from his grasp, swiping her cheeks dry with her sleeves.

"I'm so sorry," she said. "I'm not normally a crier."

"Now you're really worrying me." Grady followed her into the living room and took the armchair next to the couch. "Is it your dad? Jaden?"

"No, everyone's fine." She plopped down and picked up the letter. "I got something in the mail today."

His eyebrows were knit in one straight line, probably not all that different from the one he'd pointed out on her forehead so many times before.

"I'm one of three finalists for the design contest at the Michigan Floral Expo." Her voice lacked even a trace of enthusiasm. Not the way she'd anticipated sharing this news when she first applied for the competition.

"Quinn, that's awesome," he said. "It's what you wanted."

Her smile was faint and fleeting.

"Well, you should be a finalist," he said. "You should win the whole thing."

"But it says something about me sending in the necessary documents after all," Quinn said. "Grady, I didn't send them in."

He shrugged. "Maybe you did and just didn't realize it. Maybe they found them later?"

"I didn't. I found them in my office. They were left out of the envelope."

He scooted over onto the couch, next to her, and took her hand. "I don't understand why you're questioning it. This is a good thing. You're getting exactly what you wanted."

"There's more." It would be hard to say the words out loud. It shouldn't be, after all this time, but the news had reopened a wound that had taken years to heal. Or maybe it had never healed in the first place. Maybe it was so fresh and raw it kept her frozen, paralyzed, stuck in one place.

And for what? Why did she put so much effort into seeking out a woman who clearly did not want to be found?

"What is it, Q?"

"The letter says my mother was the judge."

Grady's face fell. "What do you mean?"

"My mother was here, Grady. She submitted the score sheet on my design."

"Oh, Quinn," he said. "I'm so sorry."

She shook her head. "No, don't be. It's not your fault she didn't even want to speak to me." Another traitor of a tear slipped down her cheek.

He stood and rubbed his temples with both hands, letting out a heavy sigh. "There's something I need to tell you."

Why did she have a feeling things were about to get a whole lot worse?

"We said no secrets, and I wanted to tell you sooner, but I was afraid of this. This exact thing that's happening now. I thought I could protect you from it."

"What are you talking about?"

"I called the Expo. I talked to someone there who figured out a way to get your entry back in the competition."

"You did what?" She felt nothing but confusion.

He sat down on the coffee table, knees touching hers. "You gave up so quickly, and I knew your design was going to be good. I just didn't want you to walk away without fighting for what you wanted. You taught me that, Quinn. You're the reason I'm still here, fighting."

"You should've told me."

"I know, but they didn't say they were going to accept the entry. I didn't find that out until the night of the ball." His face went white, as if all the blood had been sucked right out of it.

"What do you mean?"

His jaw twitched. He stood.

"Grady, what do you mean you found out the night of the ball?" Her eyes clouded with a fresh veil of tears.

"There was a woman there," he said. "She spoke to me first. She asked what I thought of the atmosphere. I told her I loved it, especially the flowers. Said I thought you nailed it." He turned a circle and heaved a sigh. "She guessed that I was the one who'd called."

"Okay, so, who was she?"

"Your mother."

"My mother." The word crossed her lips like a poison. "You spoke to my mother?"

"I didn't know it was her at first, but she had a copy of that same picture you have hanging in the shop."

"She what?" She could barely whisper.

He sat back down on the coffee table and took her hands. "I told her she should find you. I told her how amazing you are. I tried to get her to stay, Quinn."

The realization of it was like a knife to the back. "Even after all that coaxing, she still couldn't be bothered with me."

"I don't think it's like that. I think she's full of regret, and she doesn't know how to make it right."

"Don't you dare defend her." She reeled back and pulled her hands away.

"I'm not defending her," he said. "I promise. I just recognize that pain."

"The pain of screwing up so badly there's no coming back from it?"

"But there *is* coming back from it. She just can't see it. Not yet."

Quinn pushed herself up off the couch and walked toward the kitchen—why, she didn't know. Distance? Space? Clarity? None of those things came. "She's had years to see it, Grady. I guess she never will."

He stood and faced her. "Maybe not, but that's her loss. I know my conversation with her was brief, but I think she knows what she missed out on."

Quinn wrapped her arms around herself, as if that could protect her from the grief that overtook her body. She'd been waiting since she was a little girl for the chance to ask her questions. *Why did you leave? Did I do something wrong? Why don't you love me?*

And now, after this, it was clear that none of those questions would ever be asked, let alone answered.

"I think you should go." The words startled her. She hadn't meant to say them. Grady's face—solemn and concerned—was enough to break her heart. But in some ways, her heart was already broken, and there was no one to blame for being blindsided like this except him.

"Quinn, I'm sorry. I should've told you. I didn't want to upset you—I didn't want you to think this had anything to do with you." He stood in the kitchen now, too big for the small space, and suddenly she felt like the walls were closing in.

"I need to be alone, Grady, please." She couldn't breathe for the pain that had lodged itself in her throat. She pushed past him, back to the living room, feeling like a rat in a cage. There was nowhere to go.

"I can't leave unless I know you're okay," he said. "I won't."

She spun around. "I don't want you here!" The tears came hard and fast, and she was helpless to stop them. She didn't mean to be vicious, but her mind wouldn't stop spinning. Part of her wanted to sink into his arms, but he'd kept this all from her—something that he knew was more important to her than anything.

How could she ever trust him now?

His eyes—wounded and sorry—held hers for a long moment, and then finally, he shifted his gaze. He crossed the room, placed one tender kiss on the top of her head, then walked out the door, leaving her with nothing but Chinese food and the pieces of her broken heart.

Grady stood in the hallway outside Quinn's loft for seconds that turned into minutes. The light under her doorway disappeared, but still he stood, trying to think of something—anything—to make this better.

So far, his mind was empty.

There was nothing to say except "I'm sorry." And while he'd already said it, he wasn't sure she was in any state to hear it. This thing with her mother, it was brutal, and until she let go of it, it always would be.

But then, who was he to talk? It wasn't like he had a good relationship with his parents. And he was holding on to plenty of baggage of his own.

He slid to the floor, back pressed against the wall, and sat there for nearly an hour. Why hadn't he just told her the truth from the start? It would've hurt, yes, but at least she'd have him to lean on right now. But maybe she was unwilling to lean. She wouldn't let him get close again, and he hated that he couldn't take the pain away. The more time he spent in this town with these people, the more he realized there was only one who could.

He stood. "God, I know I can't be what she needs right now," he whispered against her door. "But you can. And I pray you are."

And with that, he walked away.

CHAPTER

⁓

34

THE NEXT DAY, Grady awoke after an impossibly restless night of half sleep. His heart still ached for what Quinn was going through, and regret piled high on top of him.

He was new to this kind of selfless love, and while he wasn't sure yet if he'd be good at it, he knew he wanted to try—for her. As he checked his phone for a missed call or a text, he wondered if she'd ever forgive him.

He went through the paces of his workout for an hour, probably not as tuned in as he should've been this close to his race.

After he got back to the cottage and mixed a protein shake, a knock on his door gave him hope. But when he pulled it open, it was Gus, not Quinn, he found waiting there.

He was dressed in uniform and held his hat in his hands.

"Gus," he said, trying to hide his disappointment.

"Morning, son," Gus said. "Can I come in a minute?"

What had Quinn told him? Was he here to remind Grady of his bad choices or warn him to stay away from his daughter?

Grady stepped aside so the other man could enter. "What brings you by so early?" He closed the door.

"I've got some news." Gus's face lit into a warm smile. "That daughter of mine must really care about you."

Grady's skin practically tingled at the thought. Was this actually good news?

Gus pulled a sheet of folded paper from his inside coat pocket and held it out to Grady.

"What's this?"

"It seems the work you've put in around here has been sufficient, son. They're letting you out of your community service early."

"Quinn did this?" Grady stared at the paper in his hand. Sure enough, it said he was free to go.

Gus nodded. "Judge is hard-nosed behind the bench, but he's pretty soft when it comes to Quinn. She made a strong case, I guess. Said you'd been instrumental in the success of her opening and the carnival; then she mentioned all of your public appearances and the way you helped train Jaden. He was convinced. You're not the same man you were when you first got to Harbor Pointe."

She was giving him exactly what he'd asked for weeks ago, but not at all what he needed now. She wanted him to leave.

"Why don't you look happy?" Gus stared at him.

Grady tossed the paper on the entryway table and walked into the kitchen, Gus following behind.

"Isn't this good? I thought you'd be excited."

"Yeah, it's great, Gus. Thanks for letting me know."

The old man stared at him, as if expecting an explanation. How did Grady come clean about any of this with Quinn's dad? If he wasn't careful, the family he'd come to care about would run him out of town before he was ready.

"Do you have any coffee?" Gus slid the tall stool out from under the kitchen counter and sat down.

"Sir?"

"If you're going to unload that heavy burden, I'm going to need some coffee."

Grady sighed. "I can't talk about this with you."

Gus raised a brow. "Doesn't seem like you have anyone better to talk to."

He made a good point. Grady found a mug in the cupboard and poured the man a cup of coffee. Gus took a sip, then motioned for Grady to sit. "Let's hear it."

None of the story came easily, but when he got to the part about the ball—about Quinn's mom—he stopped cold. This woman left not only Quinn; she left Gus, too. She left her husband with two little girls and never came back.

"Why do I have the feeling you're chewing on something I'm not gonna like?" Gus asked, both hands around the warm mug.

"Because I'm chewing on something you're not gonna like."

"Were you inappropriate with my daughter?"

Grady held up a hand. "No, sir. Nothing like that."

Gus eyed him, as if making up his mind whether Grady was telling the truth.

"I swear." Grady sighed. "But maybe what I did was worse?"

Two wide, expectant eyes waited for him to explain.

Grady rubbed his face, wishing this weren't a story he had to tell. But it was the truth, and whether he liked it or not, Gus was going to find out eventually. Might as well be from him.

So he told him. The whole story rolled out so quickly he couldn't have stopped it if he tried. When he finished, he couldn't look at the older man. How much more pain would he cause?

"Wow," Gus said after too many seconds of silence.

"I'm sorry, Gus. I didn't mean to hurt her—or you."

The sheriff took a slow sip of his coffee, then slid the empty mug across the counter. "Mind topping me off?"

Grady frowned.

"Now it's my turn."

He refilled the mug and handed it to the other man, who stood and walked through the dining area and out onto the back porch. The cottage had a spectacular view of Lake Michigan, and truth be told, Grady had thought more than once that he'd buy the place if he could. It felt like home in a way that nowhere else had.

It wasn't logical, of course. A professional skier couldn't make his home in a small town that lacked a decent slope, but sometimes he entertained the idea anyway.

Grady grabbed a jacket and followed Gus outside. It was cool, but not frightfully cold like January could be. Still, he wondered how long Quinn's dad planned to keep him outdoors.

"You blame yourself for this?" Gus stared out over the water, a slight wind rustling his white hair.

"I do, sir. I'd like to make it right, but I don't know how."

"This isn't your fault, Grady. It's mine."

He frowned again. "What do you mean?"

"Carly told me that Quinn's been sort of stuck for years. In a holding pattern, she said. I just thought cautious was her way, but Carly seems to think she's waiting around for Jacie to come back."

"You never asked her about it?"

Gus pressed his lips together, still staring out at the water. "I should've, but no. I didn't have the courage."

Grady leaned against the railing, facing Quinn's dad.

"Quinn's mom didn't just leave one day. I asked her to go." His eyes fell to the ground just below the porch. "I think Quinn only remembers the good about her mom. None of the bad. None of what she put us through. She's got her up on a pedestal, and I let her keep her there."

Grady watched Gus, the wrinkles around his eyes deepening as he spoke.

"Jacie was troubled. She drank too much. Usually she kept it hidden from the girls—heck, the whole town. I mean, everyone loved her. But I always knew. I begged her to get help. I researched hospitals and treatment centers, but she refused. She'd disappear for days at a time, and we always had to cover for her. Mimi was working at the flower shop then, and that's when she stepped up and learned the business. She came to me after Jacie left, wanting to buy the place. Of course I agreed—what was I going to do with a flower shop?" Gus paused for a long few seconds, his eyes glassy.

"One night I was working late, and I always checked on home when I had to work late. I didn't trust her. It's an awful feeling not to be able to trust your spouse. You tuck that one away for the future, okay?"

Grady nodded. "I got it, sir."

"It was just after eleven o'clock, and I drove by with my partner. Told him I wanted to grab something from home, but when I went inside, I smelled that foul odor of natural gas." Gus's eyes glazed over, the memory seeming to transport him back through time. "Jacie was passed out on the couch, but the gas stove was still on. The flame was out, so the gas was just leaking into the house. The girls were asleep upstairs. They could've all gotten sick—or worse, died of carbon monoxide poisoning. I still say it was the nudge of the Holy Spirit that led me there."

Gus leaned down, elbows on the railing, hands wrapped around the warm mug. "That night I told her she had to make a choice. She could go to the treatment center or she could leave for good."

Grady could see the weight of this decision, heavy and unwavering. "She chose to leave."

"Jacie was a proud woman. But I always thought she'd come back." Gus looked away. "I got divorce papers six months later and found out she was pregnant with some other guy's kid. So, in a lot of ways, she was right—the girls were better off. But in some ways, they weren't. They never had a mother, and that's my fault."

Grady wasn't used to playing the role of comforter, and he wasn't sure what to say to ease the man's guilt or pain. He didn't have wisdom beyond his years, and his life had been one poor decision after another. "You did what you thought was best for your daughters."

Gus steeled his gaze out on the cherry-red lighthouse in the distance. "But maybe it was the wrong choice."

"No sense living there, though, right? What's done is done. We only have what's in front of us now."

Maybe those were words he was supposed to absorb for himself. After all, he'd also been living with the heavy weight of past regret—and he, like Gus, couldn't find a way out from under it.

"Listen, I know Quinn is upset, but she'll come around," Gus said. "And you can't tell her about this."

Grady straightened. "We have to tell her, Gus. She deserves to know."

He shook his head. "It'll crush her. She'll lose her faith in the only parent she has left, and it won't change anything between the two of you. Only time will do that."

Grady looked away. "You can't ask me to keep anything else from her."

"It's still what's best for her, son."

Then why did it feel so wrong?

"So what am I supposed to do? She won't even speak to me."

"You go win your race and forget about this place for a while. And then you reach out to her once your mind is clear of everything else."

"I don't know if I can do that." In fact, he was pretty sure he couldn't. "I want to make things right with her, Gus. She means everything to me."

"I know my daughter. What she needs right now is time and a little perspective."

"What she needs right now is the truth."

Gus gave a dismissive wave, handed the mug back to Grady, and clapped a hand on his shoulder. "We'll be pulling for you at your race. Nothing we'd all like more than to see one of our own at the Olympics."

"Appreciate it, sir." And he did. Grady hadn't been one of anyone's own for as long as he could remember. Still, an uneasiness had worked its way into his belly.

"I'll show myself out."

The wind whipped through the bare trees, sending a chill straight through Grady's jacket and worn gray hoodie. Nothing about Gus's confession made him feel any better. If anything, he felt worse. How could he hold on to a secret like that?

But maybe Gus was right. Maybe time would help her heal, make her see he hadn't intended to hurt her.

Or maybe it would put just enough distance between them to make him forget he ever loved her in the first place.

CHAPTER

35

QUINN WASN'T SURE WHAT WAS WORSE—knowing Grady was gone or knowing she was the reason why.

She'd struggled to get through the days following his departure from Harbor Pointe, aware that her conversation with Judge sent a message: *I want you to leave.* At the time it had seemed like the wise thing to do, but now, in the aftermath of it all, she wondered if it had hurt him. And causing him pain had never been her goal.

She walked through her days zombielike and detached, going through the motions and wondering if she'd made a terrible mistake.

In the evenings, she watched the sports channel, hoping for a glimpse of the man who had stolen her heart. Just a clue as to how he was doing. After several days, with only one more week before the big race, one of the reporters granted her request. The woman was spunky and fit. Probably a former athlete and the kind of woman who would make a much more suitable match for Grady.

Quinn watched as the image of the man she'd once held in her arms flashed across the screen. She knew literally nothing about skiing, but from what she could tell, he was flying down those slopes.

"The real surprise out here in Colorado is Grady Benson," the reporter said. "This is a man the skiing world had practically written off, but what we're seeing is a new and improved version of the skier we all know and love. What's more, his constant work and the time he's put into his training have garnered the attention of the Olympic coaches, who had this to say about America's favorite rebel skier."

The shot cut away to a man with a rugged, tan face and shining eyes. The name *Brian Murphy* appeared at the bottom of the screen. "Grady's been a surprise, that's for sure. We didn't expect to see half of what he's showing us."

The reporter pulled the microphone back. "Now, in the past, you've commented on Benson's rebellious attitude. Has that been a problem since he arrived here in Colorado?"

The coach laughed. "You know Grady and I have had our differences, but the first thing he said when he rolled back into town was 'I'm here to work, Coach.' And he's proven that to be true. He's made some vast improvements to his form, and yes, he's finally listening to me." Another laugh. "I'd say Grady Benson is a changed man. I'm hopeful we're gonna see him on our team this year."

Quinn's eyes had gone cloudy as the camera cut away to more footage of him skiing. He was doing well. The clean break from Harbor Pointe—from her—it was what he needed.

Never mind what it had done to her heart.

She was a mess. She'd come home from work, put on her pajamas, and eaten leftover frozen pizza standing up in the kitchen. Now, with her hair in a messy bun on top of her head, the only thing she wanted to do was crawl into bed and wish away the last month.

If she'd never met him in the first place, she'd be fine right now.

And yet, she couldn't imagine her world if she'd never met him. He made her want to live outside the box she'd put herself in.

Nobody else had ever done that for her before.

The knock on the door elicited a groan. This would be some

well-meaning person who loved her, determined to get her out of bed and out of her misery. But she was quite comfortable wearing her misery like a cloak. It was all she wanted to do.

Another knock. "Okay, I'm coming." She hoped her groan was audible. She reached the door and pulled it open. "Dad."

He wore a stony expression. "You have a minute?"

"Of course." While she and her dad were close, he didn't make a habit of stopping over. If anything, he usually called and asked her to come by the house. "Is something wrong? Is everyone okay— Judge? Beverly? Calvin?"

He held up a hand. "Everyone's fine, hon." He gave her a once-over. "Everyone except maybe you?"

She plopped down on the sofa. "I'm fine, Dad. Did Carly send you over here?"

"No, but she did tell me you haven't been over to see Jaden at all this week."

"I've been busy."

Dad nodded, then sat gingerly on the edge of her armchair. "You don't look so hot, Q."

"Gee, thanks."

"And your apartment is a mess."

"Did you just come here to insult me?" She pulled an afghan over her lap.

"I came to check on you." He scooted back in the chair and glanced up at the muted television. "How's he doing?"

"Who?"

"Quinn, please."

She shrugged. "I don't keep tabs on him."

His expression told her he wasn't buying it. "You make a habit of watching SportsCenter?"

She picked up the remote and clicked the television off.

"He told me what happened, you know."

She flicked her thumbnail against the edge of the remote, avoiding his eyes. "He did?"

Dad folded his hands in his lap. "Are you ever going to forgive him?"

"He lied, Dad." The cloud of tears was back, and she blinked three times in quick succession, willing them not to betray her.

"But he did it because he thought the truth would hurt too much."

"A lie is a lie." She pulled the afghan more tightly around her.

"Quinn, honey." His face whitened. "There's something you need to know."

~

He was back. Top of his game. Determined to put the past behind him and move on. That meant forcing thoughts of Harbor Pointe and a certain pretty florist out of his mind.

He'd walked into the first day of training just as Matthew Phillips finished an impressive run. The cameras started flashing, and Grady realized they weren't only getting shots of Matthew, wearing the Bowman name, but also of Grady's reaction to the younger skier. In the past, he might've given the press exactly the kind of sound bite they craved. Today, with a knowing glance at Brian and the rest of the coaching staff, he chose a different approach.

Matthew came to a stop a few yards in front of him, and Grady walked straight over to him under many watchful eyes. He wore the Spectre logo, having worked out a decent deal with the up-and-coming company, and he reminded himself to keep his ego in check. He heard the camera shutters snapping as he approached.

Matthew removed his goggles. "Grady." He looked unsure, as if he'd done something wrong and was about to be called out on it.

"Looking forward to getting up there with you," Grady said.

"Yeah?" The younger man did nothing to hide his surprise.

"Yeah. Just got into town. I've got some work to do before next weekend. Hoping not to spend all my time eating your dust."

Matthew's laugh was uncertain.

Grady extended a hand in Matthew's direction. After all, the guy's only crime was being good at what he loved. And on the drive out here, Grady had determined not to hold that against him. Instead, he'd use it to spur himself on. If he was smart, it would make him better.

Matthew shook Grady's hand and more flashes went off.

"I gotta get out there," Grady said. "Here's hoping these old bones can keep up."

Before he let go, Matthew pulled him closer. "I'm rooting for you, man."

"Appreciate it," Grady said.

The drive got him thinking about more than just Matthew Phillips. He'd tossed around the footage of previous races, the missteps, the mistakes. He'd thought through the advice Brian and his other coaches had given him in recent months. He'd decided he could either tell them he'd changed or he could show them—and he knew which one of those would carry the most weight.

He'd also spent a lot of time looking back on Harbor Pointe and Jaden and Quinn. He wanted to make them proud—to give them a reason to cheer for him.

And he supposed that idea led him to thoughts of the peace he'd begun to make with a God he'd all but turned his back on. Was it possible he'd been there all along, somewhere in the middle of this messy, messy world?

Sometimes it shamed him to remember the way he'd squandered the good things God had put in his life. He'd mistakenly convinced himself he deserved those things, when he knew now with absolute certainty he did not. He didn't want to waste a single moment ever again.

In the quiet darkness of the car, he'd prayed—asked God to help him get his life right for the right reasons.

Make me new.

The words had come into his mind without warning. He didn't even know what they meant. How could someone like him—someone who'd made so many bad choices—ever be truly new?

And yet, it became his prayer. *Make me new. On the slopes and off.*

He was tired of living the same old life, doing the same things, making the same bad decisions, getting in the same fights. He wanted to surrender his anger, his frustration, his ego as much as he wanted to surrender control on the mountain. That freedom—he craved it.

Happy had agreed to clear his schedule to work with Grady, and together they'd come up with the ideal training and eating program for the two weeks before his last chance to qualify for the team. His last chance to keep his promise to Benji. His last chance to prove to the world that they were wrong about him.

The days were full. He was surrounded by people. Coaches who'd all but written him off seemed open to the new and improved version of him.

On Saturday, while Grady was packing up after practice, Brian stopped by. So far, Grady had only spoken to him in passing.

"Looking good out there, Benson," Brian said. "Seems like you finally got that left leg to cooperate."

"You mean I finally started listening to my coach?" Grady stood and faced the other man.

Brian gave him a wry grin. "Something like that."

"Figured it was about time," Grady said. "Hoping I can redeem myself next weekend."

"You keep skiing like you have been this week, and I think you just might."

"Thank you, sir."

Brian started for the locker room door.

"Coach?" Grady called out.

He turned around.

Grady's eyes found the floor. "Look, I wanted to apologize. Officially. I behaved badly for a lot of years, and I always thought I'd float through. I disrespected you, and I am sorry for that."

Brian stuck his hands on his hips and gave Grady a quick once-over. "You mean that, don't you?"

"I believe I do, sir."

The coach lifted his chin, peering down at Grady as he did. "Apology accepted."

"Thank you, Coach."

"What'd they do to you in that little town?" Brian asked.

Grady laughed. "I guess they made me want to be a better man."

Slowly, Brian started shaking his head. "I never thought I'd see the day."

"Sir?"

"When Grady Benson actually fell in love."

"No, sir, I'm not—"

"Whoever she is, she's good for you," Brian said. "That's when you hold on. Both hands. Don't let her go."

If only it were that easy.

"You going out tonight?" Brian's question felt like a test—one Grady was confident he could pass.

"No, sir. I'm heading to the hotel to get some rest."

"Good answer."

But it was in these times, when he was on his own, resting, that Grady's mind started working him over. During the day, it was easy. There were people everywhere. Coaches, Happy, other skiers. But now? When he was in his suite staring at the dark ceiling? The only thing he could think about was Quinn and how different he wished everything could be.

He'd tried texting her. He'd even called her twice, but the calls went straight to voice mail. She didn't want to talk to him—obviously.

And while he should take the hint, he couldn't get Brian's advice out of his head. *Hold on. Both hands. Don't let her go.*

If only there were someone to tell him how to hold on to someone who didn't want to be held.

CHAPTER

36

SATURDAY. RACE DAY. Nerves bounced around in Grady's stomach as he woke up early, got dressed, and did something he had never done before a race his entire life.

He prayed.

The past two weeks had been lonely ones, and while he called Jaden regularly for updates on Harbor Pointe, being separated from Quinn was harder than he thought it would be. Happy had helped him harness his disappointment, turning it into something that drove him forward, made him push harder, but he'd already decided that once the race was over, he was going straight back to Michigan to get Quinn back.

She'd taught him to fight for what he wanted. Well, he wanted her.

And so he'd fight.

But first, he had to secure his spot on the team.

He arrived early and warmed up, staying focused and keeping his goal right in front of him.

That goal? To win.

He could come in first, second, or third and be eligible for the US ski team, but first place would go a longer way with the coaches and the committee. He'd made a decent impression, but if he didn't back up his change in attitude with a stellar performance today, he could forget about the Olympics.

He could forget about the gold medal.

He stuck his earbuds in and flipped on his music—anything to tune out the crowd. He'd run the course so many times the last two weeks, he knew it by heart. He supposed he should thank Quinn for kicking him out of Harbor Pointe early—it had been good for him.

And yet, he couldn't be completely glad he'd had the extra time, not when it meant he'd missed out on days with her.

"You eat this morning?" It was Happy, checking in as usual. Grady hadn't heard him over his music, but he'd read his lips.

He tugged the earbuds out of his ears. "I ate. I stretched. I ran the course in my mind."

"So you're ready."

"I hope so." Grady let out a sigh.

"That didn't sound too convincing." The voice came from behind him. He spun around and found Quinn standing there, wearing the poofy white ski coat and a bright-turquoise stocking cap, looking every bit as beautiful as he remembered.

He blinked for several speechless seconds—was she really right in front of him? Finally, he found his voice.

"What are you doing here?"

Her eyes widened. "Should I not have come? I don't want to mess you up."

"Are you kidding? No, of course you should've come. I'm just—" *Floored? Ecstatic? Surprised? All of the above.* "Did you drive?"

"I flew." She looked proud of herself.

"You flew?" He shook his head, drinking her in. She flew—to be there with him?

At his side, Happy cleared his throat.

"Oh, sorry. Quinn, this is my trainer, Happy."

Quinn smiled—that perfect, warm smile—and shook Happy's outstretched hand.

"I guess we have you to thank for whipping our boy into shape?" Happy asked.

Grady scoffed. "He's just kidding."

"No, he's right. You do have me to thank." She grinned. "I'm very bossy."

"It's good to meet you, Quinn. I'm going to go take a look at the lineup, Grady. I'll see you in a little bit." Happy walked off, leaving him standing there, still in disbelief.

He studied her as if she were the only person there. "Am I dreaming?"

She smiled up at him, the kind of smile that made the rest of the world melt away, then sobered. "I was so stubborn and stupid."

"I understand why you were upset."

"No, it was wrong of me. My dad told me the truth about everything. And I was mad at him, too, but I know you didn't tell me about my mom because you didn't want to hurt me. She left without saying a word to me, and that does hurt. I know I may never understand all of the real reasons why she stayed away—why she didn't fight for us—but none of that was ever your fault, and I'm sorry if I acted like it was."

He reached over and brushed a stray hair away from her face. "Forgotten. I'm just so glad you're here." He pulled her into a tight hug, drawing in the scent of her, mapping the moment in his mind.

She pulled away and brought her eyes to his. "Are you nervous?"

He shook his head. "I'm ready."

"I'm going to be here cheering you on—no matter what. And Jaden and Carly and my dad and everyone else are watching the race in the clubhouse at Cedar Grove. They're all really excited for you."

He gave her a nod. "I gotta go. You okay here?"

She smiled again. "Don't give me a second thought. Go do what you came here to do."

He leaned in and kissed her. "I could never not give you a second thought." He walked off to where Happy stood and tried to get ready for the most important race of his life, a newfound hope bursting inside at the knowledge that the woman he loved was here to carry him through.

⁓

As soon as she saw him, all her hesitations about coming to the race floated away like driftwood on the lake.

Now she stood off to the side, puzzled by the scene in front of her.

"Quinn?" Happy motioned for her to come closer. She scooted through the crowd and stood next to him. "Grady wanted me to make sure you were okay. Said it might all get a little confusing to you."

"Yeah, I'm not much of a skier."

"He told me." A grin from the muscular man, whose eyes were warm and friendly. "Look, I don't know how you feel about the guy, but he's changed, and I really do think we have you to thank."

She shook her head and glanced up at the big screen in front of her, where she saw Grady at the top of the mountain. "I didn't do anything."

"You gave him something he's never really had: a true, genuine relationship. He's like a different guy. Humble, willing to learn. Yeah, he's still got some rough corners, but he's trying—he's even asked me a few questions about God, and I never thought I'd see that happen."

"Really?" Quinn had hoped—and prayed—that Grady might've finally made his peace with God. Could it be true?

"Yeah," Happy said. "It's good you're here—he needs you, no matter what happens today."

Quinn let the words soak in. She'd never really felt needed before—and she'd never let herself need anyone else. She had a feeling those days were over.

Risky as it was, it was worth it. *He* was worth it.

"Here he goes." Happy squeezed her arm, and she turned her attention back to the screen.

"What does he need to do to qualify?"

Happy glanced at her, then looked back at the screen. "Technically third place or higher, but you know Grady—he needs to win."

The realization sent a nervous chill down her spine, but her panic was short-lived. He took off like a shot just as a text came in from Carly. A photo of so many familiar faces gathered at the clubhouse at Cedar Grove. The caption read, Go Grady! Your Harbor Pointe family is cheering you on!

She wished it had come in a little bit sooner, because now she wouldn't be able to show him until he finished.

She glanced up and saw him shoot down the hill, taking each jump with the relaxed coolness of someone who didn't have a care in the world. He landed each one perfectly.

She leaned over to Happy. "He's doing well, right?"

Happy's laugh bubbled over. "He's doing awesome!"

Quinn watched, holding her breath whenever there was air between his skis and the ground, but each time, he nailed the landing and shot forward.

The crowd cheered with every jump, every turn, every smooth maneuver by a man who'd once lived for that praise. She had a feeling, though, that after this last month, maybe Grady was looking for something a bit more lasting than the fleeting affirmation of a fickle crowd.

At least she hoped so.

As he made another turn, he came into view—not just on the big screen, but in front of them, in living color.

"He's in first." Happy let out a cheer.

She folded her hands and pressed them to her lips, whispering a silent prayer as he crossed the finish line to the sound of more cheering.

Her phone buzzed as text messages from her family came in alarmingly fast.

He did it!

Grady Benson is back!

Tell him how proud we are of him!

She tucked the phone inside her coat pocket, drinking in the moment along with the rest of Grady's adoring fans.

Happy scooted out. "You coming?"

"No, no, go ahead." She didn't want to get in the way.

She watched as Grady pulled his helmet and goggles off, bent over at the waist for several seconds as if he needed time to recover. He stayed like that for longer than Quinn expected him to, then reached down and took off his skis.

Happy reached him, and Grady stood and pulled his trainer into one of those tight guy hugs, the kind that seemed to only accompany victory.

And as he leaned away, his eyes searched the spectators. Happy pointed in her direction, and Grady found her, then waved her over.

When she didn't move, he ran over to the stands, ignoring the cheers of the fans, eyes zeroed in on her. "Get down here, Quinn Collins. This one was for you."

She smiled and inched her way out from behind the teenagers who were now gawking in her direction.

He took her hand and pulled her out of the crowd, then wrapped his arms around her.

"I'm so excited for you," she said. "You have to be on cloud nine."

He kissed her—right there in front of everyone—as the next racer took off like a bullet out of a gun. "I couldn't have done this without you, Quinn. You—you're everything I never knew I needed."

She felt the smile wash across her face. How did she respond to that? She felt exactly the same way about him.

"You got some time for the reporters, Grady?" Happy stood at his side.

She expected to go back to her seat, but Grady slipped his hand in hers and led her off toward where the press was waiting.

But before they reached the expectant throng of paparazzi, Grady came to a halt. His face had gone pale, any trace of excitement gone.

"What's wrong?" She followed his gaze to a small group of people standing off to the side. "What is it, Grady?"

"It's my family."

CHAPTER

37

HOW LONG HAD IT BEEN since his parents were in the stands at one of his races? He'd lost count of the years. There was too much distance, so much that Grady had given up on ever reconciling with them.

It was only Benji he cared about now.

Even so, it had been years since he'd seen his brother too. They spoke on the phone or texted back and forth. It had always seemed like enough, but looking at him now, Grady regretted the lost time.

Quinn slipped her hand inside his, and he drew strength from her presence. She knew so little about his family, yet it was like she understood instinctively. He'd only ever alluded to what had happened to Benji—surely she must have questions now, seeing him here, in his wheelchair.

The air became tense as they approached his family, waiting off to the side as if they were just another group of fans. His mom's eyes glistened in the sunlight of the clear Colorado morning, and his dad stood there stoic and serious. Clearly it hadn't been his idea to come.

Benji's face beamed with the kind of pride only an older brother could have.

Grady stopped short of actual physical connection with any of them. "You didn't tell me you were coming."

"We wanted it to be a surprise," Benji said.

"Benji wanted it to be a surprise," Mom said. "He got his new chair, and he's a lot more mobile, so they cleared him to make the trip."

"Thanks, Gray," Benji said. "You know I didn't expect you to chip in for that."

"It was nothing," Grady said. The Spectre check had been enough to catch up on his bills and get the chair, something Benji's physical therapist said would be good for him. It was all Grady needed to hear, and he ordered it the next day.

"Who's your friend?" Mom smiled cautiously at Quinn, who straightened, probably unsure how to navigate the tension.

"Oh, this is Quinn." Grady turned to her. "Quinn, these are my parents, Randall and Charlene; and my brother, Benji."

Her smile was polite, but her eyes were full of questions. "It's so good to meet you all."

"Ah, so you're the one who got him back on track." Benji winked at her, and Grady didn't have to look over to know her cheeks would be pink.

"Oh, I don't know," Quinn said. "He was already pretty amazing."

A pregnant pause. He bet his father would disagree.

"Why don't we go get something to eat?" Benji was obviously going to power through the strain in the air.

"Grady probably has people to see." Those were the first words his father had spoken—an excuse to get out of spending more time with him.

"Actually, Grady is all yours." Happy had found them standing there, and what a time to insert himself into the conversation. Happy had made it clear more than once that Grady needed to at least attempt to repair things with his family, but Grady didn't want that reminder right now.

"Great," Benji said after Happy introduced himself around. "You wanna come along?"

Happy shook his head. "You all go ahead. I'll see you when you get back, Grady."

Way to hang me out to dry, dude.

He turned to Quinn. "You're coming, right?"

Her eyes were wide. "Do you want me to?"

"Yes, please." Did he sound as desperate as he felt? "We can just go inside and eat here if that works for you guys," Grady said.

"Sounds wonderful, Grady." His mom looked like she might burst as she lunged forward and threw her arms around him. "It's so good to see you."

The hug was one-sided for several seconds, but finally he wrapped his arms around her and hugged back. When she finally pulled away, she had to wipe her cheeks dry.

"We'll see you over there," Grady said. "I'm just going to talk to the coaches quick."

"Make sure you're on the team," Benji said. "Give us a real reason to celebrate."

Grady nodded, then walked off, wishing he could rewind to the moment before he spotted them. If only he'd headed in the opposite direction, he could've pretended he never saw them at all.

"Is something wrong?" Quinn jogged a few steps to catch up to him, and he ordered his heart to stop pounding. He'd seen the disapproval in his father's eyes, clear as day. All these years, all these awards—heck, even his race today—had done nothing to sway the old man.

Grady would never be good enough to make up for what had happened on that mountain so long ago.

"No, I'm fine." He was pretty sure she knew he was lying. "Just really wish I had a reason not to go to lunch."

The coaches were huddled near the judges' table, and since it was the last qualifying race of the season, everyone important was there. They'd all seen him ski. And he'd been flawless. He'd never felt so good up on the slopes in his life.

He'd let go of any delusion that he was in control, and before he took off, he handed the whole thing over to God. "You take control," he'd whispered. And just like Jaden said, Grady felt like he was floating—flying.

Was it a coincidence that it seemed like someone else was skiing through him? He didn't think so, not that he could ever articulate that feeling to anyone else. They'd think he was crazy.

"Great job today, Grady." Brian left the huddle and shook Grady's hand. "Real proud of how you turned everything around here lately."

"Thank you, sir. I know we've had our differences, and I made a real mess of things, but I'm back, and I'm feeling better than ever. Hoping I can show you more of my best at the games next month."

"I know you're anxious for the results," Brian said. "If I'm not making any objections, I don't think anyone else will either. I can't say this officially yet, but I think you pulled it off."

Grady let out a relieved breath that mixed with laughter as he pumped Brian's hand more enthusiastically than he'd meant to. "I will not let you down, Coach."

Brian raised a brow. "You better not." He glanced at Quinn and smiled. "Both hands."

Grady watched as the coach walked back to the huddle. He turned to Quinn. "Did you hear that?"

Her face was glowing. "I heard."

He scooped her up and spun her around, then drew her in for a much-needed kiss. "Man, I missed you." He took her face in his hands and memorized the way she looked, wishing they could just stay there, basking in the glow of good news, a race that finally went his way, and the promise of more kisses to carry him through the evening.

But the thick, dark cloud that gathered overhead threatened to pull him in. The knowledge that his family was there, waiting for him—it turned him inside out.

He pressed his forehead against hers. "I don't want to go in there."

"They're your family. They seem nice."

He pulled away and took her hand, leading her off in the direction of the resort. "Did you catch the death stare from my father?"

Quinn grimaced. "I feel like there's a story there?"

"Let's just say there's a reason we don't speak." Grady pulled the door open and let Quinn go in first. "Listen, can I just offer a preemptive apology?"

She laughed. "For what?"

"For whatever happens," Grady said. "It's never good, and it's usually embarrassing. Just consider yourself warned."

"I don't have to come along. I can go back to my room and read for a while or something."

"Not a chance," he said. "I need you."

She softened at his words, and he realized he'd never said them to her before. He'd been holding back the truth of what he felt, but now didn't seem like the best time to get into it.

Instead, he leaned down, kissed her forehead, and drew a deep breath, preparing himself for whatever came next.

He walked in and found his parents sitting at a large round table near the windows overlooking the mountains. Quinn squeezed his hand, and they approached the table. Grady sat next to Benji, and Quinn next to him, beside Grady's mom.

How he would get through this lunch without a drink, he had no idea.

Commence small talk.

Grady had little use for small talk, but what other choice did they have? It wasn't like they were going to delve into anything that really mattered.

They grilled Quinn for a while, and Mom pretended to be engrossed in the life of a florist. Grady joked that maybe his community service wasn't such a bad thing at all, which, of course, Dad didn't appreciate.

In all, the man had said maybe five words. "Pass the butter" and "No thanks."

It was Benji who kept the conversation moving forward. Thank God for Benji. "Looks like things are going really well, Gray," Benji said. "I'm glad for you."

"How've you been?" Grady asked his brother. "Keeping busy? How's the coaching going?"

Benji took a bite of his chicken sandwich. "Actually, I had an idea I wanted to run by you."

"Okay." Grady caught his mom's eye. She looked almost afraid for whatever Benji was about to say.

"Have you thought at all about what you're going to do after the games?"

Grady laughed, took a swig of his iced tea. "Considering I just found out there's going to be an Olympic Games for me, no. I haven't thought of much else the last few weeks."

Benji nodded. "I get that. But I was thinking . . ."

"Oh, Benji, just ask him," Mom said.

"Ask me what?" Grady glanced at Quinn, who looked as intrigued as he felt.

"I was thinking we should open a training center," Benji said. "You and me."

Grady frowned. "I don't understand."

"You must've thought about coaching," Benji said. "After you retire."

Grady shrugged. "I guess, maybe." After all, he'd really enjoyed coaching Jaden before his wipeout, and Quinn *had* said he was a good coach. But Benji had limited mobility, and there was only so much good a coach could do without getting out on the slopes himself.

"Think about it—we could have ski camps and training programs and raise up the next generation of skiers," Benji said.

Grady's eyes scanned the table. His mother and Quinn were both looking down, but his father—his eyes were fixed squarely on him.

"I've already started working with some young skiers, really promising kids, Gray—they're incredible," Benji said. "We could provide nutrition consulting and strength training. Maybe Happy would come on board. It could be the premier training facility in the country."

"Benj, I think it's a great idea, I'm just not sure how it would work."

Benji shook his head. "What do you mean? With your name recognition? We could really make a go of this. A lot of athletes start coaching after they retire."

"But I'm not retiring," Grady said.

"Well, yeah, but after the games?"

Grady didn't want to think about after the games. He wanted to focus on the next challenge in front of him, take it all one thing at a time.

"I figure while you're there, you could put some feelers out, get some investors, maybe a sponsor or two." Benji had certainly put a lot of thought into this.

"Benj, not to state the obvious, but how are you going to coach serious skiers?" Grady hated that he had to ask.

Benji's face fell. "I understand a lot about the sport, Grady."

"I know, man. Of course you do."

"The kids I've been coaching, they *are* serious skiers. Yeah, they're disabled, but we've got our eyes set on the Paralympics."

"The Paralympics?" Grady sat with it for a minute, trying to wrap his head around the idea. He'd never considered going into business with his brother.

"It's a big deal, Grady," Benji said. "To be able to offer traditional coaching for kids who can walk and a whole para program? There's nothing out there like it."

"I've gotta think about all of this," Grady said. "After I get home, we'll talk, okay? But first I need to make it through the next few weeks of training and traveling and competing."

From across the table, his dad scoffed.

"What was that for?" Grady heard something inside him snap.

Dad looked at Benji. "I told you he wouldn't go for it."

"I'm not saying no. I'm just trying to figure out how this is going to work or if this is even what I want."

"Do you hear yourself?" Dad's fork fell onto the plate with a plunk. "You've had a whole life of getting what you want. What about your brother?"

"Of course I want Benji to have what he wants—that's all I've ever worked for. That's why these games are so important."

"Don't try to sell that line here, Son."

"It's the truth."

"We've all seen the stories about your fast life. Don't pretend you live this way for anybody but yourself."

"Is that what this is really about, Dad?" Grady dropped his silverware on the table. "You still blame me for what happened, don't you?"

"You guys, stop," Benji said. "It was a long time ago—can we leave the past in the past, please?"

"It's not the past, Benji," Dad said. "Not when you're still living in that chair every single day." His glare lasered in on Grady. "And you think throwing money at him will make it all right."

"What else do you want me to do? I can't take it back. I've apologized a thousand times. I've spent my life trying to make Benji's dream come true, and you still can't stand to look at me." Grady pushed his plate away and stood. "When will it ever be enough?"

He stood frozen as the air turned thick. Then, knowing his father wouldn't respond, he stormed out of the restaurant and into the parking lot, aware of the attention he drew as he did.

He didn't care. He was tired of paying for the past.

And yet, somehow he felt like a lifelong penance was exactly what he deserved.

CHAPTER

38

QUINN SAT STILL AS A STATUE at the table with Grady's family.

His "preemptive apology" wasn't so off base after all. Clearly there was a painful history here, and she felt like an intruder sitting in the middle of it all.

"Why did you have to do that?" Charlene dabbed her eyes with her napkin.

"I told you this was a bad idea." Randall pressed his beefy hands against the table.

"It wasn't a bad idea until you started in on him." Charlene turned to Quinn. "I'm so sorry, Quinn. We don't make a very good first impression, do we?"

"Don't worry about me." Quinn covered her plate of half-eaten food with her napkin. "I'm going to go look for Grady."

"Check the bars," Randall said.

She met his eyes. "Your son is a good man, sir."

"She's right, Dad," Benji said. "Grady has paid long enough for something that happened when we were kids. It was an accident. It's time to let it go."

"But he still acts like a rebellious teenager, doesn't he?"

"Not so much anymore," Benji said. "He's done all of this for us, to try and make us proud. But you're so intent on keeping him humble, you beat him down. You always have."

Randall stood. "I don't have to listen to this."

"Fine, but you need to know this is your issue, not mine," Benji said. "You're not doing me any favors by holding on to all of this. The only thing I want is my brother back."

Randall stormed off, leaving them all stunned.

"Have him let me know when you find him, okay?" Benji asked.

Quinn nodded, then stood. "It was nice to meet you both."

Both Charlene and Benji stared at their plates and said nothing.

The day was crisp and cold. They should've been out celebrating, and instead he was off somewhere feeling miserable. She started with his room, but it was empty. She checked the gym, the lounge, Happy's room. All empty.

Randall's words rushed back at her: *Check the bars.*

She shoved the thought aside and went back to her own room, sent him another Hey, where are you? text, then proceeded to pace the floor for a solid hour.

Where was he? Why wasn't he answering her messages?

By evening, she felt like a hamster in a cage. She didn't know her way around town, but what choice did she have? She was starting to get really worried.

She found her rental car in the parking lot and started off in the direction her GPS told her was downtown. She scanned the parked cars, searching for his familiar SUV and whispering prayers that God would keep him safe and protected and smart.

"And when I do find him, Lord, please give me the right words to say." It was obvious Grady was hurting, but would he let her in long enough to tell her why?

Finally, after twenty minutes of driving up and down Main Street, she spotted his Jeep and found a spot nearby. She pulled her coat around her and stopped next to his car, which was parked directly in front of a small bar called Doonby's.

A nervous feeling welled up inside her as she got out of the car. She wasn't good in strange places or different states or bars. But for his sake, she had to check.

She walked toward the bar, the sound of loud music streaming out onto the street. She passed by a handful of men headed inside. One guy fell in step beside her. "You look lost."

"I'm looking for my friend," she said.

"Is your friend as pretty as you?"

"He's prettier." She shot the guy a look.

"Quinn?"

She turned at the sound of Grady's voice and found him sitting on a small bench near the street.

Heat rushed to her cheeks as she forced herself not to walk away as the guys disappeared inside.

"What are you doing here?" He stood.

"I came to find you," she said. She watched him for a long moment, and while she couldn't deny she was angry with him—for leaving her at the restaurant, for losing his temper, for coming here of all places—she was surprised to find that wasn't the only emotion welling up inside.

She saw him for who he really was—a broken man. Whatever had happened in the past, he'd carried it with him ever since, a weight that kept him from believing he was worthy of forgiveness.

She knew a little something about that. What was it Carly had told her—she saw the world through a lens of brokenness? She knew now it was true. She clung to a past that held her hostage, believing the lies that she'd done something wrong, that she was unlovable.

But it wasn't Quinn who drove her mother away. She saw that now, and she was making peace with the fact that she may never be able to reconcile with the woman she'd been waiting for. Like a child holding a balloon on a windy day, she'd simply let it go. Given it over.

Could Grady ever do the same?

"You look really pretty," he said.

"You look a little drunk."

"I'm not." His shoulders slumped. "I went in for a few minutes. Thought I could drink it all away, but . . ."

"But what?"

He shrugged. "Seemed wrong."

She watched him. He'd gone to a bar, probably had a drink or two, and then he came outside—alone? In the freezing cold? He wasn't perfect, but oh, how he was trying.

"Can I drive you back to your room?"

He shook his head. "You can come sit here with me."

"We need to go."

"It's still early," he said.

"Let's go."

He stood. "Fine."

She led him to her rental car, then drove back toward the resort in silence.

He stared out the window.

"Are you okay?" she asked.

He shrugged. "Course I'm okay."

"It's just your dad said some things I—"

"My dad is a jerk." Grady cut her off. "Always has been."

Quinn snapped her mouth shut and drove. Maybe now wasn't the best time to talk. They arrived back at the resort and headed toward his room.

He pulled his key out and let himself in, holding the door open for her. She stood, unmoving, on the threshold of the door.

"Aren't you going to come in?" he asked.

"I don't think I should."

He met her gaze. "For a minute? Please?"

She took an uncertain step inside, and he closed the door behind her. "Do you need anything before I head back to my own room?"

He touched her face. "I let you down tonight, and I'm sorry."

She looked up into his eyes and saw sorrow there.

"Tell me it's okay."

She shook her head. "But it's not okay."

He closed his eyes. "I know. I told you I'm really not good enough for you, Quinn. As much as I want you, you deserve so much better than me."

"You need some coffee." She moved past him into the suite and found the small coffeepot near the sink.

"I had one drink. I'm fine." He plopped down onto the stiff hotel loveseat. "Do you remember the first time I kissed you?"

She eyed him over one shoulder. "Do *you* remember the first time you kissed me?"

"In your loft." There was mischief behind his grin.

"You do remember." She faced him. "I always assumed it was one of those drunk things you forgot."

He shook his head. "I remember. You made me feel like I could do anything. Even then, back when you couldn't stand me."

She laughed. "You couldn't stand me either."

"But I liked kissing you." He waggled his eyebrows. His smile faded and his expression turned serious. "You're probably wondering about my family."

She handed him a mug of coffee and sat down across from him. "I didn't want to pry."

"I don't like to talk about it."

"I figured."

"But you deserve to know." A long pause then—so long Quinn wondered if he'd changed his mind.

She reached out and covered his hand with her own.

"I don't know where to start." His eyes glossed over, haunted.

"I'm not going anywhere," she said. "Take your time."

He met her eyes. "You're just so good, Quinn. Why are you wasting your time with someone as screwed up as me?"

She moved onto the sofa next to him, still clasping his hands in her own. "I happen to think there is a lot of good in you, Grady Benson. More than you know."

He shook his head. "You don't know the whole story."

"Tell me."

~

Grady didn't want to come clean or recount the story or allow his past to shape what she thought of him today. Sure, she knew a lot of the mistakes he'd made, but not this—nobody knew this one.

And yet he trusted her. She deserved the truth more than he deserved the comfort of his silence.

He drew in a deep, shaky breath, wishing he had his usual liquid courage.

She squeezed his hand. "It's okay, Grady. Whatever it is."

But it didn't feel okay. And it wasn't okay to his father. And it would never be okay for Benji. But Grady had been held captive by his guilt for too long. "I was fourteen. Benji was sixteen. We discovered skiing when we were really young. Our dad took us, and I guess he thought we had potential. That or he forced us to be good at it. Either way, by the time we hit that age, I thought I knew everything." He picked up the mug of coffee and took a sip.

"Benji was a lot more cautious than I was. And a lot more talented. I think part of that ticked me off. Even then, I wanted to be the best. We were out skiing one night, and there was a section of our woods that hadn't been cleared. Trail skiing wasn't something Benji ever did, but I loved it, and I knew I could beat him if I could get him to race me."

He'd never told this story. Not to a single living soul. Regret squeezed the back of his throat, willing him to keep the words buried where they'd been living all these years.

He found her eyes, and something in them told him it was okay to go on.

"It was a stupid bet, really," Grady said. "But he took it and we shot through the woods like we knew where we were going. The snow was deep. Deep enough to hide stumps and rocks and the roots of some of the bigger trees."

He could still feel the wind on his face as they whipped down the slope. The cleared trail was only a few yards away, but they stayed on the rough terrain—Grady in front and Benji not far behind.

"Come on, Bro, is that all you've got?" Grady egged Benji on, daring his brother to try to catch him, knowing there was no way he would. Not today. He led them through the trees and around the curve, and that's when Benji took off to the left in an effort to cut Grady off. Grady sliced left too, securing his lead as they both jumped, air between their skis and the ground.

Grady's voice shook. "I landed hard but upright. But Benji . . ."

Quinn's hand found his again.

Grady swiped his free hand across his face. "I thought he was still behind me." His eyes clouded over and he stared down, latching on to the way her hand looked on his. "The jump wasn't even high—and Benji was a trick skier. He'd jumped a lot higher and farther and faster so many times before, but because the snow was so deep, he didn't see the huge tree stump. Landed right on it. Severed his spinal cord."

Grady took another drink, an attempt to regain his composure, but the memory was too great. He'd taken his skis off and ran up the side of the hill. Benji lay there, writhing in pain.

"I can't move, Gray," he'd said. "I can't feel my legs."

Grady still sometimes heard the sound of Benji's wailing on the nights he couldn't sleep.

"I raced back down the hill to find help. They had to airlift him out. My dad took one look at me and knew it'd been my idea—my fault—and now Benji was never gonna walk again." He rubbed his temples, willing the dull ache to go away.

"He'd pinned all of his hopes and dreams on Benji, and with one stupid decision, I stole them." Grady studied the ceiling. "I don't think my father has ever forgiven me." The look on his dad's face told him as much. From that day on, the disappointment was always there, looming somewhere in the background, even when Grady won a big race or had a major breakthrough on the slopes. It had never been enough. It would never be enough. Because it was all supposed to have been Benji, and because of Grady, it never would be.

"Oh, Grady," Quinn whispered.

Another swipe across his traitorous eyes. "Thing is, Benji has never blamed me. He let me off the hook the very next day, right after he found out he was never going to ski again. 'It was my choice to follow you out there,' he told me. 'I did this to myself.'"

Finally, Grady met Quinn's eyes. "But it *was* my fault. It was my stupid idea, and I knew we weren't supposed to ski back there. And Benji—he was good. They were talking Olympics for him when he was only fifteen. It was all he ever wanted. All my dad ever wanted."

His eyes found the ceiling again. "So I promised him I'd bring home the gold. For both of us."

"That's why you won't retire," she said, her voice quiet.

He nodded slowly. "I can't quit yet. I've still got stuff to do. For Benji."

She wrapped her arms around him. "Grady, it was an accident. And you were just a kid."

"I was old enough to know better." How could she not see that? He stood and walked to the other side of the room. "Besides, you can't tell me you've just let go of everything that happened with your mom."

"I'm working on that." Her voice was quiet, and he could see the hurt behind her eyes. He cautioned himself not to wound her, not to mess this up the way he messed up every other good thing in his life.

"But you can't just snap your fingers and make it go away. You of all people should understand that."

She stood and faced him. "That's not what I'm saying."

"Then what, Quinn? What do you want me to do?"

"It's been how many years? Isn't it time to forgive yourself?"

He faced her. "I don't deserve to just go on with my life like everything is fine."

Her eyes locked on to his. "You don't deserve to be happy? Is that what you think?"

"That's what I know."

Something like realization washed over her face. "It all makes sense now."

"What does?"

"Why you sabotage yourself. Why you pick fights with people and rebel against your coaches." She studied him. "You don't think you deserve the good things in your life."

"That's just stupid," he said.

"Then why haven't you forgiven yourself?" Her eyes pleaded with him.

"Some things aren't forgivable. Your mom leaving—that's unforgivable. Me causing my brother's accident—that's unforgivable."

She stilled. "I don't think so, Grady."

"Well, you're wrong." He turned a circle, raking his hand through his hair. "Just go."

"What?" He could hear the confusion in her voice.

"I just need some time."

"You're going to push me away too," she said.

"Come on, Quinn," he said. "We both knew this was never going to work."

"How can you say that?" Tears shone in her eyes now, and he could see the wound he'd inflicted. But it was for the best. She deserved someone better—someone as good as she was.

"I want to be alone." His voice was tense and louder than he'd meant it to be.

And the next thing he heard was the sound of the door closing behind her.

CHAPTER

39

IT NEVER WOULD'VE WORKED OUT ANYWAY. That's what she told herself. Quinn went straight back to Michigan the day after Grady's race, and she hadn't heard from him since. It had been weeks.

The Olympics were just around the corner, and he'd officially made the team. He was back in the news, and she was trying not to pay attention. So far, her avoidance was working. She didn't know where exactly he was, just that he was off training and probably falling in love with a female skier or at least someone who didn't look like the Michelin Man out on the slopes.

She'd settled back into her regular Harbor Pointe routine— breakfast at Hazel's with Hailey and Lucy; Sunday brunch at her dad's house with Carly, Jaden, and the whole crew. But at night, when she was faced with the silence and darkness, her thoughts always turned to him.

For the most part, her friends and family had accepted her vague explanation that things "didn't work out" with Grady. Maybe they assumed she'd talk about it when she was ready.

Would she ever be ready?

She tried to busy herself with Expo preparations. Her mini display would be up on that stage, and even though her mother was apparently living her new life in Florida, Quinn still wanted to take first.

But not for Jacie Whitman—for herself. Because she'd seen what it looked like to be the best at something, thanks to Grady, and she wanted a sliver of that for herself.

She hoped that wasn't prideful.

Jaden was healing well, up and moving around with the help of crutches—and while he wouldn't be skiing anytime soon, he'd made his physical therapy a priority to ensure he'd be back out there this time next year.

Quinn had to admit, she'd expected Grady to leave Harbor Pointe and forget all about them, but according to Carly, he was still in touch with her nephew, and his calls always seemed to brighten Jaden's mood. His calls and the pretty, dark-haired girl who came over every day to help catch him up on the schoolwork he'd missed—she certainly seemed to lift his spirits too.

Now, Quinn stood on the porch of Carly's bungalow, praying that her visit with Jaden didn't turn into a recap of Grady's latest and greatest. She didn't think she could handle it.

She knocked on the door, then let herself in. "Hello?"

"In here, Aunt Quinn."

She followed Jaden's voice into the living room, where she found him sprawled out on the sofa watching the all-too-familiar sports channel.

"Mom's not home from work yet," Jaden said.

She sat on the chair next to him. "How are you feeling?"

"I feel good. Did you see they're interviewing Grady this afternoon after his training?" Jaden's eyes brightened. "Man, I wish I could've taken him up on his offer."

"What offer?"

"Tickets to the Winter Games. Didn't he tell you?"

She shook her head. "Why would he offer us tickets?"

Jaden shrugged. "Because he's not close with most of his family. Who else does he have to celebrate with him?"

He made Grady sound so lonely. Was he? Her heart ached at the thought. She shoved it aside.

"Stupid leg," Jaden said. "Once-in-a-lifetime chance, and I'm stuck on the couch."

"Sorry, kid," Quinn said, hoping her voice sounded lighter than she felt.

"You haven't talked to him, have you?" Jaden asked.

"Um, no." Quinn smoothed her skirt, then let her hands rest on her knees. "Wait, how do you know that?"

"He called last night. Asked about you." Jaden's eyes darted to hers. "Why don't you just talk to the guy?"

"It's complicated."

"Try me."

No. She was absolutely not going to get into any of this with her fifteen-year-old nephew.

"Never mind. I overheard Mom and Grandpa talking. I know everything."

She shot him a look.

"They thought I was asleep," Jaden said. "You're being too hard on him."

"There's a lot more to it than that, Jaden, and leaving things the way we did wasn't my decision." Quinn inched back in the chair.

"He told me that too," Jaden said.

"Good grief, is there anything he didn't tell you?" Grady's relationship with her nephew had only grown since the accident. Jaden looked up to him, like he was a big brother. That would've bothered her a few weeks ago, but now it only made her miss him more.

Jaden inched up on his elbows. "Aunt Quinn, he's crazy about you. He screwed up and he knows it. Give him another chance."

The words needled at her heart, trying to worm their way in, but she shut them out. No. She wouldn't allow this crazy cocktail of emotions to intoxicate her again. She'd made up her mind. She was better off on her own.

"Oh, look, there he is." Jaden pointed the remote at the television and turned up the volume. "They've really been talking him up. Saying he might win the whole thing."

Really? What was he feeling right now? He must be elated. "Quite the turnaround from what they were saying before."

"Yeah. He's out there proving them all wrong."

Grady shot down the mountain and came to a slick stop as two men approached him. He took off his goggles, and there was that smile. Those eyes. He looked genuinely happy. See? They were both better off alone.

Except she wasn't sitting here smiling. She was suffering, at least on the inside. She wanted to hear how his training was going. She wanted to know how it felt to prove to everyone that he was still as good as ever—maybe even better. She wanted to be in on the details of his life.

But she couldn't. Her time was spent working on her Floral Expo display and trying to forget the way she'd felt when she was with him.

The screen filled up with the image of Grady's face. He looked tan, eyes bright. He looked good. *Really* good.

Grady leaned in as he listened to the reporter, a pretty woman wearing a magenta ski cap. "There is a lot of talk surrounding this year's games, and most of the chatter is about you. How does that make you feel?"

Grady flashed that charming smile of his. "You know, Kat, I feel great. I'm glad people are talking about my skiing and not my stupid mistakes anymore."

Kat laughed. "There has been a lot of discussion about the new and improved Grady Benson, and I have to say, you do seem like a different skier out there. Do you feel different?"

He looked up, then back at the woman interviewing him. "I do. I feel strong and focused."

"And Brian Murphy, head coach of the US ski team, has taken note. He told us yesterday that of everyone competing, he's most excited about you. He said he's seen great changes in your attitude and work ethic ever since you returned from your not-so-self-imposed sabbatical." She stuck the microphone back in Grady's face.

The back door opened and Carly called out, "I'm home!"

"We're in here, Ma," Jaden hollered.

On the screen, Grady laughed, that smile doing its very best to weaken Quinn's defenses. "Well, yeah, Brian and I had our differences in the past, but I came out here ready to get humble and learn what I can from that man. He's a genius, and I was foolish not to see it before. He's the reason I'm here."

Carly appeared in the doorway. "Whoa. What's going on in here?"

Both Jaden and Quinn hissed, "Shhh."

"So what is it that's different about you, Grady?" Kat asked. "What can we attribute these remarkable changes to?"

He pulled his gloves off and looked at the camera for the first time since the interview started. "Well, you know, things weren't really going my way for a while, but I met somebody who taught me the value of hard work and faith. She taught me that sometimes your dream is worth fighting for. I guess I want to make her proud, and I want her to know I'm not done fighting."

"Will she be here cheering you on?"

Grady's eyes glassed over. "Now, that *would* be a dream come true."

"She's one lucky girl, Grady. We wish you the best of luck this weekend."

"Thanks, Kat."

She droned on about something, but Quinn had stopped listening.

"You don't think he was talking about . . ."

"Yeah," Jaden said. "He was talking about you."

"You think so?"

Carly had sat in the chair across from Quinn. "Yeah, which makes me wonder why you're still refusing to contact him."

She didn't respond.

Carly groaned. "You're so stubborn!"

"It's not being stubborn. He really hurt me." Saying the words aloud brought that dreaded lump back to her throat.

"Did you hear what he just said?" Carly asked. "Whatever happened before doesn't matter."

But it did matter. He was doing well, and she was happy for him—so happy—but that didn't mean she was supposed to be at his side.

Quinn swiped a tear as it trickled down her cheek. "There's really nothing for me to do, you guys. He made it clear that he didn't think we were a good fit. End of story." She stood. "I have to go."

"Quinn, wait." Carly put a hand on her arm, but she pulled away and kept walking. She'd had her chance with the Olympian.

And it wasn't meant to be.

CHAPTER

40

THE DAY OF THE FLORAL EXPO DESIGN COMPETITION, Quinn awoke in an unfamiliar hotel room across from the convention center in Grand Rapids. While she knew she wouldn't see her mother that day, she had to believe that somewhere, Jacie Whitman was keeping tabs on this competition. And while once upon a time that would've made her nervous, now it didn't seem to matter all that much.

When she'd let it go, she'd felt something lift—a burden that she'd been carrying around like extra luggage for the whole of her life.

Now she wanted to rise to the top of her field for her own benefit—and for the good of the flower shop.

She'd arrived at the Expo the day before and set up her display, a smaller version of the Secret Garden design that had landed her here in the first place. As she worked with those same flowers, she couldn't help but think of Grady.

Wild and untamed. If he hadn't said those words, she might not be sitting here now.

The Olympics were over. She'd avoided the viewing parties at

Cedar Grove, much to Carly's dismay. "You should come," her sister had said. "It's really fun."

"I can't, Car." She'd chosen instead to watch him from the comfort of her own loft, where she could wear every single one of her emotions without worrying about anyone else reading into them.

And she'd run the emotional gamut. From panic to fear to worry to excitement to edge-of-her-seat anticipation, she'd made her way through them all, ending, of course, with pure elation as the man she'd once loved came screaming toward the finish line to capture the gold.

He was ecstatic, and rightly so. He hadn't quit, and it had paid off.

Perhaps the best part of the whole thing, though, was watching him take that medal off his neck and walk it over to his brother, who was sitting on the sidelines, pride all over his face.

Quinn had choked back the tears long enough and melted into a puddle right there in her living room.

See? This was why she couldn't have watched with everyone else. She would've given herself away.

She was so happy for him, and more than anything she wanted to tell him, but as she grabbed her phone and stared at the blank screen underneath his name, debating whether or not to send a text, something stopped her. She couldn't. It would only confuse things.

But ever since, in spite of her excitement about the design competition, there was a hollowness inside her. A hollowness that she pushed aside as she walked through the doors to the convention center, flashed her badge, and began her trek from booth to booth.

The competition results would be announced at 2 p.m. Around one thirty, she made her way to the hall where the awards ceremony would be held. In the lobby just outside the room were the three displays that were up for Best Design. As she walked by, she heard someone comment on hers, saying, "It's just so free and full of life."

She pulled open the door to the large room and thought of Grady. *Free and full of life.* And she hoped one day she could say the same of herself. After all, that was the way she wanted to live.

The room looked like a standard banquet hall. At the front was a stage with a podium in the middle, flanked by two large screens. There were people milling about and more chairs facing the stage than she'd anticipated. She supposed it felt more daunting now that her name and photos of her designs were going to be up on that screen.

As she made her way to the front, where her seat was reserved, she stopped in the middle of the aisle. There, filling up an entire row, were her dad and Beverly (holding hands!), Carly, Jaden, Calvin, Judge, Hailey, and Lucy.

Quinn's eyes went wide. "What are you guys doing here?"

"I got them in."

She whirled around and found Mimi standing behind her. "Mimi? I thought you were in Italy!"

"We decided to come home for a few weeks before heading off to our next destination—Bali." Mimi opened her arms and Quinn stepped into a tight, motherly hug. "I'm so proud of you."

"I can't believe you're all here." Quinn pulled from Mimi's embrace and studied them all. "You guys are the best."

"Are you kidding? We wouldn't have missed this for anything." Her dad beamed. "We're all pulling for you, sweetheart."

"Miss Collins? You should take your seat now." The woman wore an earpiece and a staff badge.

"Go," Dad said, squeezing her hand. "We'll see you afterward."

She met his eyes. He'd been her mother and her father. He'd been attentive and good and kind. He'd protected her, over and over again. And she'd been oblivious to that goodness until this very moment. "Thanks, Dad. Thank you all for being here. It means the world to me."

"Good luck, Quinnie," Lucy called out from the end of the row.

"We're all going to cheer really loud," Carly said. "Hope you don't embarrass too easily."

Quinn laughed, and as she took her seat, she realized the outcome of the competition didn't matter so much anymore. What really mattered was sitting in that row—a collective group of people who were invested in her life.

She listened as Kitty Moore, a small woman with perfectly coiffed orange-colored hair, welcomed everyone to the competition. There were a number of other awards that came first, and Quinn listened dutifully, trying to keep her mind from wandering.

Finally, after nearly an hour, the words *Best Design* appeared on the screen. Carly let out a whoop and Quinn stifled a giggle. Her family had no tact. And that was only part of the reason she loved them so much.

One by one, Kitty presented the entries of the finalists. Photos flashed across the screen, ending with a headshot next to each name. When Quinn's appeared, the whole group representing her let out a cheer.

"Can we get all three finalists up on the stage, please?" Kitty glanced down to where they were all sitting, and they stood, making their way up the stairs.

"Now a quick word about each competitor from our former president, Jacie Whitman."

Quinn's mouth went dry. She met Carly's eyes as the image of a familiar yet unfamiliar woman appeared on the screen.

It was the first time Quinn had actually gotten a good look at her mother's face since childhood, and while she'd aged, of course, there was still a hint of the same woman Quinn had known and loved all those years ago.

Jacie began talking about one of the other contestants, explaining why her design was chosen as a finalist.

What was she going to say about Quinn?

Next came commentary about the man standing to Quinn's right, whose work was "edgy and moody."

Quinn watched the screen in the back that faced the stage, doing her best to connect with a woman who wasn't really there, listening as she gave her opinion about her estranged daughter's work.

"In January, I had the pleasure of visiting Harbor Pointe for their Winter Carnival, where Quinn Collins's Secret Garden display absolutely took my breath away. It was inventive and whimsical, and its magic captured my imagination the moment I stepped through the door. I wasn't the only one smitten with Miss Collins's work, as many of the guests I talked to were enamored with the beauty on display. Miss Collins shows great promise and creativity as a floral designer, definitely one to watch. If you're looking for beautiful craftsmanship mixed with incomparable artistry, make your way to her Forget-Me-Not Flower Shop today."

The screen went dark, but Quinn still stared at it, as if she could will her mother to come back. To say one personal word to her. To send her some kind of signal, some kind of hint that she still cared.

But she was gone. And there was nothing. Only a crisp professionalism that still kept her, after all this time, at a distance.

Quinn glanced up and found her father's eyes. They were drilling her, as if to ask how she was doing. Down the line, she saw face after face with the same concerned expression.

She was so loved. Her life was so good. Maybe staying away was the best gift her mother could have given her.

And as they called her name as the second-place winner, and she stood on that podium staring out at all their shining, cheerful faces, it occurred to her that there was only one glaring exception.

And it wasn't the one she'd been chasing her whole life.

⟋⟋⟋

News of her second-place achievement spread across Harbor Pointe like butter on a warm pancake. It seemed it didn't matter if you won the Olympic gold or took home second place in a floral design competition—the people of this town were going to celebrate.

The shop had gone from busy to bustling with news of her success, and she had brides calling to book her for weddings that weren't scheduled for months. In anticipation of a very busy year, she'd hired two part-time employees.

After her realization at the Expo, she'd decided she'd been stubborn long enough. Grady might've told her he wanted her to leave, but that television interview had given her reason to think maybe he'd reconsidered.

She needed to find out for sure. In person. The thought sent a jolt of panic down her back.

Now that she'd been on a plane once before, she had all the courage she needed to book another ticket. But facing him, putting herself on the line again—that took an entirely different kind of courage, one she wasn't sure she could muster.

Besides, she'd been scouring race websites to find out if he was still competing, since the season wasn't actually over, but so far, she'd come up empty. She didn't know where Grady was at the moment, and she didn't like it.

Her last resort would be to check with Jaden, which meant making her plan known. At this point, it might be her only option. And Grady was worth possible humiliation.

On Saturdays, like today, she let her employees handle the shop while she took slow, purposeful mornings with her favorite coffee and whatever book had captured her attention that week.

Now, from her spot at a small café table outside Dandy's Bakery, she watched a young family ride by on their bikes, tires kerplunking along the brick road. The sound of children laughing carried over from the park on the next block, and shoppers chattered on as they passed by, everyone making the most of the unseasonably warm weekend in the middle of March.

"Is this seat taken?"

Quinn froze. She knew that voice—she'd never get it out of her head. But there was no way it could be . . .

She turned around.

Grady.

He stood there looking as if he'd just stepped out of the pages of a catalog: chiseled cheekbones, lightly scruffy yet strong and healthy. His eyes shone bright at the sight of her.

"Hey, Q." His smile faded as he took her in.

She stood. "What are you doing here?"

He shrugged. "Heard there was this great little flower shop, and—" He pulled a bouquet, wrapped in brown paper and tied with string, from behind his back.

"Tulips," she said. "You spent money to give me my own flowers?"

He smiled. "How often does anyone ever give you flowers?"

She took the bouquet. "Never, actually."

"Then it's the perfect gift." He looked unsure. "Can I sit?"

She shook her head, as if to bring herself back to the present. "Oh, yes, of course."

He took the chair across from her, folded his hands on the table, and watched her for a long moment as she sat down again.

"So . . . why are you really here?" Did she sound as unsteady as she felt?

"Came to see you." He reached across the table and took her hands in his. "Came to make my case."

She frowned. "What kind of case?"

"Not the kind I have to make before the judge," he said, one eyebrow raised. "The kind that will hopefully show you how much you mean to me."

She had no response.

"I thought a lot about what you said. About forgiving myself and forgiving my father."

"Yeah?"

"I'm not quite there yet." He squeezed her hands. "But I want to be. I want to learn to let it go, to get past all that garbage so I can move on."

"I think that would be really good for you, Grady."

"And you were right. I do sabotage myself, and I did push you away. And I still think I'm not good enough for you."

"Grady, please—"

He cut her off with an upheld hand. "But I told you before that I want to be, and I meant it. I want to try to be the man you think I can be."

She studied her folded hands on the table. "I saw your win."

"You did?" His face warmed into a soft smile. "I hoped you were watching. Jaden said you didn't go to Cedar Grove with the rest of them, so I wasn't sure."

"I watched it alone." She eyed him. "You gave Benji your medal."

He nodded. "The medal was always for him. But the skiing—the journey—that was all mine."

She pressed her lips together. Was this actually happening? Was he really here, in Harbor Pointe, sitting at her table?

"Look, Quinn—" he reached over and put a hand on her cheek—"I'll do my best to let go of all of that other stuff, but I never want to let go of you."

She blinked, sending tears down her cheeks. "I wasn't sure I'd ever see you again."

"Are you kidding? When I won, all I could think about was that I wished you were there."

She understood that feeling, though on a much smaller scale.

"Can I show you something?" He stood.

She gave his upturned hand a skeptical look.

"Come on." He pulled her up, held on to her hand, and walked down the block toward the flower shop.

"What are you doing?"

He led her around the building toward the alley where the back door was. "Close your eyes."

"Seriously?"

"Don't ruin the surprise."

She did as she was told, allowing him to lead her on—toward what, she didn't know.

"Remember how I told you that you reminded me that my dreams were worth fighting for?"

"Yes."

He stopped moving. "I wanted to remind you of the same thing. Open your eyes."

Sunlight streamed into the alley, illuminating an old, dusty-blue Volkswagen truck.

"So, look." He ran over to the truck and pulled down the sides of the bed. "You can put crates here, and we can build a sort of shelf for the flower tins. Those galvanized metal ones you like so much. Oh, and this is the best part." He reached inside the truck and pulled out a long sign that read: *Forget-Me-Not Flower Truck.*

Tears sprang to her eyes. "You did this for me?"

He leaned the sign against the side of the truck and looked at her. "I'd do anything for you."

He grabbed hold of her sweater and gave it a tug, pulling her close and wrapping his arms around her waist. She pressed her hands against his chest and dared a glance into his eyes. Slowly, she drew her lips to his, aware that for once in her life, she wasn't thinking of everything that could go wrong.

She was only thinking of one thing: possibility. And she didn't have a single reservation about the risks of loving him. She only knew she wanted to do it from this day on and for the rest of her life.

Find love in Harbor Pointe

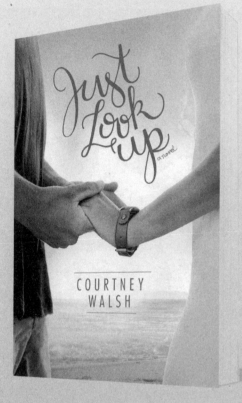

Maybe what she's looking for is right in front of her—
if she'd just look up.

Available in bookstores and online.

CHAPTER

1

JUST BREATHE.

Lane Kelley rested her hand on her knee, willing it to stop bouncing. She watched from behind her desk as Marshall ushered the client—a young guy in jeans who appeared to be valiantly attempting a goatee, albeit unsuccessfully—through the glass doors of the conference room at JB Sweet & Associates, the interior design firm where she worked as one of many designers.

You can do this. It's what you've been working for.

The chance of a lifetime.

That's what Marshall had called it—*the chance of a lifetime.* *"You're one of five people in the company who will get to be part of this project, Lane. The higher-ups are watching. This is huge. You're not going to get an opportunity like this again."*

She understood. She'd been pursuing this since she started at the design firm seven years ago as part of her senior seminar at Northwestern. She hadn't expected to stay here this long, but she quickly found a home at JB Sweet, and she was good at what she did.

The last seven years had gone by in a blur, leaving Lane with half-remembered moments of creating branded environments for new and established companies by using her artistic abilities and her love of interior design. Her college internship had turned into a career—one that afforded her a luxury loft in the city, a shared personal assistant, and now the chance to become the next creative director at JB Sweet.

Chloe welcomed the goatee guy—Ashton—and the rest of the team from Solar into the meeting room and flashed Lane her trade-mark oh-my-goodness eyes. Chloe understood, more than anyone, what this meeting meant to Lane. In some ways, this would be *their* promotion. After all, if Lane did get the position, she'd already prom-ised that her first request would be for Chloe to move up with her.

Chloe gave Lane one more knowing nod as she passed by again, and Lane actually considered pinching herself.

This was the moment she'd been dreaming of—a chance to win over the execs at Solar, to convince them that yes, they very much should give JB Sweet & Associates the honor of designing and branding their new business space, because yes, she and her team would work round the clock to make sure the branded space would reflect Solar's unique, casual-yet-trendy style.

"They love our aesthetic," Marshall had told her. *"I mean, bring your A game, but expect good things. According to Ashton, the whole team is leaning our way."*

And that was *before* her pitch. All she had to do was *not* mess it up.

She'd run through her presentation well into the wee hours of the morning, starting in on the caffeine around 4 a.m. She was ready. Excited, if a little jittery. Her designs were great. She could do this. She could wow them.

And yet, thinking of it now, she felt rocking-on-a-boat-in-choppy-waters sick. She'd never had a chance this big in her life.

Don't mess this up, Lane.

The rest of the executives from Solar, a tech company in the *Forbes* top ten last year, filed past. They shook hands with Marshall and the others from her team as they walked through the door. But not Lane. She was still at her desk, busy trying not to throw up.

Stay in control. These guys have no idea that your nerves are taking you out to the woodshed. No one can make you feel inferior in this arena. This isn't high school. This is where you shine.

The guys from Solar—she could only call them "guys" because not a single one of them actually looked like a man—all resembled their fearless leader, Ashton, aka Mr. Wanna Goatee. Jeans, hoodies, Converse One Stars. No suits for this company. Somehow she found that more intimidating, not less. After all, she'd never been the trendy type.

She shoved aside the unwelcome image of a sweater that didn't quite cover a protruding midsection.

"Honey, I tried to tell you, you shouldn't wear clothes that are so tight."

She'd been aching for sympathy, but her mother had only given empty *I-told-you-so*s and the sour taste of disapproval. She hadn't meant to disregard Lane's feelings; she just wanted to help. At least that's what Lane tried to tell herself.

Nobody here knows about that.

Marshall looked terribly outdated next to the Solar execs with his white button-down and geometrically patterned red tie. Handsome in his own way, yet everyone in the room aged twenty years in the presence of their fetus-clients.

Marshall broke away from the others and headed her way.

Her phone pinged, and she glanced at it almost without thinking. Instantly she wished she hadn't.

"What is it?" Marshall asked when he reached her. "You have that look."

She tapped on the notification. She'd set her phone up to alert her whenever a competing design firm posted something on social media, and this was a big one.

"Julia Baumann." She looked up at Marshall. "You didn't tell me Innovate was pitching your friend Ashton, too." She showed Marshall the photo, a cozy image of Julia Baumann and the goatee guy in the next room. "The caption says, 'Sweet things are happening for Innovate. Details coming soon.'" She frowned. "There's a winking emoji and *sweet* is in all caps. Is she sending a message to us?"

He took the phone from her and read the post for himself. "I'm sure you're reading too much into this."

"I thought you said we practically had this one 'in the bag.'"

Marshall shrugged. "We do, Lane. Maybe she's trying to get under your skin."

Well, that would be juvenile. Lane groaned. She didn't want to think about Innovate just before she walked into that room. Julia Baumann had a way of swiping clients right out from under her, and it was starting to feel personal. Lane found most of the design community open and friendly—encouraging, even—but Julia was none of those things.

Lane took another glance at the photo. "They look awfully friendly, Marshall, and you know Julia probably had a solid pitch."

"Maybe." Marshall squeezed her hand. "But ours is going to blow them away."

He couldn't possibly know that. She thought back to their many long team meetings—how many times had Marshall deferred to her, chosen her ideas and trusted her vision? What if he'd been wrong to do so? What if she'd misunderstood Solar and gone in completely the wrong direction?

No. She shook her insecurities away. Their pitch was ready—and it was on point. JB Sweet himself would have to take note once she presented her plans. She'd finally get that promotion and maybe even take a little vacation to celebrate.

She'd never taken a vacation.

"Come on, forget Innovate. You're ready for the big leagues." Marshall walked her over to the small huddle at the end of the room where the rest of their team had gathered.

She barely listened as Marshall gave the team his version of a pep talk. He scanned the circle and was met with overenthusiastic nodding from everyone but Lane. She didn't do overenthusiastic. She did focus. She did the game face. She did control.

And she did it well.

"Lane, you okay?"

"I'm ready." She didn't bother trying to explain her readiness or convincing Marshall she really meant it. That's what weak women did. And she never wanted to be one of those again.

"Okay. We'll start in just a few minutes. Knock 'em dead, guys." Marshall waited until the others had dispersed, then turned his attention back to Lane. "You feel good?"

She nodded as she ran through her pitch in her mind.

"Remember, this is the chance—"

"Of a lifetime." She cut him off. "I know." *Don't remind me. I'm nervous enough as it is.*

"I went out on a limb to give you this meeting, Lane. You're up to this, right?" He raised a brow as if issuing a challenge.

"You know I'm up to this." She clicked her phone's screen off, wishing she could click off the sick feeling in her stomach that easily.

"That's my girl." He clapped a hand on her shoulder. Like she was one of the guys. Very professional.

She had to hand it to him—he was doing an excellent job of keeping their relationship hidden. Even she found it hard to believe he had any romantic feelings for her at all.

"You go ahead," she told Marshall. "I'll be right there."

Breathe. She was running through her opening one last time when her phone pinged again, and as if she were programmed to do so, she pulled it out and glanced at it.

Julia had posted another image, this one a photo of the mock-up Innovate had presented to Solar only hours ago. The caption read, *We're calling it "Solarvate." Can't wait to get started.*

Lane's mouth went dry, her stomach hollow. The image on the screen looked so elegant, so regal, so not what she had planned for this pitch meeting.

"You ready?" Chloe stood at her side, looking a little more tired than usual, the way she often did after one of their all-nighters. Lane made a mental note to get her assistant a gift certificate for a massage or give her some time off to thank her for being so helpful.

Chloe had probably seen Julia's posts too. She kept tabs on them the same way Lane did. But Lane had to believe Solar hadn't made up their mind already. If they had, would they really be sitting here in JB Sweet's conference room?

She did a quick survey of Julia's design, then turned her phone to vibrate. "I'm ready."

Chloe nodded and moved out of the way as Lane passed by. She smoothed her black dress pants and sat down next to Marshall.

After everyone was seated, JB called the meeting to order. The Solar executives, with their Starbucks to-go cups, their casual shoes, their bordering-on-shaggy hair and impress-me expressions, all turned their attention to the man. Marshall might've aged twenty years in the presence of the Solar execs, but next to them, JB seemed downright prehistoric.

Lane had always found him to be a quirky kind of man, one who used words like *fellow* and had a bushy white mustache that made her doubt the presence of an upper lip at all. Ashton should take a few pointers from JB. That man knew how to grow facial hair.

Lane half listened to JB's introduction of Solar—stating facts she'd already researched on her own. Next, JB gave a short pitch about why his firm was the best to take on the massive task of creating and designing a branded space for a cutting-edge tech business like Solar.

JB assured them that the space they had planned for Solar was not only functional but truly creative at its core—something the artistic Solar execs would certainly appreciate. JB was nothing if not an excellent salesman. Maybe that's why this *fellow* was still running the show after all these years.

Lane glanced down at her tablet, mentally reciting her opening lines, when the phone in the bag near her feet lit up, vibrating loudly enough to pull Miles's attention.

"Might want to silence that thing," her coworker hissed.

She fished the phone out of her bag and pressed the button to stop the noise before anyone else noticed, but not before she saw that it was her mother calling. She sent the call to voice mail. She supposed she was due for her monthly guilt-trip phone call—it had been at least that long since she'd spoken to her mom.

In her hand, the phone started vibrating again.

Mom, you have the worst timing.

She hit the button to shut it up, then turned off the power.

Marshall took JB's spot at the front of the room and introduced himself. "I think we're ready to begin." He glanced at Lane.

Just breathe. Part of her, she supposed, would always feel like a fraud. Most days, despite her Northwestern education and years of experience, Lane still felt like she was playing dress-up in the closet of someone much older, much thinner, and much more professional than she ever felt.

And yet she'd mastered the art of playing this part perfectly, as if she were born for the role.

". . . and we're sure you'll be as impressed with her as we are. Lane Kelley." Marshall spoke her name, pulling her out of her own head.

She met his eyes and he leaned forward as if to will her out of her seat.

Had time suddenly stopped moving?

Lane stood, taking her place next to the big screen. *You can do this.* She flipped open the cover of her tablet and drew in a deep breath as the image of a mood board that perfectly captured their design popped up on the screen beside her.

She'd created the image herself. Most people were visual, and the images, all of them, needed to conjure the same feelings the space itself would. Every item on the mood board had been carefully—painstakingly—chosen.

Lane knew Solar inside and out, she reminded herself. She'd read every article, every blurb, every tweet and Facebook post that had anything to do with the business this team had built. She was wrapped up in the details—and it was about to pay off.

In spades.

She had her game face on. As she stood there, every insecurity melted away. They were in her world now, and here, she knew how to get things done.

Lane was about to deliver her first sentence when the glass door of the conference room opened and Chloe appeared. She wore an apologetic look on her face and Lane knew her well enough to tell she wasn't happy to steal the attention.

"I'm sorry to interrupt." Chloe looked at Lane. "Lane, you've got a phone call."

"Can't it wait?" Marshall spoke through clenched teeth, doing a bad job of pretending he wasn't annoyed.

Chloe's face fell. "I'm afraid not."

Marshall pressed his lips together and glared at Lane, telepathically communicating the words undoubtedly running through his mind: *Don't screw this up.*

"Can you take a message, Chloe?" Lane asked. "I'm just getting ready to begin."

"I don't think—"

"Take a message," Marshall cut her off.

"There's been an accident, Lane," Chloe said. "You need to take the call."

A Note from the Author

Every story I write seems to be a snapshot of the journey I'm on, the lessons I've learned, and the pieces of life I've grown to love. *Just Let Go* is no different. It was a pure joy to return to Harbor Pointe, this time with new characters, and to explore life through Quinn and Grady's eyes.

In so many ways, I relate to Quinn—the risk-averse rule follower who is still holding on to past hurts, so much so that she doesn't even realize how they've kept her from moving forward. I've been there. I've been frozen in the past, unable to break free of the way I thought things were supposed to go.

Maybe you can relate?

Writing this story helped me realize that letting go and moving on are essential if we ever have a hope of living a full, happy, and prosperous life. I'm grateful for the opportunity to explore the things God is doing in my heart through the stories he places there, and I'm especially grateful that you've taken the time to read this one.

I know you have a million choices when it comes to what you can do with your time, so the fact that you spent it reading my words truly means the world to me.

I sincerely hope you enjoyed Quinn and Grady's story, and I would *love* to know what you thought of it. I truly love to hear from my readers, especially when I get to know you a little better! I invite you to stay in touch by signing up for my newsletter on my website, www.courtneywalshwrites.com, or by dropping me a line via e-mail: courtney@courtneywalshwrites.com.

With love and gratitude to you,
Courtney

Acknowledgments

To Adam. Always and forever. Me + You. Thank you for being my best friend and for not letting me give up on my dreams, even when they get really, really hard. I count you among my very greatest blessings.

My kids, Sophia, Ethan, and Sam. Of course you know I love you, but did you know that I like you too? A lot. I'm awfully proud of the humans you are becoming.

My parents, Bob and Cindy Fassler. Thank you for never discouraging my big dreams. And, Mom, thanks for being my first reader. Thank you for praying for us and for training me up the way I should go. I thank God for you every day.

Stephanie Broene. I will always, always be grateful to you. You have enriched my life in so many ways, and I am deeply in your debt.

Shaina Turner. Not only are you so much fun, but you've been such a fabulous partner in this journey to turning this story into an actual book. What a joy to have the chance to work on it with you. Thank you.

Danika King. Patient. Kind. Thoughtful. Insightful. Where would I be without you? Thank you for all you continue to do to make my books stronger. You are such a gift.

Carrie Erikson. My sister. My friend. My wise counsel. Thank you for being the friend of my heart. And thank you for laughing unashamedly, even when it's slightly inappropriate.

To Natasha Kern, my agent. Thank you for challenging me to be better and write stronger. I am so thankful for your wisdom on this journey.

To Deb Raney. Always my mentor and always my friend. For all you've done to help me understand story—I am grateful.

To Katie Ganshert, Becky Wade, and Melissa Tagg, my precious writer friends who I adore and love. Thank you all for brainstorming with me, for challenging me, for talking story and publishing and life with me. Because of each of you, I feel less alone and completely supported. What a gift you are!

To the entire team at Tyndale. Seriously. You guys are the best. Thank you for what you do every day to shine a light on our stories and give your authors a safe place to create. I am so blessed to sit in such amazing company.

To my Studio kids and families. Thank you for making my "day job" so much fun. What in the world would I do without all of you?!

And especially to you, my readers. I hope you know how special you are. I hope you know that your kind words (either directly to me or via a review or social media) are so greatly appreciated. I hope you know that these stories are my way of sharing my heart with you, and I am so grateful to have that opportunity. You mean the world to me.

About the Author

COURTNEY WALSH is the author of *Just Look Up*, *Paper Hearts*, *Change of Heart*, and the Sweethaven series. Her debut novel, *A Sweethaven Summer*, was a *New York Times* and *USA Today* e-book bestseller and a Carol Award finalist in the debut author category. In addition, she has written two craft books and several full-length musicals. Courtney lives with her husband and three children in Illinois, where she is also an artist, theater director, and playwright.

Visit her online at www.courtneywalshwrites.com.

Discussion Questions

1. How does this book's title, *Just Let Go,* relate to the struggles of the two main characters? What does Quinn need to let go of? What about Grady? How successful are they at letting go by the end of the story?

2. For most of the story, Quinn's main objective is making it to the Expo so she can see her mother again. Why is she so determined to reconnect with her mother? In what ways has the Expo become an idol to Quinn? What would you say to Quinn if she asked you for advice?

3. Quinn is notoriously risk-averse: traveling, dating seriously, and skiing are just a few things on her list of fears at the beginning of the book. What is the source of her reluctance, and how does she overcome these fears in the story? What kinds of risks are you afraid to take?

4. Grady is haunted by his role in Benji's accident. In what ways do his feelings of guilt impact his life and his priorities? How does Benji feel about Grady's part in the accident? Why has Benji been able to find peace while Grady is weighed down with regret? Is there a regret in your own life that has been difficult to move past?

5. Rumors about Grady's wild lifestyle have spread far and wide via social media, and his reputation is tarnished in Quinn's eyes before they even get to know one another. Have you ever been hurt or misled by something shared on social media? How can you exercise wisdom regarding what to believe—and what to post or share—online?

6. Describe Jaden and Grady's friendship. In what ways are they good for one another? What are some of the benefits of friendships or mentoring relationships between people of different ages?

7. Were you surprised to learn that Gus was partly responsible for Jacie's decision to leave the family? Do you think he made the right decision in telling her to leave? Why or why not?

8. During the awards ceremony at the Floral Expo, Quinn realizes, "She was so loved. Her life was so good. Maybe staying away was the best gift her mother could have given her." What does Quinn learn about community over the course of the book? What is the most meaningful way you've been supported by friends or family?

9. Quinn never gets the opportunity to speak with her mother face-to-face, nor do we see Grady reconciling with his father. In spite of this lack of closure, how are Quinn and Grady able to move forward in healthy ways by the end of the story?

10. Do you watch the Olympics? If so, what's your favorite event? If a famous Olympian visited your town, what local sights would you want to show him or her?

TYNDALE HOUSE PUBLISHERS
IS CRAZY4FICTION!

Fiction that entertains and inspires

Get to know us! Become a member of the Crazy4Fiction community. Whether you read our blog, like us on Facebook, follow us on Twitter, or receive our e-newsletter, you're sure to get the latest news on the best in Christian fiction. You might even win something along the way!

JOIN IN THE FUN TODAY.

 www.crazy4fiction.com

 Crazy4Fiction

 @Crazy4Fiction